I0549239

FIVE TALES

by

Norman Giddan

Cult Classics Publisher

Dallas Texas

USA

Five Tales

by Norman Giddan

Copyright © 2015 by Norman Giddan

All rights reserved

Cult Classics Publisher

1613A Black Duck Terrace

Carrollton TX 75010

www.cultclassicspublisher.com

No portion of this book may be reproduced, or utilized in any form or by any means, electronic, mechanical or otherwise, including photocopying, recording, or by any information storage and retrieval system …except for brief quotations in printed reviews…without permission in writing from the author.

This is a work of fiction. Names, characters, incidents, and places are the product of the author's imagination or are used fictitiously. Any resemblance to actual events or persons, living or dead, is entirely coincidental. Any slights of people, places or organizations are completely unintentional.

ISBN-13: 978-0-6925468-7-1

ISBN-10: 06925468-7-1

Library of Congress Catalog Number: 2015917194

Printed in the USA

Table of Contents

No

Harm

A Novella

Chapter One

The luxury hotel suite was deathly quiet except for the muffled sounds of Middle Eastern violence on the TV. Jean Shindell slumped over in the blue patterned easy chair. She wiped away the tears and pulled herself up. She laughed for a moment. Then she screamed, "How could he do this to me? He knew… So did I." She sipped water from a plastic bottle. She hiccupped.

Finally, she did what she had wanted to do all afternoon. Vomit spurted over her dress, the chair, and the arrangement of tiny blue and red flowers of the thick Persian carpet. She wiped her mouth and fell back, half-asleep.

A handsome TV news anchor said, "Sad news tonight. Dr. Lionel L. Shindell, noted neurosurgeon from Dallas, collapsed and died after receiving the state's top award at today's Texas Medical Society luncheon. He was sixty-five years old and planned to retire next week."

She squeezed the remote and somehow managed to turn the TV off. "That S.O.B. We could have…" Then she slept.

Jean awoke abruptly after an hour, and ripped off her stinking dress. She slowly moved to the bedroom, then posed in front of the full-length closet mirror. She admired her short, silver hair and red lips, well-defined face and a sixty year old body that performed yoga four times a week. She knew he loved it.

That day had begun like so many others. She showered and dressed in a conservative sleeveless black shift, then breakfasted on dry toast and black coffee.

The next hour belonged to him. She assisted him with his clothes, shaving and showering, and also as he positioned himself in his wheelchair. He would stand awkwardly at times, but when and how were unpredictable.

He said, "Bow tie?" They argued over his ties for years—color, type, stripes, silk—whatever.

2

She said, "Not today. Grey suit looks good. Still a six footer— bald but fit. Think you'll lose weight now? Or gain?"

"My clothes are…"

She said, "Forget the clothes. Brown eyes still mystify me…skin is smooth and clear. Gold rims…perfect." She kissed him on the cheek.

"Huh? Are you my mother?"

"Don't joke."

She answered the phone. "Thank you," she said, "we'll be right down. We'll need extra help getting into the car."

"I'll push you to the elevator," Jean said.

Held under the arms by the doorman, Lion squeezed himself into the backseat of the car. Jean tipped the doorman and climbed in next to him. Their driver slid the wheelchair into the trunk.

"I'll hand you the note…at the lectern."

"What…Never…"

She said, "You'll say a few words. Acceptance of the award."

"Like fuck you buddy? Who are they? I'm the doctor. I'm the doctor."

She closed her eyes and counted to ten. What would it be like to travel with him now? He'd need a companion. He'd drive her crazy otherwise. She said, "Beautiful day, Lion. Hot and sunny with blue sky and no clouds. A golf day."

He said, "Fuck golf. I could hit those fuckers. I'm the doctor. Not them."

The driver straightened his cap. His eyes opened wide when he turned and gazed at Dr. Shindell.

She said, "Just drive."

Arrival at the luncheon turned out to be easy. The doorman at the convention center helped Lion to the sidewalk, the driver set up the wheelchair, Jean straightened his tie, and he remained silent as she pushed him into the building.

3

The ballroom packed with tables of well-fed doctors hummed with talk and laughter. The white linen of each table was offset by the bright and colorful yellow, green and purple spring flower arrangements in their center.

Jean and Lion seated themselves at the speaker's dais where their name cards were propped up. Handshakes and well-wishes all around as the president of the society introduced Jean to the prominent individuals at that table. Several patted Lion on the back and extended congratulations. Their eyes bulged with surprise at seeing him in a wheelchair.

The president of the society rose and spoke. "Please continue with your lunch. Our main speaker today comes after the next presentation—most of you know that speech will be given by the Surgeon General of the United States, a real honor for Texas. We have a highly regarded medical community here, so the winner of the outstanding physician award must be a leader in patient care, research, and community education. It is my honor to present the award this year to a distinguished neurosurgeon from Dallas, Dr. Lionel L. Shindell. The plaque I hold commemorates his decades of service to our profession and his patients. Lionel, please stand or we'll move the mic to you if you prefer to remain seated."

Jean wheeled Lion to the lectern and helped him stand, backing the wheelchair away while he held on to the wooden sides, knuckles white, with both hands.

The applause lasted for several minutes and filled the room with deafening sound. Her face contorted with sadness and tears while Lion had a rigid and blank appearance. She placed a page of notes on the stand for him to read.

His body shook. Face ashen. Words slurred. "I…I did… Fuck them. I'm the doctor."

The audience appeared shocked, as if an electrical jolt hit the room. They didn't know how to behave. Some laughed, a few clapped, most were stunned and silent. Confused and bewildered by Lion's embarrassing demise in front of them, whispers of "help him" spread from table to table.

He pushed the note away. It fluttered to the floor. "Sick. I know it. I'm not sure… Where…?"

Lion's legs gave out as he suddenly collapsed and fell backward. He crunched his head and torso against the front of the wheelchair. It rolled a few feet.

The president of the society dropped the award plaque and laid him on the floor. He began CPR. Then said, "Call the 911." Other physicians on the dais rushed over and surrounded Lion.

A large-boned doctor jumped onto the dais. "I'm Dr. Wilshire— I work with Lion." He tried to force his way through the crowd.

Jean spoke into the mic. "He's very grateful. A great man. A brilliant doctor. Thank you so much."

The EMT's arrived within several minutes. Flat-line. They couldn't revive him. It was too late. Dr. Lionel L. Shindell lay dead before his brethren. Jean moaned as she cradled his head in her arms and sobbed uncontrollably. She closed his eyes.

Her mind memorialized him as she agonized over his death. Your parents—your whole family—would be so proud and honored by your achievements. Not all your dreams came true but most of them did. You were almost always the best—Eagle Scout, interned in Africa, top prizes in science and physics in high school—the awards never ended. And now the top doctor in the state!

What a balance, too. You never put me at the very highest point—but I settled for a tie score with your career. Never ignored or pushed aside by you. I wanted you to quit this medical game sooner. I should have been louder or stronger on that, but would you have listened to me? No. You were hell-bent on this award, and you said that you'd practice medicine until the luncheon. You did.

I'll take care of everything else—your group practice, your estate, the lawyers and accountants, the IRS, the taxes, our cars and homes—everything. I love you, my darling, more than you'll ever know, more than I said, and I was prepared to take care of you forever. Maybe this way—this finality is for the best. Who knows? We've had quite a life together—ups and downs.

Chapter Two

Jean and Lionel coped with their son's stillbirth in very different ways. He consoled her. He found a way to accept it. She remained heartbroken yet determined not to allow blame or pain or sadness to ruin their marriage. That, she knew, was a likely outcome of an infant death. Feelings arose inside her that she did not share. A new day, a new hope, another chance for a child of their own.

"Honey, let's get away for a week or so. Sun, blue water, fresh fish and plenty of..."

She agreed although it had only been a few weeks. Mourning kept going and going and going. "I don't know how you do it. Whatever makes..."

Lion said, "Don't compare." He slipped on a clean shirt and a new red wool tie.

She lay covered by a blue satin comforter on the small antique French couch in the bedroom. Her hands were in a prayerful position. The tears would come in waves after he left the house. "Very dapper."

He kissed her goodbye and went to work.

She knew what he'd do. Tell his secretary to schedule a trip to Aruba or St. Maarten for a week at an upscale resort hotel on the beach. After surgery, he'd return home and flash the airline first class tickets and hotel confirmation. Then he'd say, "My secretary is a marvel."

When he returned, she still lay on the small couch in the bedroom. She'd cried her eyes completely red and puffy. Slept for only an hour or so. Dreamed of her high school boyfriend who died in a plane crash.

"Come on, honey, shower and make-up and good-as-new."

Jean sat up and arched her back. "Sadness makes me stiff." She dressed and made a token appearance at dinner. Picked at the lamb chops and mint jelly that their cook prepared. "Pills help a little."

Lionel ate well. The lamb, mashed potatoes, and peach cobbler. He sipped a Chardonnay, which he preferred with lamb. "We'll have ice cream later. Chocolate chip, your favorite."

Jean said, "Will a change of scenery help?"

"I'm sure of it. Your bikini…"

Lionel helped her pack a day before the trip. He laid out shorts, halter tops, and sandals she liked. Sunhats and sunscreen and dark aviator sunglasses.

Jean said, "Want my body exposed—maybe burned—but my head and eyes covered?"

"You're welcome. We're both packed and ready to go."

The cab picked them up at noon for the flight to Aruba. Jean felt better than she had for weeks. She loved the beach, and actually looked forward to lolling in the blue-green water near shore. Her full-piece black tank swimsuit would be just fine, thank you. The bikini was his idea, not hers. The heat of Aruba could be oppressive but a constant westerly wind kept the climate comfortable. Late afternoon rain showers helped.

Jean sipped a wine cooler on the flight and then slept. Her deepest and most satisfying rest in days. Lionel must be right—a change of scenery could bring her back to life. The view of the ocean and Aruba from the plane made her body tingle with a brief moment of peace.

Their room at the hotel—yellow and pink and white carpets and drapes, even matching bedspreads, pleased her. Management provided fresh flowers, champagne and chocolates from Europe. She allowed Lionel to make love to her, passively on her part, but she wanted him to enjoy the vacation. He did. With protection, he insisted.

For dinner, they started with a grouper ceviche followed by a broiled lobster with Vietnamese shrimp sauce and island vegetables on the side. "I hate to be an 'I told you so' but I told you so," Lionel said. "First smile in a long time." Mostly, they ate in silence. Lost in her thoughts, Jean reflected on the off-white Italian facade of the hotel, the jolly, black doorman, and the sun-browned bodies of vacationers.

The next morning, after a breakfast of sweet local fruit medley and tiny potato pancakes and coffee, Lionel said, "Beach day. Ninety degrees, tiny waves. Perfect."

7

So he led the way. On with the swimsuits, out to the beach umbrella and the white sand, turquoise water lapping at their feet. A tiny Colombian woman braided her hair and Lionel bought several silver bracelets from natives hawking goods. They were everywhere.

The fog lifted. She smiled at strangers. Threw a ball to a child. Her courage gradually built up. It had to—to overcome her depression and the fear of his response. She rehearsed in her mind: "I want to try again. I want a child. I want us to have a family." The sun and water relaxed her, as she bounced on the sandy bottom, while the mounting bravery pushed her to the point of confronting him.

She rubbed his back with lotion and he fondled her neck and pulled gently on her braids. A blissful morning of affection and dreams.

They lunched at a beachfront bar. Fried sardines with a French baguette and real butter. Then some local soft cheese filled with worms!

Returned to their hotel room for a shower and nap. Lionel fell asleep before he washed off the salt water. Jean took a leisurely bath, all the time contemplating her "mission." She knew he'd say no, that he might have a genetic excuse, that he wouldn't want to go through the experience again, and that his marriage to her, and her well-being were more important, a higher priority than a child.

They had carefully avoided the blame game so far, neither holding the other accountable for the lost infant, nor the emptiness and grief that followed. How did he do it? She never understood him on that score.

Lionel awakened from his nap, was now showered and wearing khaki shorts, a black T-top, and leather sandals. He smiled broadly, "The beach, a good lunch, a nap and thou. Wonderful day."

Jean plopped down on the edge of the bed. "I want a baby." She tried to hold back the tears but the dam burst. Gasping and sobbing and breathing heavily, "I want to try again. The doctor says..."

"No, dear, never again. Couldn't bear the thought of another stillborn. Won't... The expectation, the hope, the dream..."

He walked to the window and turned his back as he observed the afternoon beach crowd. "We have a good marriage. Many people need our help."

Jean prepared herself. She'd read several self-help books, one of which stressed simply repeating what you need or want or desire. No explanation, no logical reasoning, nothing that the other person can latch on to and disagree with or dissect. Just say what you want and keep repeating it!

"I want a baby. I want to have our children." Another cascade of tears rolled down her cheeks onto her halter. She fell to her knees before him. "I must have a baby. I want a child."

Lionel turned toward her. He placed a hand gently on her head. "Not now. Maybe…adopt later."

Her body shook. "You bastard. I hate you. You hate me. I want a child. It won't happen again, I promise." She jumped to her feet, grabbed a coffee cup from the table and threw it at the plate glass balcony door. It cracked but did not shatter.

Lionel held her. "I know you're very angry…part of the grief process."

She whispered in his ear. "I want a child and…" She fainted in his arms. He placed her on the bed. Loosened the tight halter top. Patted her hands. Poured water for her.

Alert again, she said, "I want…" She knew that they would never speak of another child again. They would not adopt. They had each other. Glued together.

Chapter Three

Several decades later, Shindell participated in an Alzheimer's study of relatively healthy seniors when he was in his late fifties. His mother died of Alzheimer's as did his brother, at age seventy. He told Jean, "I've got enough of that gunky protein called beta-amyloid to qualify for the study."

She said, "Have you thought it…?"

"Oh, yes," he said, "but I won't know if I get the experimental med or the dummy."

"Fifty-fifty," she said.

"My memory isn't too bad now. I just live with not knowing…" He scratched his head.

"Will the drug prevent memory loss?"

He smiled. Rubbed his chin, while thinking. "Could slow it down."

She wrapped her arms around him. Held him close. "We'll travel, dear. Cars, boats, planes, trains—we'll explore the world."

"You bet," he said. "My brain is so resilient. The plaques and tangles… Some bad headaches now and then."

Lion held back some of his thinking about dementia from Jean and his surgical colleagues. He'd heard of a new blood test that could tell if an individual is likely to develop Alzheimer's. He knew that exercise, a heart-healthy diet, and cognitive stimulation could help preserve memory, but he wasn't sure if he wanted to know the results of such a blood test. He thought he might get depressed, or confused, possibly withdraw from people and activities. A sense of doom could ruin his practice; even end his marriage.

A medical friend told him that changes in the blood resulted from the breakdown of brain cell membranes—in people **destined for**

Alzheimer's. Since no treatment prevented or cured it, he decided against the test. He'd be a research subject in the experimental program but skip the new blood test. When effective treatment developed he'd rethink that test. He chuckled to himself. "If I'm still alive." He felt that if he failed the current test, he might decline faster and further, so...

Then a west coast colleague told him about laboratory studies using CLARITY infuse. An entire brain is infused with a gel that fixes to almost every tissue but avoids the lipids. They block the light. The brain is washed with a detergent that flushes out the lipids. *Voilà*— nerves and structures of the brain come into view, as if preserved in clear Jell-O.

The colleague emphasized it had been tried only on whole mouse brains and portions of human brains, so far. Could help solve a range of brain mysteries in the future.

Lion was impressed with the technology, but again, he knew the application of the CLARITY technique to his situation was quite premature—maybe years or decades away. He didn't contact Stanford to find out more information about it.

He had a plan.

Chapter Four

The three neurosurgeons lingered over coffee and pineapple upside-down cake. Drinks and dinner, on the boss, grew into a tradition—every three or four months. Tonight, they met at an upscale restaurant, low lighting, quiet except for the clinking of knives and forks and swirling of ice cubes, with two busboys and two other wait-staff for their table. Food good, drinks big, and the price was right—for the two junior docs, Bob Wilshire and Kris Longly.

"I'm pleased," Dr. Shindell said, "very pleased. Practice going well. All making money, and…"

Dr. Longly said, "Saving lives, too."

"And no harm to the others," Dr. Wilshire said.

They clinked their martini glasses. Collectively, "Cheers."

The pâté de foie gras on toast arrived and then the waiter served Oysters Rockefeller and refreshed their drinks. The wait staff behaved like a big tip was in the offing.

Dr. Shindell said, "Some good news and some bad news. I've got the State Medical award locked up at the next luncheon. Top Doc. I'll practice until I get it."

They toasted again.

Dr. Wilshire said, "The bad?"

"It's obvious, isn't it?" Shindell asked. His shaky index finger pointed to his head.

"Well," Dr. Wilshire said, "you…slipped a bit. I forget things, too."

"I'm lucid tonight—here—but I may forget… Screwed up an MRI interp the other day."

Dr. Longly said, "You want us to do something?"

"Yes, that's it. Kris, you should have been a psychiatrist. Cover for me when I have a bad day."

The junior physicians observed Dr. Shindell as they sipped their drinks. A kind of watchful waiting. The next move was his.

"By cover," he said, "I mean accompany me in the OR or an office visit. Maybe a PET scan or whatever."

Dr. Wilshire drained his martini and chewed the olive. "Do your job for you—with you there? Is that it?"

"Yes. My patients need not know. No harm."

Dr. Longly abruptly pushed his chair away from the table. He stood. "Count me out, Dr. Shindell. It may be a crime. Our license..."

"You both get the practice after I receive the award. I'll be gone."

Dr. Longly walked around the table slowly. His eyes narrowed. The color drained from his face. "I didn't train at Stanford and UCLA for this shit. Wilshire, do what you want, but not me."

Dr. Wilshire leaned forward. A smile grew wide on his lips and cheeks. "They didn't mention this sort of thing at NYU either. We help you for a few months. We get the practice?" He felt the endorphins build up, like lifting weights in his gym.

"Yes," Dr. Shindell said, "but I'll be in a wheelchair some of the time. Hard to say when. If I get too belligerent or confused, take over."

"How much is it worth?" Dr. Longly asked. He sat down. "I like roulette."

"Millions. A contract... Put it in my will. Wife gets everything else."

Dr. Wilshire said, "A contract now and a codicil in your will. Can't change your mind."

Dr. Longly gulped his drink. He said, "I'm a gambler. Owe... Could get me even. The lawsuits..."

"Alzheimer's," Dr. Shindell said. "At times I'm confused or can't remember what I just did or heard or learned. Suspicious. Swear like a trooper. I'm dying. Jean helps me more..."

"You sure deserve the award. My wife thinks you're the greatest," said Dr. Wilshire.

"I was."

"What if you change your mind? Or Jean doesn't want this? Or the surgery center or the hospital administration find out and balk?" asked Dr. Longly.

"I can handle all of that. Jean gets more."

The three arose after Dr. Shindell paid the bill along with a handsome tip. Dr. Wilshire's strong build fit the Air Force Colonel and jet pilot he'd been in Germany. He dwarfed Dr. Longly, a short, skinny, nervous type who wasn't ashamed of his membership in Gambler's Anonymous.

Longly said, "You've got a family to support. Me, it's just the new Dallas Casino. I need money."

Dr. Shindell walked off quickly without saying "good-night" or "see you in the A.M." The two others didn't have a chance to say "thank you."

The wait-staff hurriedly cleared the table. The hundred dollar tip floored them.

His chauffeur picked up Dr. Shindell at the curb. He slouched in the comfortable leather back seat of the limo. His mind wandered over the past—family members and his fate.

I know what's ahead for me. It doesn't frighten me. Maybe it should. I won't know who I am or was or who Jean is or remember my family. My brother Reginald, older by nearly a decade, died of dementia at age seventy. My mother died of Alzheimer's about the same age. They were out of it for a few years before the end came. The good thing was that they didn't know it. A blank screen. Nothingness. Mistaken identities, or no recognition of anyone. Pictures of people reminded them—but only for a moment. Questions like "is that?" existed for what seemed like an eternity, maybe a millisecond, yet neither my brother nor mother could answer them.

Then their bodies shut down and the end arrived with more pain and suffering for all of us—especially for them. Hard to believe a loving and caring God could let this scourge hit a family of good, decent people.

I guess I'm next in line for this. Poor Jean. She deserves better from me. So do my patients. So do Kris and Bob.

Chapter Five

Bob heard screaming from the moment he pulled his black Mercedes sedan into the garage. It was either his wife Marnie or his autistic five-year-old daughter Lucy. He couldn't tell which one, and it didn't matter all that much anyway.

His personality shifted from offense to defense. From the ghostly quiet of the OR to the chaos of home life—terrible change of pace for him—even after more than a decade of marriage. At least his son Josh, now nine, played football.

He turned off the ignition, the engine cooled down and he stretched and twirled his long fingers now cramped after hours of surgery and driving the Mercedes.

With overheard garage lights suddenly on, Marnie said, "Come in, babe. It's just Lucy."

He still admired her appearance, not sure if it was love or lust or romance. After having two kids, sex became an issue—seldom discussed by either of them. She placed him on a mountaintop!

The screaming and yelling continued as they entered the house. Next, a thud-thud-thud... He ran to Lucy's room, only to see her banging her head against the pink wall with white angels that he'd painted for her. Thud, thud...

"Stop, Lucy. You'll hurt yourself. No more." He held her tightly in his arms. She banged against his chest and shoulders. The she cried when there was no space to turn her head. She barked some unintelligible word or phrase—like "arrdugh, arrdugh." Her blue eyes widened with excitement and fear and anger. The she suddenly stopped the guttural sounds and the aggressive movements.

"Lucy, glad to see you, too."

Marnie chuckled as she walked into the bedroom. She handed him a Scotch and water. "Lucy...three episodes all day. A **victory.**"

She smoothed her long, blonde hair, and then tied it into a knot on the back of her head. "A moral victory."

Bob gulped half of his drink. "Those behavior therapists cost an arm and a leg. How do ordinary people afford it?"

Marnie impulsively kissed the back of his hand holding the drink. "They don't. Their kids end up in a group home, or worse."

"Lucy's sound reminded me of the word 'aardvark.' Couldn't be, could it?"

Marnie convulsed with laughter. "No, the speech therapist only comes here Tuesday and Thursday. This is Wednesday."

"Will Lucy talk?"

"Dinner in twenty minutes—a Thai coconut milk and rice and chicken dish—with curry and many other spices," Marnie said.

"Living in different countries…"

"Yes, dear, or I mean Colonel, you dragged me all over God's creation." She threw her arms around him and kissed him hard on the lips. She stood on her toes to do it.

"Where's Josh?" He laid Lucy down on the bed.

"Here, Dad, here in the hall. 40—8—99—hike!" He pretended to pass the ball…

Bob grabbed the nine-year old and squeezed him. "Are you Aaron Rodgers or Tony Romo?"

"I'm me, Dad, just little Josh, quarterback of the Titans."

"Let's do punt and pass after dinner." He held Josh at arms-length and admired his body and developing muscles. "Weight training…a few years. Too soon."

Bob's love for the boy knew no bounds. Having achieved his own success in football, with scholarships and local fame, he could smell the same drive in Josh. Did he have the skills and speed for it? Dad would make sure he had the best coaches and trainers that money could buy.

The behavior people for Lucy cost a fortune, so fair-minded Bob prepared himself to spend whatever it took to give Josh a chance to make it in football. He knew it was not a good idea to tie his self-esteem to Josh's success but he couldn't help himself. Josh was his—him—the new version.

Marnie wore makeup and lip gloss for dinner. Unusual, thought Bob. Her smooth complexion and lack of wrinkles or lines in her cherubic face left others to observe what they called his "child bride." He couldn't blame her for Lucy nor give her the credit for Josh. She was a dutiful, loyal and loving wife and mother. The magic—the bells— became buried in the disappointment and chaos of their family-life.

"This Thai curry is perfect," Bob said. Three of them sat at the table. Lucy stayed in her room.

"I love to cook for you. Wish you were here for three meals a day."

"Me, too, but surgeons have crappy home schedules. We earn our keep," Bob said. "Josh and I'll play catch after dinner. Then…news once we get Lucy to bed."

"Is that her, Dad?" Josh asked. He pointed to his ears.

Lucy threw her dolls and toys at the wall. She took off her clothes and peed on the carpet. The she commenced a banshee yell that was new to the family. Like an on-off light switch, she suddenly stopped. Now she sobbed quietly.

Bob and Marnie stood motionless at the doorway to her room. "Meds need readjustment," Bob said. "Doctor in the A.M."

Marnie approached Lucy, held out both hands and Lucy smacked them with hers—an angry high-five. "Let's put your room back together, dear. Here's the photo—the picture of your room—the toys and dolls—with everything in its place."

Lucy made that sound again, something like 'aardvark' and then she barked. That was different. Next she sat on the floor and fixed her eyes on the bulb fixture in the center of the ceiling fan. Sometimes she followed the fan blades with her head.

Bob said, "I'll be outside with Josh. We can see to pass the ball around for a few minutes." He gave Marnie a hug and a perfunctory kiss on the cheek.

Marnie said, "This house is too small. I'm sick of it. There's no time-out room."

"As soon as the treatments taper off or cost less, we'll move. I promise. Get Lucy into a good special education program. I promise," Bob said.

Marnie said, "Sorry. Lo…lost it for a moment." She rolled her eyes as the tears of mascara blackened her cheeks.

Once outside, Wilshire threw a pass to Josh. He caught it and ran directly at his Dad. A mock tackle put Josh on the ground. Bob straddled him and took the football into his own huge hands. "Good catch. Always run away from the tackler." He hugged Josh. "Got to talk to your Mom now."

The inside of his home embarrassed Bob. A few antiques and mementos from overseas, but mostly stick furniture that was purchased during his training. It wasn't ugly, just not up to the standards of a surgeon. They needed another bedroom, maybe two. All the spare cash went to Lucy's behavior training. He smiled to himself—now she can arrange a stack of blocks and say "Da-da" and "Ma-ma"—sometimes.

He sighed and took a deep breath. His face flushed as he sipped a second Scotch. Seldom angry, he had become fed up with the thought of Lucy. I can't fix her but neither can the experts. A low-functioning autistic girl. I'm a leading surgeon. How could this happen to me? How can I overcome the humiliation of a special needs child?

Damn, Marnie, take me off that pedestal you created for me. At least Lucy would have the best treatment and education possible. It wouldn't be the Ivy League. She'd never be a doctor. Could she make it in any school? At some deep, primitive level, he understood those gruesome parent-child murder-suicides. He pushed that horrible thought far and away.

Marnie and Bob sat opposite each other in the living room, on dated Danish modern furniture. The cushions, an ugly brown pattern with dull yellow highlights, showed the years of wear. Bob's third Scotch, half-empty but nearly engulfed in his large right hand, helped him relax. No noise, kids asleep. As quiet as the OR when he operated. He felt that sense of control, to be in charge of himself and his surroundings, which he enjoyed and needed.

Marnie said, "I hope the news is good."

19

"Yes, it is. Lionel is going to sell the practice to Kris and me after the society's award luncheon."

"Hallelujah. Much more money that…" Her hazel eyes brightened as she punched her fists into the air. "How much does it cost? Can we pay it off over time?"

Bob Wilshire stood. He strolled to a nearby table and set his glass on it. "Not money. We help him with his patients. They don't know it. He's sick."

Marnie moved to the table and finished his drink. "Slow down. I've only got a B.A. Who knows?"

"Well, we just…"

"Those nosey nurses. They'll report… Is it legal? Patients are fooled."

Bob held her shoulders. He kissed her. "Trust me. Only for a short time until he wins the award."

She walked hesitantly to the bedroom door. "I wouldn't want to be one of the patients who think Lionel is their surgeon. Not right. Not my Dr. Wilshire. Not the jet pilot."

The door closed. Bob thought it'll pay for Lucy's treatment, a new house, whatever else we need. He poured himself another Scotch and gulped it.

Once asleep, he dreamed of Shindell dead…his wife Jean appeared. It became a blur. The alarm woke him. He operated at 7:00 A.M.

Chapter Six

Dr. Shindell's driver dropped him off around 10:00 P.M. at the front door of his Tudor-style mansion in the Fossmoor gated community. He slammed the car door when the driver accidentally raced the motor. "For Christ's sake, you…"

He fumbled with his house key, and then opened the door. Upstairs Jean sat at the dressing table combing her hair. She appealed to him. Still a ravishing sixty-year old.

He kissed the top of her head. "I've got news."

Jean said, "Tell me quickly."

"I've sold the practice. Got a good price." He rubbed her shoulders and kissed her neck several times.

"Good for you, Lion," she said. "Free as birds. Travel. Travel. Travel." She arose and hugged him, holding him tightly. "Never let go."

He pushed away. "The price is… You may not like it."

"Tell me."

Lion breathed heavily, suddenly tired. He plopped down on the edge of the bed.

"Kris and Bob bought me out."

She said, "I knew they would. Smart guys. Their ship came in." She removed his shoes and socks, then rubbed his feet.

"They'll help me. Cover up mistakes. Until the award."

"How much?" She looked up. Gazed at his face.

Lion said, "That's the price."

"How much money?" She held her breath.

"None," he said. "The practice is theirs." He fell back on the bed. Passed out. Fast asleep. Snoring loudly.

"No money. You demented fool. They cheated you. Half belongs to me now and…" she said. "Our lawyer…never agree." She pulled the down comforter over him and turned out the light.

The alcohol-fueled deep sleep strained the doctor's psyche with fragments of dreams coming and going. The final dream appeared so real to him—what he'd wished for. He dreamed that he performed near the top of his class in medical school at Harvard, but dropped out because of illness for a six-month period. Living at home, his parents cared for him. He had fallen in love with a classmate, but she'd spread a serious case of the "kissing disease." Recovery dragged on but his parents supplied the love and care and medical treatment he required. His father practiced family medicine. When he returned to school, he quietly rose again to the top of his class and a residency in neurosurgery at Mass General. Jean served as one of his OR nurses.

He awakened, startled with his mouth parched, so he gulped a tumbler of cold water. No more sleep. No more dreams. He had actually attended the University of Texas medical school, aspired to be top dog, but never quite made it. The state medical award grew into a bittersweet struggle for recognition—a revenge he never quite understood.

Lion sat at his desk and wrote "Open at My Death" on the front of a manila envelope. Then he penned a letter to Jean.

"My dearest Jean, I'm taking the medication as ordered. No promises, they tell me. Two tiny yellow pills each morning, and voilà, the plaques and tangles and whatever else, stop growing and I'm sane and ready to go at sixty-five. Go wherever you desire. We'll have money to burn I hope—so we can fly, sail, bike, ride a train, or rent an ocean-liner for all I care.

"I'll be with you and that's all that matters to me. You're still the most beautiful and exciting woman I've ever known. As a TV commercial might say, "The most exciting woman in the world." You made med school possible with your secretarial skills. Then I helped you with nursing training. Later, you assisted me when I started the surgery center. Then I played a big role in buying the house and so on. Back and forth. Helping each other at key points only enriched and strengthened our love.

"We braced ourselves for bad news when we were warned that our son wouldn't make it. Such a tiny, handful to never know a breath of earth's air.

"A terrible blow. We were stunned, shocked, nearly wiped out with a stillborn son. His name, Lionel L. Shindell, Junior already emblazoned for him on diapers and towels. But no life. The doctors speculated but were uncertain as to what happened. I guess it didn't matter—he was born dead! He lost. We lost. No chance to raise him, parent him, see him grow and develop and become his own man. A doctor? A lawyer? A surfer? It didn't matter to us. We'd have a son who lived and breathed and loved and visited on holidays.

"It just wasn't to be. Our desperate cries for something—we weren't sure what—went unheeded. We suffered horribly, each in our own way, but did not pull back and blame each other. We didn't know who or what to blame, so I convinced you that it was not meant to be and not to do it again. So we didn't. Such a loss. A hole in our lives, for sure!

"It's strange but you became even more attractive and necessary to me—your beauty, your tolerance, your understanding of life… I hate the idea of losing my mind but I'm fairly sure it's my due. Love and kisses, Lionel.

"P.S. Oops, I almost forgot. There will come a time, I guess, when I won't recognize you. My behavior will be so erratic that you'd like to forget who I am, only recall who I was. No matter, somewhere in my sick or crazy or lost brain, never forget these phrases still exist, "I love you," and "I'm very grateful," for everything you've been to me and done for me. Even when I curse or strike at you or vomit, those words are still buried in my demented brain. Listen to them. Please remember them.

"I just recalled what satin and velvet signified for me. On the outside you're like satin—smooth, silky and shiny—and you feel so good. But on the inside it's velvet and velour—rich and deep with varied degree of colors and thickness. I love satin. I love velvet. I love you. We'll be together again. I'm sure of that.

"I still remember your wink, above the surgical mask when you served as my scrub nurse in surgery. That wink said, "Good job. You got it. I love you. You're the best." How could a simple wink say so much? Yours did. I could stand on my feet for fifteen hours fortified by that wink.

"I felt like a king in the OR when you were with me."

23

Chapter Seven

Dr. Shindell pushed his disinfected aluminum walker into the ICU cubicle. He observed Marie, a scrawny, bald fifty-seven year old widow. She opened her eyes. He said, "Good and bad, Marie. Like life. We'll take it out. This is Dr..."

She said, "It grew?" Then she curled up and crumpled into sleep produced by Propofol.

Dr. Wilshire stood at the head of the bed as he read out loud from the summary chart. "Fifty-seven year old female with new onset seizure Glioblastoma, fast growing, on the surface of the right frontal, parietal region. Needle biopsy was astrocytoma, WHO Grade 3. Resistant to radiation and chemotherapy. Lesion grew two centimeters in three months."

Dr. Shindell said, "Used Phenytoin for the seizure. Prep for surgery. Head up fifteen percent, with slight hyperventilation and normothermia."

Dr. Wilshire nodded as he replaced the chart to the bracket on front of the bed.

Dr. Shindell's hands shook noticeably. "Can you take over? I'll be there, too."

"Yes," said Dr. Wilshire. "We'll use an EVD to control the ICP. There are plateau waves. Any family here?"

"No. She's alone. Widow. No kids," Dr. Shindell said. "I forget sometimes. A high ICP has a bad effect, or a good one, on Cerebral Perfusion Pressure."

"Negative. By the way, did you tell the patient that I'd be the lead neurosurgeon in the OR?" He flexed his powerful biceps and wide lats.

"No. Sh...She'll get good care. I'm the doctor."

Dr. Wilshire said, "Better keep her in a deep hypnotic state. Make sure the CPP is above 70mm Hg. See you in the OR in thirty minutes."

Dr. Wilshire thought to himself, Shindell couldn't do it. Tremors. Erratic behavior. Forgets about CPP. The son-of-a-bitch. First time for this sort of thing.

His reverie continued. I still think I can save anyone or do everything. My time at NYU got me thinking that I'm the greatest, damn near invincible. One of my supervisors said I was the best surgeon he'd ever seen. A medical genius. Plenty of technical skills combined with the intuition of a genius—like Picasso or Freud or Tolstoy. It became difficult to stay humble. I could visualize in three-dimensional space before the sophisticated MRI scans helped me in surgery—cut just enough, drain only what's necessary, suture so it wouldn't return, whatever.

My wife Marnie only made it worse. She worshipped me. After too much wine she admitted she'd…if it came to a choice, she'd take me and leave the kids behind. Later on she denied ever saying that. She loved the children and mothered them beautifully and lovingly. I hoped my son would play football—quarterback like the old man. That scholarship to college really paid off. So did military money.

A half hour later, the two neurosurgeons, four nurses, a technician and two anesthesiologists, wore gowns and gloves and masks as they gathered around Marie.

Dr. Wilshire said, "I'm here to assist Dr. Shindell. He's the lead."

Dr. Shindell pulled his walker closer to the patient. He said, "Put her head in a frame for stabilization. We'll use frameless navigation."

Dr. Wilshire sweated profusely. His eyes darted from instruments to nurses to the computer. He was good at this. New procedures he'd learned in his NYU residency.

He had to look away from the surgical site to view the navigational display. He was especially skilled at relating the location of the instruments to intraoperative images.

The tech said, "This 3-D reconstruction from MR imagery data may be a waste of time."

Stunned, Dr. Shindell said, "What? What's that?"

"She's gone."

An hour of CPR and meds and paddles followed but failed to bring her back.

"Sorry," Dr. Wilshire said. He tore off his gloves. "We didn't have a chance. I didn't even do an incision of the scalp and dissect the soft tissue. She's gone."

Chapter Eight

Dr. Shindell pushed out of the OR as fast as the walker moved. Barely taking time to remove his gown, gloves, cap and mask. Awkwardly, he showered and dressed. No need to speak to Dr. Wilshire and thank him. After all, the instruments didn't even get placed inside Marie's skull before she expired. Her blood pressure went sky-high and the ICP couldn't be controlled before the end. Dr. Shindell felt pleased that he'd been able to extend her life for six months with the radiation and the chemo.

Jean would understand. With the driver's help, he returned home for lunch. "We lost Marie, the glio…"

"Did Wilshire help?"

"Yes, he was set up for the 3-D stuff. Didn't happen. She died on the table before…"

"And you?" She passed him the broiled grouper and rice. "You?"

"Well, I was shaky. I forgot something." He spit out a bone. "Shit, I hate fish. I hate bones." He threw his napkin on the floor and tipped over the wine cooler. "Fuck it."

"Stay calm, dear. I'm sure Marie got good care."

"To make matters worse…my fucking nurse Mattie…in the hallway." He tried to clean up the mess.

"I'll do it. Mattie…" Jean patted the table top dry with a napkin.

"She said I was sick."

"Did she threaten you?"

"No…well I don't think so." He moved his walker—fast then slowly—around the table. Counted the turns. "That's six."

27

Jean nibbled at the fish. Then poured some white wine. "What about Mattie?"

"Said I wasn't the same. Should have smashed…"

"Now, Lion, you know…"

"She—that fucking nurse---yelled 'You can't operate. Shouldn't see patients.' Then she hugged me. Kissed my hands. At least, I think she… Said, 'I love you. Won't talk.' She whispered it into my ear."

Jean said, "We can't trust her, dear. She might lie. Could go to the hospital, or the police or even the State Medical Board. She knows that Bob and Kris do your job when…"

"Who gives a rat's ass. I'm the doctor."

"Yes, yes, of course. I'll mention her to the lawyer. We'll relocate…a bonus." Jean gulped the wine and poured another glass for herself.

Lionel literally fell into his chair. He stubbed his toe. "She's British, from your nation."

Jean said, "I'll take you…Urination…" She walked him to the bathroom.

"Fuck it. Piss on it. I'm the doctor." He pissed his pants. "Where's that fucking Longly?"

Chapter Nine

The white basement meeting room at the brand new Dallas Casino, suddenly crowded with people—neon-lit, plenty of blue smoke and fervent prayer, could have been planned as a storage room. The PowerPoint screen at the front read, "Life without gambling is not life without risk." Kris thought it strange that the Gamblers' Anonymous held meetings in this palace of chance. He guessed that if you can walk away from this meeting, bypass the tables, up the stairs, and go for coffee—you could do it anywhere. The test!

Unfortunately, the elevator led to the first floor. He knew he'd fail again. The need was so powerful and so all-encompassing, it forced the habit to become inescapable for him. He loved blackjack and even roulette and craps. The thrill, the excitement, win-or-lose, everything on the line. And no memories to block out or fight off. They were gone when he gambled.

He faced a choice, sort of a choice. Follow half of the fellow sinners out the side door or crowd the elevator headed to gaming. He could hear the beeps and bleats of the slots, the rhythmic jazz music from the bar, and the screams of joy or sadness as the elevator door opened—to his paradise of pain.

Big-time gamblers didn't appear before the A.M. Until midnight, it was amateur hour—and nearly all of them lost. Even small losses added up--$100 here, $300 there. It all counted for the casino.

As Kris arrived, he could feel the cold of the A.C. He could have worn a sweater or jacket but he knew he'd warm up with the action. His small frame and ordinary jeans and cowboy shirt blended in perfectly with the lower-middle and working class folks still hanging around the quarter slots, looking for a miracle.

He heard, "No more bets, please," as he passed by the roulette wheel. He'd give it a whirl later, use his blackjack winnings.

There stood Leo his favorite dealer. No one at his table, he simply smiled and tried to appear thoughtful. His white shirt, tailor-fitted, to his muscular chest and arms couldn't be missed. A tiny black bow tie at his neck.

"Evening, Doc, didn't think you'd show tonight. It's slow."

Kris sat on a high-backed stool. He lit an E-cigarette but couldn't take his eyes off of Leo. He thought to himself—he'd always felt disgusted by his own skinny, nondescript frame and his bony face. Leo was gorgeous. The ripped chest, the six-pack abs and the well-defined pecs.

"I see that. At a GA meeting. Couldn't resist…"

Leo said, "How much?"

"All I've got is $500 with me. $25 chips, okay?"

Leo's ultra-white, capped teeth shone brightly, setting off his curly dark hair.

Kris liked the background noise and smell of the casino. Steady beating sounds louder than radar with occasional police sirens that indicated a winner on slots. The simple designs, the speed, and the colors of the machines—slots, poker, blackjack—amused him and sent him into a zone where he imagined he was invincible, a surefire winner.

The neurosurgeon took over. He bet it all on his first hand. He had twenty while Leo sported a blackjack—twenty-one.

"What time do you get off?"

"In about fifteen minutes. Then I work out." Leo flexed a bicep that nearly tore his shirt-sleeve.

Kris said, "I'll drive you. Then breakfast at my place?"

"You sure?" Leo's raised eyebrows and quizzical look suggested he wasn't sold on the idea.

"Absolutely."

Kris slid off of the stool. He tipped Leo with his last $20 bill. "Pick you up in front. A new Jag convertible."

Kris drove the car to the circular driveway in front of the casino. He hailed Leo who squeezed into the passenger seat.

Leo said, "My gym is open twenty-four hours. Down the street. A mile or so in a strip mall. Nice ride, Doc. Love Jags."

Kris said, "How long?" He couldn't wait to get Leo alone.

"Wait in the lobby. Look through the glass. Watch me."

Kris parked the car. They strolled into a facility with floor-to-ceiling glass walls and mirrors everywhere. Seated in the lobby, Kris was aroused by observing Leo's workout—the smell of liniment, the grunts and groans, the straining muscles on legs and shoulders and arms. Then...

Suddenly awakened, Leo shook his shoulder. "You dozed off, Doc."

A bit groggy, Kris said, "I must have..."

"Want me to drive? I love British racing green..." They exited the gym and walked toward the Jag.

"I'm okay now. Steak and eggs at home?" He shifted into first gear and roared out of the parking lot.

Kris experienced mild panic—shaking, sweating, and shortness of breath—as he drove and anticipated what might lie ahead. He wasn't sure of himself. He'd only lost $500 this morning. GA didn't work all the time for everyone. At least he didn't carry much money in his wallet. And no credit cards. The choice of coffee versus blackjack was a no-brainer for him.

Leo slid his hand on to Kris' thigh. He smiled.

Kris trembled. His gaze never left the road.

He down shifted the Jag as he headed into his driveway. Neither commented on the shafts of red-blue sky, streaks of light of the early morning. Kris' mind was elsewhere and he hoped it was the same for Leo.

Kris rented a modest three bedroom, furnished bungalow, for less than his salary and status suggested. He spent little time at home, mostly in the office or the OR, then to the casino.

As they entered, he said, "The house... What's your last name, Leo?"

"Does it matter? It's Sanducci. Leo Sanducci, high school wrestler who dropped out before graduation. My old man was a doorman at hotels. Got me the dealer job."

Kris grabbed two Heinekens from the fridge. They toasted and clinked bottles. "To us." He pulled T-bone steaks from the freezer, then a box of eggs and wheat bread from the fridge. "Now we're set. I seldom eat this much."

He defrosted the steaks. "Uhm, sit down, Leo. Mi casa es su casa."

Kris sneezed. He touched his over-size nose and tiny eyes. He couldn't believe his luck. Leo was here—a ravishing hunk with him, a skinny wimp—a brilliant, skinny wimp who lost his money gambling.

Leo sucked on his beer. He strolled into the kitchen. "I do more than deal. Way more." He leaned down and kissed Kris on the back of the neck. Then he pulled the blinds in the kitchen to shut out the streaming bright sunlight.

The defroster timer rang. Kris had an erection while the steaks became soft, ready to grill. He said, "What more?"

Leo returned to the couch. "I'm a gigolo. For money." He smacked his lips and rolled his eyes at Kris, eager for a response.

"How much, Leo the whore?" Kris didn't know whether to scream and yell, or tear Leo's shirt off or remove his own slacks and underwear. The thrill, the excitement, the odds—all in his favor. His secret passion.

"It's $200 for fifteen minutes. Okay?"

Kris opened the cookie jar. He handed over two hundred dollar bills. "Get the fuck out of here. Leave. Go. You S.O.B. I thought you..."

"All right, Doc. Afraid you were cherry. Somebody else can pop it." Leo walked out the door.

Kris turned off the grill. Feeling hurt and furious, he wolfed down a poached egg on dry toast and put the steaks into the fridge.

Gripped by confusing emotions, he had doubts about what he'd done. Even though gambling losses mounted up, when he owned half of the practice, he'd have enough money. Affording a whore like Leo for a few hours wouldn't be a problem. The idea of a gigolo, a whore, that was the problem. Then he wasn't at all sure he was really gay. Horny, yes. No luck with women, yes. Attracted to women and men, yes. No social life, yes.

He decided he could have used time with Leo as an experiment—a glimpse into the sexual habits of gay men. He could have done that but something stopped him. Maybe, there was a mousey, skinny, female version of himself he could hook up with or **a** gold-digger nurse or tech would find him and sink her teeth in. To be or not be married. Maybe. Possibly. Perhaps. He froze in personal matters. Where was the risk-taker, put it all on the line, take a chance guy? He wasn't fearful of commitment. He couldn't even get started. Couldn't get to first base.

At least I don't have to go to that damn meeting at the hospital.

Chapter Ten

The office door sign read Rosalie Gonzalez, M.H.A. She rose to become assistant hospital administrator after just two years on the senior staff.

Inside, she started the meeting. "Thank you, doctors, for seeing me today. Wanted to talk to you, Dr. Shindell, about your health and OR techniques." The tiny Latina shuffled papers on her desk. "Coffee, gentlemen?"

"No, thanks," Dr. Wilshire said. Dr. Shindell shook his head.

"By the way, why am I here?"

"Well, Dr. Wilshire, you were in the OR when Dr. Shindell's patient, a middle-aged woman died just as the surgery began."

He fidgeted with his hands. "Yes, a very sad case. Really, no chance."

Dr. Shindell said, "Bob assisted me. Glioblastoma grew. Resection never..."

"My understanding," Rosalie said, "is that you were a bit shaky. Used a walker."

"Yes, correct. Not comfortable on a stool. Still the top neurosurgeon here."

She said, "Of course you are. Glad to hear you say it."

"Anytime."

The two doctors arose and walked out of the office abruptly. The meeting simply ended even though no one said it was over. That was it.

Rosalie pressed a button on her desk phone. "Yes, I'm pretty sure. He seemed..." She listened intently. "I understand. If there's another complaint...the committee. He's big-time." She hung up.

Then thought to herself. Be calm. No emails. Sparse notes. Just the phone call. Follow orders. Don't risk your job. More to come on this one. Much more. Her informer, Mattie, would keep her posted. Thank God for honest nurses.

Rosalie pulled up her sleeve and stroked the thick, rope-like scars on her wrist—still rough and visible.

I'm the first. The first to go to college. The first to get a degree. The first to rise to a job like this. I'll do what my boss says, but in a way that protects me—all of my family—and doesn't leave a long paper trail to hurt me.

I can still remember the sight of my mother grinding corn for her own tortillas. A magical smell when they fried. She could take a handful of pigs' feet and tails—a delicious stew poured over rice. What a woman. She always wanted me to go to school, even after my daughter Alma was born.

That husband Ahmed was a bum. Said he was Mexican. I knew he lied, but his brown skin, dark, wavy hair and dancing eyes captivated this seventeen-year old girl from El Paso.

I've made mistakes but I won't let these rich *gringo* doctors hurt me—or my chances at the best hospital job I can find.

The famous Dr. Lionel L. Shindell is losing it. His colleagues have his back.

Chapter Eleven

Dr. Longly met with Dr. Shindell late that afternoon in an empty interview cubicle.

Dr. Shindell said, "Glad you signed it. Won't be sorry. Jean will go along. About taxes…CPA and lawyer will…"

"I understand. Thank you."

Dr. Shindell slid his walker near a chair. "I'll just stand."

Dr. Longly squirmed in his chair. Wiped sweaty hands on his scrubs. "Some days better than others?"

"Yes, exactly. I've got a tough case. Old guy…chronic subdural hematoma. Drained…simple burr hole."

"Sounds like you're on top of it, Dr. Shindell." He stood and ambled toward the door.

"Wait. Now it's become acute—headaches and agitation—occasional lethargy." His hands gripped the walker until the effort pinched his face. The walker shook.

Dr. Longly said, "Bridging veins work? Congealed blood still liquid?"

"No. You turn a flap and remove the clot."

"When?"

"Now," Dr. Shindell said. "Let's prep for the OR. Got a contrast CT set up."

Dr. Longly gazed intently at Dr. Shindell. Their eyes locked. Brown versus blue. "Did you tell him before the coma?"

"I don't recall."

"OK. Let's go scrub. Remember I'm just there to assist you. Hold on to your walker. Don't say much."

Later, several nurses gazed suspiciously at Dr. Shindell as he pushed the walker into the OR. He said, "Make sure there's no infection later."

Dr. Longly said, "We won't reassemble the skull until the swelling subsides."

He observed his tools laid out neatly on white trays. The patient had a firm fixation in a three-point head holder. The doctor's armrest appeared up-to-date. A new TV camera would relay the operation to two anesthesiologists, OR nurses, and the technician.

Under his breath, Shindell mumbled "Those fuckers. Fuck them! I'm the doctor." Apparently dizzy, he twisted his head as he tried to remain steady. His eyes fluttered. His hands slipped slowly down the sides of the walker.

Dr. Longly said, "Nurse, grab him. Don't let him fall."

"Got him," she said.

"Get him out of the OR," Dr. Longly said. "I'll take over. Can't have any noise in here."

Two nurses half-carried Dr. Shindell through the double doors. A puddle of urine marked the area where Shindell stood.

The patient died immediately after the operation—just as Dr. Longly suspected. The bleeding on the rigid, large tumor bed could not be controlled. An insulated nerve hook…the sponges…suction of tissue and clot—nothing worked.

When Dr. Longly fled the OR he headed for his office and his beloved computer screen. He read about an artificial brain tumor.

Cancer cells isolated from a patient, such as the one who just died, may be cultured in an artificial brain tumor. If done early enough, treatment protocol can be tested, then developed and targeted to the individual's specific cancer cells. Until that is accomplished, he knew, most glioblastoma continue to defy medication, radiation, chemo and neurosurgery.

The first in his family to go to college, his mastery of medical statistics and patient outcomes left him with no doubt that today's patient didn't have much of a chance in surgery, even in recovery if he survived. Even a Rubik's Cube champion like Dr. Longly couldn't produce miracles.

His thoughts turned inward. I've got regrets. Plenty of them. I was so scared in medical school, so I retched before every exam and presentation. "Nervous Nelly" defined me. Sometimes I thought I was scared of my own shadow. Ashamed of my loser Dad.

But it was the shadow of Uncle Frank the soccer coach. He showed me pictures and videos and movies. He poured me wine or we drank beer together and ate chips. Then he slipped into my bunk at night. He put his hand over my mouth and told me to keep quiet or he'd kill my family. It felt good but I knew it was wrong. Uncle Frank—grown man—yet I was only fifteen. Later, I thought that he should have been a priest—he said that's what he wanted but wasn't smart enough to go to college.

I realized later on that he wouldn't, or couldn't, kill anyone. He was a coward and a liar and a garbage man who could barely read the street signs. Yet he left a strong impression—an indelible stamp—on my life. Gambling makes me feel good—real good and forget Uncle Frank.

Chapter Twelve

Once in the hall outside the OR, Dr. Shindell pushed the nurses aside. "I'm fine. Get away…bitches."

They had pulled and dragged him out of the OR while he bent over his walker and nearly stumbled. Now he moved alone, without additional help, toward the elevator.

Inside the elevator, he pushed the button for the 'roof garden.' Installed several years ago, this site became a showpiece for the hospital. Half-arboretum—bushes, trees, and flowers—half-planted with garden vegetables, benches and chairs lay scattered throughout. Paths all led to a lunch stand in the center of the roof, itself.

Dr. Shindell meandered slowly toward the middle of the garden. Feeling stronger, he now dragged the walker behind him. That lasted for only a few feet. He slipped and another visitor made sure he regained his balance and stood upright again.

"Those fuckers. I want a wheelchair."

The proprietor of the lunch counter recognized him and sent for a wheelchair. "We'll have one for you, doctor."

Dr. Shindell moved to a bench and struggled to seat himself. At last, he removed his hat, mask, and gloves. The large wet spot on his pants couldn't be missed.

"Where the hell is she? The cunt. Call Jean." Dr. Shindell yelled at the top of his lungs.

A hospital orderly appeared with the wheelchair, then pulled him up and turned and yanked him into it. "Call my wife. I'm sick." The orderly nodded.

Now seated in the chair, Dr. Shindell said, "Yippee, yippee." He wheeled himself back to the elevator but crashed into the closed door. He backed the chair away, head slumped over and lost consciousness with his eyes partially open.

Within fifteen minutes, Jean appeared, accompanied by their driver. She cradled his head, kissed him, and rubbed his shoulders.

Awake again, he said, "I'm the doctor. Who the fuck are they?"

Jean placed her face, wrinkled with worry, very close to his. "It's me... I'm here. We'll go home."

He spit on her. The driver shared his handkerchief. She wiped her nose and cheeks.

The driver pushed the wheelchair into the elevator and pressed the button marked 'underground parking.'

Jean said, "I came as soon as I could. Said you had a reaction to some prescription drug... Dr. Longly took over."

"My parents? I don't know... You smell of piss. Uhm. My walker for the dance tonight..."

Jean moved the chair toward the waiting limo. "I don't know how much longer... The strain on me is horrible. What can I do?"

Lion, now seated in the rear of the car took off his soiled scrubs. "Kiss my ass. Kiss my fucking ass."

Her mind drifted. When he was in his late-fifties, about seven or eight years before the award, now given every five years, she noticed changes in Lion's immediate and long-term memory and actions. He forgot details at home. He couldn't recall the name of his high school, or several close friends. One day he even forgot his parents' names. He couldn't remember where they went on their honeymoon. He forgot his roommate in medical school—not only his name but his personality, girls that he once dated, and so on. Memory of the past events and people grew increasingly dim. Lion brushed it off—"senior moments," he said—but Jean didn't. She had lost her father to dementia and she observed some parallels.

She pressed even harder for retirement, but Lion wouldn't budge. The state medical award meant everything to him and he thought he had a good chance—the dream of a lifetime achievement. She explored his performance at the office over a period of time, replacing nurses when they were sick or on maternity leave. Some slip-ups, but not many. He occasionally forgot to read the medical charts, often wanted her or another doctor with him when he evaluated new patients— even delayed surgery from time to time.

40

She recalled his early sixties, when Lion said, "I'm going to Tijuana. New treatments…Guaranteed."

"When do we leave?" Jean asked.

"I'll go alone. I'm not an invalid."

So the discussion, the debate, the heated arguments continued for a week or so.

He left her a note. "See you in several days. *Hasta la vista,* baby."

The S.O.B. went off by himself. No address, no phone number, just some exotic clinic in Tijuana. She thought it was a foolish, maybe crazy, move on his part. Actually, another symptom of the dreaded dementia. Left with no choice, she awaited the outcome. She feared the worst.

A phone call came early the next morning from the Phoenix police. Lionel had thrown a drink at a waiter in a bar, then stood on the table and pulled down his pants. Now in a psych ER, there were no charges pending. She had to pick him up.

Jean and the chauffeur drove way over the speed limit to the airport. The pilot and plane for the flight to Phoenix consumed many thousands of dollars, but Jean was too overwhelmed to care. "Get us there. Get us back here."

She mused. What the hell has Lion done? He didn't make it to the Tijuana clinic. Why did he go into Phoenix? What if he doesn't cooperate with us? Maybe I need a doctor to medicate him? Control his nutty behavior and that potty-mouth. That 'I'm the doctor' bullshit. Do we need his walker or even the wheelchair? Our driver is strong but we may need extra help. Will the cab driver help? Oh hell, we'll just have to see what shape he's in.

Once at the police station, Jean identified herself and made sure no criminal charges were pending.

The police captain told her that Lionel could get better mental health treatment in Dallas.

She didn't argue, just glad he could leave the lock-up and reunite with her.

The cop led her to the holding tank. The cigarette smoke, urine, and sweat—the disinfectant—stunk. The burly cop didn't appear to notice the odors. Must be desensitized to such a horrible combination.

Lionel squatted on a metal bench in the corner. An aging hooker with red hair and a purple mini-dress inched closer to him.

Jean spoke through the wire screen. "Hello, dear. We're going to take you home."

"Where's that?" Lionel asked. He arose, hugged the hooker, and strode confidently through the open barred door. "To my estate. How are…"

Jean locked her right arm in his left and they calmly left the station house.

Once in the cab, he said, "Fuck it. Fuck the Rolex."

After an uneventful flight to Dallas, the chauffeur drove them home. Again, without incident from Lionel. He provided no explanation for this fiasco.

"What happened?" Jean asked.

He replied, "Fuck it. Fuck Phoenix. I'm the doctor." Near the front door, he urinated on a rose bush.

She said, "Oh, Lion. Lion. Lion…"

Jean's body relaxed now that they were home safely again. A warm bath for him and a nap. Both seated in the study late in the afternoon. At last, Jean's breathing finally calmed down, thanks to the yoga. Her thoughts raced on.

"Lion," she said, "warm enough?"

He did not respond so Jean smoothed the blanket over his legs and propped him up with a small pillow. She turned his wheelchair toward the pond behind their home, now populated by a family of colorful ducks.

"Beautiful, aren't they?"

She pulled her chair closer to his. Held his hand. Caressed his arm. "We had some good times. Remember the farmhouse in France?

Fresh cheese every day. Red wine for our neighbor's vineyard. Beefsteak I bought in the village, freshly butchered that morning. Sunsets that were so beautiful, so memorable. You're a stranger sometimes now, but it was so easy to love you then. You've helped me understand that what you have left is important, not to focus on what is gone. The remains of a life together."

Lion said, "What a surprise. Aha... What's going on here?"

He repeated the story for the umpteenth time. "I'll practice until the award ceremony. I'm going to get it. I must be a doctor until then. I'm the doctor." Silent again.

Did he still love her, she asked herself. On rare occasions he showed kindness and love. She held on to those rare moments. Tried to forget the failing memory, suspiciousness and anger, confusion, increasing loss of his ability to maintain the basic activities of daily living. She took care of most of it.

He turned over much of the money in their charitable trust to her, so she finally signed the agreement to sell the practice. She still thought he might have been cheated by the younger doctors, preying on his obvious decline.

The family of ducks flew away. Feathers of green and blue and brown blended into the oncoming dusk.

Dinner was served in the dining room. Lion still ate. Thank God.

After dinner, Jean felt desperate. Her hands shook. Sweaty palms. She decided to call the Alzheimer's Help Line. A first time to reach out to strangers, she grew more nervous as she dialed the 800 number. She roamed the study as the call came up on speaker phone.

"Good evening, Alzheimer's Help Line. How can I help you?"

Jean moaned, and then cried quietly. She wiped away the tears. "It's my husband...Is this confidential?"

"Oh, my, yes. Of course. We do not make a recording. No tape."

"Good, my husband is a doctor. Getting worse—steady decline."

"Yes, go on. Must be terrible for you."

"Well, he can't remember things. Then he does for an hour, even a day. I think he's a risk to himself and his patients—and me." She gasped and nearly choked.

"In what way? The risk?"

"He depends on me for too much...dressing, eating and sleeping. I rescued him today from some crazy stunt. He..."

"I see. Heavy burden."

She squatted on the floor. Then arose. "Yes, he's been cheated by his partners. They hide... A cover-up."

"A legal or ethical issue? Complicated."

"I should meet with them. My husband says not to."

"Need a caretaker or even an institution for him?"

"Yes, I'll get help. I promised him he'd never live in a dementia unit. Never." She felt like crushing the phone—blotting out the call.

"If you hold on for a moment, I'll give you the names of several caretakers available near you for home assignments. OK?"

"I'll call back. I promise. I'm so upset..." She disconnected the phone.

Jean collapsed onto the yellow velvet couch near the fireplace. She wept. No sobs or gasps or screams...only hot tears.

"We'll never travel again. Waited too long," she said. "Why the medical award? Who cares? Why is it so goddamn important? Why didn't you think of me first?"

"Were you on the phone?" Lion asked.

"Yes, dear," she said, "it was a wrong number. Rest now. Don't forget the notes. They are little reminders of what to do, what to wear—you know, stuff that's so easy to forget."

"Fuck the notes."

"Are the two doctors ready to take over?" she asked.

Chapter Thirteen

Two weeks before the awards luncheon, the new owners of the Shindell Surgery Group faced each other at a small table in the doctor's lounge at Saint Luke's Hospital. Still dressed in pale blue scrubs and caps, they drank coffee and nibbled on raisin croissants.

Bob said, "The accountant values the practice at two mill. Shindell pays the taxes."

"Our services aren't cheap."

"No, but my lawyer warns there may be charges of fraud. No full disclosure. His questionable competency."

Kris swirled a spoon in his cup then added one cube of sugar. "We respected the individual patients. Acted in their best medical…the good of the patients."

He took a small bite of the croissant, and then Bob said, "What about simple ethics? Rules and standards of what's right."

"Let's get down to brass tacks. We were moral."

They high-fived and then shook hands. Bob's engulfed Kris'. "All we do is tell the truth. We assisted. Then took over. Gonzalez knew… Hospital did nothing. The State Medical Board can say we should have reported him."

Kris said, "He was our boss. Could have fired us. Our duty… No one hurt."

"We stick together. Maybe…class in medical ethics. Uhm. Possibly a disciplinary note—that's it!"

"By the way…who runs the show?" Kris asked. "Jean and Lionel are out—we're in."

Bob squirmed in his small chair. The metal legs scratched the floor. "I'm much bigger."

"It's set up as fifty-fifty. Decisions may be uncomfortable or controversial."

Bob said, "I'm much bigger."

They laughed, finally relaxed with each other. Thoughts of lawsuits or fraud or losing their medical licenses receded for the moment. As if for the first time, they both recognized that the practice was a reality—their own reality. They'd have to decide who was the boss if it came to that. Both were number one in the OR.

Kris said, "I'll flip you a coin. Heads I win." He flicked his thumb.

Bob said, "I hope you're joking, my friend."

"Sort of…it's one way."

"The lawyer said it's jointly owned by us. We can bring in associates or partners." Bob stood.

Kris said, "I'll run it six months, then you do the same."

"I'm better with people…the nurses." He feigned the fake smile of a CEO, getting rid of staff. Used his right arm as a brush. "Bye-bye, Mattie."

"I'll get an MBA. It's a sure thing." Kris shook his hand and arm as if rolling dice.

"We'll find a way out of this. Two more weeks. Then work it out."

Kris nodded. "The idea of an award ceremony at the luncheon brings tears to my eyes. Jean appears so calm. She expected…"

Bob stretched to his full height. Then he forced his body into the chair again. "I remember the good…many good things about him."

"Me too. Unless we get into trouble. Then it's his fault… His demise. You go home," Kris said, "to your wife and kids and have a drink. Me, I'm playing blackjack. I count cards even if they…" He lit an E-cigarette and puffed hard several times, then blew out a long stream.

"Almost forgot, the parents of the hydrocephalic nine-year old came in to see me. They adore Dr. Shindell," Bob said.

Kris observed beads of perspiration on Bob's upper lip. "Could have happened, no matter what."

"I promised the moon. Apologized. No charges. Follow-up. No expenses. Kid is fine now."

Kris let out a huge sigh. He glanced at Bob's huge hands. "Now they love you, Bob. Good work."

Bob's iPhone rang. Message said, "Stat OR number seven." He jumped up and moved fast.

He abruptly stopped and turned back. "Jean told me that she's nearly positive her husband got the placebo in an Alzheimer's experiment. She's a tough bird."

Chapter Fourteen

The speakerphone blared in the Shindell study. "Goldstein calling. How is he?"

Lionel's head popped up as he perched on pillows covering the seat of his wheelchair. "What's that shit? I'm the doctor. Phone company...fuck themselves."

Ignoring his request, Jean spoke. "Yes, he's the same. The awards luncheon is this week. God help us!"

"How can I be of service?"

"Well, as our attorney, I've a few loose ends. Probably nothing to worry about." Her hair flipped as she ran her hand through it.

"Yes, go ahead."

"Wilshire and Longly and I have a meeting scheduled with a hospital administrator. Lion can't go."

"Uh-huh. Makes sense." He cleared his throat.

Lion said, "Jean. Jean. Jean. Jean. The sun..."

"Yes, dear. I'll move the chair. Hold on, Mr. Goldstein." She turned him away from the windows.

"I'm the doctor. Assholes—every one of them."

"Forgive me, Mr. Goldstein. Lion became uncomfortable." She felt lucky that the new wheelchair turned on a dime.

"No problem. Go ahead."

"The hospital people will probably bring up two surgeries which Lionel didn't perform—and a mistake or two in an office visit, too." She drummed her fingers on the tall-boy antique from France.

"Yes, yes. Anyone die?"

"Yes, but Wilshire and Longly did their best. Tough cases."

"What else?" He cleared his throat again. Then he coughed. "Excuse me. Go ahead."

"Lionel created a storm after one of the surgeries. I had to get him." She traced her steps in the multi-colored Persian they had shipped from Tehran. "…an office visit for hydrocephalus."

"Jean, go ahead with the meeting. See what they have. Plan to... Consent is not a problem. Another surgeon operated. Medical Board won't… Patients didn't know."

She stood behind Lionel's chair and rubbed his head.

"Should have quit months ago," Mr. Goldstein said.

"Yes…practice until the awards luncheon. Wouldn't budge. Can I get a little huffy with the hospital people?"

"I don't see why not. Admit nothing—no mistakes or wrong-doing. Tell the others to simply say that the patients had top-notch care. My law-school buddy…uhm…general counsel for the Medical Board."

"Fuck it. I'm the doctor," Lionel said. He filled his mouth with sputum and spit on the imported carpet. "Take that, you motherfuckers."

"He's at it again," Jean said. "What about that Mattie?"

"Before we speak of the nurse, threaten to withdraw Shindell Surgery Group from hospital privileges and surgery there. Hit them where it hurts."

"The nurse…"

"Yes, that nurse. She's been spilling the beans about Lionel. Told me straight-out. Wants money to shut up."

Jean said, "As Lionel might say, 'fuck her'." She flipped off the nurse.

"My sentiments exactly. She wants a quarter mil but she'll take 100K."

Jean paused a moment, calculating the pros and cons. "Do it. No loose ends at the office."

"Consider it done. If she squawks, its extortion—a serious crime."

Jean sat down in a straight-backed rattan chair across from her husband. She adjusted her blouse. Smoothed her hair. Examined her perfect nails. She said, "Lionel is a winner."

"Bye, bye. I'll be at the luncheon ceremony."

"One more thing," Jean said. "I've read several hand-outs from the hospital. Patients have the right to know their treatment options—information about outcomes—and ethics policies."

"I'm sure there were proper consent forms in both of the surgery cases."

Jean's face reddened and her mouth tightened. "They thought that Lion would operate. Isn't that part of treatment? That wasn't..."

A huge sigh from the lawyer. "Don't worry. They were all top-flight surgeons. Lion thought..."

Jean stood again and picked up the pace of her stroll around the study. "The price of the practice."

"Yes, I know. I wrote the contract and the codicil. I'll take care of it."

"Bye. Bye."

Jean's protective armor strengthened. She glanced at Lion. She would speak for him at the meeting...fuck the hospital people.

Chapter Fifteen

Rosalie poured herself a shot of Tequila. She gulped it, then a second one. No ice. No salt. No lime. Not even any lemon.

She sat down and leaned back on the black leather couch and counted her blessings. She closed her eyes, then her daughter Alma, now twelve, would come rushing in from school choir practice any moment. The girl meant everything to her—joy, life, action, the future—everything. Her college fund…though. Not for a local community college either. Alma deserved the big time and her grades in school showed it.

Their apartment, so perfectly neat and clean and organized, mirrored Rosalie's personality and her determination and approach to the world. Nothing like the roach-infested two room shack that she grew up in with her Mom and three younger brothers. Beans and rice, then rice and beans, then… The cooking oil stunk up the place since it was the cheapest they could afford. Her mom was a seamstress. The payment for alterations, sewing and tailoring amounted to just enough to keep the kids in tire sandals, mended clothes and black beans and rice. Rosalie wore her Mom's hand-me-down dresses. Her brothers' old clothes, mended and washed, then went to the next-in-line boy. The Gonzalez boys had a reputation for wearing each other's clothes. People joked they were like twins—but of different ages. They were dirt-poor, not just poor in a neighborhood that lacked running water or electricity.

Her mother's tortillas saved the day. Several times a week she ground her own corn and scavenged onions and soft, white cheese. Out came a cheesy, soft concoction wrapped in fresh tortillas. And of course, beans and rice. That meal lasted for two or three days. She recalled how much her brothers could eat at one sitting. No wonder they turned to fat as they aged.

The door opened. Alma threw her books on to the table and hugged Rosalie several times. "Tra-la-la…" Her clear soprano voice, spirited yet controlled, brought tears to Rosalie's dark eyes. "We're doing old southern… For the black kids… I love it."

"And the math?" Rosalie asked.

"How about ninety-eight percent?"

Ex-husband Ahmed, whatever else he was, had a chiseled face and a flashing smile. Alma captured those plus perfectly shaped lips. A real beauty who grew more attractive with the passing years.

"Smart and beautiful. How did I get so lucky."

"You made me, Mama. I'm yours..."

Rosalie felt more relaxed. Her smooth brown face lost the slight reddish hue of fear and anger she'd experienced earlier during the last interview. She respected authority, maybe too much. Yet she knew when it was corrupt, or lied, or cheated someone at the hospital. Her sixth sense about people—gringos, black or Asian—propelled her career and the quick rise in succession of human relations jobs. She had to be careful, not to threaten prestigious doctors or nurses, but not let herself be manipulated by their power or control.

She was strong and stood up for herself when necessary. Working full-time while attending night school had been a juggling act. She found an older woman next door to take care of Alma. Her M.B.A. would be online, study when she wanted to.

"Let's go out to eat...maybe pasta."

"Yummy," Alma said. "Can't eat too much or the plaid skirt won't fit."

Rosalie said, "I can fix...no, I'll buy you a new one. Nuns don't like the look of hand-me-downs."

Alma said, "I'll wash up."

Rosalie did the same before they drove to Dino's Italian Café. They both ordered pasta with marinara sauce. The simplest item on the menu. Alma drank Sprite, while Rosalie splurged on a glass of the house red wine.

"Tell me more about my father."

"You know most of it. I...I must have been sixteen or seventeen when I met him. Thought he was Mexican. So handsome. Such a...hunk, so you'd say. I became pregnant so he married me—a justice of the peace. Then he left me in a few months. Everybody—my brothers, Mama—had warned me about him but I wouldn't listen. A wonderful gift arrived—you. I closed off part of myself to other men and decided to get educated and have a career here in the U.S."

Alma reached across the table and touched Rosalie's hand. "You're the best. A mother and a father and…"

Rosalie blew her a kiss. "You too."

The pasta arrived. Rosalie showed Alma how to twirl it with a fork and large spoon. She'd seen it in a classic Italian movie starring Gina—whatever her name.

Rosalie's cellphone rang. For a moment, she gazed at the creative, colorful murals on the walls—Florence, Rome, Venice—escape to Italy they said. Then she answered. The Verdi opera on the wall speakers interfered with the voice on the other end.

"Speak louder. Is this Roberto?"

"Si, yes it is. Mama is sick."

Rosalie said, "Mama…sick…what's wrong?"

She took her cell to the women's restroom so she could avoid the loud music and distracting art.

"We're at rehab place. No good here. No doctors," Roberto said.

"What's wrong with Mama?" The toilet flushed very loudly.

"Mama no speak. Yesterday put in loops…They say heart or she's just old, bad head."

Rosalie chuckled to herself. "You mean brain, not head."

"Okay, she forgets stuff. Can't remember. She fainted…"

Roberto, the oldest of her three brothers, had always been a worry-wart. Scared of school, ran from fights, and let the younger two intimidate him. He worked as a technician in a battery factory but never married. He had two children by a woman he called his fiancé, despite the fact she was already married to a policeman.

"Do this. Take Mama to the ER at the hospital. Tell them what you've told me. I'll send money to them tonight from Western Union. Understand?"

"Yes, sí. I'll do it now. Mama in wheelchair. We take her."

Rosalie could hear him relaying her message to her other brothers. He drummed his fingers on the phone. It bothered her. "I'll see you tomorrow, Friday night."

Rosalie closed her cell and returned to the table. "I'll take mine home in a box."

Alma said, "What's wrong? Pasta is delicious."

"My mother is sick. Fly to Monterey on Friday night. Western Union now. No insurance."

Rosalie paid the bill and tip. She hugged Alma for dear life when they pushed back their chairs and stood. An embrace filled with hot tears and longing and need. The cycle of life—a beautiful talented daughter and an aging, ill mother. Both part of her dreams.

She always tried to bring her mother to live with them but she wouldn't budge from the old house.

"It's home—mi casa," her mother said.

They drove hurriedly to Western Union. Rosalie sent $1000 to the account of patient Georgeanne Gonzalez, now in the ER.

Alma said, "Don't worry too much. She's strong. Had to be."

Returned to their apartment, Rosalie immediately said goodnight to Alma and kissed her. Tomorrow's interview with the Shindell Group would be challenging. She needed rest.

She had Alma. She had her mother.

Yet, she couldn't stop shaking. The yoga didn't help much. Her mom must be very ill. Not terminal, she prayed. Let her live, dear God. I'll do anything. Anything. She went to her knees beside the bed. Prayed for her mother's health, long life. Then she arose and grabbed the bottle of Tequila. She chug-a-lugged. Finally, a sweaty sleep.

Chapter Sixteen

"Nice to meet you, Ms. Gonzalez. My husband is a bit under the weather. He sent me."

"It's my pleasure, Mrs. Shindell. Glad to see you. Hope he's better. Weekend of rest..."

"Yes, it's just a mild...maybe a reaction to meds," Jean said.

And so the meeting began. Friendly, but not too friendly. "Welcome Dr. Wilshire and Dr. Longly." Not much warmth in it. Ms. Gonzalez behaved correctly but cautiously.

Both doctors nodded. No smile. No words. No emotion.

"Just a few follow-ups to our last meeting, doctors," she said. "Coffee?"

The doctors declined but Jean nodded. "It's a blend from Costa Rica with a bit of chocolate." She poured Jean a cup.

"Delicious," Jean said, "simply delicious." She sipped several more times. She wasn't sure why, but Jean sensed the enemy in Ms. Gonzalez. She braced for battle.

"Dr. Longly, you lost an elderly man with a chronic subdural hematoma a few days ago. Correct?"

"Yes."

"You were assisting Dr. Shindell but he became ill and had to be helped out of the OR?"

"Yes, that's what happened."

"Then, he became agitated and behaved...his wife and driver took him home." Ms. Gonzalez reviewed her notes.

"That's what I was told."

"Why were you in the OR? Why did you perform the surgery?"

"I was there to assist him, and, of course, to learn from his technique." He fidgeted in his chair.

"It had nothing to do with his state of mind or his behavior?" She removed papers from a file.

"No."   He looked at his shoes. Dr. Longly then lit a cigarette with a gold lighter that had a G.A. crest on one side. He took in a deep drag and blew it out. "You don't mind if I smoke? Cut way back."

"I don't have an ashtray," Ms. Gonzalez said. "Use a coffee cup."

"My supervisor is curious about an office visit of a nine-year old boy with childhood hydrocephalus. I think it was last week."

Jean said, "You know, Ms. Gonzalez, my parents used your approach—veiled threats and accusations. Supposed to induce fear or guilt and panic. They never followed through. You won't either. Not here."

Before she processed an answer, Dr. Wilshire spoke.

"Yes," he said. "I accompanied Dr. Shindell at the office visit. He knows shunts like nobody else."

Jean arose from her chair. "Be right back. Restroom." She hurriedly opened the door and then slammed it shut.

Dr. Wilshire said, "This was congenital due to aqueduct stenosis. The shunt unit didn't function properly. Local infection around it. We had a white cell count and blood cultures." He rubbed his hands together.

"Did you do a CSF sampling? Or a CT scan?" Ms. Gonzalez rolled her eyes.

"We left the shunt in position and administered antibiotics."

"My notes…other neurosurgeons state that replacement of the whole shunt is always best," Ms. Gonzalez said. She gazed at a log book.

"Dr. Shindell didn't do that. He's the expert on this. The drainage was…"

Her face darkened. "Well, the boy ended up in the ER at Saint Luke's with an occlusion and nearly died. They saved him. Over drainage…and pressure changes."

Jean re-entered the office, appearing refreshed with fresh make-up and a bright smile. "Did I miss anything?"

"My boss senses some odd things going on. Erratic behavior…two surgeons present…surgery patients lost…a botched office visit. Do you doctors hide his mistakes? Fill in for him when he can't perform?"

Jean stood and leaned over the desk, gripped the edge with both hands. "Harsh accusations, Ms. Gonzalez. Very harsh," she said. "We're leaving. The office can give you the name of our attorney. We'll probably cease surgery here. Only practice at the other three local hospitals."

"My boss might like that. The Medical Practice Committee meets soon."

In the hallway, Jean said, "She's getting inside information from our office. Let's hire all new nurses. It's not just Mattie."

Dr. Wilshire nodded.

"See you at the awards luncheon," Dr. Longly said.

NO LUCK

A Novella

NORMAN GIDDAN

Chapter One

The dark veil on Jean's small black hat hid no tears. Crying
ended when Lionel collapsed and died at the recent Medical awards
luncheon. A descent into Alzheimer's, slow and uneven, suddenly
stopped. Now, he morphed into thick brown dust layered in a gold-
flaked urn. The mausoleum held many of them, quietly behind thick,
white marble doors. Jean didn't know how often she'd visit—to pray,
and to mourn, and speak to him. He could be such a bastard.

Stubborn and insistent on working until age sixty-five, he finally
won the top doctor in Texas award. He did both, then fell at the lectern
while speaking to the medical luncheon, dead on the spot. Doctors, next
the paramedics and EMT's couldn't revive him. Even then, she felt that
he'd achieved what he wanted and needed, so he deserved a quick,
painless ending. She cried and moaned and sobbed then. Not now. No
more, she hoped.

The huge bouquet—really the largest floral display she'd ever
seen and the most colorful and beautiful—sent by the Texas Board of
Physicians already highlighted the lobby of a nearby senior center and
nursing home. No sense in letting the flowers rot near the crypt.

She walked resolutely away from the crypt, their minister
blessed her again, and the two junior neurosurgeons each held one of her
hands. They had shielded and covered for Lionel during his final
decline—performed his surgery and conducted his office visits—in
exchange for the ownership of the surgical practice. She knew they'd be
haunted for years for failing to report his impairment, lying to the
hospital and not obtaining Lionel's patients' consent. His patients
thought Lionel did the surgery and reviewed MRI's and PET scans and
prescribed their treatments and medications. Dr. Longly, small and bony
and thin, and Dr. Wilshire a huge bear of a man became wealthy
overnight, when the proceeds of their own practices combined with the
net profit in the Shindell Medical Group. They hid Lionel's dementia.

Jean trusted Abe Goldstein, her bald and short and horn-rimmed
attorney, who brought up the rear of their group. He did her bidding,
including a payoff to a whistleblower nurse, advice on how to game the

system, and investing her inherited fortune in stocks, real estate, and annuities. She accumulated wealth beyond anything Lionel mentioned or showed her. Only Abe knew the full extent of her holdings. When she reluctantly agreed to the 'sale' of the practice, Lionel substantially increased her share of the other assets in his will.

In a moment of pique, she told herself that she'd earned it all, and then some. She smoothed her black jacket and realized that the men stared at her shapely legs and the stiletto black strap heels. For sixty, a real looker—yes, there could be a future.

The sun peeped through the thin, gray clouds as the four of them climbed into the shiny stretch limo. Heavy rain that lasted for two days stopped abruptly early that morning. The humidity decreased and a beautiful May afternoon lay ahead, dry and bright with the temperature in the mid-seventies. She loved this weather and crazily thought that Lionel's ashes did too. No, she meant his soul. She wasn't really sure what she believed at that moment, but she'd done what she could for him—living and dead. She knew that she had been much too obedient, covered for him like the medical staff did.

Jean mused over Lionel's life as the limo moved slowly. The minister hit the high points—brilliance, success, generosity and leadership at the local, state, and national level. What made him continue to practice until he reached sixty-five, she thought? Until he won the state medical award?

She couldn't resist the fact that he controlled her life as well as his own. He couldn't have done otherwise, a driven, ambitious, skilled surgeon whose life outside of the OR differed little from his dominance in it. A complicated man. No, really very simple. He was fine when he got his way—almost always with her. No kids. No travel. No nursing home. No debate. No discussion. My way or the highway!

Lionel knew best. Until the dementia got hold of him and then he became vulnerable, confused, acted out frequently—swore, spit, and threw objects around the room. Used a walker but refused a wheelchair until the walker failed to keep him upright. Then he needed her like never before. She did her best, but he could be such a brute, so needy, so much of a burden that at times she was sure she'd ...

Abe said, "Jean. Jean. Let's talk for a moment. I need your directions."

Jean lifted her veil, took off the hat itself. "Yes, I'm..."

"Well," Abe said, "the problem with Dr. Longly and Dr. Wilshire won't go away. Mattie's been paid off. The hospital—maybe the medical board—even the practice may end up in court."

Jean said, "No one died. They got good care." She patted the knee of each doctor, sitting on either side of her. "Maybe better than…"

"Of course."

The doctors remained silently pleased.

Abe went on, "They did their best. No negligence from these two…fraudulent arrangements, yes, deceit on consent and release forms…failure to report… We all profited."

Jean spoke to the limo driver. "Please put on the A/C. Just a bit." It hummed instantly.

Abe said, "We must protect the practice, these doctors, and the hospital."

"Of course." She crossed her legs again.

"The Medical Board will back the arrangements I propose. The hospital and the practice pay money. Patients agree…" He squirmed in the jump seat.

"So, what do you suggest?"

"The Lionel L. Shindell Chair in Neurosurgery."

"How much?" She peered into Abe's eyes, her own dark and compliant but steadfast. She would not be bullied now into anything. "The price tag?"

Abe's face relaxed. Muscles drooped into his small double-chin. "Say two-fifty from the practice, two-fifty from you, matched by five hundred from the hospital and medical school."

Dr. Wilshire's eyes widened and beads of perspiration formed beneath his nose. "Whoa. The practice…not good for us."

"What do you want me to do?" Jean said. "Pay the entire five hundred?

Abe said, "Just a moment, Jean. The doctors have the practice…conspired with Lionel to get it—illegally, immorally and unconscionably."

Dr. Longly leaned forward in his seat. "Abe's right. We should pay. Especially if this settles it."

Dr. Wilshire nodded.

Jean said, "Whatever Abe thinks is fair. I'll go along with… He has my complete trust."

Abe said, "How about seventy-five from each doctor and three hundred fifty from you—Lionel's estate?"

Both doctors nodded.

"Done," said Abe. "This leaves Lionel's legacy intact. Celebrates his life and accomplishments. No lawsuits." A smug smile crossed his face. "The hospital and medical school love it…five hundred K is no problem."

"Don't worry, Jean, the practice will continue its high standards," Dr. Wilshire said.

Silence. No one laughed, not even a smile or smirk. The unintended inside joke played poorly.

"Driver," Jean said, "drop me off at home." She shut her eyes and leaned back in her seat.

They drove in silence as Jean thought of Lionel. She hiked up her skirt and crossed her legs again. She knew Abe stared. Lionel would like that. He never lost interest in me—my body, the clothes, stiletto heels, and scarves. If I'd been decades younger, they'd have called me a trophy wife. Too old for that. Not too old to start a new life. Grieving for the last few years exhausted me.

Time for a fresh start, a beginning that leads to travel, enjoyable work with kids and another man in her life. Someone more understanding and compassionate, who could listen to a woman's feelings and support and care for her. Someone with a thirst for adventure, a burning need to see the world and experience different ways of life, unusual foods, and a sense of excitement about life.

The limo stopped. Jean mumbled goodbye and her thanks to the men as she walked into her home. Once inside her bedroom, she ripped off the black dress and heels and tucked herself into bed. Now drained of life in only the way a funeral can do it.

The dream started with a heavy dark boulder lifted from a winding road by a masked-man wearing a cape. Jean sat in a motorized rickshaw, driverless but staying ahead of the traffic. She called out to the masked-man, thinking it might be Superman, but there was no answer. In fact, there was no noise at all—no birds, no animals, no wind, no thunder—and even her words were soundless. For some reason the masked-man jumped into the rickshaw and guided it along the road. He did not peer at her, and said nothing to indicate that he was aware of her presence. She tried to touch his shoulder but couldn't. She tried to speak to him, to ask him who he was, what he wanted, if he could help her— but words failed her.

Suddenly the bedside phone rang and she awakened. "Yes, yes. Who is it?"

A click on the other end but no words. The end of the dream? She thought she heard the melody from the Beatles' song about 'help from my friends,' but she couldn't be sure. She desperately hoped that good things were ahead. It just didn't seem to be enough to simply be rich. She hungered for more from life.

Chapter Two

Jean leafed through the travel brochures on her desk—Europe, Asia, a Kenya safari, or a Danube River cruise. She wanted it all, every last drop of adventure and sightseeing and shopping and romance. She'd dreamed of a long ocean cruise with a stop at every sunny beach, every ancient city and every cathedral and church—tasting every ethnic or regional food and wine. She wanted it all. Now!

She couldn't resist thinking that Lionel might have enjoyed any one of these trips—or vacations—or sightseeing, if he had only slowed down and retired before the big "A" hit him—and her.

She pushed him out of her mind. He's not here, she thought, so why wonder or speculate. Please thyself. That's a variant of 'Know thyself'. She was amused. She smiled. The L'Oreal white face cream and mask soaked up some of the lines and wrinkles of aging, most appearing while she served as a caretaker.

It's time. It's now. Don't dawdle. She called her travel agent. She told her maid to serve her breakfast in bed. She told her driver to be ready and to clean out the ashtrays. The car smelled, even her new white Lincoln sedan.

She called Abe's wife for advice. They traveled extensively.

"Marsha, it's me. Feeling restless," Jean said.

"You sound good. Lunch soon?"

"Yes, but I want to see things, do things...get the hell away from hospitals and doctors." She wiped off the cream. "A voyage to..."

Marsha said, "As they say on TV, 'travel moves you'."

"Where should I go? Cruise? Do you like them?" She patted on a cleaner and conditioner.

"Yes, of course. Careful...that damn virus. Go on a long one. Meet people. Settle in."

"Thanks. Bye-bye."

Jean knew her need to explore was healthy, hoped it wasn't premature.

She booked a three-month cruise from her agent.

She called her maid upstairs and told her the plan. She wanted the house to stay open, kept clean, and ready for her return. The driver could help the maid with the house while she traveled.

The agent said, "Sure you're ready?"

Jean said, "You have no idea how ready." She smiled to herself. "Very ready. Finally finished the last thank you to condolence cards."

"Then I'll book you a first-class cabin with a private deck on a ninety day tour of the Caribbean, Europe, and then the Danube River. No, strike the Danube, you'd have to change ships... Next time."

"Sounds good. I'll do it. Hooray! You've got my credit card."

Jean rested comfortably in her blue and gold brocade armchair with her cellphone on her lap. She closed her eyes. The stored-up worry and dread of the past few years momentarily lifted. She ran her hands through her hair, smoothed her dressing robe and felt better than she had in a long time. She'd remembered the slogan 'Just do it.' She did it. Her driver would drop her off at the dock in Galveston. This was so easy. She dozed.

Her agent dropped off the travel itinerary and tickets later that day. Only three days to pack. The ship, *Queen of the Sea*, one year old, carried two thousand passengers and half that many crew, with three pools, a day spa, gambling, a Las Vegas style theater, movies, a museum, an elegant shopping mall, an exercise area, and so much more. At the tail end of the colorful brochure the phrase "Health Services Provided." Oh, no, Jean thought, no more doctors, hospitals, medicine, state medical boards, even nurses. That's all behind me. The future is so easy.

She packed three suitcases, then added a travel trunk. Jean liked clothes, wanted to look good at dinner—maybe the Captain's table. A few days later, her driver got her as close to the ship as possible following a brief tour of Galveston.

In the 19th century Galveston grew into a bustling city with a vibrant important port. Decline set in. Other ports turned more of a profit, horrible storms and hurricanes damaged property and hurt business ventures. Ships moved on elsewhere.

Galveston promoted a set of streetcars which moved tourists and locals alike through the beautiful stretch of Victorian homes. Many were restored and painted in pastel greens, blues, and yellows with white or black trim on the curly-cue lattices and doorways. Gentrification caught on at the same time as the port became a hub for cruise lines and passengers primarily from the southwestern U.S.A.

Now a busy port again, Galveston became home to several cruise lines about twenty years ago. Jean's porter carried her bags to the loading area. She stood in the line of people checking their passport and travel destination, and tickets. Carry-on bags opened and examined at a separate table by staff. Seasoned travelers hid booze in water bottles. Most got away with it.

Another sixty-ish woman, groomed and dressed in a beige summer Burberry suit and suede boots stuck out her hand. "I'm Marie. My husband and I didn't get along. Boom! Divorce court." Her almond-shaped turquoise eyes matched exquisite jade earrings.

"Nice to meet you. I'm Jean Shindell. My guy died."

Marie said, "We can fight it out for the Captain." A subtle laugh, then a wide mischievous grin crossed her face.

Jean shifted her purse and the carry-on from one hand to the other. "Me. Just R&R. He's all yours."

"If you get bored, join me. I'll be a volunteer at the youngsters' daycare."

"Love to. Don't have my own kids. I'd…love to help out. Uhm… Raised my sister then…"

Their line moved slowly. Jean's black slacks were tight, her white turtleneck graced her figure without forgiveness.

"You look good in that outfit. Dark eyes—white skin—great combo," Marie said.

As Jean moved closer to the staff members at the table, someone touched her shoulder. She turned, startled and annoyed. She faced an ordinary looking man—about forty, nothing remarkable about his appearance except a yellow bow-tie and snow white caps on his front teeth.

"I'm Serge Koussef, an attorney in the DA's office in Dallas. A few questions before you board the cruise. Okay?"

Jean said, "Credentials? Card? Badge?" She held out an open palm.

"Yes, of course." He opened his wallet and flashed a set of cards. "Can we sit over there? You'll still have plenty of time." He pointed to a nearby bench.

After they seated themselves, Serge revealed an audio recorder and a notebook.

"What's this about?" Jean asked.

"A probate judge reviewed taxes and noticed money missing in your husband's philanthropic trust fund. Referred it to the DA. A few questions..."

Jean said, "Talk to my attorney?"

"He says you authorized him to remove one million from that five million dollar trust fund. Correct?" He made notes in a small leather-bound book.

"No, it's not. Abe handles all my legal and financial work. Ah. Uhm. I trust him completely."

"The withdrawal was not authorized by you. Did you receive any of that money?"

"No. As far as I know, the full five million is in the trust... Scholarships." Jean stood and turned to walk back to the line she'd been in earlier.

Koussef said, "Please wait. Would you testify in a deposition or in court?"

Jean looked over her shoulder. "Of course. Nothing to hide."

"By the time you return from your voyage, Abe will be indicted... If he pleads guilty, he could be in jail. Thank you." He walked away quickly, heading to the Men's Room.

Jean caught up with Marie who saved her spot in the line.

Marie asked, "Things okay?"

"Yes, yes, some technicality in my husband's will." She removed the passport and tickets from her purse. "I'm sick of lawyers…looking for problems. So are doctors…"

Jean hoped to see young families with children, so the aging passengers disappointed her. She realized that the expense of a several month cruise ruled out many young travelers. Here were four women in wheelchairs, an old man with a walker who stumbled along, and for contrast, several mid-life well-heeled couples in Brooks Brothers and Chico clothes—most of them in soft yellow, pink, or bright orange. She chuckled to herself when she thought of what Lionel would have commented—"So this is…travel."

Jean observed two Middle-Eastern couples, one woman completely covered by the chador except for a lattice-work cloth over her eyes. An African-American middle-aged lady, beautiful in a flowered, dark red, green and purple gown and matching turban. Interesting fellow travelers to meet and enjoy. A handful of children.

Marie said, "I met the head of childcare. A real bitch. They've got sick kids and crazy kids—only a few. Plenty for us to do."

She stood before a uniformed woman at the desk showing her passport and tickets, who said, "The next line is to check your carry-on bag. Um. Hmm. No booze."

Excitement built up. Jean soaked up the atmosphere. Luggage and bags dropped and picked up and moved along the lines. Honking horns and blaring sirens from the boats and huge white ship near the dock. A faint odor of gasoline or kerosene from engines. A slight echo in the huge staging area.

At last, up the boarding ramp. The Captain greeted each passenger. Jean thought he appeared to be out of central casting in Hollywood. Tall, tanned, brown beard speckled with a hint of grey, dressed in all white uniform with delicate swirls of black on his billed hat. Probably about fifty.

"Ah, hah," he said. "I'm Captain Louis Jardot. Two for the Captain's table. Tomorrow night at eight. Welcome aboard." His hand felt a bit damp.

Marie said, "We'll be there with bells on."

The Purser directed them to their cabins. Both had expensive one bedroom cabins on the top deck. Their luggage and bags would arrive later.

"I'm Paul, your cabin steward," said the tiny Asian man in the hallway. "Call me night or day. My duty is to serve." He opened Jean's cabin door for her.

Throbbing with excitement, Jean thought of this spectacular new cruise ship. Tidy cabin with a separate bedroom and a fourth level balcony. What a view—dawn and dusk. Occasional fog arrives, then lifts to show a cloudless blue sky with receding burnt orange and purplish-red in the background. Maybe layers of steely grey and white rain clouds. Even puffy cotton balls. Shapes of dogs, cats, elephants, monkeys—the whole menagerie painted in silhouette in the sky. God's work? Who knows?

She also mused about the vivid descriptions in the travel brochures. A cruise. Movement. Shimmering waves pounding the ship but hardly noticed. Thrust. Going forward to new places and different ports. Shaking. Occasional shimmy from side to side in a wild storm.

Then there were secrets. All anyone knew of you is what you told them or what they observed. Most too drunk or stoned to notice. You could be anyone. Any background. Any status or married or single or widow or whatever. Reinvent oneself or stay the same. Authenticity or fake it—lie—hide—be someone else!

Chapter Three

The Captain's light stubble and chiseled features stirred Jean, especially in full moonlight, a romantic backdrop. Such an attractive man, cosmopolitan, learned, and utterly charming, she thought. Too bad he's only around fifty.

"Thank you, for dinner. The Dover sole—so perfect with that dry California Chardonnay—and the…"

The Captain said, "My pleasure. Marie flirted. Uhm… My interest…you." He held up her left hand and kissed it. "Only you, dear Jean." Then he held both of her hands to his chest.

Jean couldn't decide. Move away. Pull her hands back. Kiss him.

He decided for her. He kissed her lightly on the lips, still holding both hands.

Now Jean backed off. "It's been a long time, Louis. A very long time. I'm not ready…"

He kissed her again. Firmer and sweeter and longer. She threw her arms around his neck. Moved her body closer. Such wonderful lips.

"I understand. Believe me," he said.

They walked leisurely around the upper deck, arm in arm. Jean thought that this was too soon, too quick, yet a soothing balm for her isolation and loneliness. Yes, she'd been lonely with Lionel—his "fuck this, I'm the doctor,"—became a mantra for her loneliness as a caretaker, watching over him, never knowing what he'd do next, what outrage would come out of his mouth, what demand he'd make, what craziness he'd act on.

The Captain said, "Don't let our age difference bother you. My marriage made me an old man. I feel young with you. I feel…"

Jean said, "I'll bet you say that to all…"

"Don't mistrust me. I won't rush…We have time." He slipped his arm around her shoulders and squeezed lightly.

"I know…My husband had dementia. Slow decline over years. He collapsed and died. He was a successful neurosurgeon. So stubborn and pig-headed...did my best." Sobbing and trembling, her tears poured out. "The memories…still hurt."

"Before we both jump overboard, I'll see you to..." He smiled, touched her shoulder with patience and understanding in his heavy-lidded grey eyes. "Let's go." He kissed her on the tip of her nose. "My story…You've probably already guessed that my ex-wife got bored. I was away weeks, even months at a time…angry and vengeful."

"Oh, my..."

Captain Jardot said, "I'm not supposed to fraternize with the crew or date passengers. Taboo…"

"Why me?"

He said, "You're the first. Your appeal…Your allure…" He kissed her hands.

Jean said, "I'm not that special…really?" She smoothed her hair. "The flattery is…"

"It's time," the Captain said. "I could fall in love with you. Even if I…my job here. You're worth…'

Jean turned and walked to the railing. The Captain followed her. She said, "Let's change the subject." The pleasure of a man so attracted to her…willing to risk it all…grew into shame. She hid her blushing cheeks from him.

He said, "Got a text today that some big-time crook may be on board. Paul Picconi. Ran out on a felony conviction. Phony name here?"

"What will you do?"

"Go over the passenger list. Figure it out."

He took her by the shoulders and kissed her very hard and long.

"So strong, my Captain."

Once in the hallway, Jean blew the Captain a kiss and unlocked her cabin door. She experienced wave after wave of feelings—excitement, fear, acceptance, and pride. A man desired her. She quickly undressed and admired herself in the full-length mirror. Lace bra and panties highlighted her ivory white skin and lustrous dark hair. She vowed to become a blonde with streaks. Even at sixty, she thought, I'm still damn attractive, but the Captain is only around fifty, maybe forty-five. Face it, I'm just a horny cougar leading a lamb to slaughter—at least to romance, maybe sex and intimacy. This Captain…quite a guy.

She answered the phone. Marie said, "Couldn't resist calling. You got him, girl. Ahah. I tried but…"

Jean sat on the edge of the couch. "Not really. We just walked the deck and kissed—early movies of Katherine Hepburn and Spencer Tracy."

"So, what else on the second night…after dinner…"

"It's so new. So different. Very handsome and very nice and very patient." The ship swayed slightly.

Marie said, "Sounds good. By the way, I met again with Maryanne to discuss the kids. Don't forget…both volunteers."

"Great." Jean stood before the mirror again.

"She's got one kid who she thinks is 'not right with the Lord'—that means crazy and nutso. Then there's a little boy who she thinks is autistic or Asperger's. As if she'd know. His parents drink all day."

Jean dropped the phone and picked it up quickly. "Our work is cut out for us."

"Yeah, she wants both of us. Okay?"

"You bet. Can't wait." Jean turned so she could see her rear end.

"You'll still have plenty of time for whoopee with..."

"Good night, Marie." She hung up the phone.

Moments later it rang again. "Jean, I just wanted to say how wonderful… My cellphone rings and my beeper won't stop. Grease fire in the main kitchen. Smoke in one Level Two hallway—free breakfast to all those rooms that can see it or smell it. A ninety-year old man lost one of his suit cases. The porter found it in the man's closet. Only way to be alone with you is..."

Jean said, "A busy, busy man. I like busy men. See you tomorrow, Louis. Thanks again. Some fire here but not a bit of smoke."

Marie and Jean entered the Kids' Club at 8:00 the next morning.

"Hello, ladies," Maryanne said. "You must be Jean. Marie mentioned you. I'm Maryanne. I thought you'd be younger but..."

"Nice to meet you," Jean said. They shook hands.

Maryanne said, "Here are the rules of the club." She handed a color brochure to Jean. "Safety and security come first, last and always."

Jean kept her cool. She didn't like her from the start. Thinning white hair cropped short, a high white turtleneck sweatshirt, and black leotards. The potbelly didn't help. The remark about Jean being "younger" sealed Maryanne's fate.

Marie said, "We don't work with the Splash group, do we?"

"Oh, heavens no, our instructors for that are trained professionals."

Jean turned to Marie and whispered, "That pink scrubbed skin...what a bitch."

Maryanne smug and self-satisfied said, "We have swim classes for kids ages four through eight—Safe Splash—we charge extra for it."

"What else do we need to know?" asked Marie. She twisted her torso. The plastic chairs were so uncomfortable.

"I want you both...anybody loitering near our center or paying undue attention to kids...whatever. Tell me or the staff."

Maryanne brusquely handed over an information form to each of them. "Please fill this out...who you are...in your cabin and give it to me tomorrow."

Jean said, "Fine. Those shelves are low, so the toys and games will distract autistic kids. You need several more small tables and chairs... Where's the bathroom?"

Maryanne stood stiffly behind her desk. "Parents assume liability for their kids here. You may want to back out. There are a few other volunteers…"

Marie said, "The parents…"

"Yes," said Maryanne. "The parents are spoiled brats. Should be at home raising good Christian children. Jennie and Bobby tomorrow."

Marie and Jean marched out of the center, having been rudely dismissed by Maryanne's shake of the head.

Marie said, "She's an ex-nun, retired as a teacher. Dropped out of her order. Rumor has it she got involved in an affair with her roommate there. No one likes her." They strolled leisurely down the hall near their cabins.

Jean said, "Good news is the Captain. He's divorced. Wife couldn't take his travel schedule. Very romantic. Wanted to be a doctor. Studied maritime stuff—British Academy of Maritime Management. Worked his way up. Quite a…"

Marie said, "Wow, and so handsome." She studied a slip of paper. "My girl Jennie…tomorrow. Been sick. Help her read and play. Yours is Bobby, a four year old with autism. We'd better fill out the questionnaire now. The Nun will dump us if…" She turned to enter her cabin.

Jean said, "You're a quick study. You learn so much about people." She hugged her. "You remind me of that Beatles tune with a little 'help from my friends'."

As she entered her own cabin, Jean realized that she hadn't had a close trusted female friend for a long time. Her life with Lionel left little time for herself. She liked chatting with other women—clothes, children, men—even talking about serious topics in current events and world affairs.

Jean felt liberated. A new wonderful friend. Marie liked her and she liked Marie. Happened quickly. She trusted her gut instinct. Without planning it Lionel kept her close to him and away from other men and women. Possessive as he was, he didn't realize or admit to her need for other companionship, especially with like-minded female

74

friends. Was he afraid she'd spill the beans—his illness, his control, his steadfast decision to keep working until age sixty-five?

Now she could befriend whom she wanted and share with another—a confidante. It felt so right and so good. She knew Marie had a story. Everyone did so what was hers? Did he beat her? Abuse her? She'd find out during the voyage. Marie would confess, just as Jean would open up. The time had to be right for soul searching and reaching the bottom-line of existence—life itself with all its craziness and confusion and uncertainty and pain.

Caretaking had been a full-time vocation. She knew now that she should have taken more time for herself. Lionel wanted her available 24/7.

She recalled his attitude. "No nurses. No nursing homes or rehab centers. No assisted living. No burial plot either. Burn me up...a bottle or jar or urn. Dust either way. Nothing lasts."

Jean soaked up the sun on her balcony. The salty air, blue-white waves, an occasional boat horn or whistle, a cloudless sky, and a delicious aroma wafting up the side from the kitchen on the second level. Before she drifted off into a sun-sleep, she eliminated more burning redness on her stomach, face and thighs by covering herself with a huge beach towel. The empty chair next to her—that could have been Lionel with... The good news—she'd met Marie, couldn't stand Maryanne, and felt attracted to the Captain. Lionel's last few years anchored her to him, to serving him, hoping he'd throw her a bone of thanks occasionally...rarely.

Jean stumbled from the balcony to answer the phone inside her cabin. Still hot from the sun, she said, "Yes. Yes."

"It's me, Louis," he said. "I can't see the movie and take you to a late supper."

"What's wrong?"

"Going to Dr. Parkson. A couple of passengers...some damn virus. Interview them. Precautions..." His voice cracked slightly and did not hide worry over an outbreak.

Jean, now alert, said, "I'll see you there. I used to be a nurse."

"Good, Dr. Parkson needs..."

75

Jean found her way down four decks using steps, then the elevator, to the infirmary. With a small doctor's office, and ten beds it served as a makeshift space for passengers with real and imagined illnesses, mostly the latter.

Louis hugged her. "Jean, this is Dr. Parkson, the ship's sawbones."

The doctor shook hands. "Nice to meet you. Louis says you're a retired nurse—mine is only part-time, so…I'll email the company about you."

Something about him attracted Jean instantly. Maybe…a doctor. A shaved bald head with rimless glasses, and the grey-polka dot tie, the pressed grey slacks with polished black shoes. A little like Lionel…different. And riveting blue eyes.

"If I can help out later," Jean said.

Louis said, "Have the three patients go back to their cabins. I'll see them there. Not much we can do for a virus."

Dr. Parkson, "You're right. Control fever and aches. Reduce vomiting. Uhm. Hum. Hope it's not all over the ship. God help us…"

Parkson's eyes never moved from Jean's face.

She noticed. Flattered but a bit uncomfortable with Louis standing next to her. Her heart raced as she ran her hands through her hair. She turned her head away.

"I volunteer…kids in childcare. Need me…I'll come."

Chapter Four

Marie and Jean ate an early breakfast of steel cut oatmeal and honey in one of the ship's large main dining areas. The noise in the room—busy foot traffic and crowded tables—spoiled it. Early risers still half-drunk either sat hunched silently over black coffee or yelled and argued with each other—no in-between. A few minutes before 8:00 a.m. Marie and Jean were happy to leave for the childcare center.

Maryanne introduced them to Jennie, then moved away from her. "Jennie's head...cancer treatment. Spread... A determined eight-year-old. On her last voyage." Maryanne walked another few feet from Jennie. "Mom and Dad drink all day." She pursed her lips and feigned spitting on the floor.

Next, it was Bobby's turn. "This is Jean, Bobby. Jean will be..."

He cried and ran to the far wall, hiding his face. Maryanne said, "Bobby is four. Uhm. No language. A speech teacher at home, but..."

Jean walked cautiously to Bobby. He repeatedly banged his head on the wall. Continued crying and sobbing.

Maryanne then held him from behind. "This is what I do. Sick of it."

Bobby's wide dark eyes poured venom when he turned to peer at Maryanne. He kicked her in the shins. She let go of him and walked away. Bobby stopped, then rocked back and forth in the corner.

As if on cue, his mother stumbled, nearly fell, as she entered the childcare center. Slurring her words, she said, "How's the little...how's Bobby?"

Bobby screamed, an unintelligible groan or grunt and threw a toy fire engine at his mother.

She said, "You ungrateful S.O.B."

Jean said, "I'm a volunteer with Bobby."

"Good fucking luck, lady." His mother walked out, unsteadily, slipped on the deck outside the door. Righting herself she said, "Good fucking luck." She slid again.

Jean moved closer to Bobby who still faced the wall. He turned to her. She held out both arms in a welcoming, open gesture. He ran to a small table. Then he rearranged the four chairs and plopped down in one of them.

Jean placed a picture of a tree on the table in front of him. She said, "Tree." She pointed at it. "This is a tree." Bobby glanced at Marie and Jennie on the opposite side of the room. Jean placed a picture of an apple on the table. She said, "Say apple. This is an apple." She pretended to munch on one. "We eat them. Yum. Yum."

Bobby shut his eyes. He banged on the table. He pushed over his chair. Jean reminded herself that significant communication and social skills were not developed in Bobby and to go slowly with him. He played rough, just short of hurting himself or destroying his environment.

By accident, Jean hummed a few bars of a southern spiritual— Old Man River. Bobby perked up. He tapped his fingers on the table. Fast, then slowly. Jean moved closer to Bobby and sang a few words less than a foot from his face. He didn't move. She hummed again, louder this time. She sang slowly, then gradually faster and faster. Bobby's fingers tapping matched the rhythm and loudness of her voice. She couldn't believe it but Bobby grunted something that sounded like "love" or "God."

Without planning it or understanding exactly what had happened, Jean discovered that Bobby responded to music—to rhythmic sound—to her orderly and systematic voice—and translated it into tapping with his fingers on the small child's table. "Hurrah," she said.

Bobby blinked his eyes again. Then he ran to the toys and games. He rearranged the books on the lower shelves by size.

Maryanne said, "Take a break ladies. Walk on the deck."

Marie locked arms with Jean as they strolled. "How wonderful Jennie is. Bonded immediately. We...played word games and even learned a few Spanish words. Parents are billionaire New Yorkers with no time for kids. Older brother and sister...attend boarding school in Switzerland. How about you?"

Jean said, "Bobby likes songs." She waved her hands in the air like a symphony conductor. "This breeze and the ship's gentle rolling, I feel—so wonderful. It's good here. Met you. The sun is strong...clouds collapse to make way for it. Maybe I'll write music."

Maryanne yelled from the doorway, "Phone for you, Miss Jean."

Marie said, "Sarcastic bitch."

Jean ran and picked up the receiver. "Be right down." As she hung up the phone, she said to no one in particular. "Tit for tat...Emergency...help Dr. Parkson."

Maryanne glowered. "See you in the morning, Miss Jean."

Jean used the elevator. When she reached the infirmary, Dr. Parkson greeted her. "I didn't say it over the phone...a woman claimed she was raped. She states the man pulled out in time. No semen in her or on her panties. Vagina and skin not torn...no sign of physical violence or harm. Will you..."

"I'll talk to her. Who...?"

"The Captain." Dr. Parkson, face and ears flushed, sat behind his desk.

"Really?"

"Yes, no joke. Help me." He wiped his brow. "Please."

Dr. Parkson led Jean to the patient's exam room. He said, "Mrs. Elsinon, this is one of our volunteer nurses, Jean."

What a beauty, Jean thought. The woman was no more than twenty-five, long blonde hair, ruby red lips, and bright hazel eyes—very bright and luminous green-brown. Maybe 5'3" and 120 pounds.

"How do you do. Nice to meet you," Mrs. Elsinon said. "I'm Cindy."

"Do you feel like talking about it, Cindy?" Jean sat in the small chair.

"Not really. I'm okay. I went along with it. Champagne. Louis took me to his cabin. I don't remember if I said "no" but I thought "no". Never passed out. He's a...stud."

Cindy wiggled her legs as she set upright on the examining table. "I felt angry when I woke up. I'm fine now. Wanted someone here to know. My husband is…he's home with our two kids." She slid off the table and dressed.

Jean mused she's more beautiful than… At least, Louis has good taste.

Cindy abruptly left the room and reached the door to the infirmary.

Jean said, "Anything you want me to say or do? Police?"

Cindy said, "No. Warn women. Uh…He's one horny S.O.B."

Jean reminded herself that this cruise—between Bobby's autism and the Captain and Cindy's blatant sexuality—promised to end any lingering need for Lionel, living or dead. She'd done all she could for him and now she'd help Bobby. And one more thing. Get better acquainted with Dr. Parkson.

Dr. Parkson motioned for Jean to come to his office. "Well, what…"

Jean said, "She seems to want it dropped. No police. My hunch is that it was consensual."

Dr. Parkson said, "Thanks. Let's have a drink some time."

"Okay, love to."

Life on the ship shielded cruisers from the clean balmy air, white-blue waves, and hot sun that surrounded the liner. Air-conditioning and ornamental ceiling fans kept people cool and comfortable but blocked off from the natural beauty of the churning, white-capped ocean, grey gulls overhead, and the hazy beautiful colors of dawn and dusk. If one only gambled, danced, saw Broadway shows and enjoyed the sauna and massage, then the darkness of life inside took priority over the light and wind and water outside.

Without any warning, the doctor abruptly grabbed his bag, and ran to the elevator. "Going to Deck Four. Problem. Emergency phone call."

Jean trailed behind him. "I'm on Deck Four, too." They rode the elevator together.

At Deck Four, Jean could hardly believe the sight. At least a dozen people gathered around the small swimming pool. Everyone stood, speaking in hushed tones, with all the lounge chairs empty and inviting.

"I'm the doctor…please back away. Stand back." He opened his bag, then used a mirror to see if the small boy laid out on the deck was breathing. He said, "A faint pulse, shallow breathing, but he feels cold to touch." He started CPR and continued for at least ten minutes. "I'll give him a shot directly into the heart if…" The boy's head lurched upward and he retched, covering his upper body in a mix of swimming pool water, yellow bile and scrambled eggs. He lived.

Dr. Parkson muttered, "Thank God. He'll be fine."

Bobby opened his eyes and through half-closed lids he peered warily at the crowd of onlookers. He closed them. Shut tight. Then he screamed and yelled and sobbed. Groaned. More vomit and fluids poured over his chest.

Dr. Parkson covered him with a white blanket from one of the chairs. He massaged his arm and legs, then carried him to a deck lounge chair.

Bobby's sobbing stopped. He shuddered and threw off the blanket. Then he ran into the childcare center nearby.

Dr. Parkson said, "Hey there, young man. Wait a minute…I."

Maryanne spoke. "His parents are rich drunks. He's autistic. Jean Shindell…volunteer teacher. This damn woman…" She pointed her finger at Jean. "The woman Bobby followed. Accidentally fell in the water. Doesn't swim. Can't read."

Jean fought a blast of fury and anger toward Maryanne. Her face reddened and her body trembled with unusually strong emotions. She thought—to be blamed by this head of the school—Impossible. Horrible. Despicable. This bitch took no responsibility.

Bobby's mother staggered toward the group. "Did something happen? Where's my…?" She slipped on a wet spot of vomit and pool water. Then regained her balance. "Why didn't someone get me sooner?"

Dr. Parkson said, "Please bring your son to the infirmary. He'll be fine."

Maryanne said, "He ran out of the center. Followed Miss Jean… She no longer volunteers for me." She did an 'about face' military style and walked away.

Marie put her arm around Jean's shoulders. "I'll take you back to your cabin. Maryanne is crazy as hell. I'm not sure I'll volunteer there again."

Jean, overcome with sadness and hatred, cried bitterly until they reached the cabin door. "A shower and a glass of wine." Her words slurred.

Once inside, the paper-thin veneer of bravado broke apart completely, and drained by the cascade of feelings, she slumped against the door, and slowly slid to the floor, devastated by Bobby's actions. She'd had such hopes for him, sensing that the musical connection could be the beginning of some kind of language. Her disdain and contempt for the lies of Maryanne, however temporary, did not outweigh the optimism she felt earlier for Bobby's life and future.

Then it hit her like a ton of bricks—another grim reminder of her dead son—that nagging guilt and loss haunted her daily, but now it took over her whole being. It must have been her fault, not enough woman, too weak, her body not prepared to host a living, breathing son. Lionel gave up, never again willing to try for a child, convinced that it simply wasn't meant to be. No son. No daughter. No grandchildren. No heirs. Would God forgive her? She couldn't forgive Lionel, nor could she diminish the pain of her own conscience. Here, with Bobby, the jinx again—he'd followed her, fallen into the pool, nearly died.

Jean's mind mercifully shut down and she slept, lying spread-eagled on the carpet near the cabin door. She awoke with a horrible headache. Several aspirin and two glasses of white wine later, she showered. The stain of Bobby's episode, the lost connection to him, did not wash away as easily as the teary, dried mascara on her cheeks. Alone with her memories, she climbed into bed, pulled the blankets over her head and slept again.

This time she dreamt that Lionel screamed repeatedly that "it wasn't meant to be" until she awakened, briefly, her body sweating and shuddering with fear. She thought, he never really understood me. He just wanted what he wanted, kept our life as smooth and predictable and certain as he could—at least before the dementia got him.

Around midnight, she awoke, had a glass of water. "Maybe Dr. Parkson…"

Chapter Five

Jean and Dr. Peter Parkson lay on the sandy beach away from the crowded food huts and picnic tables. The both refused a massage offered by a native and concentrated on their cans of cold Modelo beer to wash down sandwiches of pulled pork with con queso from the nearby carry-out.

Most of the ship's passengers migrated to the small shops and jewelry stores in this quaint Aruba port of around several thousand people. Their business was tourism—silver jewelry, colorful blankets and rugs and orange glazed pottery.

Jean and Peter's business, simply each other. The mutual attraction, strong as it felt, needed substance and background and explanation. Their beach towels with green and red outlines of Mexico City's urban landscape, touched at the edges. Peter up on his haunches, rubbed oil on Jean's back. Her one-piece as revealing of skin as most bikinis.

He wore a large straw sombrero to cover his shaved head. Both used the cheap, brown sunglasses bought at the carryout.

"No one knows, do they?" she said.

"I hope not. I fell in love with a passenger."

Jean said, "Whoa. Do the back of my legs, too." She wiggled her toes.

Peter did as asked. "I don't need to know much. Like a teenager. Head over heels."

"My husband died."

"My wife died."

Peter rolled her over, held her and kissed her tenderly on the forehead, nose and lips.

She threw her arms around him as she arched her back. Then she pushed his shoulders up in the air and kissed his chest and neck. "Yum."

Peter said, "You know what I'd like to do now?" He smiled lovingly as he caressed her arms and shoulders.

"Yes, I know. Me, too. On our third real date?"

He sat up as she removed her hands. He crisscrossed his legs yoga style. "My flexibility is returning. The arthritis cure is love and romance…a second chance." He poured lotion over his arms, legs and chest. Jean removed his hat so she could spread it evenly on his face.

The sun beamed down with intense heat and the baked sand finished them off. The cloudless sky with a light wind cooled them. It felt like being in a sun tan parlor with the light and heat on both sides. Waves of two or three feet lapped the beach with small whitecaps that were easy to splash through. An overhead helicopter hugged the shoreline, evidence that the local government protected its tourists.

Peter drew a heart in the sand with P.P. + J.S. in the middle with an arrow through it. "Love."

He went on, "I've got great plans for us. Aha. The Great Wall in China, Galapagos Islands, beef noodle soup in Macao, steak frites in Paris, the museums of Florence, the sweltering beaches of Thailand. You name it, we'll go there, be a part of it…the culture, the language, the wine and food…don't forget the fried octopus in Venice. Trust me."

She kissed his hands. Long artistic fingers that had probably saved hundreds of lives as an internist, maybe thousands. Another doctor, she mused; it must be my fate, my destiny as a nurse to love a doctor again. He is handsome, slight paunch, and the penetrating eyes reached her soul. She wished she had seen his full head of grey, curly hair before he shaved it. She'd ask him to grow it back. He had two grown children but that was just about all she knew of his past.

He knew what she had told him about herself. The life and death of Dr. Lionel L. Shindell.

Jean and Peter returned from the beach. Showered and rested, she applied more aloe body lotion to several crusty areas on her stomach. Hope for dinner with Peter at a local Aruba hotspot was dashed, since his replacement, a part-time physician only gave him five hours of freedom.

No time to eat. So, she called Marie and planned to have dinner with her.

Marie said, "Can't. Got a cold. Ah... Bring food here."

"Sandwiches and soup. See you soon."

The cabin attendant, Paul told her she had a call. Abe telephoned on the ship-to-shore line. Jean sat in a small booth near her cabin to receive the call.

Abe said, "How's it going? Met people? Fun?"

"It's been good so far. The Captain...", Jean said.

"I need your help." His voice was barely audible.

Jean said, "Please speak up."

"Well, I'm in trouble. Some money..."

"Yes," Jean said, "I know about it. Trusted you. So did..." She stood hunched in the cramped space.

"I'm embarrassed to ask," Abe said.

"Go ahead." Her voice snapped a sharp command.

"Could you say you instructed me...the one million..."

Jean said, "You want me to lie?"

"That's a terrible way to ..."

"A lie," Jean said, "that's it?" She sat down again, very slowly.

"Yes. They'll go easier on me. Horrible. Jail. Prison. Uhm...I..."

"I can't," Jean said. "Sorry. You...You betrayed us. A real S..O..." Tears clouded her vision.

Abe slammed his receiver down with a loud bang.

An hour later, Jean kicked the bottom of Marie's cabin door several times. She had food on a tray held with both hands.

"Come in. Door's open."

Jean put the tray on the floor, opened the door, then set the tray on Marie's bedside table.

Marie appeared ashen, her eyes watery and deep-set, perspiration covered her forehead. Propped up by several pillows, she lay back covered by dark brown blankets.

"Do you need a doctor?"

"No," Marie said, "a nurse is fine."

Jean opened the soup container. "Chicken with rice."

Marie spooned a mouthful. "Tell me everything—every single detail."

Jean sat at the foot of the bed, not ready to eat. "We spent several hours at the beach. Oiled each other's bodies. Held hands. Kissed. Fell asleep in the sun. Woke up. Deserted his internal medicine practice in Chicago. Older patients...chronic diseases.

"His wife had a headache that wouldn't go away. A brain tumor. She died during high-risk surgery. That was a few years ago. Depressed for a year. Two grown daughters, both married. Loves them. Cleared up his medical and hospital bills---decided on a change of pace—new life on a cruise ship. I'm his first..."

Marie mumbled, half-asleep, "Wow." She slid down the pillows and developed a beatific smile as she snored.

Jean felt her forehead. Fever had broken. She quietly left the cabin after closing the blinds. She'd eat later in the cafeteria.

Returning to her cabin after dinner, Jean penned a note to Marie asking for an update on Bobby. She pushed it under Marie's door. She lay down and napped.

At 7:00 p.m. Marie called. "Hi, it's me. Feel better. Chicken soup and sleep—perfect combo. Anyway, thanks so much. Bobby is fine. Kids recover quickly. His new volunteer... Bobby hit him...spit in his face. The guy held him in...TV wrestling. Maryanne just..."

"Thank God he's okay. I miss him already. Could have..."

Marie coughed, then sneezed. "Woulda, coulda, shoulda,...Bye for now."

A knock on the door. "It's me, Louis."

Jean opened the door, but kept the chain locked. "Yes, what's up?"

"Have you been ignoring me? I miss you. Ahem... May I come in?"

Jean unlocked the door. Louis tried to hug her but she turned away. "Please, sit down. Make yourself comfortable."

Louis appeared amused, "Why so formal? Still love me?" He grinned at his own sarcastic joke as he sat in a corner armchair.

Jean couldn't help but still admire him, resplendent in white slacks, starched white shirt with braids on the shoulder, and the ever-present Captain's billed hat. Still tall, muscular, and handsome, the blue eyes captivated her with the glints of yellow-green.

She said, "Let's go outside... Spectacular sunset."

"Okay with me. I've got an important matter to discuss." He followed her.

Jean said, "I do, too. Beautiful, isn't it? Puffy pinks and blues in the sun..."

"Yes. You know...the rape business?"

"I do." She stretched out on the pillows of a lounge chair.

Louis pulled a deck chair close to her. "It's not true. Baloney. Malarkey. She's a cunt...oops, sorry, shouldn't have said that."

"I'm not judge and jury, Louis. Our relationship... Over. Caput." She put on her sunglasses.

Louis appeared shocked. His eyes widened and she could see his hands tremble. No movement in his face. "Why? Isn't that something we... Together?"

"No, not this time."

He reached for her as he stood close to her chair. Grabbed her shoulders. She couldn't move.

"Stop it. That hurts." She struggled. Tried to push him away.

Louis tightened his grip. "How do you think I feel? You are…"

She kicked his legs as hard as she could. He bent over. She pulled herself up and ran into the cabin and out the door.

Louis yelled. "Jean. Jean. Please."

"Go away. Don't come back. It's no good," she said. The hallway reverberated with her words. "If you don't, …uh, uh…I…I'll report…"

She observed the Captain slam her cabin door shut and walk away in the opposite direction. He screamed. "What a bitch! Who needs her?" Then he straightened his tie, took off his hat and smoothed his hair, and put on his toothy, commercial smile. He found Marie's cabin door and knocked. No answer.

Still shaking and flushing from the encounter with the Captain, Jean hoped relief was ahead. She needed Peter. She rushed to the infirmary

Chapter Six

There he stood, saying goodbye to an elderly male patient. "Don't worry one bit. That bug bite won't itch after…

"Oh, hello, Jean. Hello. Hello." He hugged her. She held on for dear life. They kissed. Then again.

At the door, the patient said, "Good… Thank you, doctor." He smiled and lingered a moment, then shuffled through the door.

Peter spoke to Jean. "I've got a secret."

"Me, too."

"I'll go first," he said. "I'm crazy about you. Don't think of anything else. What's yours?"

Jean pulled away from him. "Um. Um. Well…That Captain. He accosted me… Held my arms…Couldn't move. I told him to get out of my life and…"

Peter's lips and cheeks contorted. He gathered his emotions. At last, he said, "A real bastard. Should call the police and…"

"No. No. Don't. I don't want any trouble. Said the rape stuff isn't true."

"Well, if I hear one more report about him, I'm…Coast Guard and local police." He removed his long, white physician's coat and hung it over a chair. Then he grabbed a blanket and small pillow and placed them on the examining table. "Room for both of us?"

"Yes," Jean said, "if one of us is on top."

They embraced again and literally lunged for the table. Peter landed on the bottom. He helped her out of the sweater and blouse. She undid the zipper and pushed his pants to the floor.

Peter said, "Infirmary closed."

They were gentle with each other. Kissing and hugging. Caressing and rubbing. Soothing and satisfying.

Peter's breathing heated up. He panted. "So very beautiful, Jean. Such a darling. How did I get so lucky." He moved deliberately and slowly inside her. "So very…"

"Do you mind me on top?" Jean asked.

"Oh, no. It's so wonderful. So very, very…"

They nearly rolled off the table when he climaxed. He held her as tightly as the Captain had. But this time it felt wonderful, so right, so good, so liberating, so free of the past, so… Her own finish, in gradual spurts, lasted for what seemed like hours. She lay flat against him as she kissed his neck and face.

She said, "I took care of my sister. Next Lionel. His Alzheimer's grew worse. No children to share my burden and my worry and my helplessness. Nothing changed the downward spiral. He wouldn't go anywhere… And yet…"

Peter did not budge. Stayed semi-erect inside her. "A doctor's wife…an awful existence. Not for us." He snored. Asleep.

She pulled the sheet and blanket over them. She mused, not bad for people sixty. She dozed.

Peter opened his eyes once awake. "Do you want to gamble or go night fishing or see a Broadway-type musical with dinner?"

No answer. Finally, "The choice…um…hum…I'm hungry."

They used the bathroom next to the infirmary waiting area to wash, clean up, and straighten their clothes. No telltale signs of what had just occurred on the examining table remained. Only love.

"I got us tickets for a musical with drinks and dinner. Music and food—perfect together."

Once seated, Jean said, "I love it." She raised her champagne glass in a toast. "To us."

Peter's smile stretched his face. He hummed the melody to 'Getting to Know You'. "Getting to know all about you."

"It fits," she said. "This room is perfect. Dinner and drinks and a Broadway show. What fun." She sipped her drink again.

"I've seen the Yul Brynner movie but never the live show. It's wonderful...you'd even make a Clint Eastwood movie a joy for me." He poured them each another glass.

The waiter appeared. "Rare roast beef with sautéed mushrooms and mixed veggies...Bon appétit." He gracefully placed the food on the table. "Another bottle?"

"Yes, please," said Peter. "Very, very cold."

They listened to the music again without talking. Glanced at each other. Doubling the enjoyment of the show, multiplying the warm glow of the cold wine.

"Earlier," he said, "I didn't mention your gorgeous eyes, your silky skin, the firmness of your pink nipples, the burst of..."

"Thanks."

In no hurry after the show and dinner, hand in hand, they walked slowly on Deck Three. The gambling casino couldn't be missed—the beeps and sirens and clangs of the poker, and blackjack machines and the row-upon-row of quarter slots both beckoned and warned them.

The doorman said, "Good evening, Doc. Good luck."

Peter said, "Jean, let's spend $25 on the quarter slots...free drinks."

"Sounds good." She yanked the slot handle.

Jean thought to herself that she could put up with the smoking, the ever-present smell of booze, and sweaty players for a few minutes. She didn't like this place but she humored Peter.

He lost the $25 quickly. "Damn it. I had two roses but never three...I...I won you. Who cares about slots." He nodded at several of his recent patients, who greeted him.

"Any more secrets?" Jean asked. "I've got one. I love you. I knew...when it's..."

"Me, too," Peter said. He slipped a filigreed silver and pale green jade ring from his pocket. Mexican silver. "First ring I gave my wife. Cancer finally shrunk her fingers so it didn't fit." He held the ring in the palm of his hand.

"Such a sentimental so-and-so. I love it." She slid it on the ring finger of her left hand. Held up her hand to admire it.

"I've got another secret...not a good one. Uhm...I...I lost my medical license."

Stunned by the news, Jean nearly fell off the stool next to the slot machine. She said to herself that it couldn't be—was it déjà vu? Everything seemed so perfect. Now, the knot in her stomach grew. She choked back vomit, determined not to embarrass herself. She was afraid she'd faint so she grabbed Peter's arm to steady herself. She didn't know if she wanted to hear the details or not.

"Tell me...tomorrow."

Chapter Seven

During dinner the following evening, the dark purple Merlot wine relaxed her. She ate herb-crusted, broiled salmon with scalloped potatoes as if there was no tomorrow. But there was a next day and many more ahead. She needed to know the facts. "How did you lose your license?"

Peter peered into her eyes. The waiter poured each of them a second glass of wine. "Your eyes—so mysterious in this candlelight."

"Please, tell me."

"My wife's ovarian cancer got progressively worse over several years. It metastasized. We had insurance...hospital and oncology bills, the cost of radiation and chemo grew oppressively."

"Go on, my dear."

"I violated my honor and integrity as a physician. First time. Terribly ashamed. Horribly guilty, to this..."

Jean placed her hand over his. "The ring is so..."

He said, "I referred several of my patients for surgery. Other treatments could...should...have been tried first. One nearly died. Another...bedridden after a botched stent procedure."

Jean shuddered. He was so open and trusting with her. "Then?"

"To make a long story short, several families sued me, the hospital and the surgical team. Claimed I got kickbacks from the surgeons." He gulped wine.

"Did you?"

"Yes, not enough money to cover the bills but it helped. The Medical Board took a dim view...I...I told the whole truth. Lost my license. Did not...the cruise line."

"You were desperate. Your wife dying. Bills piling up. You didn't harm anyone directly." Teary eyes. No crying.

Peter said, "Thanks but no thanks. I behaved badly and perhaps illegally. Paid the price."

The waiter appeared and removed their plates. "May I offer either of you dessert?"

Jean shook her head.

Peter said, "Yes. French apple cognac for both of us, please. A cheese plate…sourdough, too."

He observed Jean, then said, "I had a strange dream last night, or early this morning…just before I woke up."

"Oh…Tell me." Jean moved her chair closer to the table. She placed one hand on his.

"Here goes. I'm in a grocery store. I order a duck. They are…well, no feathers gone but head and feet left on…I search for black-eyed peas, and yams. Look all over…can't find…them. Closing time. The owners blame me for keeping them. Then a woman cooking the duck in marinade sauce drops it. She says it's her fault that the owners are kept after closing hours. She tells me to roast the giblets, not sauté…"

Jean said, "What's it…?"

Peter raised his glass in a mock toast. "Broke the rules…I…Couldn't find what I wanted. Saved by a woman's gesture."

The dining room cleared out, only three tables of guests still eating and drinking.

An old Sinatra melody about sentimental love played in the background. Food, wine and Peter's story, following their love-making, left Jean in a fog. She wanted to hold Peter close to her, soothe him, and stop his shame and guilt. He had wanted to protect his dying wife and pay for her necessary treatment. She hummed the melody 'when somebody loves you…'

"That's not the end of it." He sipped cognac and nibbled the dessert Gruyére cheese with sourdough bread chips and sea salt rye crackers. "There's more."

95

"What else?"

"Well, the bill collectors came after me. Fast and furious. Still owed a lot—the deductibles didn't...twenty-four hour nurses at home for the final six months. Uhm. Uhm. Took a job with a pharmacy company...I...I lost a lot of income."

"You did... You loved her."

"Yes. Very much." Chugged another cognac. His face and neck flushed quickly.

"What else?" Jean asked.

"A neighbor of ours held himself out to be a bigtime real estate and land developer. I gave him every penny. Borrowed...my life insurance...sold my 401(K)." He sniffed the third cognac, then gulped the entire tumbler.

"Went all in."

"Right."

"Gave him several hundred thousand. Good...no, great...return for several months. Should I go on?" His eyes blurred. Watery tears of naiveté and shame.

"Yes. What's the rest of it?"

"Well, it went sour. Ponzi scheme. Lost most of it. The neighbor escaped his court sentence. Police searched. Lived somewhere in the Caribbean..."

"How much do you need? Lionel left. I'll borrow. You're not alone. We'll get...married." She held out her hands as she stood. Then she leaned across the table and kissed him.

Peter paid the bill. "There's one more piece of the story. Tell you tomorrow." He pulled out his handkerchief and walked out alone.

Jean sat again and sipped her cognac. Did Peter sense that their relationship might be in trouble—even the end of it. Too much stimulation. Too much guilt and shame and embarrassment. His need to be punished and then redeemed. She could help. She didn't feel rejected or isolated, rather that he needed momentary space and that he'd be available to her again in the morning.

Jean's insides churning from all that Peter told her, slowly returned to her cabin. She sat on her darkened balcony. She sensed that a very hot, humid tomorrow stretched out before her. Perspiration dripped easily, almost like tiny rain droplets from the heavens. Thunder from distant layers of grey and black clouds promised heavy downpours approaching, the lightning flashes every few minutes. No peaceful sleep ahead.

Chapter Eight

That next morning Jean and Peter rode exercise bikes in the fitness area on the stern of the fourth level. The doctor's navy blue shorts revealed a small potbelly inside his white long sleeve jersey. He couldn't stop staring at Jean's black and white body suit, a biker's outfit. He said, "Jean, you remind me…"

"Tell me, Peter. Tell me the rest of it."

"Here it is. Once I realized…I helped him…I lied…Uhm. Hum… Pretended no problems existed. Shielded it for a few more months."

"Yes."

"The shocker. I saw him yesterday on the ship. He didn't…"

"What?"

"Yes. Stays in his cabin. Meals there. Goes outside when the maid and porter clean it."

She upped the incline and speed of the bike. "Catch me if you can, Peter. I'm going fast. Out of breath. My face red?" Hot sweat dripped from her head and neck.

"Yes. Red and gorgeous." He pedaled as fast as he could.

"What's your plan?"

"His name is Paul Picconi. He skipped bail. He begged me to…" Dr. Parkson gradually slowed down. "Using the name Mark Adams."

"Shall we get off in Panama and lose ourselves…"

"No, I'm going to call the F.B.I. and local police…the truth. Turn him in." He stopped pedaling.

Jean slumped over her bike's handlebars. "Could we buy him off?" She closed her eyes as breathing slowly returned to normal.

What had she gotten herself into, she wondered? Parkson appeared to be just what she wanted and needed and had hoped for. A fresh start. A new life...a mate she shared...values, ideas, lifestyle, and best of all, romance and love. Goes broke carrying for his wife, so be it. Takes kickbacks. So do others. Loses investments. She could not only cope with it, she could make up the financial difference. Complicit in a fraudulent scheme? No. No. No. Please God, not that. Not another felonious doctor.

She hummed the melody of the Ames Brothers' song 'Love is a many-splendored...' Yes, love is so complex, so layered, so difficult, and must be so strong as to withstand any kind of disappointment or failure, even success, for that matter. She'd stand by her guy, not walk away. He needed her, now more than ever. She admired Peter's forthrightness and his courage to hand over Picconi. Maybe if the authorities had actually tracked him down without Peter's information?

"What about...?" Jean asked.

"I'm going all the way. Tell them what I did. Beg for mercy...reduced sentence...for my assistance." He slid off the bike.

Jean wiped both seats with a disinfectant cloth, then returned to her cabin. She needed time to think and plan.

The overhead whir of the helicopter's blades caught her attention. She wouldn't admit to herself that it might haul Peter far away. She padded back into her cabin from the balcony and held her hands over her ears. Maybe Peter changed his mind. If someone else notified cops about Picconi, Peter's role...possibly not widely known. He might have escaped once the police and F.B.I. nailed the mastermind.

Marie called, "There's a Policía helicopter. They're taking away two men. Dr. Parkson and some other guy in handcuffs."

"I know. Some kind of a scam. Peter...involved." She hung up. Showered and dressed in shorts and a small halter top. Wore huge dark sunglasses and thin flip-flops. Then sat in the sun and tried to sleep. Too devastated and drained to rest.

As the ship approached Panama, Jean observed other objects on the horizon. At a distance, it was difficult to know if it was a fishing boat, cruise ship, a small island, or the edge of the port. Squinting into the brilliant sunlight so that identification remained impossible. Jean's life had taken on a chaotic flavor again, lousy surprises which forced her to make decisions. The uncertainty of where she was matched the uncertainty of who she really was and how she'd behave when it all hit the fan.

Jean felt alone and very isolated.

She called Marie. "Please come to my cabin." She needed a friend, and decided to confide in her. The only person on board that she could trust. "I need you."

A knock on the door and Jean answered it. She hugged Marie and kissed her cheek while Marie stood in the doorway.

Marie said, "That bad, huh?"

"Yes," Jean said.

They lowered themselves into lounge chairs on the balcony. Jean's sunglasses hid her watery, red eyes while Marie teared up before Jean said a word. Marie's understanding and warm empathy, though unspoken, strengthened Jean's desire to open up, to share the whole story, and to seek her advice.

Jean said, "His wife died of cancer. He had huge bills, so he took kickbacks and lost his medical license. He foolishly invested...uhm...in a Ponzi scheme and lost everything. He lied to police. He was involved."

She removed her sunglasses. Tears poured out amid the sobs and moans. She shook. Thought of jumping into the water. Lost her love to crime and punishment. Not the guy she'd fallen for. Fooled again.

"A goddamn crook. Small investor but he tried to hide the scheme. Lied for his neighbor."

Marie arose and walked to the balcony, peered at the waves, and then sat at the end of Jean's chair. She held Jean's hands and smoothed her hair.

Marie said, "What a story. Not the ship's doctor you fell in love with. Or is he? You never really know people completely that is, on a cruise. Many kinds of baggage. Some secrets, most better left unsaid."

Marie lit a cigarette. "I quit, but…"

"Marie, I need to think this through…decide…what to do?"

"You love him—all else follows."

Jean said, "I'll set up a trust in his name. Money for the best lawyers—a new practice—a fresh start after we marry."

Marie hugged Jean. "I've got a great lawyer. Use him."

"Yes, ours is a thief."

"If you don't like mine, he'll refer you to…"

"I'm sure he's good. Thank you for listening to me." She arose and straightened her blouse and put on fresh lipstick. "The years will go by in a flash."

Marie said, "We met because of this cruise. A fantastic coincidence. Friends for life."

"I know what you mean," said Jean.

"Most of the time, you never see people again…those you connected with. Told all about yourself. Made it sound good—maybe the truth—or hide something important." She hugged Jean again.

Jean said, "I hope I'm not acting foolishly. Sometimes not sure where I am…or who."

Jean stopped shaking and dried her tears. Put on her sunglasses. "I must look horrible."

"Well, here goes," said Marie. "I told you that my husband and I split up. My ex is in jail now. The federal penitentiary in Colorado for high-risk inmates. He killed his mistress…guilty…life without parole."

"Oh, no…"

"Yes, I didn't know about it. Young, beautiful, a model and dancer in a local club. He's a Bill Clinton clone." She flicked the cigarette overboard.

"My God."

"His girlfriend evidently wanted to marry him. Threatened to tell me. Begged...divorce. The usual. Did some drugs. Uhm...strangled her. Voilà."

"Police caught him?"

"Yes, he confessed. I...I washed my hands of him. Never saw him again. Got a divorce. He didn't object... My story."

Jean sat up and hugged Marie. Held her close. "And the family?"

"For another day," Marie said. "Everybody was sickened by events, and so stunned and frightened they may never recover." She arose and leaned on the railing and gazed at the sea.

"Life sucks," Jean said. "What should I do? Peter will serve time in prison. With my luck..."

"You'll know when the time... Think it over. Don't rush. He didn't kill someone."

"Let's drink some champagne and eat red meat—a steak. I'm starved."

Marie said, "Yes, my treat."

Nearly a month later, Jean picked up an English-language newspaper in an Australian-port-of-call. Picconi got fifty years in a federal penitentiary but Peter only got two years. He'd pay his debt to society, maybe get his medical license reinstated, but still be flat broke. What could she do? How to help him?

She decided to write him a letter. With pen and paper she sat at the empty doctor's desk in the infirmary.

"My darling, I can't tell you how much I miss you. Your honesty humbles me. When you finish, I'll find the best lawyers. We'll get your license back and I'll buy you a new medical practice where no one knows either of us. It's not because I owe you anything, but because I love you, want to spend my life with you, and feel it's only my fair share to help with redemption and a fresh start for both of us.

All my Love,

Jean

102

P.S. I recently learned that my lawyer, Abe Goldstein, is incarcerated in your cell block. Have you met him? Lionel and I had complete trust and confidence in him."

Jean worried that Peter could die in prison or be forced to prolong his sentence if he violated any rules or orders. Of course, to be honest, she reasoned, he was a committed felon...no medical license, and flat broke. She could help but what if he continued to refuse any assistance from her? Would she still want to marry him, still love him? She thought yes, but doubt crept in. He'd be frustrated and disappointed in himself and his career. It could rub off on her and their relationship.

She questioned whether he was a felon at heart. More crimes ahead? Or was the Ponzi scheme and his medical malpractice in the past, never to reappear. His crimes were understandable ways of making money to pay debts and survive to help his cancer-stricken wife. Jean had no way of knowing the complicated history of his life when she met him. Was she being foolhardy, hoping for the best, unprepared for the worst?

Jean's overwhelming sense of doom and futility surprised even her. No luck. She rushed out the door of her cabin, through the double-doors to the deck, and crossed to the railing. With both hands, she reached for the top rail, holding tightly as she placed one foot on the metal cross-bars.

Paul the steward saw her from the hallway, and hurried out to the deck. "A problem?" he asked. "You run fast."

"No. No. Things are fine...Go away."

Jean paused as she saw she couldn't get one leg, let alone both of them over the top bar. She realized she'd have to somehow force her body over by using her hands and arms, then the power of her legs to propel her. The dive that followed would be easy.

Moving closer, Paul said, "Sure madam. Everything okay?"

"Yes, go inside."

"Paul not sure," he said.

Jean realized her last...her final moment on earth was with a cabin steward. His behavior—uncertain but knowing, confused yet caring—affected her, but had no impact on her decision. Paul tried to serve. Nearly saved by a man she didn't know.

103

In a trance, Jean peered at the blue-white waves far below. Calm wind. Bright sun. No clouds. So inviting. Eternity, at least oblivion, lay beneath the water. She'd tried but had no control over the consequences of her choices. The outcomes befuddled her. She gave up.

With a frantic surge of conviction and raw strength, Jean sprang upward and plunged overboard, with Paul's screams echoing in her ears.

THE PAPER PEOPLE

A Sci-Fi Novella – I

Norman Giddan

PART I

To Love and Die

PREAMBLE

The small, dark cave in the hillside smelled musty and slightly damp. Carved out of the hills, it hugged the land where the Paper People finally settled. Two white, flickering candles on a simple wooden table created dancing shadows on the curved, stone ceiling.

Wearing a blue dress shirt and dark slacks, Papa Beard stroked the foot-long silken, white hair streaming down his chest. The table held a scroll, which he pulled open with two bone handles, revealing a parchment-like book inside. Papa knew the temperature and humidity inside the cave would keep the story alive for many decades.

"You kids are old enough to understand what I'm going to read now. My wife, Myra Beard, your grandmother, wrote a family tale for you both. She died last year, 2030."

"I'm twelve now," Ben said, "but Roberta is only ten."

"You'll understand most of it. Plop down on those thick cushions. Close your eyes. Here comes history," Papa Beard said. "I'm going to use this loupe system to help me read."

Roberta clapped. "Oh, goody, a long story. Is that like reading glasses?"

"Yes, but much stronger. Makes tiny words look big. Uses lenses to reflect and focus light."

Ben said, "Hurry up, Papa!"

Papa Beard bent over the scroll. Tears momentarily clouded his vision. He blinked his eyes several times. "Here goes," he said. "I plan to read this book every year."

Chapter One

I felt blessed to see both of you born so healthy and strong. Our family reveled in this pure, simple ecstasy. Your parents provided the best of care. To help out, we eventually gave them what little money and savings we had.

Ben, you had so much hair. I'd never seen that much before on an infant. It gradually grew from ink black to light brown before you were a year old. And, Roberta, you were so smart. You sucked and grasped better than any other baby in the hospital. What a lovely pair. I'm saddened to think of not being part of your life as you grow up.

Around the mid-20s, Papa and I lived on the street as homeless folks, both of us unemployed. Previously, I taught school and your grandfather developed instructional technology. We found a tent under a bridge, repaired the holes, and slept and ate in it for many months. Hot summers lasted longer than usual, so at least we kept dry and warm.

Every few days we ate and showered at one of the homeless shelters. Hundreds of thousands lived as we did. It was not a pretty time with all the wars and destruction of the earth.

Papa often scrunched up his cheeks and turned up his lips. He looked like I felt—frightened and lonely.

An announcement on the shelter job board jumped out at me. Food, a place to live, and a job with decent pay were promised if an individual qualified. It briefly described the job, and several of the qualifications required. I kept a copy from the Homeless Shelter Bulletin Board:

JOB AVAILABLE

Adult to serve as the skin for books, providing location for the art and script of lasting and significant stories. The provider of the skin for this visual and written project must agree to have his or her body virtually covered with high-grade tattoo art, inking, possibly color. At death, the skin will be carefully mummified, removed, and treated appropriately to preserve its integrity, then arranged in a permanent scroll for historical purposes. Payment for this enterprise is dependent on the general health of the individual, a dermatological assessment, and a commitment to engage in the process of writing on skin for a period of at least one year. Unfortunately, anyone who has tattoos currently will not be considered for the project. The entire skin of an adult must be available. Viewing and interviews will commence immediately, final selection within one week. All applications held in strictest confidence.

You may be shocked by what they wanted from applicants. It should seem inhumane, disgusting by current human standards, reminiscent of primitive Amazon head hunters or Hitlerian medical practice. There is little comfort in the knowledge that some volunteers for this project may die of a totally unrelated illness shortly after it is completed. Extremely unfortunate for them, yet the timing is perfect for readers of the surviving classic stories and novels.

The Human Resource Laws of 2019 offer homeless felons the opportunity to become skin donors, and also mandate that convicted adults deemed legally to be homeless may become part of the program in exchange for a reduction in prison sentence and eventual expungement of court proceedings. We were informed that no felons or convicts were included in our experimental group.

The Zoots, a gang of Hollywood shysters and promoters, hired seventy-five of us homeless folks. We had no tattoos and we spent no time in prison. We agreed to give our bodies, in particular our skin, to the experimental project—the Paper People Project, as they called it—when we died.

Frankly, things were so bad that we grabbed at the chance to become a part of the project. My tattered multi-colored, print dress hung on me like a sack of bones. Friends hardly recognized me any longer. We had each other—thank God. Mildly optimistic, we hoped that the job we'd been selected for would pay off so we could survive.

Papa said, "Still have it?"

"Of course. Nobody gets this." I traced the heart-shape with my finger. The gold locket and chain hung low inside my dress. I pulled it out and opened it. "Could use a cleaning. The pair of pictures still..."

"Let me see," Papa said. "Our looks changed. Not our love."

We gazed at the photos together for what seemed like an eternity. My heart raced. Sweat on my upper lip. Hands shaky. Held back the tears—the tears of memories, joy, youth, success, so many possibilities.

"Don't tell me. Left side is our wedding. The right side is from a few years ago."

"No Alzheimer's for you—not yet anyway," I said. "What were you? Six feet and one-hundred-ninety pounds. Good body. Handsome guy. Straight nose, dark blue eyes and smooth skin. But such a wide mouth."

"On the left or the right?"

I said, "Hah! Hah! Our wedding. You tease."

"You looked mighty fine a few years ago. Before the... Low cut, strapless dress. Heart-shaped face with a dimple in your chin. Flashing hazel eyes with such long lashes. Maybe a few more wrinkles and lines, but I like them. A mature look. Very nice. Kept your weight down, too. Gorgeous legs hidden here. Hair upswept. An educated look. You're even slimmer now, but all to the good."

He leaned over and kissed me, then the locket. Dear man. Quite a guy, your Papa. "You're such a liar."

The months of life on the street, our homeless plight, took their toll. If the locket were a triptych, it could reveal a third photo of us. Better not, though. The wedding and recent photo made for much more beautiful memories. I hated being homeless, living as we did, searching for food in dumpsters and garbage cans. A dramatic comedown in our lives that I simply hated when I stopped being sad and disappointed. The suffering of so many others here and globally lessened the pain—but not always.

When I said things were bad, I really meant it. More of this later, but here's a brief glimpse. Earth had seen two small nuclear wars and most of the Middle East was a wasteland. Deadly toxins and poisons spread over many countries. Climate change, very hot weather, ate away at the trees and forests, so wood products and paper were no longer abundant. The short supply of petrochemicals, the basis for electronics, severely limited the production and repairs of all of our gadgets—cell phones, computers, TVs, and GPS devices. It felt like the information and digital age would slowly shut down. Paper became worth more than the money printed on it. Hoarders loaded up on it.

On the afternoon of the final selection by the Zoots, while on our way to their encampment, the Paper People marched in the El día del Muertos Parade. This parade took on a life of its own. Designed to remember and celebrate the lives of the dead, it had a history of a different meaning and purpose for the living. The parade planners invited diverse groups to participate—minorities, gangs, disabled, homeless, poor, and addicts—with a vague hope of celebrating these marginal folks. Maybe march them to a better life, with a sincere desire to serve and save the outcasts and the weak and the needy. We fit in perfectly.

Dark skies threatened rain that year. Our group stayed together as a unit, such a rag-tag bunch, to walk in the middle section of the parade. Zoots guarded us, protected us, and told us where to go and what to do.

I was sweaty and jittery. My feet hurt. My stomach ached.

Papa said, "We're property for the Zoots."

Jeremy Sledge, a slick promoter from Beverly Hills, dressed in two-thousand dollar Italian suits, dark sharkskin to match his long, wet-looking hairstyle, said, "Folks, I'm the head man of the Zoots. Your experiment—I mean your project is very important."

His phony smile and perfectly capped, white teeth scared me. Your grandfather and I held hands as we walked. Our bellies would finally be full but I wasn't sure what else lay ahead.

Papa stayed close to me and occasionally swung one arm around my shoulders. He leaned over to kiss my hands. He said, "Out of the frying pan and into the fire."

Sledge said, "Stay near each other. We have enemies. They hate the homeless, especially street people who read books. They may try to stop us."

Steady drumbeats from a Catholic group established a serious, measured rhythm to the march. Zoots, so proud of themselves and the project, surrounded us with at least a dozen or so protectors. We didn't fully understand the reasons or the risks for us, or them.

Huge crowds packed both sides of the street, heads bowed in reverence, followed by sighs and screams as the Virgin Mary statue passed, cheers for the remembrance of the day. Assorted piñatas, colorful and fluffy in red, green and white, appeared at random intervals, full of candy, I supposed. When would they be popped? With so little sweet in our diet, we could hardly wait for even a small piece of licorice.

Sledge said, "Our enemies are just behind us. They're called Diablitos. Their leader is El Diablo."

I glanced back at them. Wearing military berets over dark faces and heavy beards, they wanted God knows what. I overheard one of them say, "Big bonfires soon."

Another one said, "Only El Diablo knows what's good. He'll show them. He'll take over."

I shuddered, grabbed your grandfather's hand even tighter, and hoped for the best—at least we were safe for the moment. So many hated the homeless. I was used to it. Thugs lived everywhere.

Midway through the march, Sledge handed out ghastly skeleton masks for us to wear, similar to those that scare young children at Halloween. He said, "These will make you more interesting. Maybe scare the enemies."

We wore them with pride. After all, in some sense we'd been saved from starvation, possibly death in the streets. I thought that the Diablitos should have been wearing them, with their cruel attitudes and beliefs. They probably had shaven heads underneath their berets.

Your grandfather said, "Look at the reviewing stand. That must be El Diablo. He's in a crisp, white, military uniform. So many medals and ribbons. The others wear orange scarves decorated with marigolds."

I said, "I wish we could get out of here."

El Diablo yelled from the reviewing stand, "Kill them! Kill them all!"

Your papa said, "Listen to the jack-boots of El Diablo's gang. The thud, thud, thud of neo-Nazis."

"Yes, dear," I said.

The Diablitos threw their fists into the air as they marched. They feigned shooting guns or rockets. Chants of "burn books" and "kill the homeless" reverberated throughout the streets. A popular gang, vicious and unforgiving, their large following among the populace cheered them on. Youngsters stoned us with tiny pieces of concrete the size of marbles. Parade onlookers waved signs like "Hitler Lives" and "We Hate Homeless." A global crisis breeds both cruel politicians and violent gangs, while ordinary citizens like us simply do their best to stay alive.

I told Papa, "I believe the soul lives on in eternal life in heaven. So much hatred and misery here in the street. It hurts. What's next?"

"We'll have to wait and see." He let go of my hand, his body trembling.

Finally, we were herded toward a waiting bus at the end of the parade route. I'll fill you in on the gangs and their leaders later in my story. Just wanted you to have a taste of it for now.

Sledge said, "Come on, slow pokes."

"Is that an order?" Papa said.

"Take it any way you like. Your future is safe. Next stop, everlasting life. What I mean is that our compound is located at a clearing in a federally protected forest in Northern California.

"The Zoots and the Diablitos have a bloody history. Drugs and booze. Their cartels scared us. Threatened to kill all Zoots. So we went straight! The Paper People—one of our business deals—I mean scientific efforts."

I was now shaking in my boots. "Sledge warned us. Some gangs don't like us. Who's the 'us'?"

Papa said, "This parade is perfect for the Day of the Dead—if a person can live through it."

I said, "Are you being prophetic?"

The Mariachi band, simply strings and brass instruments, cheered us up after the taunts of the gang. The last remnants of the parade headed to St. Christopher's Cemetery to honor the dead. We missed that. I wanted to remain as hopeful and upbeat as possible in light of the situation. I trembled at the thought that we'd sold our souls to a gang of devils in fancy suits and ties from Hollywood. Exhausted from the march, my body and mind tried to move on its own—out and away from the craziness.

We reached the bus. We stood in line to board it, one of the Zoots carefully placed each mask in a black net bag.

"No need to cover up," Sledge said. He adjusted his tie and ran his hands over his slick hair. "You are like the monk scribes of the Middle Ages."

An awful thing happened. I don't like to remember it, but you should know about it.

A Diablito ran at full speed toward the bus, eyes glistening, shirt billowing in the wind, and cap missing to reveal a completely shaved head. He drew a long dagger and repeatedly stabbed one of our Paper People who fell to his knees. Minutes went by. Blood splattered everywhere, on clothes, the ground, and smeared on the bus door. It was a terrible sight. I think I heard the death rattle. The Diablito escaped.

Too stunned to react, many of us screamed and yelled for the police to help. To my amazement, the Zoots quickly herded us on to the bus, which drove away at break-neck speed, leaving the dead victim abandoned on the ground.

Sledge smirked. "I'll talk to the police later."

Papa put his arm around me. He said, "They can't protect Paper People."

"Saved the rest of us." I huddled closer to him.

Papa said, "It's horrible. A horrible end. A horrible beginning." He rubbed his eyes on his sleeve, and then stroked the long hair covering his face.

I was hot and sweaty and confused. I shook. "Who was the dead guy? Are we slaves? A frightening thought."

Papa folded his arms over his chest. "Look, Myra, we'll eat. No pauper's graves for us."

He dozed for the ride to the compound. My head rested in the hollow between his neck and shoulder. So, I slept, too. I dreamt that as we rowed oars in the hold of a slave ship on its way to the New World, one of the men slumped over dead. What would happen to the rest of us? Dreams don't always make such good sense.

Chapter Two

A tiny bit of personal history may help you understand. We experienced an unending number of unpleasant, dangerous events before we became Paper People. You wouldn't believe what happened in society. It horrified me. Electricity and food were in short supply. Factories closed, city parks went brown as they lost most of their trees, and many service stations shut down when gas was rationed, major electronics stores disappeared, and electronic-gadget repairs became outrageously expensive, with no guarantee of the work.

I don't like to remember most of our life on the street. We bent over and searched the dumpsters one evening at dusk. Hungry and thirsty at that moment, a deep, bass voice boomed out from behind us. "Give me money. Don't turn around." Some guy had snuck up on us.

Scared and surprised, but unhurt, we raised ourselves to a standing position. I said, "We have no money. Go away."

"Give me money."

Papa said, "Leave us alone. We live..." His hand rested on my shoulder.

"Money--now."

I took off my right shoe and awkwardly removed a thin gold bracelet stuffed into the tip. A piece of jewelry I'd saved. Without turning around, I held it high in my hand. The robber grabbed it and I heard him run off. The locket still nestled snugly between my breasts.

Minutes later we moved. Papa held me tight. We both shook. His grip did not stop my shaking.

"It's okay. We're still here," he said. "Jewelry is such a burden."

That same day we finally calmed down and returned to hunting inside the garbage cans and dumpsters. We weren't alone. Others jumped into the piles of trash in the dumpster, searched with eyes or hands, and shifted feet to find something to eat or drink or sell or to trade.

Hold your breath and sit down now! Papa found a newborn baby, covered in dried blood, and a piece of the uterus, with a dangling umbilical cord. He gasped and said, "Oh, no. A dead..."

"What did you say?"

He held up the tiny life-less human being for me to see, probably no more than four or five pounds. "Beyond belief. A dead..."

A horrifying sight to behold. The face was unrecognizable. The skin of the head and neck was beginning to turn greenish. Much of the body still appeared rigid. Maggots fed on some of the purplish-brown tissue now. The odor of rotting meat.

I retched. Then cried and sobbed. "My God. What a world."

Papa covered the newborn with his undershirt and wrapped it carefully like a Christmas present with his belt as both the tie and a carrying handle. "Hold this while I climb out," he said.

I retched again. I felt like burying my head in the ugly, stinking rot in the dumpster.

A dead child, an unlived life, and a horrible reminder of what the world had become. "What should we do? Where can we take it? Who will pray?"

I retched once again but nothing came up this time. My stomach emptied earlier, now my soul.

My mind saved me as it jolted me into the past, how my feet bounced comfortably when I wheeled you kids in a two-seater stroller— you were four and two years old. Once around the park, then to the zoo. Well, what was left of the zoo as the older animals died or were returned to their natural habitat.

I was scared to death of the old, dark gray elephants, but not the two of you. You watched and laughed and even screamed at times as they flipped their trunks around, eating some nuts, splashing or drinking water. Then they were ready to take you both on a ride. It cost so much but was worth it, to see you each settled safely into a seat on the back of an elephant as it stumbled around, then lurched and kneeled as the guard helped you from the seats. "More, Grandma," Roberta said. "Again.

Again." Ben, you simply smiled and petted the thick, tough furrowed skin of the elephant's leg when you dismounted.

I knew you'd keep riding as long as I could afford it. "We'll come back. We'll do it again." When you were back in the double-stroller, the elephant ride and the hot sun and the rhythmic movement of the wheels led you both to the same comfortable place—sleep. I actually stopped midway home to make sure you were both still breathing. Then I sat on a bench and flexed my feet.

As I returned to the present again, that deep, basso voice boomed out near the dumpster. He'd been hiding. "Don't turn around. Found a piece of meat for me, did you?"

"No, no it's…"

"Hand it over. Then the two of you put both hands on the dumpster. Close your eyes. Count to one hundred."

We did as commanded.

My arms crawled with tiny worms that like decayed food and garbage. I brushed them off before I grabbed Papa. Everything swirled around. So dizzy. I passed out.

He must have carried me to one of the missions. I woke up laying on a cracked leather love seat, a cold towel on my face and Papa holding my hand.

He said, "I prayed for the child. Did what I could."

I said, "I'll never forget that ghastly voice. Never. Never. Never."

I raised up and buried my face in his chest though I knew he smiled, and grimaced at the same time. I held him even tighter and closer. My face hammered his body.

I'll never be able to forget another morning when Papa and I found several cans of food that had fallen behind the shelves in a food mart. The abandoned store stunk of urine and rotten fish. Two guys came out of nowhere with knives. They wanted our cans of food. Papa threw a can at them. We ran to the storefront.

One of them chased us. "You bastard, you hit me."

117

He caught up with us and slashed Papa on the arm. We ran outside. We weren't very fast, but this time, thank God, he didn't follow us.

I patched up Papa's cut. "Police?"

"No," he said, "These guys might find us and kill us. They're desperate. Got off lucky."

We even tried panhandling one day. It was a beautiful blue sky, no clouds, and not too hot. We felt lucky. Just perched on the sidewalk and held out an old hat. A few coins dropped in but not enough to buy a meal. Our city block in the downtown area had at least one hundred other people chasing passersby for money or simply sitting cross-legged on the sidewalk begging.

The crowds jostled each other, while panhandlers followed people and bumped against the sedentary beggars like us. In movies those asking for a hand-out are few and far between each other. We were part of a faceless and homeless and hungry and angry mob of street people.

"Better shave those legs, lady," a passerby said. He laughed and pointed at me.

"That ugly beard," another said, "is very, very ugly and too long, old timer. Methuselah."

Papa said, "Hate you, too."

We didn't even enjoy what little dignity and respect life on the street deserved. Outcasts among those with nothing to eat or sell or trade. Papa put his Old Navy watch cap back on his head, after shaking out a few coins and a Chinese fortune cookie. The slip inside said, "You will find happiness in family life."

Papa stood. He pulled me upright. "This would be a joke if it wasn't so serious." His cheeks bulged as his mouth scrunched up so tightly that his eyes closed.

Too much competition for too little loose change. This may seem strange, but thank God, we'd already given the last of our money and savings, plus a few pieces of jewelry, to your parents. No one could steal it.

118

I could go on and on with terrible incidents from street life. I don't want to scare you grandchildren, or just seek sympathy, yet I did want you to have a feel for the near impossibility we faced as homeless during this period of history. It will help you understand why we jumped at the chance to become Paper People. My feet hurt most of the time—no, all of the time.

Your own dad kept his job as an accountant part-time, while your mother took in laundry and ironing to help make ends meet. She also worked part-time at a food bank, occasionally sneaking a little extra home for you kids. Your parents scrimped by so they could live in a garage after they lost the house.

We were scared to death by all that we saw.

I'm not ashamed to admit that more than once, I felt like giving up—finding a quiet, clean place to curl up and die. I didn't confess to Papa. He'd try to cheer me up and talk me out of it and say better days are ahead. I don't know if he ever felt like ending all the deprivation and suffering of street life. If he did, he'd die before admitting it. Men and women do differ. We did on issues of heroism and bravery, even simple day-by-day optimism.

Since I was child, I'd bathed or showered nearly every day, sometimes twice in a day when the pollen count skyrocketed. Homelessness equated with dirt, grime, mud, fleas, and lice, even when we could take a lukewarm shower twice a week. The disinfectant soap and de-licing powder made me nauseous. Hair clogged up the shower drain. It shook me up so much that I stood several feet back of it, on the outer edge of the narrow, weak shower spray.

I'd been spoiled by middle-class life and, moreover, middle-class values like 'cleanliness is next to godliness.' I had never lived in a muddy tent or a military-type foxhole, like soldiers in the rainy season in the Asian wars.

Religion, my higher power, or spirituality was another matter. Papa and I attended some revival meetings at a small tabernacle crowded to the rafters with a motley collection of drunks, addicts, homeless, and the "down-on-their-luckers" as we referred to ourselves. Thick stale bread and a strangely tantalizing, steaming bowl of soup, maybe mush or goulash, awaited those who stayed for the entire service. The preacher, who bragged he was a reformed alcoholic, sober for ten years, screamed about abstinence but had a magnificent baritone voice for Christian songs—heaven, God, Jesus, survival, hope, tomorrow, gratitude, and the angels and, of course, the devil.

I sang my heart out, reading the words printed on a few dog-eared pages remaining in a much-used song book I shared with Papa and three others. He simply hummed along when the out-of-tune pump organ played something about praising 'His Glory!'

Sometimes he had two bowls. I couldn't stomach that much of whatever it was in those bowls. Rusty spoons didn't help matters, failing an English butler or downstairs maid to polish the silver.

People called each other by the name of Brother or Sister when they spoke, which was actually very seldom. Head down, spoonsful from the bowl found their way urgently into mouths still gurgling with the preceding slurp. The old adage 'wash your hands before dinner' did not apply. Grimy, blue-veined hands with long, brown nails—they stunk, too—made for unpleasant dining companions. I hate to sound like a snob, but my usually social nature hid during these prayers and sit-down meals.

I could hardly gaze at Papa, who shared a joke or pleasantry with whomever sat next to him. Truly, I don't know how he did it. He'd pull a tiny roach out of the soup, laugh like he couldn't stop, and blame it on his neighbor. Then that guy laughed too. Sometimes, they each ate part of the roach for effect. I'd vomit if I watched these shenanigans too closely.

I prayed that the garbage cans on the street would have tempting morsels in them—stale bread, decaying veggies, a sip of orange juice or soda left in the bottom of a container. I prayed very hard for these items and sometimes, a few times in each day, they appeared. We ate. I asked Papa to join me in this spiritual exercise, but he declined. Instead, he tickled me under my arm and kissed the top of my filthy, stringy hair. I'd never been a real beauty, but I felt so ugly and unattractive. He disagreed, but I didn't really change my view.

I'd better back track again. Before things got really bad in our world, we could find most foods in the stores or at open-air markets early in the morning. Ben, you preferred small berries and nuts that you could eat without spoons or forks. Blueberries and strawberries ranked high among your favorites. Cherries weren't as popular because of the seeds-- you swallowed a few when you were quite young.

120

Roberta, you liked meats, especially pork by itself or mixed with chicken. It's hard to believe but Spam, lightly fried was your all-time favorite. Ham sandwiches on pure white bread. I should say the promise of one of them could encourage you to do almost anything, like pick up your clothes or make your bed in the morning.

After the year 2020, the availability of quality foods gradually diminished year-by-year. From 2025 on, we ate what we could find in the stores, mostly rice and potatoes and canned fish with questionable dates of "use by" crudely crossed out. We suspected that the cans had been altered by the authorities.

Papa and I had codes to reveal our emotions to each other, for how we felt about ourselves and the world around us.

If I said, "My feet hurt," it meant I was unhappy and disappointed.

Papa joked that it must be comparisons with pictures in the locket. Not so! Well, yes and no!

When Papa scrunched up his mouth that meant he was upset and annoyed, maybe angry.

Speaking of angry, we disagreed on a lot of things when we first met and then married. He loved the beach, the water and the sand. I was so-so on the beach since sand got into everything from food to clothes to hair. What a mess.

The parks were my preference—just to sit on a blanket on a large expanse of thick green grass while a horizon of trees shimmered in reds and oranges from a setting sun. That was heaven, especially with a glass of cold white wine. My "feet hurt" at the beach, and he often "scrunched up his mouth" at the park, so we went to both places. We took the two of you when you were toddlers and you enjoyed yourselves with nature.

Of course, Papa and I differed on more basic issues, but I'm not sure that I want to air all of our dirty laundry in this story. Suffice it to say, we managed to usually cooperate and work out our differences, and to respect those differences when we couldn't reach a compromise. Men and women, boys and girls, simply differ in a number of ways. Makes life much more interesting.

Papa and I did come to blows now and then. Somewhere inside me I was angry—just the anger borne of sadness and frustration.

121

He said, "Unhappy with me? Lost my job. Can't support you. Family life gone."

"I am not."

"Yes, you are. I know it. Your face and your eyes give it away. Tiny bits of hate sent my way."

I walked away. Loved Papa. Wonderful man. Shouldn't blame him for the worldwide crisis. Not his fault. Sometimes I did blame him. It wasn't fair but I did.

Oh yes, I forgot to mention that Papa rubbed my feet with strong squeezes and short strokes when I complained that they "hurt." He's such a dear man! When he "scrunched up his mouth," I listened to him and tried to sympathize, followed up with a big smooch.

Let me give you a better written, expanded summary of the situation the world faced. You'll understand more of this as you get older. Then I'll show you some more of the ways it affected us personally in our daily lives. I cobbled together the following digest from a few torn, charred pages of a *National Geographic* I rescued from a dumpster.

"Intense heat withered the green earth and trees suffered previously unimaginable trauma or death. Amazon forests dried up, lumber in most countries commanded a premium that priced it out of the market for homes, buildings, or other wood-based products, let alone fuel for stoves or furnaces. A limited amount of paper was available but inordinately expensive. Libraries outnumbered banks in the frequency of thefts or robberies, and easily outpaced them in what accountants termed 'book value.' Traders stored boxes of books in huge container ships under armed guard for their worth as wood products. Cellulose, a polymer which is the main constituent of wood and paper, was in very short supply.

"Electronic devices and digital media technologies couldn't really be trusted into the future, even the electronic ink of e-readers. Paper had been used originally in many printed circuit boards. Computers, smart phones, TVs, digital cameras, and so on declined sharply in quality and availability due to the interlocking relationships with oil-based production, distribution, and storage, let alone repair or replacement. With the Middle East shut down, petroleum shortages affected many of the chemicals used in the field of electronics, so the devices we took for granted drifted into a painful, unwanted obsolescence.   High-tech data storage and retrieval increasingly belonged to the past.

"This was the post-apocalypse world that writers, poets, or prophets anticipated for centuries. Fear, panic, and angry guilt ruled the emotional life of survivors. With all of this, care for others and genuine concern for their welfare did not fade away completely. Hope stayed alive, drenched with skepticism and downright despair. Many individuals who lost loved ones found time to set up or volunteer at make-shift hospitals to care for the injured and malnourished."

People on the street grew moody, temperamental, and pessimistic, often downright angry and vengeful.

This is a grim view, but that's the world we lived in. Just as you'd expect, ordinary survival was the name of the game we played. To wake up the next day. Naturally, I prayed my grandchildren, the two of you, would enjoy better times.

Papa and I personally felt the effects of all this in several ways beyond losing our jobs, our home, and two cars. Some losses weren't so bad. We ate little meat or dairy products. Sleeping in a tent or box or doorway became easier with the climate change warming us. We walked everywhere. Living outside produced healthier, tanned skin and even left-over veggies were healthy for us. We followed a few harvests, and salvaged bags full of overly-ripe apples and pears, and enough grain to boil up as gruel.

We didn't pollute with as much soap and disinfectants and deodorants, so our clothes were filthier, we were dirty, and this lifestyle reduced the practice of doing laundry every few days or washing dishes several times a day. A little dirt might be healthy but not this much. I let my nails grow and cut the end of my grey-streaked hair with a pen knife, giving it a jagged, classic look. With no makeup to worry about, my skin and face looked much younger according to you-know-who. I was still just a bit over five feet tall.

Papa said, "Not bad at all."

You probably won't believe this, but I let the hair on my legs and under my arms grow. I felt like an Italian actress in a classic WWII movie. I wish I looked more like one, Sophia or Gina or whomever.

Papa grew a magnificent beard, black speckled with white, not a uniform grey. His long hair fell nearly to his shoulders, so I cut it now and then and tied up the back in a long pony-tail. I did trim his nails weekly, since he said he didn't want to look like many homeless men with long, dirty fingernails. His toenails were another story, cracked, long, curled, brown, and dirty. Scrubbing them with the corncob soap didn't do much to change their appearance or eliminate the aroma of his feet. I surmised that the odor of his single pair of socks filtered through the holes in them onto his skin and settled there for good. Every few weeks he obtained a fresh shirt and pants at the shelter, but jackets were hard to come by. He never was much of a clothes-horse.

One cold day he wore a long fur coat donated by some rich woman. I told him if he added a dress, high heels, and some lipstick he'd really be something. I wished he'd laughed harder and longer but he evidently wasn't as secure in his manhood as I thought.

I'm no scientist or businesswoman, but I do know that good things, for a single individual or a state or country, even the world, usually take time—sometimes a generation or more. The loss of wood pulp and the shortages of oil, for example, occurred over many years. Petrocarbons suffered at the hands of tactical nuclear wars, which spelled the end of the age of gadgets. I loved my gadgets—the phones, watches, PCs, tablets, GPS, and so on. They were "oil-based" to put it in terms I understand. Something new, an invention, will come along to replace that whole technology. I hope and pray it comes soon.

We had coal until terrorists found ways to destroy the mines to such an extent that coal production plummeted. That was a big problem, because I had heard of a new, cheap process to change coal into a liquid that could replace oil.

We try to control nature but it doesn't always work out. Sometimes nature rules us. During my lifetime, technology unlocked gas inside shale basins. We had horizontal gas wells, drilling across wide areas and very deep. But we weren't prepared for the negative effects, as we felt so desperate for an abundant supply of gas. The drilling uses toxic chemicals and some radioactive materials are released. At first, the effects on air and water quality appeared tiny, and climate stayed the same despite this kind of drilling. It all changed when research proved this approach was dangerous for us and not worth the risk of contaminated ground water that led to an increase in cancer. So there you are.

Technology can take over, and lead us down a primrose path. Experts make mistakes. Humans correct most of the errors, but it takes time, a lot of it in some cases.

I couldn't get the human cost out of my mind. Millions of people died worldwide from radiation poisoning, hunger, and malnutrition. Two tactical nuclear wars contaminated the water, air, and soil of most of the Middle East. Large parts of the world resembled the area referred to as the "Chernobyl incident" of the prior century.

Yet, we were alive. Did we deserve to be? Why us? Feeling guilty and ashamed of my doubts and complaints, we were lucky to have been chosen for this experiment. To stay alive, even on a day-by-day basis was a blessing. To survive, to live, to have hope—that was our basic need.

Chapter Three

The bus driver jolted me back to the present when he slammed on the brakes before he made a hard right turn into a narrow side road. I returned to the Zoots. I stopped thinking about the past and the condition of the world when we closed in on our destination.

Papa hugged me. He squeezed my hand. "We're nearly there. This is it."

After an hour's drive in a steady rain, we followed Sledge to the three military barracks with one-third of us housed in each. I peered out of the window of our new home at the white tips of a mountain range, virtually stripped of any living trees or green brush.

Each of us had a comfortable cot, sheets, blankets, towels, soap and, best of all, toothbrushes and paste. Heaven! The first thing I did was throw my arms around your grandfather. Then I pushed our cots together. Next, I showered and washed my hair.

Sledge announced a meeting of all of us just before our evening meal. We sat primly at tables in the mess hall. Questions about our future were deflected or ignored by the Zoots. They said we'd know soon enough, that we had been carefully selected and would have a specific purpose and function.

A lanky man in his early thirties with long hair, a dark beard, and a chiseled faced tried hard to pin down Sledge. "I am Cristo. Tell us our jobs here. What do we do? The mystery is are we to die?"

Sledge said, "We all die. Your death leaves you immortal. That's all for now."

Cristo said, "I'm confused. I don't like it." Exasperated, he suddenly raised both arms above his head, much as priests do.

Chants of "yes" and "tell us now" met with indifference from the Zoots. Several of them conferred briefly in the back of the hall.

126

Sledge said, "Our experiment—our project—is called the Paper People Project. You know that much." His eyes narrowed into ruthless slits.

When the dinner bell clanged sharply, chefs and waitresses streamed through the kitchen door. I told Papa, "English history night." The thick-sliced beef, roasted potatoes, caramelized carrots, Yorkshire pudding, and apple tarts put all thoughts or feelings to rest. Life on the street, even a decent meal in a shelter, could never compare with this food and service. How bad could life be here?

We slept late the next morning. Then we casually strolled over to the mess hall for a tempting breakfast buffet—eggs, bacon, sausage, fruit, milk, and croissants and coffee. We lingered over coffee and sweet cakes.

A smug smile crossed Sledge's face as he spoke to the assembled group. "I want to introduce Chief Toyanta Togadoloppo, the Dean of Mortuary Science at the Community College of Samoa. He decorates bodies for a living, and then mummifies them later on."

A huge, muscular, brown man stood and grinned broadly. His body was replete with beautiful, intricate, black art—waves and swirls, zigzags, lines with bands and scrolls, dots and circles.

I said to your grandfather, "I'm not sure I like this." My feet were sore.

He rubbed my shoulder. "Don't worry. Remember where we were before this."

Sledge said, "Your skin will last—a cross between chicken pox and the black plague. Imagine tiny black dots over all of your body from shaved head to feet and toes—even eyelids."

The chief applauded loudly as he smacked his hands together, then stood, and bowed. He said, "Special dye. Special dye."

Cristo said, "No one could do it or read it."

Sledge said, "We supply a technologically-advanced loupe for the body artists. It's a small lens device like eye doctors use. Much more powerful. Makes tiny things bigger and easy to read."

127

Cristo twisted in his chair. He stood, arms at his side. "Something funny here. A little strange. We want to help... I don't mind martyrdom, but this..."

"If anyone wants to leave, now is the time," Sledge said.

Not one person moved. The alternative, so unappealing and uncertain, prompted all of us to sit tight, voted to stay with our bodies, so to speak. We had a lot to learn.

"Our education committee from Beverly Hills has just selected the books that will be among the first. For example, the *Bible* and several novelists like Mark Twain, Hemingway, Faulkner, and Sylvia Plath, even Ken Kesey, but also Machiavelli, and Eudora Welty, Mary Shelley, and poets like T. S. Eliot and Pound, and the lesser-known Swinburne, and *Beowulf* and the *Canterbury Tales*." Cockily, Sledge slicked back his hair and puffed out his chest. "We hope to include dramatic plays, scripts of operas, movies, and TV serials later on. Buster Keaton's comedies and Stanley Kubrick's films are masterpieces."

Cristo stood. Could he become our spokesman? A youthful leader with obvious intelligence and clear logic. "Where do we fit in? Why are we the Paper People?"

Sledge feigned worry as he walked from side to side, wringing his hands and then wiping his brow. "Well, what if we lost famous works of literature or poetry or history forever. What if Frost, T. S. Eliot, Pound, Faulkner, Melville, Hemingway, the Bronte sisters, or the Canterbury Tales or Beowulf simply disappeared, never to be recovered or taught to our descendants?"

He regained his slick composure and sipped coffee. "So little paper and the steady decline of digital processes. How do we preserve books in this perfect storm?"

Cristo said, "Scientists will solve this. They'll invent something."

"Exactly," Sledge said. "That's what our project is about. You folks, you Paper People, will have books of all kinds, the most necessary and important books, tattooed on your bodies."

"Then what?" Cristo said. "We'll die off one by one."

Your grandfather whispered in my ear, "Oh, my God. What else could happen in this life? We'll be sold."

Sledge turned on the charm, smiled and patted people on the back or shook hands as he shuffled around the room. He removed his tie. "Our dyes are non-toxic and there is an antidote just in case one of the chief's artists makes a mistake. While you're waiting your turn, please enjoy the food, get plenty of rest, take in the sunshine before, not after, you have the tattoos, and get pumped up in the exercise room we've built near the swimming pool. Enjoy. We want you to be fat and happy here." His mouth now widened into a toothy grin. "At least for forty days. I'm joking."

The chief's three tattoo artists appeared that afternoon and screened each of us, head to toe. They said nothing while they drew some rough sketches.

Sledge spoke pompously at dinner to identify and praise the primary professionals cooperating with this experiment.

"I'm going to lecture a bit. To be specific, the entire body, front, back, and both sides of the torso, from head to toe, serve as the page-by-page locations. Without the inordinate skill, extraordinary patience, and tireless perseverance of Dr. Lawrence 'Mo' Tinsley, Professor and Head of the Department of Body Art at the American University of Samoa, this project would not have been possible. I regret that he's not here tonight. He personally trained the team of artists, including three graduate students from his doctoral program. They write, draw, and ink simultaneously, applying their craft to the four views of the body.

"You've already met the Dean of Mortuary Science at the Community College of Samoa, standing on my left, who will shave and otherwise prepare your body to receive maximum lasting imprint from the artists, laying the groundwork for later preparation of the skin for drying, mummification, slicing, and scroll arrangement. Chief Togadoloppo kindly mixed the special non-toxic dyes employed in this multi-colored ink project, employing sterile dyes, ink, and instruments to prevent infection.

"I should add that the chief is the absolute best at what he does. In case you don't know it, tattooing originated in Polynesia. It has great emotional significance in addition to the beatification of the human body. In Samoa, it is called *pe'a* for men and *malu* for women. The latter are only tattooed from their knees to their upper thighs in dots, straight lines, and zigzags. The chief tells me that when the body art is completed in Samoa, an egg is broken on the individual's head and coconut oil is poured on the scalp. We'll simply have an outstanding Samoan dinner here.

"Gratitude of the highest order is also due, the late James Lee Bucklay, M.D., M.PH, Ph.D., Research Professor of Ophthalmology at the Harvard Medical School. He arranged the prismatic loupe system, which uses lenses and prisms to reflect and focus light. This resulted in the highest degree of magnification, which enables the artists to adorn each of you Paper People with an entire book."

After dinner, when all of us were stuffed with steak, fries, Caesar salad, and double chocolate ice cream, the chief stood, smiled, and announced, "Hurt a little. Start in morning. Bingo now. Okay?"

We had never had tattoos, though many people enjoyed them—a commonplace choice. Current or past loves, important births or deaths, romance, angels, demons, good luck, threats—all found their way on to arms, legs, back, neck, face, and hands. How painful could it be? Each page would be very small, essentially a dot. Evidently, only living human beings were fit for the procedure. Dead skin couldn't absorb the dye properly.

I nuzzled your grandfather's cheek. "Let's find some of the antidote."

He kissed my ear. "Good idea."

Cristo walked very slowly, nearly falling, as we returned to our barracks after bingo. "You know, we get paid a stipend for participating. They deposit the money. It's there for us, plus interest."

"What happens if we leave the project? What if we break our agreement?" Papa asked.

"Good question. Very good," Cristo said. "Better not ask." An index finger crossed his lips.

Sledge overheard us. "You bolt, we'll find you soon enough." He smirked and rolled his pig eyes triumphantly.

A big part of me felt that we should be grateful for what we had. It was impossible to forget that human existence is much worse in those parts of the world where the devastation caused by radiation and global warming is worst. I knew there was a horribly similar pattern. Ghost towns are creepy, people disappear, rats and mice eat human food, coyotes and wolves roam freely, electric power is out, and the radiation eventually kills most people, animals, and trees. Oceans overrun cities, yet ironically there are fires everywhere.

As years go by, and to the extent that climate change allows it, cities are then swallowed up and choked by greenery—grass, plants, and even some trees eventually grow over the cities. Cars rust out. Any remaining wood houses burn and finally collapse. Stone houses and buildings last much longer. Cellulose film decomposes, and this runaway environment ruins paper. Mold spores take over libraries.

Back to the present. Sledge strutted before us like a peacock—small, prancing steps offset by an arrogant demeanor. His gaze circled the room seeking as many of us as he could—penetrating directly into our eyes. "Once you settle in, you'll love it here. Accommodations are five-star." He chuckled to himself, alone with his brand of humor.

Cristo said, "What if we don't love it?"

Sledge said, "The bargain. The contract."

"Well, I'm sure we can contact friends and relatives, even have visitors."

Sledge stood immobile now. "Not really, you read the contract. Did you think it's only simply to satisfy some lawyer?"

Papa arose. "You're going to hold us to every word?"

Sledge nodded.

We were stunned.

Cristo said, "After the tattoo process, what assurance… How do we know that you won't kill us? Sell us to a carnival?"

"Trust me."

I knew we were trapped. We had signed some agreement without reading it very carefully. Hungry, tired, miserable street people aren't careful when they desperately seek a way out—something better. We were bought and paid for.

Sledge said, "By the way, I'm taking two of you on a trip out of the compound when your books are completed. We'll visit Hollywood. Meet people in the arts and movies. They'll invest."

Sledge eyed a middle-aged man and woman—apparently a couple—walked over to them and placed a hand on the shoulder of each.

131

"You two will go with me. You'll be first. Steinbeck on you, sir, and Faulkner on you, my dear."

Nonplussed, the couple held hands sheepishly. The man said, "We're not married."

Sledge said, "That's fine. By the way, we don't want any of you to have children. It's good if you're too old, not married, whatever..."

Cristo whispered to Papa and me. "No visitors, no kids, no furloughs, no promise of old age or natural death. A sacrificial bargain."

This meeting provided a lot to think about. I decided to try to be fair. I wanted to talk to the two folks that Sledge chose to take to Hollywood for the investors to oogle.

Curiosity got the better of me, and a few days later I sought out the couple, whose names I had not previously known. I asked around and told others that I wanted to talk to them. They had been seen leaving with Sledge, but no one recalled that they had returned.

When I asked Sledge about them—how the trip went, whether the investors ponied up—he said, "Business is business. Mind yours."

I met Cristo, who tried to reassure me that our lives were not at imminent risk. He knew how to stir up hope and patience.

He said, "The Zoots need time. The process of saving our skin and preserving the tattooed written material is tricky."

I didn't fall for it and I was constantly worried and discouraged by our situation, not just a life term in prison but now death-row, itself.

Papa held my hand. "Cristo knows. Listen to him."

"I know what everyone wants of me. Grateful for their faith in me. Just don't want to be the leader," Cristo said.

"Why not? You're such a natural..." Papa said.

"We all want you to be the top dog," I said, "to speak for us."

The three of us roamed the compound. Bellies now full of ham and cheese sandwiches and a lovely light-brown chicken consommé, we gathered steam as we walked arm-in-arm. I embraced Cristo's right arm automatically without thinking about it, Papa the left.

His arms were not heavily-muscled yet so strong and resolute, as with a swimmer not a weight-lifter. I felt close to him, like family, and it appeared that Papa did, too.

Cristo said, "My vision inspires others. Really more of a philosopher, a prophet."

I dropped his arm. "We don't have anyone else with your commanding presence. The Zoots listen to you."

Papa released his other arm. "You're the man we need. Please reconsider. You're special. All of the Paper People want you, and I do mean everyone."

"Let me sleep on it. Perhaps prayer or a dream will help me decide what's right."

"Good," I said. "That's very good to hear."

The next day Cristo assumed command of the Paper People. No more discussion. He just did it.

We spoke to him after breakfast.

He said, "I'm meeting with Sledge and several other Zoots tomorrow. We need better treatment. I'll lead."

"Thank God," I said. "Must have been a wonderful dream. You'll make a big difference. I'm sure…"

Papa nodded. "There'll be plenty for you to do. This tattoo business is new to us. It may backfire someday."

Chapter Four

We went for a swim at dusk. Cristo scurried to the swimming pool and jumped in feet first and thrashed around comfortably in the water. He dunked me gingerly and then Papa. "You're my team."

I said, "Cristo, at times you seem—different people--psychiatrists might call it a multiple…"

He gazed at me for what felt like hours but said nothing. Then he swam underwater to the far end of the pool. "The eye of the beholder is the key to this. You'll see and experience and know different versions of me. Don't let it scare you off."

Papa said, "Myra, the multiple stuff is far too personal. A kind of craziness. To avoid something worse." He rubbed my shoulders. "It's creepy. You must think we're all nuts."

Finally Cristo smiled. His eyes danced with light, the angular, tanned, good looks of his face bright with pleasant humor. "It's okay," he said. "I know what Myra refers to—distinctions in my behavior. She sees it and senses it."

"She can be awfully inquisitive. I ought to know," Papa said. He peered at me with mild disapproval but I didn't defend myself.

Cristo said, "I'm really only one human being, but there are three parts to me which stand out at various times—when needed. I lead and teach, I'm a motivator, and sometimes, old and very wise." He rubbed his face and hair with water. "Only you and Papa will observe these momentary changes. The others will only notice that I speak with a new viewpoint."

"See, Papa, I'm right," I said. "Why us?"

Cristo continued. "You are both very special. I may look different from time-to-time. Sometimes the me you're familiar with. Other times more robust and energetic, even muscular, and occasionally much older and frail."

134

Papa said, "You say we'll be the only ones to see it all. Why, Cristo, why? It's just too mystical."

Cristo said, "You are with me." He pulled himself out of the pool and toweled off.

I climbed the pool's ladder to stand on solid ground, since the water gave me an uneasy sense of movement and instability. I thought that I'd try to remain level-headed, calm, and dispassionate. Otherwise, I might feel that I'm seeing things that shouldn't be there—aren't there. Hallucinating. Psychotic. Far crazier than Cristo's explanation!

Sometimes I didn't understand him. He always seemed to know what was on my mind—the two missing Paper People preoccupied my thoughts now.

He said, "It's murder—probably outright murder of those two Sledge kidnapped. The Zoots must have another holding pen. They're perfecting the process to skin us and turn it into a parchment-like roll for reading."

Papa held up his right hand, index finger and thumb in the shape of a gun. He dropped it and then simply pointed to his right cheek. "Defend ourselves or turn the other cheek?"

Cristo said, "We must help each other. Stick together. Have faith."

I thought to myself. He's such a powerful presence. So persuasive. So forceful in his quiet, unassuming way.

He said, "I've been in worse situations. We'll survive this."

Cristo's hands, powerful and heavily calloused, didn't quite fit with his lean, lithe body. Dressed now, his baggy look engulfed his torso in a billowy, simple shirt and slacks. His olive skin shone against the all-white clothing. Heavy brown beard gone, the piercing green eyes still shone. He was truly a charismatic leader who inspired us without really trying, simply by his behavior and actions.

A major event started the next day. The inking project turned into reality for all of us. The chief employed three of his young Samoan warriors, each trained carefully in the complexities and nuances of body decoration. They were called *tufugas*, and enjoyed prestige and respect in Samoa. The young men could read and write English, but spoke little of it, so the only direct communication during the tattoo sessions was

135

with the chief. He then relayed any necessary information to his acolytes. He was messenger and the supervisor and mentor.

Sledge chose three of us to begin the regular sessions. The chief mixed the dye. Sledge asked me, your grandfather, and Cristo to be among the first guinea pigs—the first of the Paper People. Cristo portrayed the *Bible*, I revealed Hemingway's *For Whom the Bell Tolls*, and your grandfather was covered in Ken Kesey's *One Flew Over the Cuckoo's Nest*. It seemed an odd assortment of literature.

Sledge said, "The education committee planned it this way."

Cristo abruptly stopped in the middle of the first afternoon. He said, "No more. No more." He slapped the needle to the ground and ran towards the barracks. "I'm sick of it. It hurts. I don't want to finish— even the *Bible*."

Later he relented when the chief said, "If pain bad, Zoots hold you down. No move. No move body."

The chief tattooed me. I suppose it was a special honor. He strapped a specially equipped loupe onto his forehead, covering the broad, wavy black tattoos that morphed into empty dark squares. He began his job.

"Ouch," I said. "That hurts my arm. That really hurts a lot."

He smiled and went on inking.

I grimaced. "May I have an aspirin, or a stronger pill for the pain and my nerves?"

He smiled again but continued his work.

The chief said, "You Americans have saying—suck it up. So, suck it up. Get used to it, old woman." No smile now. He undulated the art on his face perceptibly in a menacing manner.

All I could see was a black dot for each page. I suppose it was a page, maybe a chapter. I couldn't tell. I fell into a kind of zone and my suffering diminished into annoyance, more like several mosquito bites or bee stings.

His stylus, so razor sharp that no additional needle was required, consisted of a long feather with white fringe on the end. He placed a quiver of them on a table next to my chair. The black dye appeared thicker than ink, so he stirred it every few minutes.

I tired quickly. Before I slept the chief said, "We use safe dyes and non-toxic ink. Not like Samoa. Use burned kerosene there. No boar's tusk here. Go very deep."

As he stirred again, he turned and almost as an aside, he said, "My people die of infections. Antibiotics here."

Once asleep, my dream took me back to life on the street. I eyed Papa carefully. The gray beard, thick and wild, began where the hair over his ears ended. The hair, still more black than white, set off his dark eyes which danced and twinkled even in the worst of situations.

Papa said, "Are you staring at me?"

"Yes," I said, "Doing just that. You handsome devil."

"I miss it," he said, "I miss my job—the people—I was good at it."

I smoothed my own hair. It felt stringy and had lost its luster and shine. I prayed it didn't fall out or stick to my hand in bunches.

"I was about to become the Director of my department in Instructional Technology. Vice-presidency after that. Who knows?"

I slipped Papa's hand, the skin toughened from street life, into both of mine. "Jobs—careers—plans—promotions. Not there now."

Papa removed his hand. He walked toward the dumpster. "When they let me resign, I thought…"

"You were mad as hell."

"Yes," he said, "I was angry and hurt and disillusioned. Why me? I hadn't done anything wrong."

"Your face is scrunched up—mouth turned down. You're pissed-off. We're a pair, aren't we?"

"Come over here," he said. "We'll do a dive in the garbage. You just got sad, very sad when the principal merged the third grade classes. Hung you out to dry. All those years."

137

I held onto his shoulder. My eyes burned and tears slowly formed. "I loved the kids."

"And they loved you." He held me close to him.

We smelled like the street but it didn't matter. We weren't alone. "A lot of good years to remember. Probably should have taken that principal job."

Papa opened the dumpster lid. "Principals lose jobs, too." The lid stuck. "It's the damndest thing. We volunteered in soup kitchens and food banks. Not us. Never us. I even created a virtual reality training program for the volunteers…"

"Let me help you with that lid," I said. "You know, I was Teacher of the Year. Global warming, wars, inflation—they even got the Teacher of the Year." My feet killed me.

A light drizzle began. We hurried with the foraging so that the contents of the dumpster didn't get any soggier than they were. Wet garbage—we called it leftovers—was the worst. Crumpled, sticky brown, lemon rinds refused to make decent drinkable lemonade. Who knew?

Awake now, my mind is still wandering. Before we lost our jobs and lived on the street, Papa and I had been very happy. Social and economic concerns prevailed in the world, gradually worsening, but we had a steady income and a home, and of most importance, we had each other. We had fun together and enjoyed each other as best we could. Your own father, Joey, was out of the house, so we re-built our empty nest.

We met shortly after college and stayed married more than twenty-five years before I got deathly ill. I can't say it was love at first sight, but I can't say it wasn't. Very close to that.

Papa listened to me when I had a bad day at work, then said, "Chocolate?" He found a way to cheer me up. Then he rubbed my feet.

When he had a bad day at work, I gave him an oil and body powder massage. Sometimes more than a massage. "Enough?" I asked.

"Absolutely not," he said. Clean shaven, his soft, dark blue eyes were bright and his teeth very white in those days.

138

Papa had the energy and intelligence and humor that complemented my more serious, yet expressive personality. We were both curious about life, what made human beings tick, and we anticipated a long life together—ups and downs but we'd work it out and prevail over any obstacles that came our way.

When newly married, we often found ourselves near water— ocean, lakes, and rivers. Both of our mothers were deceased and the water soothed us.

Papa said, "Poets equate mother with the sea. Sometimes rough and frothy, but always returning to a calm, serene smoothness."

I said, trying to be clever, "Just like you."

He smiled, gazing straight ahead as the ocean's tide turned.

Then the world-wide bust, with wars and suffering and starvation on a global level. Our dreams quickly dissolved, the foundation of our family's security broke apart, and, *voilà*, we lived on the street.

We were lucky to live in Northern California. At least we were alive and together and our immediate family survived.

Northern California and sections of Oregon and Washington State were included in the areas of the US that had decent water, breathable air, and a portion of its soil that could be planted with selected fruits and vegetables. Some animals reproduced and a few even flourished. In short, contamination of nature due to radiation had luckily skipped much of this region.

We were so fortunate here compared to most of the world. Our forests were inescapably drier and browner, but control and management shifted to those living in, or near them. That change promoted the forest cover and animal life. Local people relied on forests for nuts, honey, and mushrooms for food.

In Northern California, long lines of people circled supermarkets simply to buy stale bread and moldy cheese. Available food was so expensive that many individuals planted their own gardens if they could afford to buy seeds or young plants—and could pay the exorbitant rental fees for the plots.

We had always owned a car, sometimes two. Without a steady supply of oil, gasoline was rationed so cars couldn't go very far. The ugly litter of huge piles of rusted-out car parts grew everywhere.

139

I can't avoid the unpleasantness of the here-and-now any longer. The bright sun loomed directly overhead so I had to shade my eyes, though my entire body was protected by a large yellow umbrella with the wingspan of an eagle. My upper arm and shoulder ached, both covered with black dots and some red welts. My feet really throbbed now.

The chief cleaned the feather pens with a special chemical or solvent. With a twinkle in his eyes, he walked away. He said, "Lunch."

I sauntered over to your grandfather, still asleep under his protective, huge white umbrella, seated a few yards away. He opened his eyes slowly, blinking.

I said, "Not too bad."

He said, "What's for lunch?"

Other project members, scheduled for tattoos later on, played volleyball, Ping-Pong, or swam or sunned that morning. They were starved for lunch, too, and none of us was disappointed.

Dark ale, crisp fish and chips, and blueberry tarts with thick yellow cream for lunch. All English, but Papa observed there was no newspaper to hold the chips.

Papa and the chief walked out of the dining hall together. I trailed behind. "Do you plan to stay in our country?" Papa asked.

The chief flexed his biceps so that the intertwined swirls of black, decorative tattoos rolled and glistened in the bright sunlight. No birds or trees or mountains for this guy. "Maybe. Depends. Tattooing big here."

"Yes, you could earn a good living here."

The chief said, "In my country I'm big shot. Tattoos and body art very important. Part of life. At puberty and when get wife. Women get circles inside circles when baby born." He tightened his abs now so that his ribs were visible, marked by small interlocking stripes. From his mid-torso to his knees was an intricate tattoo he called a *pe'a.*

Papa said, "You're very proud of your body."

"Yes," the chief said. "People in Samoa happy. Love bodies. Body painting good."

"Our people tattoo dragons and flowers—names of people and crosses," Papa said. "We couldn't be Paper People if we got tattoos earlier."

The chief smiled as he hugged Papa. "You come Samoa. Get what want. I know English good."

I encountered Sledge near the door of the dining hall. I wanted to be brave and speak up to him.

He said, "How are you, Myra? The dots are very becoming on you."

I said, "Fine. Just curious. What will you do with us?"

Sledge stood next to me. I moved ahead of him so that he couldn't slip his arm around me.

Sledge said, "Lease you or sell you. Marketing, later on."

"After we're dead?"

"Yes." We now walked in tandem again.

"You know," I said, "we feel like slaves. Why not emancipate us? Let us go."

Sledge chuckled. "We'd lose a lot—money, prestige, power. We..."

"We'd be free," I said.

"That's the marketplace. Capitalism in action."

What he said was true. Why should they lose out? We had no resources to pay them for our release. They would not do it out of the kindness of their hearts. We were an experiment. Just a small group.

We strolled near the dining hall together, middle-aged slave woman with her manipulative master, bellies full of another delicious lunch. We needed Lincoln!

Our group napped for an hour or so, then back to tattooing until late afternoon.

A tangy, red wine accompanied the rare pepper steak and fries for dinner that evening. I succumbed to it. Chocolate biscuits and

141

strawberries with cream for dessert. Then an engaging classic movie. I think it was *The Invisible Man*.

Your papa moaned that night curled up alone in his cot. An infection grew red and swollen in his right arm, enlarging it to twice its normal size. The Zoots provided antibiotics so it cleared up quickly, thank God. Another bitter reminder of the ordeal we suffered to become their walking bookstore.

And so it went for many months. Despite our serious concerns, we were happier at that moment than we'd been in a long time. We both gained weight, even wore some new, clean, clothes provided by the Zoots. Papa's six-foot frame filled out. Very sexy. We were healthy, felt it and looked it, except nearly everyone was covered with black dots. Were we patients in an adult hospital ward of black chicken pox? Maybe the lost tribe of polka-dots from the Amazon? Or, had scientists found a way to put microdots on human skin instead of paper?

Our fit bodies failed to fool us about life in the experiment. Papa itched and scratched until his arms nearly bled with the redness and welts. Believe it or not, he had scabies. The Zoots found a lotion in their medicine chest to cure it. They said it was a derivative of the flower chrysanthemum.

"We have to take care of your skin," Sledge said. "Paid a fortune for the lotion."

It took several weeks for the tiny critters hiding in skin folds to disappear. Papa said, "These Zoots aren't so bad, are they? We can sleep in the same cot again. Keep the linens clean."

We had a group meeting one evening during the inking process. I said to Cristo, "What if we all used the antidote and then left here?"

He said, "You fear death at their hands?"

"Sure do. After we're all fully inked why should they let us live? Thought we'd reach old age, then..."

Papa joined in. "They'd find us one way or another." He held my hands, too tightly.

Cristo said, "If the antidote failed, we'd be easy to spot."

A new Cristo took center stage. It's illogical, but he appeared to be so powerful that he could make almost anything happen. He still showed beautiful green eyes, now almost turquoise—yet I noticed that his neck muscles bulged.

He said, "I've got two ideas. Forget the two missing people. Stop all shaving and inking. Go on strike."

Another Cristo, much older and noticeably frail, roamed the rear of the room. "That's not right. We've agreed."

"They'll kill us," the muscular Cristo said. "When we're dead, there won't even be enough in our bank accounts to pay for a decent funeral. Clam up old-timer."

The Cristo I knew best said, "Old is good."

The athletic, 40-ish Cristo said, "Well, maybe a strike won't work. We don't know how the Zoots will react. Instead, we could sell our own skins when we die." He rubbed his now magnificent arms and shoulders, to emphasize their eventual market value.

Our Cristo as I referred to the man I was most familiar with, shook his head, first slowly, then with gusto. "No. No. No. We're not Zoots. We want the books removed."

And so it went. Our Cristo morphed into his two alter egos as they argued, raised possibilities, then shot them down with logic, with emotion, and with justice. The cumulative effects of this heated discussion: avoid a strike, refuse to sell our own bodies, consider how and when to escape with the antidote in hand.

Papa said, "Three brilliant, voices of one man. The Zoots can't match this quality. On the negative side, we..."

My feet were very sore. The frustration of having trapped ourselves in all of this haunted my thinking.

The room emptied, most of the Paper People trudged out with their heads hanging and eyes glazed with confusion, facing uncertainty mixed with gripping fear—the grim reaper edged closer than ever unless we extricated ourselves.

The pessimistic mood didn't interfere with Papa's inking but a few days later he broke his little finger playing table tennis. He'd been a champ twenty-five years earlier, but now he slammed his paddle-hand into the edge of the table during a kill shot. A nurse in our group yanked the dislocated finger back into place and created a small splint. This time he said, "I'll just play left-handed. I can beat anyone here with either hand tied behind my back."

Instead, he lost badly in the first game of our round-robin tournament. I expected him to laugh it off, but he didn't. He sulked and blamed it on the lack of proper medical care. He even scrunched up his mouth in an ugly display of annoyance.

So life went on before, during, and after the tattoo process. Fall-out from the Middle East continued to be blown in unexpected directions, reaching the west coast of the US again. It was the first round of nuclear fallout, microscopic debris and dust, to grace our skies. The Zoots provided us with safety masks to wear and inoculations against low, non-lethal doses of radiation poisoning. No one became ill, pleasing us and the Zoots who didn't want to risk their perishable assets during a time of high value.

As more and more of us completed the "print" process, our bodies now marked from head to toe, Papa said, "I'm ugly. I want disability benefits."

I said, "Our government is too poor." Then I kissed him.

We were disfigured in a strange, but permanent way. My hunch was that people would hide their eyes if they saw us, or look away, pretend that they weren't grabbing a quick stare. The black dots encased our bodies, unique even for unwieldy prison tats, and set us apart from ordinary humanity. Individuals with such markings appeared destined for the grave—our market value lay in death.

I felt stuck between the Zoots who would sell our "books" and the Diablitos who wanted to destroy all "books." Maybe the Diablitos would sell us, too, if they could figure out the details and make money. I shuddered at the thought. They were a continuous worry—provoking tears of sadness and fear—about the future. What would become of us?

Chapter Five

The tension stimulated by El Diablo's gang frequently tormented us. Diablitos used binoculars, telescopes, snipers hiding in trees, and an occasional drive-by in an all-terrain vehicle to spy on us. They viewed our life in the compound and appeared to spend hours and hours observing the inking of books and photographing it. No frontal assault, yet.

The Zoots' protective warning net of armed men with guns and sensors, carrying video cameras surrounded our camp. Maybe the Diablitos didn't want to risk themselves in a knock-down battle. Perhaps they were patient, mainly curious how successful the Zoots would be with their experiment. Then they could copy it. All I knew was the discomfort, the fear, and the worry of being spied on with an unpredictable outcome. Why? What would happen?

At dusk, after a quick dip in the pool, I took a short walk between the pool and the boundary of the compound. Finished with a long day of tattooing, Papa fell asleep in the lounge chair under a wide-spanned, striped, blue and white umbrella. So, I walked alone in the shade, still in my hand-me-down black two-piece, feeling relaxed and safe and secure for the moment.

Suddenly without warning, a huge hand forcefully wrapped itself around my mouth and jaw. Stunned by the attack, I hardly fought and couldn't scream or yell as two more bearded men dragged me into the shrubs, then carried me to a large tent about a half-mile away. I gave up all thoughts of crying for help, and simply moaned and trembled. I closed my eyes, fearful of recognizing my enemies.

They plopped me scratched and bleeding from the shrubs and underbrush, into a simple chair covered with rough horsehide. I opened my eyes at last.

One of the bearded men, middle-aged, removed his cap and used it to wipe some blood from my body. He said, "Are those dots the books?"

I must have been partly in a state of shock—numbed by the unexpected attack yet with a growing sense of futility and anger. How dare they grab a woman like me? Were they going to torture me? Kill me? Would the Zoots mobilize to search for me? Protect me?

My life did not flash before my eyes, so I reasoned that they weren't going to kill me. What did they want? My feet ached terribly, toes stuck together, even curled up.

I said, "Yes, each dot is a page from a book."

"We're Diablitos. We hate books. We watch day and night," he said. Cap back on the top of his head, his narrowed, dark eyes looked even more sinister. A single gold lower tooth enhanced an evil appearance. The dirty, black beard made it worse.

"What do you want? Take me back," I said. "My cuts are red and sore. You dragged..."

"We want information. What books? How do they do it? What will they do with you people? They shaved your head, lady."

"What's your name?" I said.

He stroked his beard as a crooked smile appeared briefly. "I am El Diablo, the boss. I wore a white uniform—the parade. We burn books. We torch libraries. I write on stone."

"I'm Myra. I'm one of the Paper People. They tattoo books on our shaved skin. They use light in a certain way. That's all I know. Take me back, El Diablo. Please. Please." Several cuts started to bleed again. "Do you want a war?"

"No, no war. We're not ready. We just watch and learn. What books?"

I didn't know how far to go with this guy. What did they learn? They hadn't really hurt me badly. Cuts heal. No torture. No deprivation. His clothes and body stunk to high heaven. But, no handcuffs or horrible spotlight in my eyes. My heart raced as I was scared to death but a little voice inside me said, stay calm. Answer as best you can. They won't kill you. I hoped the little voice was correct. I tried to save most of the shaking until later. Even so, my hands trembled visibly.

"What books?" He took a long swig out of his canteen, wiped his mouth with the back of his filthy hand, and then offered me water.

I drank. "Thank you. All kinds. Old, new, famous, historical, fiction, non-fiction—all kinds. One book on…"

He stood before me, then pulled up a chair and lifted one mud-caked boot on it, a haughty, arrogant posture which fit him. "Don't shit me, lady. I want the truth. Want to screw one of my unwashed soldiers?" He lit a foul-smelling tiny cigar.

My heart raced even faster, with nowhere to go. I hoped it wouldn't explode, but that could be better than what El Diablo offered. I experienced blurred vision. It cleared up when I rubbed my eyes. If El Diablo's odor was an example, his troops must stink to high heaven. Speaking of heaven, I crossed myself several times and prayed for salvation later on. I wanted to return to Papa yesterday.

"What will it be, lady, or Myra?"

"Specifically," I said, "the books save important works of creativity. Many have survived for hundreds of years. Civilization must not lose them."

"What will they do with you? Kill you?"

I said, "I hope not. They'll have our skin when we die. Books will last. Like a mummy." I thought of the dry, taut skin and light brown, scrawny, bones of ancient bodies I used to stare at under glass cases in museums. There but for the grace of God go I.

He said, "How do they fix the skin?"

"I don't know their process. That's the trouble."

El Diablo kicked over his chair. He held my arms as he helped me stand. "You're shaking. Relax. Return to your people."

My knees wobbled. I was afraid they'd shoot me in the back. I half-stumbled through the bramble, bleeding from open cuts again. Near the compound, I finally screamed, "Help! Help! I'm hurt!"

Papa ran to me. He held me for an eternity. I must have fainted, because the next thing I recall is Papa placing cold, damp rags on my forehead and repeating a short love poem. "Myra, Myra, Myra. Stay close to me. Always. I'm so happy that you're here now. The Zoots—

such cowards and bastards—refused to send out a search party until daylight."

I repeated the story of the incident after dinner that night to a spell-bound crowd in our barracks. A local celebrity of sorts. Other Paper People hugged me and congratulated me on my bravery and strength. I was a heroine. I accepted the accolades but didn't deserve them.

I felt lucky to be alive and back with Papa. The only way in which I felt at all special was that I was the only member of our compound to have met and talked in person with El Diablo. He never did tell me what his specific beliefs and goals were. All I knew was that he wanted to destroy all that I valued. Gangs—not a pretty picture of the future of civilization given their autocratic, cruel, and tyrannical leadership.

I said, "Papa, should I ask for pills? This life—the world—is so distressing. I'm nervous and sad and…"

He said, "No, don't show weakness or give the Zoots anything to use against us."

So, I suffered in silence, even at night when Papa held me and wiped away my tears. He couldn't do anything about my dreams.

Gang members and, of course, many others in society perceived the chronically homeless as a lower caste, marketplace assets for the likes of the Zoots, as well as the weakened class of the poor and downtrodden. Without hope for redemption, jobs, or other self-sustaining efforts, society compared us to humans in the classic movie *Planet of The Apes*, thought to be a lesser species, not as intelligent, motivated, or competent as our captors.

There were many of us now. We did band together and form close bonds and friendships. In our collective mind, the Paper People had superior talent, a genuine source of self-esteem, and a remarkable reason to look forward to a valuable, long-lasting legacy after death. In life, we could be seen as slaves, outcasts, and renegades, while in our own eyes, we held out hope for the future, the chance for social change to endure, and selfishly, the opportunity to be well cared for while alive.

Both the Zoots and the Paper People harbored unrealistic ideas!

Don't ask me how I knew it, but I felt certain that the Paper People would find a way to cope with their well-fed, comfortably clothed isolation and imprisonment. You might wonder why we would ever consider something else. Why not just enjoy the comforts given to us, then compare them with homelessness? We couldn't do it.

We knew it was wrong to be enslaved as Paper People. It degraded us as human beings with a body and a soul—beliefs, ideas, plans, needs—an image of goodness. We felt good about doing good. Very old songs flooded my mind: Michael Jackson's The Man in the Mirror and Simon and Garfunkel's Bridge over Troubled Waters.

Life on the street left me with clear ideas about the need for help. Even in global meltdowns, homeless individuals should have a comprehensive program—though all of it may not be put into effect immediately. Such an effort, the need for which is supported by our time living on the street, must cover food, housing, education, social services and job retraining.

If the program works out, even on a limited basis, the homeless will not be as reckless as the Paper People had been. They'll be more careful and cautious as to the arrangements or contracts they secure. Their own individuality and independence will be a top priority, not to be sold or traded to the highest bidder. The boundary that separates homelessness from the rest of humanity is very porous and malleable. Believe me, I know!

We had to discover a way out of this compound, to leave while alive, to escape.

Cristo perched on the top rung of our political hierarchy. I was so glad he'd changed his mind. His natural leadership skills fit perfectly with a charismatic, inspirational personality, a man who commanded respect and admiration. He bargained single-handedly with the Zoots for continued good food, warm blankets, clean sheets, and the promise of steady employment once the books were completed. Followers met in small groups, agreed upon what was needed, and then relayed their wishes and needs to Cristo.

Papa said, "He's going to speak tonight. All of us will..."

"Good, we need a good gripe session. Life could be better. Warm blankets and good food are not enough." My feet were plenty swollen and red.

149

Cristo's shaved head featured the Psalms, though his lean build allowed only one-half of the Holy Scriptures to be placed on him, the other half on someone else about his size. One needed a loupe to be able to tell which person showed what part of the *Bible*.

Cristo scratched his bald head. "This meeting is confidential. I want out of here. They're only paying us what prisoners earn working in jail. It's bogus. We're simply..."

Applause and loud cheers hurt my ears. I guess everybody shared my disappointment and felt cheated and angry. Papa scrunched up his face, wide mouth closed and lips downturned.

Cristo said, "You know who these Zoots are, don't you? They only care about profit. We're just modern papyrus."

A hushed silence overcame the Paper People as we listened to Cristo's impassioned plea. We all knew in our hearts that he spoke the truth.

Now the contrarian, Papa whispered, "He should have been a preacher on TV."

"Say something nice," I said. "Such a caustic remark."

"You're right. I withdraw it." He kissed my hand. "He could have been a demigod."

"Oh, you're impossible." I squeezed his arm with as much strength as I could muster. The skin grew red underneath black dots.

Cristo suddenly appeared a bit older, stronger and more powerful. He said, "So that's the way it is! We need to mobilize. We won't hurt them."

I noticed that his well-defined chest and arms left no creases in his tight, short-sleeved tee-shirt. Dark blue jeans showed off thick thighs attached to his narrow waist. Now with the chiseled face of a body-builder, his penetrating green eyes set in a wide brow complemented his athletic physique perfectly. Life at the compound had been good to his body. Was I deceived?

Hands clapped respectfully. Then cheers. The momentum grew with loud chants. Voices cried out: "Yes. Yes. We must go." "We must leave." "They exploit us."

150

It was almost as if a spontaneous dance erupted—half conga-line and half a nondescript swirling and twisting of bodies. We felt the future, the music in our souls.

We shared a collective guilt over what we'd done, what we'd become. I may exaggerate things, but we lose integrity and humanity as a result of a shameful contract with the devil. The Zoots and the Diablitos share a common ancestry—power, control, and greed. Their narrow-minded contempt for intelligent, fact-based dialogue about critical social and political issues could not be ignored.

Believe it or not, your grandfather slowly stood and talked, steamed up by the conversation. "Who are we to cast the first stone? We knew what we were doing. They're more cruel than we thought. They did what they said they'd do. No law or judge can help us."

Cristo, now appearing to us as an old man, rose awkwardly to his feet. He nearly fell. "Who is he to say these high-falutin' words and cheap philosophy. We eat. We sleep. We sun. We're healthy."

Papa and I felt no surprise when the hurrahs and applause and screams overwhelmed the group. They exclaimed, "Yes! Yes! Yes!"

The Paper People cheered and agreed with whoever spoke last. What did they really believe? Would they bolt in the face of a death-row existence? Would being incommunicado, even if voluntary at the beginning, move them to run away?

The question of eventual escape never left my mind. We must go!

Chapter Six

Legal scholars could argue about what we knew, what we expected, what we promised, and what dangers we bought into when we agreed to be experimental guinea pigs. We didn't think far enough ahead. Desperate people do desperate things. We failed to think through our plans, taking into account the possibility of surprises and unexpected reactions or consequences. At one level we were treated well—no beatings, physical restraints, or leg irons. On the outside, it looked acceptable.

From the inside, it was a much different story, one we should have, but failed, to anticipate. It was a moral outrage, an assault on us as human beings, wanting freedom of action and movement. We were now prisoners kept in the encampment against our will. We didn't peer into the future, only filled our bellies and hoped that this crazy experiment would be legal and useful and helpful to us.

We did not look ahead to conflict with the Zoots, to the harm to our bodies, or the anguish in the inking of the stories. We gratefully dedicated our bodies, such as they were at the beginning, to science, to knowledge, to eventually helping others where we had failed. The Zoots, of course, did not discourage this line of thinking. If honest and straightforward, they should have told us we became a profit center, first and foremost, and a scientific breakthrough as a lucky by-product.

Even their process of selecting printed material was biased and consumer-driven. Instead of establishing an independent committee of professors, writers, and artists, the Zoots relied upon a Hollywood group of ad and con men to develop a catalogue of books. Later, movies, TV shows, and poetry could be tattooed on people. Luckily, the initial selections were good ones.

Our group would be a harbinger of things to come, the first wave of the future of commodities and entertainment. The Zoots told us all of this, conceited and arrogant as they were, in an attempt to demonstrate the accuracy and usefulness of their approach to the arts—and to us.

152

The meeting continued in the barracks as your grandfather spoke up. He said, "Don't forget how things were before we became Paper People. Sheer survival..."

I hugged him as he stood there, so proud of his practical approach to life.

He sat down to silence. They appeared to like him as a person but not his views on revolt. No one cheered. Several men slapped him on the back, a small consolation for saying what he thought. Papa scrunched up cheeks, lips, and nose. His wide mouth took a downturn, revealing his anger at the group's reaction.

Never much of a rabble-rouser or activist of any kind, I wanted out in the worst way. I would have given anything for the chance to see you kids grow up, go to school, do sports, have fun with your friends. We were valuable property, though deformed by the dots. A prison in two places—here as well as in the city.

Still, I wanted to escape with gratitude and honor and dignity. I wanted an "Honorable Discharge," though none of us had enlisted for a fixed period or a specific war or to fight off terrorists. Our agreement with the Zoots was a forever deal—till death we do part—part with our skin, that is.

I brazenly marched up to the front of the barracks, eyed the others, stood as tall as I could, and said, "How do we do it?"

They all chanted, "How? How? How? How?"

Courage moved down to my feet. No soreness or stiffness or throbbing now.

An insurrection began, with mutinous strength and trustworthy allegiance to each other. The Paper People were going to escape and leave the Zoots holding the bag.

I felt the group's support, so I said, "We need the antidote before we leave."

Chants followed of "Yes! Yes! Yes!" and, "We need it. We need it now."

I don't know how to explain this: as much as I hoped to escape the compound, and rid my body of the ink covering it, I sensed that I wouldn't live long enough to enjoy a long, normal life as your grandmother.

Both of my parents died in their early fifties despite good medical care and rehabilitation. They had inoperable and untreatable cancers. I hoped for the best, as they say, but prepared for the worst. With no money or property to leave you both, I struggled to find a lasting expression of my feelings—a will and testament for you that told the story of the Paper People episode.

If they paid us more money, or if the Zoots were less eager to loan us out, or sell us to the highest bidder, would we have been actively seeking the outside world? My answer was always "yes."

There is nothing more inhumane than being held captive, even voluntarily choosing slavery over oblivion. Our freedom to choose, to select where we lived, to decide with whom to share our lives—these issues inevitably led to escape. And yet, escape might lead to life on the street again. Not a pretty thought to choose to be homeless, and poor, and eat from trash bins. Better to live under the thumb of a cruel, heartless gang leader, always feeling scared and frustrated and full of hate? Stay or leave could both be ugly choices!

The meeting ended. I went outside for a moment. I caught sight of a bearded face topped by a beret near the boundary of the compound, but only a fleeting glimpse. I thought that it was up to the Zoots to protect us. It was their project, so security belonged to them.

We slept fitfully. Then we were suddenly awakened that night around 2:00 a.m. by a loud voice booming over a nearby P.A. system. World War II was ancient world history to you guys. Tokyo Rose sent alluring messages, hurtful reminders of home, complicated patriotic themes over loud speakers during the 1940's Japanese-American hand-to-hand combat for islands in the South Pacific. We now experienced a tiny replica of that.

I turned on my old digital recorder as El Diablo spoke loudly and persuasively. "Hello, Paper People. How are you tonight? Sorry to wake you. It's me—yes, it is—El Diablo, himself, the leader. We're looking at you. To see what you're doing. We won't attack. I promise."

Papa and I sat upright in our bed. The loudspeakers blared El Diablo's voice over the compound. Papa said, "Is that the same guy?"

"Yes."

"Does he think we're complete fools?" Papa slid out of bed and went to a window. "My God, they're shooting off fireworks, short-lived showers of green and red, followed by huge white stars."

El Diablo said, "The sky is beautiful. Life with me is beautiful. My beliefs. You're important. We love you."

I joined Papa at the window. The fireworks were glorious but burned out quickly. "He's a cruel dictator. Nothing more."

"Join the Diablitos and no more tattoos. Hair and beards again. Our food is better. We travel a lot. We ride motorcycles. We'll tell you what to believe."

Assorted voices in our barracks screamed and yelled at the top of their lungs, "You hate us." "Go away." "You hate books." "Knowledge is power."

Then more quietly, "I'm going back to sleep." "Pull the covers over your head." "Don't listen to that garbage." "He's a liar."

Papa and I remained at the window. It sounded as if canons fired shells that burst into colorful glimmers of falling stars, with resounding booms and echoes that hurt my ears. We held each other, afraid to let go.

El Diablo said, "Our ideas are simple and true. I rule. My word is written in stone. It's not finished. We honor all dictators. Books confuse people."

Our barracks door flew wide open. Sledge marched in with several Zoots in tow. We gathered around them in our bedclothes and robes.

Sledge's face, shining with perspiration, appeared in silhouette against the backdrop of light from the open door. "He's a liar and a cheat. He is head of a drug gang. Hates books and knowledge—fears open and unfettered ideas and thoughts. He knows nothing of history or languages or literature. They hate us. We have money. We're college graduates. It's breeding. We read and think and easily solve problems." He wiped away the sweat on his face with a handkerchief. "See you at inking."

The Zoots slipped out quickly. No goodbyes. No questions. No answers. Just Sledge's brief soliloquy. So, we went back to sleep, just back to bed for me, since my thoughts were punctuated by Papa's

155

snoring until nearly dawn. I felt confused, frightened by both the Diablos and the Zoots, ready to finish the tattooing and somehow get on with our lives—whatever that meant and wherever it led us.

At first sunlight Diablito shots rang out in the compound. I went to the window again. A Zoot lay motionless on the ground, his torso covered with spurting blood and contorted in spasms. Then he was motionless. Fellow Zoots carried him to their private barracks. Smoke arose from the chimney and I assumed that Zoot's body was cremated. They never said anything to us, didn't explain the shooting, and acted as if nothing had happened, just like the earlier murder of one of the Paper People. What else could we expect from individuals with no mercy. My toes wanted to disconnect. I yearned for safety and protection.

Their weakness exposed for all to see, their lack of retaliation, convinced me again—if I needed it—that the Zoots were incapable, or uninterested, in saving their own or us. To evade such guards might be possible.

El Diablo proved his power, his military superiority, as well as his capacity for deception. An outright liar who only wanted to watch us, my foot! Better to be dead than misled by such an outrageous, deceitful tyrant.

Sledge spoke briefly about these concerns after dinner that evening. "Don't worry. You're well defended by us."

Papa and I went to bed early! Voices awakened us. We went to the window and observed and listened. A full moon hung in the cloudless sky.

In the compound, a middle-aged Diablito arrived in the dark under cover of a white flag. Long beard, cracked grimy skin, and ragged, dirty clothes, urgently in need of a complete makeover. He said, "We need anti-venom stuff—a snake bite. Rattler. Made a noise."

"Put down the flag. We respect it," Sledge said. "Go away. You killed one of us. We don't have anything for you." He smoothed his oily hair.

The Diablito literally collapsed on the ground. "I need water. I am El Diablo."

Sledge handed him a canteen full of fresh water. "You're lying. What do I get from you?"

"Twenty-five of us here. We buy. We sell. We use drugs." He gulped half of the canteen water, then raised himself to full height and shook the dust and sand from his tattered uniform. "Not much food but *mucho* drugs."

Cristo wet a cloth and held it to his forehead. The visitor was dehydrated so he might have double-vision. Something made him appear dazed and a bit confused, as his gaze quickly moved to each in this small group. Maybe a drug reaction.

"They don't trust me. Several men want to leave," El Diablo said.

Sledge said, "Maybe you thought we'd shoot you. Tell me more."

He stretched his arms and legs. "Feel better. My eyes are better. We watch you. See what you do. How far you'll go? Your Paper People... Sell them and make a profit. You belong to us."

"Attack us?"

"No, not now. Just watch. Books are bad. Bad thoughts." For some reason, El Diablo walked closer to Cristo. "Who's this guy?"

Cristo gazed at him, green eyes bulging through heavy lids, unblinking in an immobile head. To us, he now appeared older and quite weak and frail, trouble standing, in need of a cane.

"Don't stare," El Diablo said.

"They say I'm wise."

"Well," El Diablo said, "we know the truth. My ideas are..." He brushed off his ragged uniform again. Then he removed dirt from his cap. Dust flew when he scratched his head.

"What ideas?"

El Diablo paused before he answered, "Brown people are best— not white, red, black, or yellow. Brown. We purify our race."

"What else?"

"We have great civilizations. Incas and Aztecs. Our people from the Amazon—superhuman with magical powers."

157

Cristo said, "What's wrong with books?"

"Only my book—my story—is true. Written in stone and lasts forever." He slurped noisily from the canteen.

Cristo, the venerated patriarch, a tiny white cap perched on top of his bald head, gestured lazily with bony fingers covered in loose hanging skin. A blousy shirt hung low over his wide-legged white slacks, held up with a knot tied by a pair of strings: simple, direct, and immediate but different—really one of a kind. He said, "You may not understand, but written language in books... We pass on our cultural traditions. Written words are very precise."

Cristo now squatted awkwardly on a small stool. His breathing grew faster and more shallow. He sighed. "There are many truths. I'd like to save you. You are not a god."

El Diablo said, "I have a blood oath with my..."

Cristo stood off-balance. "You don't believe in God, do you?"

"No. It's bullshit. God is dead."

Cristo said, "I tire easily now. At times I'm strong but I feel weak and vulnerable at the moment." His shaved head bowed and barely able to stand, he shuffled to the side.

Suddenly, we observed an energetic Cristo, as if on cue, walk forward. "Why do you sell drugs and commit terrible crimes? Such violence. You threaten..."

El Diablo said, "Who are you?"

An open, almost boyish, countenance also revealed Cristo's new wide-eyed innocence. He said, "I'm a passionate person. I throw myself into everything." His arms and chest bulged. "I guide others."

El Diablo said, "I'm leaving. The snake-bite story is not true. I lied."

Sledge grabbed his shoulders and faced him. "You're not really El Diablo, are you?" He surprised him with a sucker punch. "I should kill you. You have killed Zoots."

El Diablo turned his head, coughed, and spat some blood. He did an about-face and marched away. The limp white flag lay on the ground. A canteen now dangled from his military belt.

Still at the window, I boiled over with rage. I whispered to Papa, "It's dark. I'm sure it's El Diablo. He's a beast—a tyrant and liar—he'd kill us. I hate him."

Sledge screamed, "Don't come back you devil. You're a traitor. You're a killer. A murderer. You're stupid. I'm in charge here. Stay the hell out of here." He threw several stones at him. Then he kicked dust in his direction. "You don't have a process to save human skin. You want to steal our way."

He turned to Cristo. "You baffle me."

Now seeming to be middle-aged, Cristo stood with his hands crossed behind him. Much like a weightlifter or the way European men walk. "I can be very wise."

"Did you need to control the conversation?"

"Sort of guide it," Cristo said.

Sledge said, "You Paper People are really something. You could be a Zoot."

The next morning Sledge entered the dining hall during breakfast, strutting cockily to show how pleased he was—with himself.

Your grandfather turned to me. He said, "I assume we have a perimeter defense. Prevented the Diablitos from sneaking a frontal attack."

I said, "Hope you're right. These Zoots couldn't fight their way out of a wet paper bag."

He laughed. "If they could afford to buy one at today's prices." He laughed again, more of a wise chortle this time. "We do have fun, don't we? You know, if I ever get this Ken Kesey off of me, I'm growing the world's longest beard, just like the Amish or Hasidic."

We strolled around the compound after breakfast. Arm in arm— it felt so good to love Papa and be loved by him.

"We need the antidote to the tattoo dye," I said. "We'll have a big 'white out' party—erase all of it so we look normal again. Let the Zoots and Diablitos fight. We must get out."

Chapter Seven

The full moon beamed light on Cristo, Papa, and me seated on a narrow bench installed near the swimming pool. Cristo disrobed and dove into the water, quickly jumped out, shivering as he wiped the water from his hairless body, lean and strong.

Papa said, "Why do they spy on us? Why do they hate us this much?"

I said, "Come on, you know they talk about books as poisonous snakes. Kills different ideas."

"Yes, yes," Cristo said. "But it's more than that. They're afraid of ideas. They're scared to death that book knowledge will gradually influence their movement. Devil in Spanish is *diablo*. The devil won't allow books or movies or TV to survive in any form—even on human skin. That undermines their future plans. No forgiveness from them and no repentance."

I said, "They really are the bad guys. They'd skin us and sell us too."

Papa nodded. "My dear, you're not just another pretty face." He kissed me. Then he hugged Cristo. "You both teach me and honor me with your presence. And that's no joke."

Papa's body language—upright stance, serious demeanor, expressive hands—revealed no ambivalence or uncertainty, just bushy-tailed integrity. Brutally honest and completely sincere. This was an example.

Cristo said, "My alter egos help me. I make a lot of judgments and act myself. I'm never really alone." The early evening warm temperature dried his body, so he pulled on his slacks and shirt.

Papa said, "What do the other parts do for you? You make big decisions."

161

"Well, they give me a lot. The muscular one pushes me to action, and the old man, well, he provides the underlying wisdom and life-and-death force. Changing the world—even one society, or even the Paper People is not a quick, one-person job."

I stood ram-rod straight and tall as I could, threw my shoulders backward after sitting hunch-back on the bench during our discussion. Papa called me nosey. "What else does the old man do for you?"

Cristo circled the bench and then inched closer to us. "You're right, of course. One is a decade older, but larger than I am, Father Time is much older, now in his mid-seventies. The Zoots saw something in me that they liked, something profound. A lot of the Old Testament is inked on me."

Papa said, "Yes, but you call the shots. We chose you to be our leader. No baloney from you." He stroked his smooth face and bald head.

Cristo said, "Without my patriarch, I'd be an ordinary one of us Paper People. The wise one makes me what I aspire to be—loving and good and just."

Papa now walked toward our living quarters. He bent over and lit a blazing fire in the pit. "That's quite an explanation. You are remarkable, Cristo—quite remarkable. It's sort of science fiction, but I've seen it. So has Myra. Not zombies, or witches, or the undead. Just Cristo."

I cried, not enough so that the two of them noticed. But I did cry. I had no idea why, and I don't to this day. I knew we were leaving, one way or another.

The chief approached us. Cristo followed up in conversation with him, part of the planning for our departure. Papa and I were onlookers. We overheard everything.

The chief said, "I don't go. Should stay here with my people." He sat cross-legged before a raging fire pit.

"We must have you with us. You apply the antidote. You speak English," Cristo said. He pleaded with uplifted palms. "Please, chief. Please come with us."

The chief arose and circled the bonfire, finally booted several stones into the fire. "Zoots been good. Good money. Good food. Good life."

Cristo dumped several more logs on the fire. The fire sparkled, like hordes of lightning bugs. "Well, what do you think the Zoots will do to you when we leave?"

"Give money to go home."

Cristo said, "Do you think they'll spend another penny if..."

"Just leave me here?"

"No," Cristo said. "They are cowards. They'll kill you. Several Paper People have disappeared. They left another one dead when..."

The chief trembled with fear, shook his head in disbelief. "Say that so I'll leave. No, no, no..."

Cristo said, "Yes, they will. They don't value human life." He stirred the fire pit, appearing calm, but with a sweet glow of kindness in his eyes. "We must make life go on."

"Can return when want to? Pay more than Zoots?"

"Yes to both questions," Cristo said. "You can leave after the antidote does its job. That's it. Or, you can stay. I'll help you develop your tattoo business. You could be rich."

Rumbling thunder in the background, the sky lit up with streaks of zigzag lines of light. Heavy rain suddenly pelted all of us. The fire was soaked and died.

"Yes," chief said, "I'll go. I'll help. Come back here. Then go Samoa."

"Thank God," Cristo said. He embraced the chief, barely able to get his arms around the huge, muscular torso.

Papa said, "Good night, Cristo. You amaze me." He led me to our barracks for sleep.

Later that week, the Paper People, scared and angry, crowded into the dining hall to decide on a course of action. Infuriated by El Diablo's actions, one segment demanded violent retribution.

"We can't let them do this to us—the shooting, kidnapping Myra, and then those loud, deceitful messages," Papa said. Loud applause followed.

I beamed with pride. He defended me even though I was not tortured or ransomed by El Diablo. What would the Zoots say? We didn't invite them to this "team only" discussion.

Our intent was to take matters into our own hands, though we were ordinary people, easy to spot with the black dots covering us, and no weapons or other means of attack.

I held Papa's hand, leaned over, and kissed his cheek. He slid his chair closer to mine. He moved his hand so he could place his arm around my shoulders. He loved me and valued my strength and ability to bounce back from tough times. He said, "Such big shoulders for a little lady."

I said, "How would we fight back? No weapons that I can see."

Nods all around: "You said it." "We're not soldiers." "The Zoots should do it."

Papa addressed the group again. "My fellow Paper People. We come not to bury the Zoots but to praise them. They are pledged to protect us. Retaliation…"

I clapped and others followed my lead. Papa's reference to Caesar. A standing ovation for Papa's ideas followed. He smiled as he returned his applause to the assembled Paper People.

I said, "An eye for an eye. We should do something. They are horrible."

Sledge surprised us when he stormed into the dining hall. He somehow knew that this opportunity presented itself. His leadership could shine. "I heard about this meeting. Decided to join in—though no one invited me. The Diablitos are a drug gang, killers and thieves. We revile them."

Someone in the rear of the hall yelled out, "Protect us! We're insecure. We want justice!"

I said, "Draw a line in the sand. They grabbed me!"

Sledge took center stage. He slowly groomed himself: straightened his tie, buttoned his suit coat, puffed up his hair, and stood before us with supreme confidence. At last he said, "Relax, everyone. You can count on us Zoots. We will obtain more guns and shoot and kill Diablitos—an eye for an eye. Trust me."

Cristo arose so that his stance blocked Sledge from the view of the audience. "Never. Never. Never. It will only lead to more bloodshed. Revenge. More violence. More killing."

The Paper People apparently agreed with his simple logic They sat quietly but thoughtfully. Several closed their eyes and others held their head.

Sledge pushed him aside. "What should we do? We have to answer violence with an equal dose of the same."

Cristo moved in front of Sledge so he again occupied center stage. The angular face showcased his green, penetrating eyes which reached out to each of us with a gentle, loving quality. With arms upswept his quiet demeanor, even when he was so confrontational, connected with our deepest emotions. "Our answer is to pray, to look at ourselves, and to seek inner guidance. We will be protected by God's divine wisdom."

"God helps those who help themselves, doesn't he?" Sledge asked.

"Yes," Cristo said. "We must be more careful in the compound. Do inking indoors. Stay away from windows and doors. Go out at night instead of during bright daylight. Upgrade our perimeter defense."

"What about leaving?" Papa said.

"Yes," Cristo said, "if it comes to that."

I asked, "Why not revenge?"

Cristo circled the room slowly. He gazed at us carefully, turning it into an uncomfortable, silent tug-of-war. "We cannot take a life for a life. There are other ways to defend ourselves. As martyrs we'll rest in peace." Tears wet his cheeks. He didn't bother to wipe them away, but simply stood tall in the center of the room with his eyes half-closed, rocking slightly back and forth, quietly singing what sounded like a Gregorian chant—at least I recognized the Latin.

Sledge tried to satisfy us. "I've got a plan for killing Diablitos if they attack us. Our current outlying defense will hold only for a time."

"So?" I said.

"I'm bringing in experienced military snipers who will hide on the rooftops. And guard dogs. Very mean and ugly trained German Shepherd dogs who will maim and kill Diablitos."

"Aha," I said. "Aggressive Diablitos will be shot on sight or else killed by the dogs. Is that it?"

Finally, I thought. At last the protection of the Paper People became a priority for our captors. I didn't care if it was their selfish greed or just a tiny bit of human charity. Either way, we'd live and the Diablitos would get their comeuppance. Maybe they'd just vanish into the wilderness to stalk and intimidate others.

Papa said, "Sounds good, Sledge. A simple but workable plan. We're the bait for them. You insist that we trust you to follow through on this."

Sledge said, "Yes. Trust me. I'll do it."

After the meeting, we strolled around the encampment with Sledge, then joined by Cristo, still opposed to violence. We examined the rooftops of the buildings, and an old horse barn which would house the guard dogs and their training staff during the day.

Cristo noticed that a railing was needed for two of the rooftops. He wanted more barbed-wire rollups around the edges of the camp.

Sledge agreed at first, then told Cristo it would cost too much, without the necessary benefit. The two argued forcefully.

Sledge said, "If you don't like it, tough. You lead them, not us. Go to hell."

Cristo trembled with loathing and resentment when his muscularity and strength took over. He grabbed a door handle and slammed it shut. Then he punched in the screen covering it.

He said, "Either protect us or let us be killed. No halfway measures."

Sledge said, "You can trust me. You'll be safe."

I whispered to Papa, "It's a hoax. No snipers, no dogs, and no barbed-wire. No protection plan. Just a dirty, scheming trick to..."

Sledge said, "You Paper People are impossible."

I hated Sledge, who saddened and disappointed me more than ever. The meeting was over. We parted ways with Cristo and Sledge. Sledge was a boastful liar who tried to mollify us, while Cristo preferred martyrdom and eternal peace. No more killing, I hoped, though I wasn't certain.

If we ever escaped, there could certainly be a war—for us— between the Diablitos and the Zoots. I couldn't help thinking about a key question: Who was Cristo? What about violence? How did we get so lucky to have him in the Paper People? If he was a multiple personality, they were an impressive threesome, without whom we would not have survived. His capacity for planning proved that point time and time again, though he didn't always succeed immediately.

Chapter Eight

A lot happened so quickly that I could barely keep up. Cristo miraculously ensured our departure. He located the antidote and then convinced chief to steal the antidote cream and, in case it was needed, additional tattoo dye. We realized the chief faced life in the compound at best, not a return to Samoa. More likely death at the hands of the Zoots. We couldn't let him stay or die. We needed him.

As a next step, Cristo worked out the details of the escape plan. Under cover of darkness, our tattooed books remained hidden. Long-sleeved shirts and slacks for all, hats and scarves, too.

We faced the prospect of concealing the break-out from Sledge and his fellow Zoots, maybe a dozen of them. Their defense force was the final obstacle after the compound emptied.

Cristo threw the dice one day. "Sledge, why not take us into what remains of the forest? Just a chance to get away, enjoy a new environment. Maybe a day trip?"

"You know," Sledge said, "that isn't a bad idea. Could be good for us Zoots, too. Change of locale and a change of pace for a day or two." Sledge brushed lint from his jacket. "If we lose a few of you, that's fine. We'll find you. We'll get more. There are plenty of street folks."

Cristo's idea turned into reality. The Zoots' bus dropped us near a clearing just off the only passable road. We walked about one hundred yards.

After the tents were staked, we gathered so Sledge could talk to us. "Don't think of leaving. Your bodies are marked and we'll easily find you." Our six-person tents stood several miles from the inking compound.

After an hour or so, we heard a huge blast followed by several smaller explosions. Next we viewed thick black smoke, and sky-high, red-brown flames shoot up from the compound. I found out later that Cristo bribed a guard to start the fire in a hut that contained books, movies, videos, and so on. An ingenious plan. All of the Zoots hopped on the bus, which drove quickly to the compound so they could fight the fire.

We darted into the scraggly woods, singing and holding hands and skipping like school kids off for the summer. Cristo's committee mapped out a route to a nearby town. We marched all night and arrived pre-dawn, then hid ourselves in an abandoned warehouse located in an outdated industrial park.

No Zoots in sight. We didn't observe or hear Diablitos. It seemed too easy. Only scratches, hunger pangs, and very swollen, red, sore feet. I wanted to complain but decided to bite my tongue.

Cristo and his allies really took care of business and surprisingly in our small community, kept it to themselves. They provided each of us with a kitchen knife to forage, to protect ourselves, and to give us a small weapon for use in this potentially rough urban scene.

Your grandfather said, "We'll eat from trash cans. Maybe unpicked fruit. We'll make it." He rubbed his hands together, anxious to start a new life.

I said, "I'm not so sure. At least we're free and able to choose."

I felt more relief than excitement and joy. The Zoots did not understand our degree of suffering with them, nor our resolve and desire to escape. Free of the Zoots, life in this warehouse—no water, electricity, or food—posed obvious drawbacks.

We slept most of that day, which became our pattern. Rested by dark, a few of us crept out of the warehouse to check out our location. A Diablito sharpshooter sent a bullet near us, then another, and another. The signature beret and beard showed above the ledge on a rooftop several blocks down the street. The Zoots had their compound fire to manage, cocksure we'd never bolt, but some Diablitos obviously trailed us. If it came to a dogfight, they easily out-gunned us.

I'll spare you kids some of the details. Diablitos' guns ruled, our knives simply provided too little self-defense for lengthy combat. We acted carefully, hidden until nightfall, walked close to buildings, remained in the shadows, avoided all other individuals, set up guards at the doors of our building, ate garbage or stolen fruit—still none of our tactics prevented four Paper People from being shot and killed.

169

We were grievously hurt, and unprepared for burial or cremation. Cristo led religious services for the dead heroes, as we remembered them. No one sold their skin! Though he now appeared to me as a lacking strength, a somewhat wobbly old man, he nonetheless carried the bodies into an empty room, a small kitchen in an earlier phase of the warehouse. After the service, Papa and I foraged.

"Oh, my God. It's a Twinkies wrapper. Nothing in it," Papa said. "Here's a couple of apples, spoiled but..."

I said, "Goes with this cheese—green and white crust. Ugh. I cut away the edges." A sour, moldy odor overwhelmed me.

"Dear, find me some sourdough bread from San Francisco."

"Very funny, very funny," I said. "I'm going to the warehouse for my snack. White wine would be perfect." My feet balled up with pain, so I walked very slowly and carefully. The blisters, cracks and lesions—well, I probably needed a cane.

Once inside, Papa said, "I'll boil you some water." He grabbed a pot to make some dandelion tea.

Further complications occurred while we were holed up in that warehouse. Cristo and his pals got us there but couldn't entice everyone to remain. Two Paper People, a man and a woman, became so frightened and disillusioned that they simply walked out one morning with their hands held up high above their heads. Their estranged daughter Samantha stayed with us.

All I heard was, "Don't shoot. We're going back to the compound. Please don't shoot."

Papa told me that Cristo discussed the decision of staying versus leaving with these two folks for long hours during the night. They said they'd just as soon take their chances with the Zoots as with us. The painful traveling, moving and then relocating without proper food or water wore them down. Even Paper People, have a personal limit.

They never had a chance to go back to the Zoots. Diablito snipers shot and killed them both on the front walkway of the warehouse. It was easy pickings for the snipers in broad daylight. The Diablitos stole their bodies. Only God knows if they had perfected the process to salvage their skins for sale. I hoped and prayed that they had not.

170

Exhausted by our life, my mind drifted to memories of your father Joey and you two grandchildren. Our son, your father, held a special place in our family, not simply because he was our only child. That was part of it but little Joey—so active, so smart, so handsome—tried everything. He crawled early, walked beautifully at age one, and mastered swimming before he was three. Of course, he didn't reveal himself as a child prodigy with memory games or math skills or the piano, yet he learned quickly and showed a nice balance of obeying our rules with a style of independence and "Doing it myself," as he referred to it.

Your Papa and I, quite biased about Joey as parents usually are, felt he was special to us. Others thought so, too. A teacher in his pre-k class said, "I don't exactly know how or why, but Joey is unique—in a good way. He's a special kind of kid. You're very lucky to have him." Joey was named after Papa, whose full name is Joseph M. Beard, but we never called him Joseph Beard, Jr.! He stayed Joey to us, then and now.

Our pediatrician said, "He's growing just fine. Nothing wrong here. Quite a young guy." He nodded and smiled at Joey. "Always like seeing you, Joey." He listened to his lungs and said, "Perfect."

Then the doctor turned to me and said, "I don't usually say this but I feel good here with Joey."

"Yes," I said, "He's got a certain quality—hard to define."

The doctor said, "Well, Mrs. Beard, it's kind of a magical quality, really a spiritual sort of feeling. Maybe a shaman in another lifetime." He patted Joey on the shoulder.

"Yes, I agree."

Joey sat on the edge of the table and squirmed until he stood again. He said nothing but he embraced the doctor's legs and held on tightly.

The doctor said, "Bye, Joey. See you, Mary. Oops, I mean Mrs. Beard."

"Call me Myra. That's my name."

"See you both in six months, Myra," the doctor said. His face and neck flushed. "More immunizations."

171

Joey continued to mystify us as he matured. He spent time alone in his room, reading, watching TV, and quietly observing the heavens through a telescope Papa found at a garage sale. "I love it, Mom. The galaxies are beautiful. The stars arrange themselves in perfect designs. I could watch forever."

But Joey showed strong leadership skills, too. He ran for class president in the ninth grade and won in a landslide. His class raised money for children with disabilities. Then he was elected head of the religion club. They learned about all the different religions in the world and held a meeting once a year to honor the major faiths.

Papa tried to get Joey involved in sports such as baseball or basketball, but without much success. Instead, Joey loved to walk long distances with several friends, lost in nature and the out-of-doors. On our family camping trips, he climbed hills, rode donkeys on narrow trails, and hunted for berries and mushrooms in the dense brush and forests. I don't know if it was odd or peculiar or special, but he always preferred open leather sandals as opposed to hiking boots or sports shoes.

At fourteen, Mary Goldberg emerged as the apple of Joey's eye. I should say "eyes" because she shone brightly at the center of his universe. Very pretty, Mary appeared equally enamored of Joey. I wasn't sure she was smart enough for him and I hadn't made up my mind about her being Jewish. I'm not proud of feeling that way.

Joey said, "Mary and I are going to the sophomore dance together. What should I wear?"

That was the first time that clothes, and his appearance, had surfaced in Joey's life. Generally, he just didn't pay that much attention to those things.

I said, "What's Mary going to wear?"

"A white dress, I think." He covered his mouth to hide a sheepish grin.

I said, "So you could wear brown slacks. How about a white dress shirt with a matching tie?"

"Sounds good to me." He danced around the room and gave me a powerful hug. "You know about things like that. Thanks. I'd just as soon wrap myself in a white sheet."

I laughed. "Very funny. What would Mary think of that?"

172

Waving his arms and strolling around the room, sometimes Joey sounded like and appeared to a grown-up philosopher or minister. He spoke of good and evil, the way we should relate to others, the need for generosity in the face of oppression and so on. His future knew no limits.

"Clothes are just a covering," he said. "They hide important things. The way we care for each other, and trust people. Forgive them."

I said, "Joey, your ideas are profound, way beyond those of a high school student."

He said, "I could lead a church. But I like commerce and business. I'll study accounting in college and marry Mary later. Get that "marry Mary"—sounds like "merry, merry," which I hope it will be."

He was funny, too, which I enjoyed immensely. Just like Papa, so the apple doesn't fall far from the tree!

When Joey turned eighteen, the bottom fell out. A more-or-less idyllic family life changed forever. Joey was diagnosed with multiple sclerosis, a degenerative muscular disease. He missed most of his senior year, sick and weak at home. Some days he didn't have the strength to get out of bed. When he did, he was clumsy and his body shook. Papa and I were devastated. New medications helped to some degree.

He said, "I hurt so much. I'll never give up. Never."

Papa and I cried much of the time. We felt helpless, unable to find a permanent cure or medication to completely arrest the course of the illness. The doctor warned us that Joey might only live into his early thirties. We spent many sleepless nights damping down our dreams for Joey. We expected less—for a shorter period.

We told Joey about the prognosis. He said, "I'll make the most of it—whatever time I have. Suffering is part of life. I'll help others."

But here he is today, still alive after the horrible global meltdown, working once again as an accountant. His health is restored and the MS has been in remission for years, even through the worst of times. No wheelchairs or walkers for your father. He's been down but now he's up again and able to be a good parent and loving husband to Mary.

I couldn't be more proud of your parents—their resilience, ability to adapt to difficult circumstances, and to move ahead with their lives despite smaller expectations and reduced dreams. Ben and Roberta, learn from them. They are excellent role models, especially for this crazy world your generation will inherit.

Joey credits his recovery largely to the love and support of Papa and me. I don't know if that's the proper medical explanation but we were there for him, as the saying goes—feeling crushed, sad, and helpless—but there for him, to share his occasional tears and to be uplifted by his unrelenting optimism.

He was there for us, in a word. He inspired us. He taught us the meaning of hope and optimism. Is that what families are all about, mutual help and joint support? I think so. We all face problems and disappointments, most not so serious as your father, thank goodness. Overcoming frustration and failure is critical, not only to survival but to eventual success in life.

Mary took our place, increasingly, once they were married. Her parents were deceased, but I always was curious as to their feelings about Joey's MS. Mary built upon our efforts to empathize with Joey's whole MS situation, the fearful baggage that comes with it—some perceived accurately, some not, but all of it survivable until one is curled up in a nursing home bed unable to sleep, rest, or eat without assistance.

Mary and Joey fell in love as young adolescents and their appreciation of each other grew stronger through the years. I had lunch with Mary when you both were toddlers. She said, "Joey is strong again—a six foot frame full of muscle and meat. There is an increased tenderness to him, an understanding..."

I said, "I know. Couldn't have asked for a better son. Times are getting worse and worse. Don't know what will happen to all of us." I twirled my curly brown locks. "No more hair salon visits."

Mary said, "With all the wars, and all, Joey thinks that some of us may lose our jobs. We're plenty worried." She sipper her coffee and took a small bite from a plain croissant—no butter or preserves. "Still struggle to look like I'm in high school."

"Oh, Mary, you're very attractive. Beautiful, clear skin and such a good figure. Wish I had it."

"Thanks," she said. "I don't want to spoil lunch but I have a question. See the kids enough? We don't want you to think that we hog them."

"We'd like them to stay with us for several weeks in the summer." I took a huge bite of fettuccini.

Mary slid on fresh lipstick and powdered her cheeks. "Sorry, Mom, but you and Papa. Well, it won't be possible..."

"Why not?"

"To be honest," she said, "you give in to them all the time. Too indulgent. Not good for them."

"Who the hell are you to say that? We raised your husband. The man you married."

Mary said, "Oops. Didn't mean to offend you. Joey agrees with me. The kids are ours, after all." She didn't flinch when confronted.

I said, "Do you want dessert?" I knew she didn't but maybe I could ruin her figure with some sugar and fat.

"No thanks. Have to run."

"We could change. You teach us. We'll do it." I straightened my dress, and then ran a comb through my hair, trying to control a seething rage. How dare she...

Mary stood, wiped her mouth with a napkin. She leaned over and gave me a peck on the cheek. "Wonderful to see you. Love to Papa. We'll talk about the summer again."

"Give hugs and kisses to all. We love you." I meant that, at the moment, for three of the four of them. What is that, seventy-five percent?

If I recall correctly, I wolfed down a banana split with double-chocolate ice cream. It cost a fortune. A son is a son until he takes a wife, or something like that. I hardly tasted my salad or the remains of the pasta.

Papa and I hadn't lost touch with our very special, and only, child but it felt like it at that moment. He was off somewhere in the ether with Mary and you kids. Now in good health, he enjoyed a happy and loving family life. Where did we fit in? I wasn't sure that there was enough room for all of us. After all, you two kids were our only grandchildren!

I choked back tears until I saw Papa that evening. They cascaded down my cheeks and neck the moment he hugged me.

He said, "What's wrong? Bad day?"

"Yes."

He didn't let go. "Tell me. It couldn't be that bad."

I broke loose and plopped down onto our much-used, soft, velvet couch. "Mary won't let us have the little ones this summer." I cried hysterically as I buried my head in my hands.

Slowly, Papa sat next to me. He ran his hand over the smooth maroon velvet. He said, "Why not? Have we done something wrong?"

"We're too indulgent."

He said, "I can be the toughest and meanest disciplinarian alive." He stretched his face into a contorted glob, shielding his surprise and hurt, faking it beautifully.

"Not me. I won't change. I'm a grandmother. Don't know how many good years I've got left."

Papa held me again. "We weren't too indulgent to help Joey."

We had that nice little house near the park, comfortable for now but the winds of war were blowing along with the other man-made and natural disasters ahead. How long would we last? The house? The jobs? Money? Now was the time to be with the grandkids. Not later. This summer would be great fun and we could swing and climb and slide and go to the zoo and picnics and swim and all the rest. Now, not later.

Papa said, "I'll call Joey."

He did and Joey backed down with certain conditions: limits on candy and ice cream, scheduled times for rest and sleep, and following through on any reasonable rule we established.

I said, "I'll sign an oath."

Your mother and I never discussed the summer plan again. We enjoyed a memorable time during that vacation. I'll never forget how happy and content Papa and I were.

When we delivered you both home, Mary said, "The kids look great. Tanned and healthy. We'll do it again."

I was jolted into consciousness. I must have fallen asleep recalling family events, but I wasn't sure. Papa shook me several times. Then I awakened fully. He handed me a hot cup of tea. I was thirsty. Our dreary present again. Inside the warehouse. More guerilla warfare!

Chapter Nine

Cristo's alter ego, a middle-aged motivational speaker inspired us with his nightly pep talks. Strong words mirrored his body, the result of years of training and exercise. Sporting the build of a Roman warrior, he argued passionately that God would want us to protect ourselves against the Diablitos. The large central atrium of the warehouse echoed with his words.

Rusty iron stairs creaked and swayed dangerously but we felt safer upstairs. Ancient brick walls chipped with missing mortar, still sturdy after years of disuse, held up an old, flat tar-paper roof. Our strongest and fastest used an outside fire escape to roam and to protect us.

A youthful, better known, and familiar Cristo finally relented. He said, "Self-defense is permissible now. We face certain death. Sometimes might is right when the enemy is so cruel. I've changed my mind—but only for now."

I don't really know how they did it, but Cristo and others located a nest of Diablito sharpshooters, and then stabbed them to death. They captured rifles and ammunition. Several Paper People, military vets, knew how to use them. We felt just a bit safer.

When they returned, Cristo said, "Never take a knife to a gunfight."

Papa and I roared with belly laughs. "Get serious."

"Here's the gory, horrible truth. We stabbed two of them. Both unconscious. No breathing and no pulse. They started to turn blue. Blood spattered everywhere."

I said, "Even a doctor couldn't..."

Now it was Cristo's turn to guffaw. "Who said I wanted to save them?"

Cristo and others perfected the techniques with the guns. They now had knives and guns and ammo. Dressed in black clothes, heads and faces covered with charcoal dust and moist dirt, they developed into formidable opponents of the Diablito snipers, who of course, expected little resistance from us homeless victims. I guess they thought we'd just give up.

Three Paper People crept out of the rear door, one at a time, unseen by the enemy. They were barefoot and clearly at risk of injury. Plenty of broken glass or sharp cans and rough stones made even walking a dangerous undertaking.

Huddled against the inside walls, we listened to shots fired outside. Primal fear entered my soul, not rapid heartbeat, not bodily tension, or jittery anxiety or sweaty angst, but the deepest, darkest fear for us, for you, for them—for the world. I closed my eyes and held tight to the brick wall until my fingers bled. Papa's scrunched-up face looked frozen with terror and hatred.

Cristo and the others returned safely in an hour or so. The shooting died down. They said nothing to us. No time for talk. Blood spattered over their dusty, dirty faces. We said nothing.

Several Diablitos roared by the warehouse on huge choppers, driving fast while gunning their engines to horribly noisy, ear drum shattering, RPMs.

I actually feared my ear drums would burst, so Papa tore his only handkerchief into strips and stuck them in my ears. "That should help," he said.

The Zoots directed their huge searchlight into our warehouse windows. They'd mounted it on the rear of an ancient Humvee. The light danced around the windows and walls, a kind of hide and seek.

"Get lower against that rear wall," Cristo said. "Lie flat and don't move."

Your grandfather and I did as Cristo urged. He was right. The Zoots drove on without entering the building. They didn't try very hard to corral us. Cowards to the end.

Later, two Zoots passed by slowly in their green Hummer. They kept traveling on the road that led directly back to their compound.

The bloody insurgency-style war continued. Hiding in small enclaves, without weapons of any significance except a few guns and homemade knives, we fought several pitched battles with well-armed Diablitos and Zoots. After an attempted assassination of Sledge, the Zoots' security forces were demoralized and tended to fight half-heartedly and only in daylight.

The Diablitos made a tactical decision to only fight at night, reasoning, I suppose, that if they could threaten and intimidate us, eradicate several of us, they could capture most of our group and take their time to finish off the Zoots. Later I learned that many Diablitos felt they should not waste valuable military resources on a spineless group such as the Zoots, that technology and climate change would eventually reduce them to job-hunting, maybe, beggars on the street.

The Diablitos snipers picked us off using infrared scopes on long-distance Kalashnikovs, Russian-made rifles stockpiled in the Cold War of the previous century. El Diablo bought them, in all likelihood, cheaply in unopened cases once the tension of the mid-20th century subsided.

After five more Paper People had been killed by sniper fire, with sixty-five remaining, we moved quickly from building to building, spreading into smaller three-or four-person teams. We used the garrote to kill several Diablitos and slit the throats of two snipers, who were unaware that we would put up a fight at all. Surprised by the resistance, the Diablitos adjusted their strategy and placed even more snipers at the point of attack. Then, we retreated. We held a meeting of the entire group to determine future strategy.

Cristo gathered us together that night. We held hands, seated in a wide circle. "We're stiff from sleeping on the floor. We're hungry. We're tired. We must leave. They'll pick off a few more of us."

No one disagreed. I said, "How do we do it?"

Cristo smiled at me. "I like a woman who thinks strategically. Several of us will lay down fire with the guns. Everyone else will walk or run—a few at a time—to the outskirts of town. Into what's left of the forest, to live, or to die."

An older Cristo, craggy face encased in a long, gray beard, steeped in wisdom, appeared and said, "We have the power and strength to do it."

No one argued. Your grandfather nodded.

Thank God the nights were starless, pitch-black, and warm.

Cristo moved to the center of the group. "I had been a builder. Then I studied to become a construction engineer. Then it all hit the fan. No place to live. I always wanted to be a preacher—have my own church. Funny how things work out."

I said, "You are fantastic. Tell us more of your background."

Cristo squinted, shook his head, then rubbed his powerful hands together. Several heavy sighs, then he said, "All in due time."

"I'll wait. So will Papa. We're just curious."

Cristo said, "The past is important. Sorry to be so vague."

I reached out my hands to Cristo, who then held them. "The secret is worth waiting for."

"It is a big one."

I dropped my hands. Then I hugged him. I laughed through my tears. "Stop playing God."

Cristo's hands then formed a prayerful pose. "We're all good together."

Cristo's strength and brilliant leadership finally reached the bottom line. How to survive? How to live? Who cares about us? Why should the world protect us? Others will take our place? Are we merely cogs in a media campaign of change and adjustment that will play out, whether we live or die?

Cristo's answer: "Humans will find a way out of their dilemma, as they always have." He then said, "We deserve to live out our natural lives! We must have freedom."

Somehow, the world—a just world—would free us, help us, protect us, and hopefully value us beyond the Zoots' commercial interest. Perhaps the world would find a way for paper, and those writing on it, to survive in another form, but one in which the humanity of the individual is respected and guaranteed.

181

We couldn't sit back and wait for universal justice. The world had higher priorities than the Paper People, regardless of what we deserved. History was on our side, yet time was not. One hundred years from now we could be a footnote in someone's story, or we wouldn't matter at all, totally forgotten by future generations. Bold action, under Cristo's command, appeared to be the best choice. Survival of the remaining Paper People required us to find another place to live, hopefully in peace without the violence of self-defense. We had to help ourselves.

Papa's sense of humor—oh, how I loved it. He called our exit, "Stone, Paper, and Scissors." Stone, instead of rock, was an irreverent slap at El Diablo's writing his ideas on stone! Paper covers stone and wins. It was not at all clear to me that we would win our freedom and independence, but the risk didn't stop us. I simply preferred to believe wholeheartedly that the Paper People would recover, be re-born, and rise up again.

Our guns fired at the Diablito sharpshooters, horribly loud with continuous crackling, blocked my hearing. The firefight worked, though. All the remaining Paper People, plus the chief, our turncoat tattoo expert, traveled in small groups to the edge of town. Hungry, I almost nibbled on a few strands of brown grass. The gunners stayed on, the last to leave safely. Cristo said later that they might have shot two more Diablitos but he wasn't certain.

We planned our departure carefully, though it was almost as easy as walking away from a U.S. minimum-security federal-prison compound. We remained in small groups, using hand signals to communicate, only foraging for food and drink at night. We wore dark clothing to cover all of our bodies except the face, which we painted to hide the tattoos. Unusual appearances to be sure, but not so surreal in this world of late-night city creatives. Once we were identified as Paper People, Diablitos' agents would kidnap, detain, and maybe kill us on sight. We carried as many weapons as possible to fend off enemies—the Zoots and Diablitos. Both gangs wanted us. A horrifying kind of popularity!

It became common knowledge that the Zoots hired private guards and security teams to track down the escapees who were so valuable and necessary to their business. Such guards received instructions to be cautious, and bring them back alive. If necessary, only to shoot the Paper People in a spot that did not obliterate, or at least did little to damage their tattoos. Next, to bring the bodies to the Ink Compound as quickly as possible for preparation and scrolling.

We knew that even El Diablo, who was more violent, instructed his followers to do as little damage to Paper People as possible—shoot, knife, burn, explode—so that when they survived an attack or imprisonment temporarily, their utility as "books" was not completely nullified.

The Zoots, who wanted to recover the Paper People, and Diablito's confederates were at war, too, though the Diablito's immediate priority was us. No Paper People, the Zoots became a less urgent threat, since their current cash cows were dead and buried. El Diablo never forgave the Zoots for being educated, middle-class, and white with access to considerable financing for their vicious schemes. They read books, enjoyed movies, and went to plays. He wanted to destroy what they took for granted.

Cristo somehow got inside information. He mentioned that El Diablo's favorite memory was of the book-burning bonfires in Nazi Germany. The notion of control over public will through propaganda slid easily from one social and political approach to another, from book burning to roasting Paper People. Yet, El Diablo felt that our skin must not be so deformed that it could never be sold. A true despot, he longed to become the autocratic dictator of the hordes of uneducated, cruel forces that shared his beliefs. But money meant power to him, so he didn't give up on the idea of selling our skin.

The Zoots never recovered from the shock of a revolt by us— ungrateful, clearly tagged and marked Paper People. They hoped, macabre as it was, that the Paper People would be shunned by civil society, even more unwanted than they were as the homeless, and eventually would be killed, or commit suicide if they bolted. Their lovely skin could then be sliced, dried, mummified, and scrolled for the future of mankind.

The top ten movies of all time! The Man Booker award winners! Nobel Prize winners' manuscripts! Mark Twain! Those beautiful novels of history and culture from Africa and Mexico and South America! The Romantic poets! All of it could be saved and savored by future generations.

Scientific virtuosity supplanted scientific rigor, now that conventional science was crippled by scarcity, war, violence, and the earth simply running out of things previously thought to be necessities. The Zoots could be Jonas Salk or even Einstein!

Here's a bit more of what I learned from Cristo about the gang leaders.

El Diablo, now forty-seven years old, was raised in a Mexico City orphanage after his parents died in a fireworks factory blaze. He always carried a pinch of cheap snuff in his left cheek.

The Zoots led by Sledge, reflected the style and values of Beverly Hills, where, indeed, Sledge grew up in an upper-class environment. His parents were both attorneys for movie producers. He looked younger than his forty years, tall and sleek with a smooth, tanned face and expensive, tailored clothes.

El Diablo and Sledge reflected a study in contrasts. Brown was best to El Diablo, while Sledge preferred white. Sledge read books but El Diablo destroyed or sold them. Drugs to use or drugs to peddle, control by one or the other. I could go on and on.

They also shared horrifying values and beliefs. I hardly need to mention again the manipulative leadership, the style of violence and murder and hatred of anyone or anything different from them. Hated both of them!

How could the gangs beholden to such leaders ever alter their viewpoints, let alone what they did to others? Society at large, the majority of decent citizens had the capacity to change, to become more tolerant, less discriminatory, but these gangs and their leaders appeared stuck. Not much hope for them.

Thank God for Cristo, our leader. At thirty-three, he was the son of a shoemaker whose mother abandoned him shortly after birth. With a body rendered hairless due to inking, he was covered head to toe with biblical stories and Psalms.

During our journey, I slipped off my shoes when we sat cross-legged and enjoyed a rest period. As it ended, I finally stood and leaned against Papa. "We'll have quite a story to tell, dear."

Your grandfather said, "I don't know if we'll be here to tell it. We've got to get deep into these woods." He laughed. "Before they dry out completely." He hugged me tightly and we both hid our fear of the next trail.

I said, "Even if I die, I want my book gone."

He said, "I agree. No bookstore business." He wiped his hands over his face and arms.

We marched single-file into the darkness, following a path Cristo found. Once again, we walked all night, tired, hungry, and worried as could be. The stored-up fear gradually left us and hope replaced it—baby steps to be sure. Cristo discovered a small stream, and we kneeled to drink from it, much like John Wayne did in the prior century's classic cowboy movies.

Your grandfather said, "I wish I had a wide-brimmed hat to fill with water."

I said, "Splash it over your head and face?"

He said, "Yes, ma'am." He patted his dirty, dotted scalp, shaved and covered in his book.

The Diablitos probably followed our route and most likely concocted a plan to capture or kill all of us. The Zoots might chase us, but I wasn't so sure of what they would do. Usually without critical weapons, they couldn't fight off the Diablitos, and maybe not even poorly armed Paper People.

Collective worry over survival turned out to be just that—worry, worry, and more worry. It weakened me. I needed help. I didn't know how much more shaking and trembling and throbbing my body could endure. Or my mind.

My suffering in this journey deserves a special note. I was one of the few who didn't fare well, reminiscent of classic World War II movies depicting the forced marches of captured soldiers through jungles and swamps. In those movies some became ill, a few gave up, and many perished. My situation, of course, didn't compare with those screen portrayals.

Papa said, "Shall we leave you here?"

I didn't laugh. "Just use towels and shirts—wrap my swollen feet, kind sir."

Papa did just that. Then he and the well-developed, powerfully built, Cristo half-carried me the rest of the way.

185

"All I need is crutches," I said.

"Lean on us," said Cristo.

I didn't mention the mosquito bites or bloody scratches from bushes and low-hanging tree limbs. I was also bitten by a small black snake, fortunately not spewing lethal venom.

A heavy rain pelted us near the end of the journey. Our path now muddy, walking while carrying me became even more treacherous for Papa and Cristo. Warm air holds more moisture, so the rain fell in buckets.

Papa said, "You are one tough bird." He shook the water from his shirt. Still soaked from head-to-toe.

Cristo chanced upon a small plateau, protected by hills, with a narrow river of clean water—at least it looked clean. A fresh morning sun now blazed down upon us. The summer heat would last for several more months, while we re-located and built shelters.

Military vets showed the rest of us how to make soup from dead tree bark, brown grass, insects, and wild berries. We lost weight but lived, free of the Zoots, and without visible signs of the Diablitos. I sensed they were out there. Thank God, no nuclear fallout here!

We worked as a team to build lean-to shelters from dead branches, stones, and crunchy leaves, for protection from sun and rain, but not from the cold of approaching winter. Berries and the military soup kept us alive at the beginning. We roasted some wild game and fish, too.

We sat around the campfire, relaxed at the end of a long hike into the woods to capture wild game in homemade traps and nets. I said, "Cristo, tell us more about these gangs."

Cristo said, "I have my ways. Sorry, but I can't reveal everything."

Papa held my hand under the makeshift table, then tickled my fingers until I squealed.

"Is that funny?" Cristo said.

I said, "Oh, no, not at all. Sounds very important to me. So sorry." I left the table and refilled my coffee cup at the large container set on a small camp stool.

The campfire area emptied out except for the three of us. I knew Cristo planned to update us on El Diablo. My skin crawled with anticipation, not knowing if the information would be grisly or ghastly or only fearful.

Cristo said, "As you know, El Diablo has his own gang or cartel or cult, whatever you wish to call it. Ultimate destruction of us." He stirred the fire. "The Zoots are no heads-on match for the completely motorized Diablitos. They drive old Humvees, ancient Jeeps and motorcycles."

I sipped coffee and nibbled at a stale chocolate chip cookie. "Why not make peace? There's plenty of crime for both."

Cristo's lips spread with a faint, empathic smile. He shook his head and appeared as if he might cry. Tears pooled in his eyes but his cheeks were dry. "The gangs are a sad bunch, to say the least. Forgive me, if I lecture. El Diablo enjoyed a military background and eagerly participated in a counter-revolution in Mexico. He exiled to Cuba. There, he became a trusted subordinate of loyal followers of the national hero, the long-deceased Fidel Castro, their leader for decades. Cuba finally became a fledgling democracy around 2020. El Diablo played both sides of the street.

"The rich landowners were overthrown by Castro's version of Socialism, which took hold for decades. Cuba, if you know your history, received much help from Russia and some degree of aid from others in the Communist bloc.

"It didn't work out so well, as the economy faltered, the infrastructure and public education suffered, and the people didn't prosper as he promised. Equality of a sort but not growth!

"When El Diablo returned to the US-Mexico border area, his drug money attracted a group of followers. For ceremonies, he was always meticulously attired in a white military uniform, his chest heavy with muscle and rows of colorful ribbons and medals, eyes covered with huge, dark aviator-style sunglasses. The glasses and uniform made him look younger than he was. Quite an imposing and charismatic fellow."

187

Papa said, "Do we have a replay, on a very small scale of part of the second World War?" He puffed up his cheeks and tightened his mouth. Big time!

I really didn't understand his question. He followed current events and political history more than I did. So I simply gazed at him quizzically.

"In a way," Cristo said. "That's it. El Diablo and Sledge, coming at the world from different philosophies of government and the individual's relationship to the state, are both manipulative leaders." He pursed his full lips and squinted angrily.

I guess Papa understood more than even I supposed he did. Cristo shook his hand in acknowledgement and appreciation. I simply hugged him. He was mine.

Papa said, "The Zoots are doctrinaire capitalists. Entrepreneurs without a conscience, or any genuine concern for society. Driven by profit, pure and simple." He knocked over his coffee. Then he grimaced with his lips turned downward and growled like a hurt, cornered animal.

Cristo said, "Yes, that's right. They cover themselves with platitudes about freedom and wealth. They try as hard as they can to load the dice in their favor. Unfortunately, we're the chips they were gambling with."

Papa and I had lived in a casino.

Papa said, "The Diablitos would love to have the money and other resources, such as the Paper People, that..."

"Yes," Cristo said, "but the Zoots will run and hide. They won't fight the Diablitos directly. They'll curl up in a corner."

I needed a respite from the intense political discussion, so my mind moved on to you two grandchildren. You'll see why.

I tried to focus on the special moments I had with your grandkids, not what I'd probably miss in your lives—graduations, marriages, children of your own, and a secure, happy life. Fights and arguments took over as you grew up and attended a pre-k program. You two could argue over anything and everything. Who was smarter? Who knew more? Who had more friends? Who was more lovable?

I prevented bloodshed, though it seldom reached that boiling point: Reasoning didn't work very well. I'd say, "Look, you've each got one sibling, so love and protect each other."

"No."

"I hate him. He's mean to me. He won't let me use his basketball."

"I hate her. She's selfish and wants everything her way."

Punishment didn't work very well. "Grandma won't take you out for ice cream if you keep fighting."

Separation worked sometimes. "Ben, please go to your room now and stay away from Roberta."

Ten minutes later I'd find the two of you together, going at it again.

Mediation was a complete bust. "Wouldn't you like to have a pleasant relationship?"

"No, we love fighting like this."

At last, my thoughts left family as I returned to the present discussion. "I'm going to sleep, gentlemen. Good night," I said. I kissed Papa, lay down nearby on a blanket, and closed my eyes.

As sleep took over, I wasn't certain if Cristo's hands made the sign of the cross, or not. I dreamed of an end to sickness and fighting and violence and warfare. A safe and peaceful world. Is that called wish-fulfillment? My dreams didn't fit the real world at all!

Chapter Ten

We built a series of cave dwellings, underground bunkers, and camouflaged tent-like structures, then returned to our real strength: living on the land without malls, stuffed with shops, supermarkets loaded with food and drinks, cars, or digital gadgets. Wild game, fish, berries, and mushrooms replaced the night-time scavenging for leftover garbage in an urban ghetto. More and more of the city people also found their way into the forest. They were worthy competition until irrigation became problematic.

We actually flourished as the weeks and months went by, surprising ourselves and the Zoots—if they even knew about it. The Zoots survived, too, but they didn't flourish even as parts of the world returned to some kind of normalcy. Cristo informed us that many entered lesser occupations, such as waiters, bartenders, and dishwashers, earned smaller incomes, and suffered the humiliation and costs of their failed project. Diablitos still hunted Zoots even though they did not hold, or guard the Paper People.

Ironically, life in the out-of-doors with plenty of sunshine, clean air, and fresh lake water to drink, combined with the antidote, to produce a remarkable phenomenon: our tattoos gradually faded. Children might have been highly educated and cultured by reading our stories, but not now, as the body ink gradually absorbed into the skin. Some of the sharpness of the indentations did not disappear as quickly. A few credited factors such as the healthy lifestyle, the absence of local stress, the relative safety of our new compound, the demise of the Zoots and the death of several Diablitos. Most thought the antidote did its work successfully. I perceived another hand at work.

The chief spread the antidote cream on our bodies each day. A pharmacist told Papa that something called IPL or lasers could harm the skin, but that the chief's antidote strengthens the body's immune system. It worked quickly so we estimated the "bookstore" would disappear in a few months.

I said, "That hurts. Ouch. It hurts me."

He continued to spread the cream over my body. The burning sensation actually pained me more than the original body art.

"Ouch. Can't you be more gentle?" I wiggled my torso.

Papa said, "Why don't you swear at him? Tell him off."

This time the chief smirked. "Suck it up," he said.

Papa and I roared.

The chief smiled in appreciation. He gave in and painted the cream onto my mottled skin with a small, soft brush this time.

We planned and planned and planned on the assumption we'd live for a protracted period of time in these woods. We'd grow crops, veggies, and berries in those few protected areas in the hills, just as many city folks did wherever they found arable land with water. One idea was to domesticate baby wild boars for protein, in addition to trapping or shooting squirrels, coons, and ducks. Children would come along so schooling and educational programs would be required.

Late one morning on a sunny, warm day, clouds descended on the valley as a fierce wind took us by surprise.

I'll briefly tell you about something awful that happened that day at lunch. Cristo sat next to a twenty-five-year old beautiful woman named Samantha. He taught a class in hiking and climbing for the younger Paper People.

He said, "Samantha, you okay?"

No answer. He didn't know it but she couldn't tell anyone what was wrong. A piece of broccoli stuck in her throat.

Cristo touched her arm. "What's wrong?"

Still no words from Samantha. Then she waved her arms, flailing in panic, and gasping for breath. She grabbed her throat with both hands as she gradually choked to death, unable to explain with words.

Cristo then understood. He arose from the bench seat, stood behind her and wrapped his arms tightly around her chest while he squeezed repeatedly. Called the Heimlich maneuver, air in the lungs forces out food stuck in the throat.

191

It didn't work. She lost consciousness. Her heart beat for a few minutes. She began to turn blue.

Cristo felt her neck and wrist. "No pulse and her pupils are fixed," he said.

Samantha choked to death on the spot. A wave of sadness washed over the encampment. Such a waste of a young, vibrant life.

Earlier, Samantha refused to leave with her estranged parents— the two escapees from the warehouse who were shot and killed by Diablitos. She remained loyal to the Paper People and lived in the compound with us. So it's doubly sad—parents who couldn't take any more and daughter who survived everything else only to die like this.

Your grandfather broke down when Cristo, appearing older and weaker to us, a frail priest, conducted the memorial service for her. No humor could help Papa this time. He held me closer than ever that night.

I was sure he was thinking of you grandkids. What if it happened to you? That was on my mind, too. I didn't sleep a bit that night.

A very big miracle was in the making, yet I knew nothing of it at that time. After several weeks, Cristo discovered that the Diablitos had indeed located us, and constructed a huge piñata filled with a lethal bio-chemical agent—a gas that would destroy us in one fell swoop.

Cristo surmised from a Diablito informer that their concept was to send the "Great Piñata" to our camp as a peace offering. Once gouged open, no candy or sweets, but ultimate death for all the Paper People, with more wealth from our skins for the Diablitos. The Diablitos, maintaining their distance, never knew that our antidote had successfully removed the dots. The books were gone. They would have killed us without anything but death to show for it.

Cristo discovered later on that a lowly Diablito guarding the piñata accidently punctured it. The wind direction veered just enough so that the entire Diablito contingent was wiped out. Fortunately, the toxic effects of the bio-chemical agent, anthrax in aerosol particles, did not reach our people several miles away. Occasionally, we did catch a whiff of the decomposing bodies. Horrible odor especially on warm days without wind.

192

We were simply lucky because we had only a limited supply of antibiotics to counter the anthrax. Was there another interpretation? Whatever the cause of this amazing event, we were now truly free, able to return to city life, completely unmarked by the books.

Cristo, in a skull cap and long white prayer shawl, conducted a very beautiful prayer service of gratitude for our freedom and future possibilities. Spirituality now dominated the Paper People, not a party-like atmosphere that could have prevailed. Yes, we were happy, very joyous, and pleased to be free of our books. He even said a brief prayer of forgiveness for the Zoots and the Diablitos.

Our inner serenity, so precious to us when we lived off of the land, would soon come face-to-face with the gritty reality of life in the city. Would we be homeless once again? Starve? Rootless? Out of work? How would we live? What about new gangs? Racial conflicts? Corruption in government? Would we band together to survive? Papa will live to find out the answers, but not your grandmother.

Months went by and then we returned to the city. Things seemed better. Science, especially bio-chemistry, led the way again. Biofuels became popular with crops raised in drought-resistant conditions. A cheaper way to produce solar panels worked out, and the panels were produced in factories largely powered by wind. Such factories were, of course, strategically located in areas where wind dominated the landscape. The forests grew more sparse and increasingly brown due to global warming. However, a synthetic wood with associated paper-like products became possible. It was still in a development phase, and too expensive to be produced and used on a mass scale—but that was simply a matter of time.

Attempts to revive the oil and gas industries largely failed, not only because of the havoc of the two nuclear wars in the Middle East, but due to the spillover destruction of gas and oil wells worldwide. Insurgents struck back in retaliation for injustices perpetrated on the Arab nations. They fought back in the only way they could—sabotage and explosions of prime wells and coal mines that raised the nuclear-power issue again.

It may be a surprise, but people were still divided on the issue of nuclear power, though it had developed very fast for decades. Doubts lingered due to the atomic bomb massacres in Japan, the near meltdown in the U.S., the catastrophe at Chernobyl, and the Japanese shutdown of all nuclear power after the earthquakes and tsunamis of the early 2000s.

I'm no scientist, so I don't know how to evaluate all of these issues, but I knew in my bones that nuclear power would return as a major supplier of energy for the world. Then we needed a way to turn global warming on its heels, to make it work for us, not against the trees and forests and oceans. The advance with crops made it seem likely that trees and ground cover would return, requiring more heat and very little water.

Water would become what paper and all of our plastic and oil-based commodities and social toys had been earlier—the key to culture and civilization being passed on to you young people. TVs, smartphones, i-pads, computers, tablets, and all manner of digital communication equipment—functionally dinosaurs—might become the mother of invention once again.

Once our skin cleared up—Papa said he wanted to thank our immune systems, tattooed stories gone, so most hair grew where it had once been. More grey for me but larger bald spots for Papa. Our joy and relief knew no bounds at last, as we enjoyed the freedom and independence of our return to city life.

Nearly a decade had gone by. Still no picnic, since now we camped out in your family's garage, using stick furniture we scavenged and hand-me-downs from your parents and their friends. The local economy stabilized very slowly, everyone feeling the pinch of lower wages, sky-high prices, and a slow rebound in energy production based on rationed coal, uncertain wind, and that blessed sun.

During the worst of times, your parents also lived in the very same garage. Barely a step above our life on the street. As city life began to regain some sense of order and stability, they rented the small, adjoining house constructed entirely of wood. Termites, rot, and mold will eventually win out. For now, it's a place for all of us to live.

Your parents made it through the worst of it. Only one of them had a job at any particular time, never both at once. We pledged all of our money and savings and property to them, so their survival, and yours, would have a safety net. Life on the street, the homeless experience, ruined the lives of far too many children. Shelters, even half-way houses, interfered with the normal growing pains and pleasures of childhood.

You might wonder how I knew that Papa would live a lot longer than your grandmother. Well, as I mentioned, my own parents, your great-grandparents, both died in their early fifties. My father had a massive heart attack, and my mother suffered from pancreatic cancer for a horrible, painful last year of her life. I didn't inherit the long-life gene, if there is such a thing.

When I turned fifty years old, I experienced a sharp, stabbing pain in my side. Papa took me to the ER. After tests and an MRI, we got the news—I'd be lucky to live a year, maybe less. They could help with some of the pain but not all of it. Surgery was impossible.

Papa said, "I'll take good care of you." No jokes or humor, just straight out deep concern and love from him. Frustrated by his helplessness, and angry that he couldn't cure me, his jaw tightened repeatedly. "What's that classic country western song about loving you until the day you're gone? It should include after you're gone."

Chapter Eleven

My year-long descent into weakness and eventual confusion picked up steam. We had little money, so expensive travel was out of the question. My plan was to preserve the story of the Paper People—on me, of course. I was assured by the doctors that my insides were cancerous, but even if I lost a bit of weight my skin would be suitable for tattoos.

Papa said, "You've given your body to science—called Ben and Roberta."

He tried to make me laugh. So, I went along with this macabre idea and cried with his humor.

Papa checked with other specialists, but healthcare deteriorated during the period of the Paper People. I hoped for medication or radiation or surgery, anything to save me. A miracle would have been fine, too. No such luck.

The chief understood and wrote reasonably good English, and I had my trusty digital recorder, now on its last legs. Papa always assisted with the writing and any translation issues prior to the body ink.

Inking and my health were in a perfect perverse harmony. The cancer got me as the inking progressed. The book for the two of you took all of the months I lasted—less than a year.

As I prepare to go to whatever is next for me, I envision a new world ahead for the two of you. This view is based on several lectures Papa and I attended before I spent most of my time as a "sickie" in bed. When I went out, I covered up head-to-toe to hide the new dots.

Here is a brief summary of what I learned. Saudi Arabia is recovering after the two nuclear wars and leading the way in securing a stronger integration of the Middle Eastern region. They're all scared to death of a resurgent Iran.

After many decades of strife, Syria is still torn apart by the on-and-off civil war. Part of it may become a region within Kurdistan. An independent Kurdish homeland has been a long-wanted dream of the Kurds. One theory is that it will become a hodge-podge of states and so-called city-states. Who knows? Only history.

One of the speakers at the lectures said that Belgium will split up. Arabia will break up, and the Congo, too, will splinter. On the other hand, it is thought that Korea will unify at last.

Wish I could be there to see this new world with you.

Papa found me a much-used wheelchair at a second-hand store called St. Vincent de Paul. He scraped off the rust, cleaned and oiled it, so that he could push me soundlessly. Actually, it was sort of fun for the both of us—me, too weak to walk very far, and him joking that he loved to "push me around."

I said, "You hold on to the handles to help your balance. You're getting old, my man." I blew him a kiss. He heard it, but couldn't see it while standing behind the chair.

We went out on cloudless days with hot sunshine and no wind or rain. Papa placed a blanket over my legs. "Who is that politician in the middle of the 20th century, who had a blanket like this? Wasn't it F.D.R.?"

"You're so smart. Such a good memory, too."

He stopped near some flowers—coleus, I think—popping up above ground. A few shrubs had survived in this small neighborhood park, but I could count the few remaining dead trees on one hand.

"Well, if you mean the gangs we faced---"

"Yes," I said. "The gangs—the Zoots and the Diablitos. What about them?"

Papa said, "You know the bad stuff."

"Some good stuff?"

"Yes," he said. "I've been informed that the Zoots finally recognized that their approach didn't take care of everyone. Many suffered. El Diablo was pure evil. The Diablitos met their maker."

"Don't forget, written in stone."

"I'm afraid," he said, "that you're going to ask about what we have left here, back in the city. The Paper People are no longer slaves." He loosened the brake on the chair and we moved on. He picked several flowers and laid them on my lap.

"You're a wicked man, destroying public property. I'm going to miss you very much."

He chuckled. "Not as much as I'll miss you. Why are you doing this to me? Wish I were the sick one."

"Sorry," I said. "We don't have that choice."

I debated whether I should go into the lurid details of my demise. Sparing you the specifics, I simply became weaker, spending more time in bed or in a chair, and then in the used wheelchair. My suffering increased as did the use of strong drugs including narcotics and a new synthetic—at the end, they didn't do the job.

I do want to brag about Papa. He fed me, remained at my bedside, spoke of his need and love for me, recited brief romantic poetry, and even got me a special hospital bed at a closeout sale.

The last few months marked a social withdrawal of sorts. I seldom saw anyone—you or your parents or friends. Just didn't feel like it, though I appreciated the kind feelings and genuine concern. I wanted or needed to be alone most of the time—alone with my thoughts.

My thoughts centered on the story for you children, my legacy for you. Papa understood my ways and didn't force other relationships on me, especially when the inking took place. I felt guilty that I shut out your parents who wanted to do more for me and visit more often. I hope they understood. I'm sure they did. Joey knew my love never faltered and Mary forgave my shortcomings. I was blessed that Papa knew me so well.

He said, "Whatever Myra wants, Myra gets." Holding my hand, sliding his other one over my newly inked, now hairless scalp, he comforted me. "Whatever Myra wants…"

Our favorite love poem was Shakespeare's Sonnet 98. Papa memorized it and repeated it many times. These lines were especially meaningful to me—his love for me.

Nor did I wonder at the lily's white,

Nor praise the deep vermillion in the rose;

They were but sweet, but figures of delight,

Drawn after you, you pattern of all those.

Ironically, I usually fell asleep somewhere around the middle of this sonnet, before he actually spoke these words.

I think the Paper People story kept me going, gave me life, so to speak. Even on mornings when I wanted to suffer alone in silence, the chief arrived and we went to work.

Papa didn't have to do much motivating. Occasionally, he said, "Whatever Myra wants…"

That did it—a gentle reminder that I wanted to complete the story for you kids and that my time was running short. Once or twice I said, "Whatever Papa wants…" It didn't make any sense.

He said, "I've got it all. For now, that is." He suddenly walked to the door, opened it and slammed it as he went outside. I knew he wept.

Before I died there were two things I had to do. One of them, obviously, was to complete the job with our tattoo artist, the chief, who inscribed the story of the Paper People on me—our personal story and the Paper People Experiment—from beginning to end. My second priority was your grandfather, who would clearly outlive me. He needed a nest, a comfortable arrangement for his life as he aged, in all likelihood, by himself. Living independently, but not alone, the two of you, his only grandchildren, could become the center of his existence. Maybe he'd do something else—I had no idea what it could be. He had tremendous inner strength.

Luckily before I was totally bed-ridden, I found some landscape oil paintings at a hotel going-out-of-business sale. A leather couch, gently used, beckoned me at a Goodwill store tent sale. Your mother gave me two tiny lamps, which fit nicely on a bedside table. And so on. Papa liked his nest. So did I, even though the garage grew chilly at times from a perpetual draft which blew in beneath the sliding door. My feet throbbed and burned—especially when I ruminated on the sadness and eventual loss we faced.

The chief worked on me with great care for months. The pain, excruciating as it was, turned into pleasure at the thought of Papa reading our story to both of you one day. Hopefully, it would take place in that same small cave in the hillside where the Paper People had enjoyed a taste of freedom and life in the country.

The tattoo project turned out to be as much for me as for both of you. It gave me a reason to keep going, to stay alive though my days were numbered. The legacy of dots gives my death a lasting purpose and meaning.

Once the chief completed the Paper People story on my skin, I requested that the story be preserved and read to you both when you were old enough to understand it and appreciate your roots and family history and, of course, your grandmother.

Near the end, our story tattooed, my body shaved and covered with black dots, Papa held my hand, and quietly from memory recited several short love poems. I slept listening to his melodic, rich voice. I understood the messenger much more than the poetry. He probably held my hand, hugged and kissed me. Such a dear man.

We had few guests, but one day I heard a gentle knock on the garage door. Papa opened it. There stood Cristo, tattoos gone from his lean body. He ran both hands through his shoulder-length hair.

Papa said, "What a pleasant surprise." He hugged Cristo, then held him at arm's length. "You're not a book now."

Cristo said, "No, just a former member of the Paper People who luckily escaped."

"You and your guys planned it. Almost perfectly. I'll never know your secret."

Cristo put a finger to his lips. "We won't tell."

"Please sit. Here's a chair. Coffee?"

Cristo remained standing. He said, "No, thank you, Mr. Beard. Oops. I mean, Papa Beard."

"I know you're here to visit Myra," Papa said.

"Yes, if that's possible."

Papa tip-toed into the area now used as our bedroom. A pock-marked black, green and orange oriental screen provided a sense of privacy—not much, of course. He leaned over my bed and whispered, "Cristo's here."

"I'm not deaf."

Papa said, "Cristo, please come in here. Myra can't wait to see you." Papa walked away and left me to enjoy my own crankiness.

Cristo padded into the bedroom area quietly, with his powerful hands before him in a prayerful repose. "Myra, Myra, Myra." He craned his neck to kiss me on the forehead. Then he held my bony hand in his as he sat in the chair next to the bed. The chair—we called it the throne—nearly threadbare, brown, cotton fabric with two arms of pecan wood and leather, had surely been a dining room seat before the neighbor gave it to us.

We gazed at each other. Closed our eyes. Peeked. Then opened them. Not sure of what to say or how to feel or the best way to communicate in this awkward situation.

"You look refreshed and uplifted," I said. "A new day after all that Paper People stuff." I coughed some blood onto the sheet.

Cristo wiped it up with a small hand towel. "I expected you to be weaker. No sense of what's going on."

I said, "Sorry to disappoint you. I'm dying but still have my mind—much of the time. Did I ever properly thank you?"

"No need."

"I'm glad."

Cristo awkwardly placed my hands in both of his, difficult as it was to carry off. He stood so that the arrangement was easier.

"You know I care about you. I want to discuss the future."

"Mine or yours?"

He chuckled. "Ours. We all... Every path..."

"Boom. We die. We're gone," I said. "Death everlasting."

Cristo let go of my hands. He strolled around the bed, stroking his long hair and appearing to be lost in thought. "Would you prefer life everlasting?"

"Who wouldn't?"

"Well, if you believe in God—your soul goes to heaven and lives on forever. Life everlasting."

My lids grew so heavy that they finally hid my eyes completely from Cristo. I still recalled his beautiful olive skin and shining green eyes and youthful, handsome angular face. Life everlasting had a nice ring to it, but death everlasting is true too. Life and death together, part of the same thing. We die but we live. In death there is life. The body goes while the soul moves on. Very comforting. Even more comforting, Papa lives!

When I awoke, the Cristo I knew best was gone.

Papa said, "He's a fine person. Always doing things for others. Never for himself."

"Should have been a priest. Such an aura. Did you slide that jewel-encrusted cross under my pillow?"

Papa propped up my pillows and spread out the blankets again. He smiled lovingly. "Cristo."

I was still half asleep when Papa sat down on the foot of the bed.

"What do you remember about us?" he asked.

"We had an interesting life. Neither of us liked bowling or golf. We liked tennis and swimming." Now I was fully awake. "I always wanted—a boat and a horse."

"Boats are a pain in the ass. Too much to take care of. I never knew about the horse." He inched his chair closer to my bed. He stretched his legs and then raised them on to the blankets.

I said, "I didn't mention it. Better uses for our money. Education for Joey. A nice house." I touched his leg. "This is crazy but here's what I want now."

"I promise."

"Don't let me ride in a hearse. I want a horse-drawn carriage. Tell the driver all about me—big lies—wonderful person, great wife, and marvelous grandmother. Tell him about the Paper People story on my skin."

"I promise." He sobbed and held his face in his hands. Papa quickly regained control of himself. He said, "You grew a lot over the years. When our son was growing up, you were a stay-at-home mom. Such good cooking. House immaculate. Ravishing looks."

"I'd still be that if I could." I gently rubbed the bottom of his foot.

"Well, at the compound, you spoke up, assertively. Let people know what you thought about things like escape and violence and the Zoots."

I said, "Yes. You said less. We're like an apothecary scale—yin and yang—up and down—loud and quiet—live and die."

"Yes, dear."

In case you wondered, until the very end I retained a very good memory for places, people, and what they say. So does Papa. He helps me recall conversations. God knows how, my ancient digital recorder worked perfectly while we were the Paper People. That's how I got the conversations close to perfect—a word, or phrase, even a sentence may have been wrong or missing, or in a different context, but no serious mistakes in your story. I made sure of that.

The Paper People project failed for the Zoots but we learned about ourselves and our humanity. It was a scientific failure since we escaped and the tattoos could be so easily removed with the antidote cream. Even had the tattoos remained, no way to prevent the eventual degrading of skin had been perfected. The scrolls would crack and crumble due to the effects of the environment. Even El Diablo's stone does not last forever!

At the human level, the project was an even larger failure. People are not assets to be bought and sold. Or enslaved!

Sometimes I was in a dream-like state—partly conscious, maybe confused. Papa reminded me one day that I had another visitor, so I sat propped up by pillows in the hospital bed. The lever on the side raised or

203

lowered it. Sometimes it was fun to go up and down, when I had the strength. I fell asleep, or into some kind of fantasy.

Papa opened the garage door and said, "Cristo is here again." I'd swear he had married us more than twenty-five years ago. That was a wonderful memory of him—vigorous, long dark hair and those captivating green eyes set in such clear, white skin.

In walked a shop-worn old man with thinning gray hair and a dirty collar and shabby cassock. His skin had a yellowish tint. His mouth gaped open with labored breathing, and his eyes half-shut under thick lids.

"So nice to see you," I said.

He leaned over the bed and kissed my cheek. He held both of my hands. His felt leathery, the bones hold together by white parchment. "It's been such a long time," he said. "Too long, Myra."

Papa arranged a deck chair for the priest before he edged out of the door.

Cristo said, "One of my parishioners gave me blood. I got Hepatitis. Plenty of jaundice, too. Not much time before..." He squeezed my hands again.

I smiled with an open countenance, my eyes closed as I peered at the past, a remembrance, my stored-up image of a young, vibrant, handsome Cristo. Yes, I was very attracted to him. I'm not ashamed now to admit it. I said, "I want you to give me the final rites."

"My honor," he said. "I'd better make arrangements for myself... A race to heaven." His head and upper body sank on to the bed. The bed creaked loudly. "I hope I didn't hurt your leg, my dear. My body doesn't always behave."

I patted his head. "If you hadn't been a---"

Papa opened the door. "What's up? You okay?"

"Oh, yes, things are good. Cristo is taking a brief rest. Even God..."

Papa said, "Better leave the jokes to me."

While Cristo rested, I dreamed of another early memory of him, which remains with me forever. Believe it or not, children, Cristo held your own father in one hand and sprinkled water on his forehead with the other. "In the name of the Father, and the Son, and the Holy Spirit I---"

Plunk. Down went Papa. Passed out cold during the service. Too much excitement with the son we were so blessed to have.

A wet cloth on his head, a friend sat him upright, then he stood again. "Sorry, folks. It got to me."

Aunts and uncles and cousins crowded around, anxious to assist Papa's recovery. That young Cristo sent your own father, Joey, diving into Christianity. Wearing a tiny filigreed dress-like bodice in white linen and satin. How could he miss? The outfit came from my mother. While dressed in a perfect fit, Joey whined and cried without mercy during most of the christening.

Papa was so happy and proud that I could have cried myself. I felt like one of the parents should stay strong during the ritual. Even Cristo teared up when Papa passed out.

What a day for us. Who knew what the Lord had in mind for us in the years ahead. At that point I couldn't have imagined the story of the Paper People, even as a work of pure fiction.

Cristo slipped out again. Sleep that night proved to be erratic. I'd be wide awake one minute and then sleep soundly for at least an hour or two. In and out, back and forth, here and across. Each time I awoke, Papa held my hand and smoothed my hair and bathed my face.

For some strange reason, I dreamed of being in labor when your father was born. A nurse said, "You've got a beautiful boy, a son. You've named him Joey."

Papa kissed me and held our son up high with both hands so I could see him. The nurse used our camera to take a picture of the three of us.

The dream changed abruptly and for no apparent reason, a 40-ish, vigorous, muscular Cristo appeared, dressed only in white silk running shorts, without shirt, or slacks, or hat, but wearing flimsy brown leather sandals. He ran along the bank of a narrow, swirling river with the chief. Both were sweating profusely, breathless and near exhaustion.

The chief said, "Too much. Long run. Not in good shape." He walked slowly.

"Me, too," Cristo said. "You've returned from the compound?"

"I met Zoots. My people gone." He stopped walking, bent over to catch his breath. "I told what you do."

"That's fine," Cristo said. Hands on his hips, he smiled at the chief. "It's okay. I'm pleased we got away and proud of the Paper People. A very human group."

"You led them."

"Yes, I did. We had a plan which worked. Those who survived still suffer, but returned with personal freedom." He smiled again at the chief. "I forgive you. The Paper People followed me. We made it back to the city. We believed we could do it, we hoped, and we did it. The Zoots will try to kill me sooner or later. I regret my mistakes. There is a price to be paid. My enemies, El Diablo and Sledge didn't learn or change."

A single rifle shot rang out. The heavily muscular, athletic Cristo slumped to the ground. The Zoots assassin arrived and stabbed the defenseless Cristo repeatedly with a huge Bowie skinning knife. Blood splattered everywhere. Cristo died. Doctors would call it a severe hemorrhage, followed by his heart stopping. Then, no breathing.

The chief said, "I stay here. Zoots got Cristo. He was trouble."

The Zoots assassin then stabbed the chief several times in the heart. He said, "We don't need your kind either."

I'm awake again, at least for the moment. I hope the final dream of a motivated Cristo is not prophetic. The dreams of him came to me in so many different shapes—old, weak, young, strong—making things happen by his energetic actions and bold leadership.

So, my dear Ben and Roberta, my message to you is simple: Stand up for your beliefs. Stand up for justice and fair play and cooperation and sharing and loyalty and all those good things. They are worth it. Life without them—well, life without them and love is simply not worth it. The excitement and joy and pleasure of choosing to have chief tattoo this story for you is my final way to stand up for what I think is right and good.

I don't know for certain if your grandfather would be the one to read it to you, but I hoped Papa would still be alive. Goodbye and remember I'll always love you both very much, just as I loved your Papa.

A final word to Papa. Never regret what happened. We did the best we could to live and survive. It was actually an exciting adventure to be with you throughout our many ordeals. Humbled by losing our jobs, our homeless life imitated that of so many millions of others. Those who perished as the world whirled around us had no chance at all to be Paper People.

We enjoyed that opportunity, however brief, to be valued, to be fed and housed, to be tattooed, then to erase our "books" and become ordinary citizens again. This once-in-a-lifetime experience is to be treasured, not to be hidden or eschewed or forgotten. Some history book will include us—at least it should. Perhaps the remaining Paper People will strike back some day and fight hard for justice and fair play.

I suspect you'll miss me more than you imagined. That's fine, and I would have felt the same way. Do get on with your life. If you find the right person, marry again. If not, you have our son and his family, those precious grandchildren, Ben and Roberta. I'm always there with you and with them. Always. My love is eternal.

I have achieved a special kind of quiet peace and serenity. It's a very spiritual feeling, seeing the world as a huge ocean of rolling white-capped waves, then blue stillness, but not necessarily a religious feeling. If God is everywhere and is everything then it couldn't help but be religion.

There is no despair, no isolation, no loneliness; just a sense of belonging to the familiar cycle of life—the beginning, middle and the end.

The end, of course, appeared to me as a fresh start. It is the beginning of eternity not oblivion, of participation in all things, secure in the warm feeling of oneness with the universe, without any promise of return. Goodbye for now.

POSTSCRIPT

The smoke twirled gracefully to the cave's ceiling as the candles died out. Papa Beard put down the loupe and closed the scroll. He held it to his lips.

"You know, Myra, you always said I'd outlive you. I have, but except for the family and grandkids, I'm not sure it's worth it. I couldn't wait until I could finally read your story to them. I miss you so much. I want you back. Yes, I just scrunched up my face."

Then he kissed both sleeping grandchildren, so dear to him. He stroked his damp beard several times and wiped away the remaining tears, still wet and hot on his cheeks.

In his heart, he knew that family and love nurtured survival, and kept alive the natural optimism of the human condition, especially in the young. Myra was a very good teacher. Her strength and fighting spirit lived on. He needed both as he faced the unexpected challenges of an unknown future life—alone.

THE PAPER PEOPLE

A Sci-Fi Novella – II

Norman Giddan

Part II

To Die for Love

PREAMBLE

The damp, airless cave held the smoke twirls from the white candle in a state of suspended animation. Dim light from the candle bounced off the ceiling to reveal two adolescents and an adult woman.

"Grandma, is that you? Really you?" asked Ben.

"Yes, big surprise."

Roberta said, "But Grandma, you were…"

"Yes, dear, I know. But I'm back now." She threw her arms around both of them, hugged them long and hard, and then looked down as her tears drenched them.

"We heard Papa read us your whole story of the Paper People a few years ago."

Roberta broke away from Grandma's embrace and edged to the corner of the cave. "This is too weird. It can't be you. You're not the undead, or a zombie, are you?"

"No, I'm not."

Ben said, "Where's Papa?"

"You'll know soon. I'm going to read his story to you." She lovingly moved her hands over the scroll.

"Is he dead?" asked Roberta.

Grandma said, "Let me read this story. You'll have all of your questions answered."

She wiped the tears away and waved off the smoke from the candle. Then she opened the scroll which took up most of the space on the table before her. She leaned over and kissed it.

"You guys relax. Now you're seventeen and fifteen. You'll understand Papa's story. He was an amazing person, the love of my life.

211

He's written you the story of his life and the Paper People after I moved on. He gave me back my life."

Ben said, "Grandma, is it really, really you? Papa read us the whole story of the Paper People—you wrote it on your skin. Is this scroll written on...?"

"Be patient, Ben. Just be patient and listen to Papa's story. We'll have time together afterward."

She adjusted the loupe to her blurry eyes and began to read. Her eyes burned with the effort.

Chapter One

It was a miserable time after your grandma Myra died. I blamed myself and felt so alone in the garage. I didn't much care if I lived or died. You kids, your parents and a few friends kept me going. They convinced me that Myra had good care and that the doctors said that there was no known cure for her form of cancer. It was inevitable that she would die of it. They said I should be proud of all the time and energy I put into her months of infirmity, especially her final week of life.

Of course, I didn't buy it at first. I think that everyone said what they said because it was the right thing to say. I believed them to some extent but it really didn't sink in—at least not very far.

Everywhere I turned in our garage reminded me of Myra. I guess I didn't realize how much I loved her and how much I'd miss her. Her spunk, her knowledge, her love, her honesty—all inspired me and left me in an abyss with her finally gone.

One night I shuffled to the garage door and flung it open. I screamed—low and loud and deep—followed by a high-pitched screech. "No. No. No," I said. "Come back, Myra. Don't leave me. Please come back to me."

I fell to my knees. "I curse God. I hate God. There's no answer. None at all. No one can help."

As I grieved, I went through a kind of metamorphosis. I had crazy thoughts. I had Myra's skin on the scroll which I'd read to both of you. I thought to myself that maybe—just maybe—there was some medical society, perhaps a doctor, or maybe a secret research program that could restore her life. Sounds like a witchcraft kind of thing. I guess I was a little off-balance.

The global economy, off balance too, currently grows in fits and starts. Synthetic oil is being developed, natural gas is in wider utilization, and the forests are slowly regenerating. Food and household "fuel" are available, but the prices remain high. Soup kitchens and homeless shelters still flourish. "Freedom" gardens supply much of the

213

produce for the city's stores, and directly to those families that have the resources to plant and harvest them in outlying "plots" they rent from landowners.

Much of the world, especially the Middle East, remains decimated by the two nuclear wars, the ruin of petrochemical industries, and the global warming which has killed off forests and raised ocean levels to dangerous heights.

I'm sure it's not the end of the world, the extinction of all mankind. But we cleared too many forests before the warming trend took effect. Nuclear fall-out and carbon dioxide permeated the earth's atmosphere. We haven't been hit by a huge life-changing asteroid or invaded by aliens yet, but our reliance on computers, software, TVs, and other technologies leaves us vulnerable to oil-based manufacturing. Governments and corporations can easily manipulate these toys of ours in ways we never imagined—the individual suffers, sometimes without knowing it, as they protect us in the name of national security.

Our local political situation has gone from dictatorial mayors to pols that specialize in acquiring money and fueling corruption. Money and gang power rule. Ordinary citizens feel powerless with no chance to use the ballot box to influence their lives—elections are obviously rigged. There is an uptick in local extortion and kidnapping.

My son Joey and his wife survived and you grandkids are doing well for the moment. Papa is there for you.

I put aside thoughts of family and the confusing world to march again in the parade on the Day of the Dead which grew in beauty, pageantry and length since the Paper People participated nearly ten years earlier. Déjà vu. Then we were seventy-five, now reduced to sixty. Books erased, dots gone, we now proudly strutted as a group of liberated once-homeless folks living in freedom. Our suffering and liberation united us. No Zoots to harm us, sell us, or protect us.

Crowds cheered and whooped it up on both sides of the street. Huge balloons of red and green and black hung over the floats, revolving like a miniaturized solar system. The papier-mâché Virgin Mary and Child, done in bright lime green with white carnations drew applause and reverence.

I marched proudly but sadly. No Myra at my side though I sensed her loving presence. She was always with me, rain or shine as they say. A hot, bright sun, hung in a cloudless baby-blue sky, with heaven smiling on us. The parade usually stopped at the huge St. Christopher Cemetery outside of the business district, for prayer, reflections, and to pay respect to the deceased. Remembering the dead and honoring their contributions.

The Mariachi band stirred us with its exciting yet steady beat—trumpets blaring the melodies and drums and string instruments playing counter-point to these lonely and lovely tunes. I could hear the polka and waltz influences. The Zoots and Diablitos no longer existed in the parade, replaced by new marauding gangs which found their way into the event. Local merchants sponsored floats to sell their products, high school bands featured patriotic marches or 'America the Beautiful' type songs, majorettes twirled batons while stuffed into their tight costumes. The Mariachi band members traded their traditional white pants and shirts for Charro outfits.

The plaintive music brought tears and so many memories. Oh, Myra, there is so much to admire about you. A wonderful, loving grandmother to Ben and Roberta. You had fun with them, taught them, and set an example that will be hard to follow. You stayed so strong when Joey became ill, helped me see that we had to be realistic about this life and career—to let him lead the way with his own choices. Then you stood up to Mary, asserted our rights and needs as grandparents, even though you had raised objections privately to their marriage.

You suffered with me—those disappointments of the way the world changed under our feet. Life on the street didn't throw you, nor did that miserable time as a well-fed "book" lady.

You grieved the loss of your parents but moved on with your life. This led you to me and I guess my sense of humor appealed to you as well as my own strength and decisiveness. We felt like we had it all, even when we didn't have it all.

Several escapes from the Diablitos and Zoots left us free in the city, but too late for much of a life. Then you became ill and all I could do was be there for you in all of your suffering—our suffering.

The celebration and respect for the deceased obviously conflicted with the two powerful gangs represented. I knew them to be purveyors of violence, drugs, intimidation and corruption. Still, they demonstrated for all to see, the controversial inclusiveness of gangsters, and the criminal diversity of the parade—especially skins of brown and white—two gangs called the Diamonds and the Ivories. They were notorious in the local culture, and took every advantage of this post-apocalyptic cityscape to which we returned. Old wine in new bottles.

The leader of the Ivories, one huge bear of a man—a tattooed biker who called himself Big Elmer—sat awkwardly in the parade stands surrounded by his acolytes, skinheads who hated America and worshipped Hitler. Big Elmer's gang was the Ivories—lily-white and proud of the fact its members dropped out of high school and none had GEDs. Big Elmer screamed in a high-pitched voice, "You brown bastards eat shit, or is it shitty beans?"

He pounded his huge fist into a pal's gut, then held him close and kissed him on the lips. "Sorry, I lost it." He twisted open a candy bar wrapper with his teeth.

"You tell them, Elmer. You know what to say." "Fuck the wetbacks." Various Ivories chimed in with their chants of hate, safe to echo their leader's murderous aggressiveness toward all non-white ethnic or racial groups or gangs.

The parade abruptly halted. No music. No marching. We stopped dead in our tracks to gape at the tumult in the Ivories section of viewers.

Sirens blaring, the police appeared as the crowd dispersed in all directions.

"What's happened?" I said.

Cristo said, "Shots fired. Someone is hurt." His strong but graceful hands came together in prayer.

Judy Tobin said, "I think an Ivory killed someone. I heard screams of 'muerte, muerte.' What a world." A sexy widow of sixty, she looked to be the same size as Myra. She wore a black jacket and slacks.

She stood too close to me. I felt titillated and repulsed at the same time.

I yelled to a bystander. "What happened up there?"

An old man said, "I don't want to get hurt. An Ivory guy shot another Ivory and a Diamond woman. Someone said she's pregnant. Both died."

The roar of motorcycles told us that the Ivories hurried away. The Diamonds would find them later. Retaliation—tit-for-tat—had become the norm. No romance allowed between members of different gangs, especially no children born of white father and Mexican mother. Gang mentality seemed impenetrable!

Ideas floated around the city of bringing the gangs together to discuss racial issues. Tolerance might be taught when multicultural beliefs and attitudes became pinpointed and clearly stated. Stereotypes could be assailed, shown for what they were, and negative contacts overcome. Greed and power and cruelty marshalled the gangs' behavior toward hatred and violence.

The liberal elite favored the "positive contact" approached aimed at the huge majority of citizens, with hopes that the community could find other avenues to eliminate or reduce the influence of the gangs. Without the gangs, there would be less fear in the city, an increased sense of community importance and hope for breaking up the prevailing drug culture. Mixed race dating and racial intermarriage were no longer novelties!

A police loudspeaker blared, "Anyone who saw this shooting or has any relevant information, see me now or call police headquarters." Cops lazily went through the motions when murder involved gang members. Gangs took care of things later.

The Ivories and the Diamonds were archenemies. They wanted each other's territory, competed for drug sales and distribution, and bribed city officials such as the mayor and police to get what they wanted. While the brown and white gangs had no love for each other, they agreed in their hatred of Asians.

Ricky Rubio, head of the Diamonds bragged of connections to several Mexican cartels. The crowds threw marigolds in the path of his Diamonds and chanted, "Mexico sí, China no." Ricky was surprisingly short and fat. He nearly burst out of his purple and blue guayabera shirt. His bloated face showed smooth, brown skin but no hair, except a droopy mustache. Nothing sophisticated about this guy, I overheard him say, "Later, mi amigos, beans and rice and tortillas and Tecate. Ignore white shitheads—gringo assholes."

It was a real shame because most Mexicans I'd known were family folks, helpful, even-tempered, and took what life gave them. The sugary drinks of Chiapa and the honey sweets from Puebla were lingering, pleasant, yet distant memories.

217

It occurred to me that while we were primarily white, we had several black and brown members of our entourage. After all, the recovering homeless come in all sizes, shapes, and colors. The real surprise was that no one in the gangs paid much attention to us. We were older, represented no threat to the organized gangs, and were known only as the group who had luckily outwitted and outfought two earlier gangs—which had totally disappeared.

We were innocent of any connection to current crime or violence in the city. There we were, sixty of us, the survivors of the Paper People experiment, marching years after being signed up for our skins. We were free now. The two new gangs acted with no more immediate threat to us than to any ordinary citizen who wanted safety and security in daily city life.

On one side of me Cristo marched with Judy on the other. It felt good just to be there so many years after escaping from what we got ourselves into.

Cristo said, "We're here again. Hurrah!"

Judy said, "It's strange. A few dots are on my leg now."

Cristo put his arm around her. "Not to worry."

The parade now stopped near the old cemetery at the edge of town. Huge, colorful bouquets held sway on the graves, some **with** simple crosses or headstones, a few with marble statuary honoring **the** occupants. While all paths lead to the grave, yet death is disguised and remembered in many forms and different ways.

Some created private altars on this All Souls Day. Originally an Aztec holiday, I watched as sugar skulls, marigolds, and the favorite food or drinks of the deceased decorated the altars.

Judy said, "I taught anthropology before… Specialized in Oaxaca. Has the most sites."

I said, "Tell me more." We three now sat on a bench near the archway leading into the Mexican section. Cristo relaxed between us.

"To the Maya, the conch allowed communication with the gods. The spiral shape meant eternity. Particular trees connect the three levels of life—underworld, earth, and after-life."

I said, "So many architectural shapes—cornices, pillars, balconies—on the grave sites."

"Yes, of course," Judy said. "The sites are full of flowers, beauty and grace. Candles are everywhere. The Mexican way celebrates joys, and reality—also the humor of life." She arose from the bench, turned and gazed directly at me.

I shifted my eyes, but couldn't resist laughing. "A large stone dog sits over there. Waits for his owner's return."

Judy said, "I don't know whether it's meant to be funny or just so very sad to see the lonely dog." She hurried through the archway into the cemetery proper. Then she turned to us and waved good-bye.

Cristo and I remained seated outside the graveyard. My guilt and doubts stopped me from entering. An unwillingness to part with Myra served the same end. I couldn't or wouldn't or shouldn't join in the laughter, the tears, or the prayers of those people surrounding the graves and headstones. I wasn't ready to celebrate Myra's death, nor could I pay my respects and show my love here.

Cristo put his arm around my shoulder and pulled me closer to him. He said, "You'll get unstuck soon."

Chapter Two

I had another idea. One of the original Paper People became a funeral director. I know he thought I was outrageous and demented, but he agreed to maintain Myra's organs suspended in a life-giving, nutrient fluid. Her skin was on the scroll. Her bones were now covered with olive oil and lay in a large aluminum case in my garage home. Her voice, though weakened by cancer, remained intact on my ancient digital recorder. I did not part with Myra. She was dead but not for me. She'd return. Gone for a while.

I spilled the beans to Cristo. I told him everything. I should have kept my mouth shut but somehow I knew I could trust him with my plans for Myra.

As though he'd received an electrical shock, his long, grey hair sizzled and his torso momentarily froze. "No, Papa. No. No. No."

I said, "I must."

Cristo said, "You're violating God's will. He creates life! Gave us his son." His eyes roamed the sky, searching for something.

"I know all of that. I must. I'll find a way." I rolled my eyes toward the heavens, too, maybe seeking forgiveness, certain I was on the right path.

I said goodbye to Cristo and a few of the others. Given the choice, I'd trade my life for Myra's in a second. She wasn't far away. I'd find a way to help her cross over, return to me. Cristo and his pals will never approve but that didn't stop me. I sensed, almost magically, that I'd find the medical or professional skills needed to accomplish my goal. I might be crazy but I knew in my heart that I was right. Then I could celebrate, treasure her love, pay respect to her life, and be grateful for all that had happened.

I knew I'd find the perfect doctor and researcher to help me in my quest. Such certainty shortened my protracted grief.

The shock that literally ended the mourning, yet brought on a whole new sadness and disappointment, was the discovery that the dots returned to cover my entire body. Judy's experience foreshadowed it. I spent hours in the sun to rid myself of them; next got them wet, and finally soaked in a tub for hours in the vain hope of ridding my skin of them. No improvement!

A week or so later, I met Judy by accident one evening as I walked around the city aimlessly, dressed in black attire. She covered up the same way, including a floppy, black, velvet hat and a veil over dark glasses.

I said, "Judy, so good to see you." We hugged.

She surprised me when she pulled away quickly. "You, too?"

"What do you mean?"

She said, "Many others—former Paper People—have regained their..."

"I hoped it was just me—maybe a few of us. Tried everything." I pulled up the sleeve of my shirt to show her my own.

Judy said, "Waste of time. Nothing works." She coughed and gagged, then held her head up and sobbed as only a devastated middle-aged woman can sob—deep, throaty, and without shame. Her soaked veil clung to her cheek.

"The others?"

"Yes," she said, "as far as I know. There's a reunion tonight on that mothballed destroyer from WWII. Even an exotic doctor who has a lab on board."

"I'll be there," I said. "Maybe we can find an antidote that lasts a lifetime."

Judy said, "I always loved your humorous support. I know your wife did, as well." She wiped her glasses dry with a corner of the veil, then replaced them as she strolled next to me. "See you tonight."

I returned home. My ruminations stretched out endlessly. I smashed an old wooden table against the garage wall. It broke into pieces which I simply left on the floor. Feelings burst. Not only furious that we had once become homeless, but cheated now that Myra was gone. I was alone and disappointed that the chief's antidote failed. Why me? Why us? What had we done to deserve this? Where had my sense of humor and perspective gone? My mouth was not big enough or wide enough to fashion the scrunch that I felt.

That chance encounter with Judy proved to be a pivotal moment in my return to the city. Well into my late-fifties I knew that I wasn't totally alone. In concert with the others we might discover a new antidote cream or ointment that could help us. Action would help me, a job to be done, some function to perform.

As a cloudy sky brought on evening, I arrived at Pier 10 where the USS McCarran had been in dry-dock for many years. I expected an old rust-bucket, but the gangplank led me to a series of conference rooms which were clean and freshly painted ochre and pale green. The remaining Paper People were there, seated at round tables laden with Styrofoam coffee cups. Overhead bright lights encased in wire frames gave the room a flickering yellow glow.

Despite the occasion, I smiled and shook hands and hugged my old comrades. There was Cristo, literally changing before my eyes: a bit more grey in his tousled hair and neatly clipped beard; yet stronger than ever; for but a brief moment his face showed the signs of aging—with creased skin and a turkey neck.

Cristo said, "Hey, it's Papa Beard. So good to see you again."

"Same here, wonderful to see you people." The unspoken name was Myra—since they knew she had not survived the bout with cancer.

Judy came by our table. "I'm back," she said. "They're back, too." She pointed to her arms and face full of the original dots. "I'd like to choke the chief. He promised..."

The several sides of Cristo played a remarkable role in the history of the Paper People. His strength provided us with hope. When reason failed, he turned plowshares into swords and his spirituality altered our beliefs and helped us shift to action—especially with the escapes into the forest and rural life. Escape meant that buying and selling us in the inking compound eventually met the same fate as buying and selling in the biblical Temple.

Cristo said, "We confronted evil and miraculously, we won."

Myra never quite understood the implications of his "work as one" phrase. He did save us, and it must have taken all of his wisdom, power, will and capacity for action. Without giving us a full explanation, Cristo said, "It was salvation."

We shoved the various cruelties and punishments and inhumane attitudes of our captors on to the back burner. Taking good care of our bodies never hid the threats of premature death, even the last-meal-on-death-row implication of our five-star treatment. The eat, drink and be merry philosophy of the inking compound failed miserably to satisfy our human souls. We Paper People grew to know, collectively, that we would be killed ASAP after the inking.

Cristo moved to the front of the room. The floor swayed slightly as the tide came in—an old destroyer that must be in the process of being refurbished for some kind of living or working arrangement. Definitely in dry-dock and mothballs, but not quite dead in the water.

"I'm back, too," said Cristo. "There are sixty or so of us here tonight. Welcome. It's good to see everyone. Even under these circumstances. The "books" are here. The chief was wrong. We must make plans—make decisions about how we want to live."

Judy said, "If the dots go away again, what will happen?"

Cristo, suddenly much older again, drew upon wisdom and understanding. He held onto the back of his chair to balance himself as he arose. "Books will last centuries in the libraries. They'll hold all the digital material that survives, too. Scientists will invent paper substitutes."

"Yes," Judy said. "Our lives should be normal."

Cristo waved off this discussion. "We must take care of ourselves. That's God's will, my friends. I'm sure of it."

"We're outcasts again," I said.

Judy said, "Who would want to associate with us? Looks like the black plague or AIDS or maybe something worse. Are we infectious? Friends or family want to know."

Cristo said, "We're just different." I now observed his well-defined, rounded biceps. He flexed them. "No one can catch this from us." Laughter followed.

"Seriously, friends," he said, "we must stick together—a community. We have endured a lot and overcome most of it." Applause followed, then a standing ovation. Now an old man with a bent back, he nearly slipped to the floor, then caught himself as he sat down awkwardly.

I brooded and felt depressed at the thought that our bodies would be permanently marred by the books. In that sense, our captors would be the winners. No longer needed for our value as books, the experiment having completely failed, still the vestiges remained.

The first problem was the stigma, the disfigurement of the Paper People, the humiliation and embarrassment that followed from the fact that the antidote worked temporarily. Judy hit the nail on the head, stating that we looked like the black plague, or AIDS, or worse.

People would glare at us while trying to shield their gaze. Some individuals might be offended or frightened or nauseated by what they saw. We could become the objects of scrutiny, eager to explain or apologize or simply to drift away from others.

Might we become comfortable enough to face the public and ourselves with these dots covering us from head to toe? Affected individuals with disabilities, those who lost limbs, others with prosthetics, some in wheelchairs or using walkers, struggle to come to grips with their own worth and self-perception, and then adjust to the reactions, often well-meaning, of family and friends. Could we adapt as burn victims do? Would we find a way to accept our limitations in appearance? What would the dots mean for employment opportunities or marriage or travel?

Our easiest, and most obvious, reaction was to cover up, hide the dots, and hope for a new permanent antidote. Failing a new and different, more effective ointment or cream to remove our tattoos, we'd have to face up to the issue of hiding the truth from others permanently or revealing to the world what had been done to us.

Concentration camp numbers tattooed on one's inner arm remain a grim symbol, a proud reminder of evil-doers. Perhaps, our plight could have a similar impact on society—illustrating the harm that humans inflict on each other in the name of showmanship and personal gain.

One of the younger men whose name I couldn't recall spoke now. "We're not just victims. Let's strike back. The Ivories and the Diamonds are a blight on our city. The government screws over people."

Arms flailing, face now beet-red, shaved head dripping with sweat—he was a picture of vindictiveness. "Gang members carry bags of cash to the mayor's office. An honest grand jury... They'd indict him."

He lit a fire in me, a flame of energy and hope and optimism. When I arrived at the meeting all I cared about was visiting with friends and finding a way to get the dots off of my skin. I thought that we would track down the chief or someone more professional. Maybe the needles hadn't been sterilized properly, or the dye was imperfect, or we got too much sunlight before the scabs had healed, or some other cause to be remedied.

Maybe, just maybe, we could do some good while we tried to find a new antidote. I said, "My wife Myra would approve. She became an activist, as you all remember. I could become a ..."

Judy flirtatiously smiled at me. "Vigilante."

"Yes, that's it. I could become a vigilante. We all could."

Judy said, "Wear black. Cover our dots. Wear masks or burkas or heavy veils to hide who we are."

Cristo said, "Slow down everyone. We can't impose our will, our idealism without thought and prayer and planning. It'll be easy to hide the dots and disguise ourselves but... Do we have the drive and energy to fight city hall and the devastating effects of the gangs? Vigilantes operate outside the law. They only last for a while. Outlaws. No violence. No bodily harm."

Dead silence, quickly followed by cheers, screams, and loud applause as the group rose to its feet to approve our new mission.

I said, "Vigilantes take justice into their own hands. We'll need weapons. To scare off the bad guys."

And so it began. A straw vote was unanimous in favor of the vigilante concept. We would work nights so we named ourselves the Bats. Those who had jobs in the city would quit or take a leave of absence. We'd hide and cover-up as best we could—at least for a period of time.

Cristo said, "That's good. Bats were one of the ten curses of the Pharaoh before the Exodus."

The old man knew his *Bible*!

225

The argument over violence continued for a long time. There was still great respect and admiration for Cristo. We recalled that he'd changed his mind before when push came to shove, and our people were injured or killed by gang members. He would again. The die was cast. We'd get the Ivories and the Diamonds, sooner or later!

Cristo said, "Let's name the McCarron. I've seen bats which like water spend the day in crevices or warm cracks in this old destroyer. It's the Vampire."

"Yes," I said, "the Vampire is a perfect name."

Hoots and hollers from the assembled group signified a unanimous voice vote of approval. So, the Vampire was christened as home base for the Bats.

Judy stood. "The bats on this ship don't kill mammals. Vampires do. We do, too. We're Bats who kill."

Standing applause for Judy. She curtsied before she sat down.

The meeting ended on a high note.

As I walked out, I overheard the young firebrand talk to Cristo. "If we die as vigilantes, it's a righteous ending. I can't live much longer with these dots all over me. I'm not that strong."

I couldn't help wonder how many of the others sensed it might be their last hurrah. I did.

The times grew worse again, even in a protected area like ours. Harsh winds and flooding hit the city, as the water levels in the ocean rose. Drought struck the small gardens that city folk had depended on to supplement their meager diet. Ponds dried up, as did the small streams used for irrigation. Fruits and vegetables withered in the fields. The cost of irrigating a small family vegetable plot grew exponentially, even if enough water could be found to complete the task. A torrential rain finally broke through the clouds one day, followed quickly by a terrifying ice storm.

It began to feel like the worst of times again, but there was still high-priced, though limited, food stuff available in the stores. Feeling like a wild-west cowboy, I bought huge bags of cornmeal and sugar and salt. Enough for months of cooking on my two-burner propane stove. Survival, at least.

226

I felt in my gut that some good things were ahead. Maybe it was just blind optimism, crude denial of the lingering downside of my personal situation and the loss of Myra. I called it "survival plus."

Chapter Three

With nothing to do one evening, I wandered into the bowels of the destroyer, only to come upon a short man, heavily-bearded with thick round glasses, quite pigeon-toed. "Hello, I'm Dr. Stine. You are in the lab of labs." He held out a small hand with blunt stubs for fingers. I shook it.

"I'm Beard. Here for meetings upstairs, top-side as they say. Glad to meet you, Dr. Stine."

Dr. Stine said, "The pleasure is mine." A thick, guttural English betrayed his Eastern European background. This only reinforced the image of a mad genius at work. He removed his long white coat, dragging on the floor, and perched on a stool. "I have no assistants. I prepare my own slides and cultures. And such a low-power microscope. Yet..."

I strolled around the tables loaded with piles of books and pamphlets and data sheets. I pointed to the cot and said, "Guess you sleep here, too."

"Oh, yes, I love being alone. I worked on a cruise ship. Just research now. My old books... Only discoveries now. They called me, 'that wonderful, strange, little doctor.'"

"My group holds meetings and social get-togethers," I said. "A mothballed ship but not empty."

Dr. Stine gazed at me, his dark, small eyes, magnified by thick lenses. He listened intently. "You're curious about me?"

"Very much so."

"I don't blame you. Most others avoid me. I'm involved with life and death—and in-between." He waved his arms as he nearly fell off of his stool. "I've studied cancer, robotics and jellyfish." Now his eyes widened, crinkled with humor, carefully observing my reaction.

228

"That's quite a combination." I quickly peeked through the microscope. "Couldn't see much."

"Well, I began as a conventional cancer researcher at Hopkins. Wiped out one kind and another type came back."

"What then? Not so technical, please."

"My research assistant, the wife of the college president, and I... I lost my position. Did robotics at a private medical corporation."

I said, "From cells to skeletons?" I was more than just impressed by this guy. Something else but I couldn't put my finger on it. Elation and excitement jolted my body. My knees wobbled. How often in life does a dream come true?

"Yes, exactly. I developed the exoskeleton for paraplegics. Treated the injured or cancerous human being. Combined cell biology with engineered robotics. That's my shtick."

"How? I may not understand."

"Activated immune systems. Reprogrammed extracted T-cells. Analyzed DNA and RNA of different cancers."

I said, "Skip the other details. I wouldn't be able to follow it."

Dr. Stine said, "Fine. How about some cognac?" He poured us each an identical amount. He quaffed his.

I sipped mine. "There's more to your story."

"Well, since you ask. Yes. I've adapted earlier Asian studies of the jellyfish. They return from adult back to the beginning of existence. No death. I want to do something similar on humans, at least to life at the time of death. Not immortality and not a clone. The identical adult will..."

I poured us each another brandy. Both of us gulped it down quickly this time.

"I've moved way beyond electricity." His chest heaved in a wild horse laugh.

I didn't get it. So I smiled in appreciation of his raucous joke. "I've got to go. I knew I'd meet someone like you. I want to bring my dead wife back to life."

He stood, clicked his heels and bowed slightly. "Anytime. Next visit you'll tell me why you are covered up. Yah?"

Several days after meeting Dr. Stine I invited Judy for dinner. Her husband had died at the hands of a sharp-shooter just before we left the warehouse.

She knocked on my crumbly wood door. "Guess who?"

We embraced. It felt good to me. A human body next to mine. The embrace quickly turned into an embarrassing series of squeezes and hugs. Myra would smile on this carrying-on but I just wasn't into it. Grief and loss and hurt leave a long bitter frozen trail. That's all I'll say to you kids on this topic—at least for now. Except for this observation: I sensed that the months of mourning your grandmother finally ended—I could now imagine how she felt if I were near another woman. She wouldn't mind at all. But I did.

"I need to pick up some cheese and crackers, or a piece of sausage to have with wine. Okay with you?"

Judy smiled and nodded. "Sounds great."

We walked to an all-night corner market a short distance from my garage apartment. As we entered, I observed some shelves full and others completely empty.

The young Asian who stood behind the cash register appeared bored and sad, dull eyes half-shut and lips curled down.

"Snack foods are in the corner, aren't they?" I asked.

"Yes," he said. "Not much choice. Stuff sells out quickly. Especially the junk."

Judy admired herself in a large mirror near the door. She puffed up her hair, and then smoothed it with a clear cream. "Could be worse," she said. "Much worse. There are so many sayings about age that I..."

I found the snack area, prepared to make a quick selection and go home. Two teenagers argued loudly in the next aisle. At first, the dispute centered on which potato chips to buy. One said that the chips were dated, too old to sell and eat.

The other argued that "all of this crap is too old to be safe."

Then the argument escalated over their money. "You can't spend mine on old shit," one guy said.

"Fuck you!"

A struggle fired up between the two and stale bags and broken bottles flew off the shelves near them. Screams accompanied the shoving and fisticuffs. Shelving fell on one of them. He yelled that his leg was crushed and cut. A loud thud told me that one of the youngsters had been knocked down and lay on the floor.

The cashier yelled, "Stop it! The police…"

I didn't intervene. No need to show the dots to strangers. I ran to Judy, grabbed her arm and we were on the sidewalk in a flash.

Judy said, "Fights and arguments over food. Saw it all in the mirror. I hate it." She reached for a handkerchief in her purse. She wiped her eyes and blew her nose. "I hate fighting. Only breeds more of the same."

I said, "Me, too. I just want to live in peace and freedom. We don't really need anything but the wine. That stuff is so awful."

"Absolutely, I want a very big glass. I need it. That store did have bags of rice and sacks of potatoes."

I said, "Only good with the finest French champagne."

Judy drank some white wine when we returned. She plopped down on the old velvet couch which I had covered with a brown plaid blanket. Her feet found a torn leather hassock. "I always admired your Myra, grits and gumption. We never bonded. I'm still hurt and angry about my husband and everything…"

"The gangs?"

"Yes," she said, "and the horrible city government. They steal and get bribes. That mayor—those cruel thugs."

I drank two glassfuls. "I need your help."

"Almost anything you want or need. I've got extra bottled water and canned food."

"No. Not food. Thanks. I've got a hunch—a fantasy about bringing Myra back to life," I said.

She held out her glass. I filled it from the open wine bottle. "The strain must be terrible. I know. I'm alone, too."

I roamed around the garage, touched some old family photos. "Bear with me. I really mean it. Restore Myra—alive again."

Judy drained her glass. I emptied the bottle into it.

"You need this wine more than I do. That's just plain nutso. We die. We're gone."

I had to take a chance. Judy was my best bet for what I needed. "I want your help."

Judy flirtatiously rolled her eyes, and then unbuttoned her sweater. "Anything you want or need." She put the wine glass on the hassock and patted the seat next to her on the couch. "I'm strong. Touch my arm."

I scurried to the door. "You're a great person. I'll tell you the rest of it soon. I don't want to shock you."

"Fine, just walk me home tonight. The offer stands," she said as she buttoned up her sweater.

We strolled quickly to Judy's apartment. The cool night air and lack of conversation encouraged a perfect cool-down.

I slept fitfully that night. More wine might have helped.

Several weeks passed by as the Bats organized themselves. Cristo and I were among those who planned to get training and arms to fight other "gangs" and the corrupt politicians. Gangs threaten each other with violence, kidnapping and "disappearances."

Under these circumstances, Cristo slowly changed his mind about the use of violence in self-defense. He reported a dream in which God tells him that "fighting against evil" is okay if nothing else works to stop it.

His prophetic words at a Bats meeting still echo in my soul. Now professor and minster, he appeared much older when he spoke, shaking and frail but with a firm voice. "We need courage, dignity, honesty, and bravery is to face evil directly. With as little violence as possible. We don't always turn the other cheek. Bats must fight."

We returned to the valley where the Paper People lived after leaving the warehouse. One gang died with the Great Piñata, but our former captors simply gave up and returned home to Hollywood. The land and forest nearby were, to put it simply, drier and browner and more barren than I remembered them. The lack of irrigation and proper fertilizer added to the effects of climate change. This valley retained a certain nostalgic attraction for me, now the site of our military training camp.

Ten of us, including your Papa and Cristo, were the designated "shooters." Other Bats were assigned tasks concerned with clothing and uniforms, weapons maintenance, ammo, food and cooking, transportation, and so on.

We slept in old army pup tents, two of us to each tent. Up at 6:00 am we did low-level calisthenics and stretching, then ate a light breakfast of fruit and yogurt. After we relaxed and cleaned up our living areas, serious training began. I'll tell you about several other groups and their activities first, before I focus on the arms and weapons experience that were my part.

Some made Ninja-type black hats, scarves and blousy shirt and pants so that all of our bodies were covered. Shoes consisted of black cloth sandals.

Others were taught to clean and repair weapons and insure a steady supply of ammo, car bombs, various size knives and throwing stars. No suicide vests for Bats!

Another group, largely the older folks, took on the jobs concerned with securing food, cooking it, stockpiling cans and bottles of non-perishables, and driving the rejuvenated school bus that became our primary vehicle for the encampment. Sounds like basic training for the army and it did have a strong resemblance—except our evenings and weekends were our own and we prepared to fight gangs and other evil-doers, not another country, nation-state, or outside terrorist group.

All of the rifles and pistols had some type of "silencer" on them. We were to become quiet as Ninjas, whenever possible. Bats only come out at night. Attacks would be surgical, kill one or two by sniper fire, bomb a car, or kidnap family members of the corrupt politicians.

Our drill instructor who taught marksmanship turned out to be a complete surprise—Judy Tobin. She had been a sniper in the Israeli Defense Force as a teenager. She never told us who, how many, or the cities in which she had killed Islamic radicals. We knew only that she had been successful. God knows what she could have done in that all-night market if the fighting involved us!

Our D.I. said, "Okay, folks, listen up. I count seven men and three women. Ever shot an assault rifle, an AK-47 or a Bushmaster?"

Not one hand was raised.

"Well," she said, "anybody shot a pistol or a sub-machine gun? Or a shotgun?"

One of the senior citizens in his late sixties said, "I went hunting with my grandfather. Used a 12-gauge."

The D.I. said, "Deer, that sort of thing?"

"Yes, but never got one. No antlers on our wall."

And so it went. We were green—novices, really. I had shot a BB gun but never even fired a paintball, so I kept my mouth shut.

Judy lined us up at a target range about six feet apart. She held an AK-47 in both hands. I'd swear she smiled at the gun, but the shiny glints on the metal play tricks with the eyes. She turned toward the targets about forty yards away, held the foldable stock on her shoulder and fired a short burst—target nearly gone. "You don't have to take a long, careful aim. They just demolish what you point them toward." She smiled at the trainees this time.

She then moved behind us, dressed in army beige fatigues and high-top suede boots. Her voice now hoarse, she said, "Fire to your heart's content. Then we'll talk."

I remember that you squeeze a trigger, don't pull it suddenly. I aimed the assault rifle at the target, or generally in its direction, and fired. Nothing hit the target, but I didn't hit anyone else and the recoil was slight.

"Okay," the D.I. said, "none of you hit anything or anyone. Good. Nothing to be scared of. Take your finger off of the trigger." She walked in front of us.

Judy sauntered out to the target area and moved the concentric target circles to an area thirty yards in front of the firing line. "That's better. Give it a go. Don't shoot me." She jogged back behind us. "Now."

What a difference! Just pointing the rifle without a fancy sight or scope did the trick. We all shredded paper. Then we hit a second burst. Then a third. I hate to admit it, but fun it was!

Judy said, "You see how quickly you can become lethal. The same with a 9mm Glock, a 20 gauge over and under—or a digital-timed car bomb. Take a break now. Nothing to be afraid of here. Just ways to kill…"

Suddenly, I shook like a leaf. My armpits flooded my upper torso. My heart raced. I feared I'd have a seizure or a stroke. The woman next to me on the firing line held her hand over her mouth, then vomited through her fingers all over her weapon. I'm embarrassed to admit that I wet my pants.

We retrieved our targets, or what was left of them. Cristo turned out to be the best shot. He said, "Killing others is not my thing."

The day was sweaty hot and bright with sunlight, so the men took off their shirts, hoping the sun would blur their tattoos. The three women rolled up their sleeves and their blouses to mid-torso, just below the bosom. We all knew that sunlight alone wouldn't do the trick. We desperately needed a new antidote, though we'd wear the black Ninja outfits for our vigilante missions until we could remove the dots.

Lunch worked out well. The ten Bats on the food selection and preparation detail did a bang-up job, making delicious veggie pasta covered by an original tomato basil sauce which used only tomato paste, basil flakes, and grapeseed oil. The pasta itself came from a food bank overloaded with bags of quinoa pasta and potato noodles.

This group planned ahead for the time we'd all live on the ship. They had developed a meal-plan that included the canned, dried, and pickled foodstuff that we'd use to survive when Bats hid themselves during the day and made their pre-determined raids and attacks under cover of darkness. The Ninja outfits hid the dots, so our true identity was not known, and as vigilantes we hunkered down in the Vampire during the daylight hours.

Our plan was for a two-month siege, during which we'd be away from family, friends, and jobs—which only a few people actually held. Most older Bats worked only part-time or at menial jobs which they could easily leave for a time. Our two-month blitzkrieg had one goal: eliminate or substantially weaken the two gangs and their corrupt, dishonest, political beneficiaries and allies.

Cristo provided the U.S. Navy with a cock-n-bull story about the Bats protecting the destroyer while it was in dry dock. They bought it hook-line-and-sinker, so we gradually moved limited personal belongings, sheets, pillows, and blankets into the sleeping quarters. Cramped, but we made do. Along with the ping pong and pool tables there, we also played cards and board games. We left all of our electronic gadgets behind. Guns, knives, bombs, and so on were welcome. Vigilante justice after dark. Like true vampires, we slept during the day.

The slight rocking motion of the ship lulled us easily into sleep, despite the reversal of our usual day-night pattern. Even the hammocks and iron frame bedsteads grew relatively comfortable. The shared bathroom and showers had a fixed women—men rotation. Most Bats were at least in our fifties and sixties, so there wasn't anything we hadn't already seen and nothing to shock us. Ho! Ho!

Our rotating chefs and cooks did us proud. Twice a week our meals were designed to provide insight and help us understand **the two** gang cultures that were our sworn enemies. I'm not talking about major food groups you preferred as kids, such as pizza, burgers, or chicken strips. With Big Elmer's Ivories, the white supremacists in mind, our cook grilled or barbecued wild game—deer, rabbits, squirrel and possum. For cultural information about our Mexican foes, we were served beans and rice with molé sauce, and hot chiles and pork in queso cheese sauce. Stereotypic food preferences of the two gangs, but they tasted so good— especially with the knowledge of what lay ahead for the gangs.

I have no idea how the kitchen staff acquired the foodstuff for these meals, and I never asked. They were fantastic and got us in the mood to decimate the gang members, strange as that may sound to you. We liked their food, tried to appreciate their culture, but hated what they did to businesses, citizens, the city, and to each other.

Vigilante justice always traveled on a full stomach, no matter how bad things were in the city—the usual continued inflation, high unemployment, scarcity of much foodstuff, and chronic violence and corruption at the highest levels. We had a big job to do and needed the energy to do it.

Preparation is the key to success in all things, whether it's rekindling justice or restoring Myra.

Chapter Four

    The first big project for the Bats involved money. The ancients knew that the love of money is the root of all evil. Without all the profits from drugs, prostitution, murder, and extortion, the cartels and gangs could not survive. So, we planned to steal their drug money from a central location which laundered it on its way to Mexico City and Berlin.

    Our information was that the Northern California Bank, N.A. held the money after two gangs made deposits, then sent a wire transfer to their companion banks abroad. More limited income earned by the gangs was deposited in a small community bank in the Napa Valley as a "cover" for tax purposes.

    Our heist was exquisitely planned after weeks of observation and spying on two of the gangs. The "treasurers" of the gangs collected the proceeds from their mules and street salesmen on Fridays, counted it, and then deposited the cash later that evening. I did reconnaissance on the Ivories.

Classified FBI Information

Elmer Jones – Ivories

Called Big Elmer, he is the leader of the Ivories, a gang of uneducated, white racists who formed their initial alliance in federal prison. The Ivories hate all immigrants, foreigners, non-white groups, as well as Jews, Catholics, Hindus, and Buddhists. Big Elmer hopes to assassinate Ricky Rubio, head of the rival Diamonds. The Ivories largely engage in small-time pot distribution, theft, robbery, assault, and carjacking, but if he kills Ricky, Elmer plans on the Ivories moving into lucrative hard drugs. The Ivories are recognized by their signature black-matte Harleys, Confederate flag bandanas, and amateurish black tattoos. They worship Big Elmer and think he is the third anti-Christ. Big Elmer is a huge man given to sleeveless t-shirts, a big gold cross, dirty, torn jeans with military insignias worn over oiled black biker boots. He is addicted to Mars bars, and eats only the meat of wild game animals and birds, which he kills with an AK-47 or an AR-15. Big Elmer resides in a double-wide trailer with Billie Jean, his common-law wife. He regrets that he didn't finish high school, but swears if he had, he wouldn't have learned how to open Coors beer bottles with his teeth.

Cristo followed the Diamonds' money trail. Armored sedans with heavily armed gang members picked up the money around 8:00 p.m. Fridays and took it to the bank. Strangely, both gangs used the same time and same procedure but different portals. Maybe they assumed it was a safe way to do it. You rob us and we'll rob you. I guess they thought they could do anything—even be careless. It made our job that much easier, as there were no other bank patrons present.

At the appropriate time, we struck.

"The gangs worry about each other," Cristo said. "They hardly know we exist." He drove the stolen van which held five more of the Bats. His hands encased in black leather gloves tightly grasped the steering wheel.

"That's the entrance and the alley is on the side," I said. I felt calm in a strange but confident way. We had prepared carefully. The planning paid off.

Our van had identical lettering on both sides—Knight Electrical. We parked it near the doorway used by the gangs. A bank manager typically answered the door when a buzzer rang, then a bio-metric vision device opened the door.

Earlier, Bats tampered with the system, so we made sure that there were minor issues with the buzzer and the bio-metric system. To anyone observing, it made sense that Knight Electrical was on hand to monitor the ongoing concerns and repair anything that needed it.

The bank night manager failed to pry open the door. The buzzer sounded but the bio-metric vision system malfunctioned. I used binoculars to read the lips of the Diamond carrying several bags of cash. "What the fuck?"

He stood at the doorway confused, and then emptied his gun into the lock, the buzzer, and the bio-metric unit. Out of bullets now, he was a sitting duck for Cristo who shot him and then ran behind the Diamonds' car and killed the others before they realized what was happening.

Clever Cristo. Blue-red flames could be seen and minutes later a loud explosion. Done!

"It'll take less than a minute to rush to the opposite side entrance for a repeat performance with the Ivories," I said. "Don't kill the bank employee, though."

After the Ivories were warned by the firebombing of the Diamonds' car, all four of them exited the sedan in order to provide maximum protection for the courier with the bank bags.

As the van pulled up, I said, "Trouble with the buzzer?"

Three Bats immediately shot the Ivories' gangster with the cash, and then bombed that sedan, after killing three more.

Something in that car blew sky high. Not just the gasoline in the tank, but a type of explosive which produced a three-story fireball that quickly burned itself out into a billowy cloud of black smoke. The air turned putrid with a stench so horrible that the Bats slipped on masks to protect their breathing.

What was stored in the Ivories' car? Perhaps a powerful explosive to blow up the Diamonds' safe house? Maybe to attack and finish off the Bats? Could the Vampire's hull have withstood such force? Who knows?

We never knew exactly what the smell consisted of, but it was noxious—maybe a type of fertilizer bomb that never reached its target. The odor, the thinned out gray smoke, the sheer devastation to the car and its occupants left no doubt, however, as to our intentions. Death to all Ivories and Diamonds!

If only the explosion to the Diamonds' car had been so dramatic. That firebomb simply burned the occupants to death and destroyed the auto in what seemed now to be a mundane blast and fire.

The evening's totals: eight dead Ivories and Diamonds, two armored sedans demolished, and several million dollars in cash recovered that was headed to cartels outside the country.

Though we'd worn gloves, we wiped all of the van's surfaces. Then we steered it off a pier into a watery grave. No prints or weapons or money left behind.

High fives all around as we walked to the Vampire to celebrate the operation. Gangs were the top suspects, so with both **side** entrances used after normal banking hours, the Ivories and Diamonds must have blamed each other.

Sooner or later, they'd be on to us. Bank security cameras only pictured individuals in Ninja attire.

The level of tension and uncertainty about this job rose perceptibly as we arrived at the destroyer. We'd all been in a zone, focused on carrying out the mission, creating chaos and death, and then obtaining the money for our current life and future activities.

Now, there was the guilt and shame of this immoral and illegal conduct, the outright murder of eight human beings and the theft of their drug money. I knew we were righteous and doing the right thing, but still the means were awful. I kept reminding myself and the others, "They kill children and ruin lives and stir up violence. Vigilante justice is..."

I turned my back on our common room now full of beer barrels and microwave popcorn. Once up on the deck, I leaned over the railing and retched. My legs buckled as I partly sat and partly fell. I vomited again. The boat swayed as I shook from head-to-toe. Survivor's guilt, I wondered? I survived the Paper People experiment, the ongoing global crisis, the loss of Myra, and now my criminal behavior with the Bats.

I knew what we did was so wrong, but perhaps some redemption would come from using the drug money to pay Dr. Stine to create the antidote. I must have passed out on the deck, because the next thing I recalled was someone shaking me and half-carrying me as I stumbled down to our sleeping quarters below.

A few days later, my next assignment required me to interview the owner of a laundry and dry cleaning shop. We'd gotten word that he wanted to go to the police, but decided to speak with a vigilante before doing that. He trusted us. I met him at 9:00 p.m. in the rear of his store.

"Hello, I'm the Bat they call Papa."

"Me, my shop." We shook hands. "Why black? Look like Ninja."

I said, "It's our uniform. Tell me what's going on. We don't tell the police. Don't know which ones are honest."

The owner poured tea. He handed me a tiny cup. "Special. From Hong Kong." He sat back in an old rattan chair that had seen better days. Even the subdued light in the room couldn't hide its age, or his, for that matter. The distinctive odor of cleaning solvents stopped just short of anesthetizing us.

Through several missing and crooked front teeth, he hissed. "If no pay, they kill family. Take shop."

"Yes, go ahead," I said.

"Come here. Like old Tong gangs. Say help me. Pay ten percent."

"Did you?"

"Yes. Too much. Can't do it. No pay, they own half." He held out his left hand. The thumb and index finger were missing. Ugly scars. Still, he sipped tea with it, forcing a sad, painful smile.

"That's horrible." I raised my scarf and drank my tea also.

"Dots? Scabs?" he asked.

"Old wounds from a long time ago. Remind me of bad things in the world." I replaced the scarf to cover my face. "Call themselves Diamonds?"

"Yes, Diamonds." He stood slowly and the woven, crinkled rattan tried to restore its original shape. Too old. Too broken.

"We'll watch the store. When Diamonds return here, we'll take care of things." We shook hands.

"How much, Papa?"

"No pay. Don't worry."

Two nights later around 10:00 p.m., just as the elderly owner closed for the day, a late-model green Mercedes sedan parked in front of the store. Three Mexican men, well dressed, walked up to the window and knocked on the glass. One of them yelled, "Tomorrow is last chance. We'll own half if you don't pay." They all laughed sarcastically and pointed fingers at him—menacing in the shape of a gun.

He remained inside the storefront and said nothing. He simply bowed before he disappeared behind the counter.

I planted a car bomb with a forty-five second digital timer on it under the left rear fender of the Mercedes.

The Bat with me and I walked down the nearby alley as fast and as silently as we could. I saw the Mercedes pull away from the curb, move half a block, and explode into a fireball. The three bodies were burned beyond recognition, according to the police report. The weekly business gazette carried a small story headlined "More Tong Wars in Chinatown", with photos of a large crowd of cheering Asians peering at the metal chunks and debris scattered over the street and sidewalk. The owner of the store could be seen off to the side of the crowd. Did he have a sheepish grin on his face?

A week or so passed, before I discovered that one of the Bats had a distant cousin loyal to us inside the Diamonds. He kept us informed of their plans and future arrangements. So we knew a great deal about the flow of drugs from Mexico and other countries in South America through Texas and California into the U.S. and Canadian markets.

Several things happened which caused an interesting development, a coincidence giving us an opportunity. Global warming raised the temperatures of the earth's oceans and many fish became diseased or eventually died. The Ivories then made a killing shipping chicken, and pork, when they could find it, to Asian countries to substitute for the diminished fish supply. We knew that the Diamonds also mistakenly blamed the Ivories for their three soldiers burned to death outside the dry cleaning establishment in Chinatown.

Our informant told us that the Diamonds' leader, Ricky Rubio, discovered that the Ivories were going to attack them again—accurate information this time. He told his gang, "We go first..."

His next-in-command argued against it. "Maybe the Ivories didn't do it."

"No way, José," said Ricky. His short, stocky frame bristled with fury. "A handmade white silk Mexican wedding shirt for... a good plan. Something different."

The next-in-command said, "Kill all their chickens and pigs."

"That's it! A white shirt idea! Fuck the fish," said Ricky.

243

Our informant was part of the crew sent to the main Ivories' farm. They poisoned all of the hundreds of pigs and thousands of chickens. Then they killed and skinned the dozen Ivories operating the farm and delivered the human meat salted and iced in boxes to Big Elmer.

Ricky told his crew, "Muy bueno. Mi amigos each get a bonus. Extra meth."

Ricky killed and maimed first, and asked questions later. He hated the "yellow sneak-fucks," almost as much as the "gringo bastards." "Brown is better than white or yellow anytime, anywhere." He laughed so hard that when the top buttons on his shirt broke off, it flew open revealing a huge hairless chest tattoo of a thorny cactus with the letters L.S.D. inside of it and diamonds surrounding it.

The Ivories took a big hit. They must retaliate or lose face. The Diamonds stayed on high alert. So were we.

The blitzkrieg continued. Our next mission found us kneeling on a hilltop. Cristo and I used small military binoculars with pale green night vision, to spy on the Ivories. We could see Big Elmer; plenty of tats covered his neck, shaved head, and arms—just handmade black and white crosses, swastikas, and sexy angels from his prison time. A biker from head-to-toe in a black leather jacket with a bandana around his neck, roach clip, and an AK-47 hung loosely from his coon-skin shoulder strap.

Cristo said, "He's a very, very bad guy. His father was an itinerant farmer who drank. His mother was an addict who did go-go dancing part-time. A great high school wrestler, no surprise given his size, he got into meth which led to prison. Then to skinhead gangs and to killing his cellmate."

"How do you know all of this?"

"I have a unique way to research these gang leaders, so I learned about Ricky and Big Elmer too."

I handed the binoculars to Cristo. I said, "Let's get back to the future, or the present or whatever. What are the Ivories doing to those women?"

Cristo said, "The women wear boots and tight jeans but they are naked from the waist up. Oh, my God. Their heads are shaved." He dropped the binoculars. "There are four of them. Oh, no, it's horrible." He pounded his clenched fists into the dark earth, until the knuckles were swollen and bleeding. "He's very bad."

I picked up the binoculars. The women were slapped, slugged, whipped, and thrown to the ground. A Big Elmer look-alike yelled, "Fuck, fuck, fuck," before he jumped on several of them.

"Geronimo! How do you like that? You'll be Ivories," Big Elmer screamed at the top of his lungs.

Cristo carefully unloaded his backpack, then he wiped off his hands. He opened the tri-pod and set up his M40 sniper rifle and telescopic scope so that the front of the gun fit snugly in the **tri-pod** for stability. "I'll insert centerfire cartridges—.338 Lapua Magnums."

"You've come a long way, my friend," I said.

He lowered his scarf so that his entire face and eyes were free of the Ninja attire. Now a very powerful, resolute, and strong version of Cristo. He took his time, played with the scope and sights.

He said, "I'm ready. Bright moonlight, no wind, and excellent probability of hits." He glanced at the moon and momentarily bowed his head. "I shouldn't. God forgive me."

Then he shot three of the Ivories in the forehead between their eyes. They fell over dead.

We immediately fit our gear into the backpack. Neither of us spoke. We walked back to the Vampire.

At last, Cristo said, "Very bad people. I wait for the second coming. They wait for the third antichrist."

"Who are one and two?"

He said, "Hitler and Bonaparte."

As we started up the gangplank, I said, "I've wanted to tell you about my progress in bringing Myra back to life. Dr. Stine is..."

He stopped short. The gangplank wobbled slightly. "Oh, God, not that. You're still thinking of..."

"You heard me. I've saved her skin, bones, and organs. Judy is the model. Myra's voice is on... All the building blocks."

I could see tears in his eyes, dripping onto his face scarf. "It's not right, Papa. Not right. Only God gives life. Get on with your own life. We're both sinners."

Shaking noticeably, he grabbed the hand-rail tightly, as if he might jump in or stumble or pass out.

"That's my plan. Only you and Judy and Dr. Stine know it."

I held him upright to avoid a fall as we managed to enter the ship proper.

"Reconsider," he said. He turned into an old and weak man, so I helped him as he stumbled toward his bunk and fell on it. He snored when his head hit the pillow.

I would not reconsider. Myra must return to life. That's it! I'd rather die trying.

Chapter Five

Late that same night, I decided to introduce Judy to Dr. Stine as part of the plan to restore your life, Myra—my dearest one. Judy had no problem playing the stand-in. She hid her fear and seemed eager for the experiment to begin. In the back of her mind she might have been aware that if it worked for us, it could work later on, for her. And if it didn't, then…

Myra, your name remained on the tip of my tongue and your memory in the front of my thoughts. So, you'll understand that regardless of Judy's wishes, she did not become my girlfriend, but rather a close friend who would "model" your body for Dr. Stine.

Anyway, Judy and I made our way down two floors of vertical, slippery ladders to Stine's office and laboratory.

After introductions, Dr. Stine asked Judy to simply stand and make no movements while he walked around her four or five times. He pushed his spectacles lower on his nose. He nodded. "Yes, she's perfect. Same everything. My measurements will be perfect. Perhaps some sherry?"

We all sipped from small German, crystal wine glasses. Dr. Stine had style.

"Maybe Papa hasn't fully explained things. You will help us bring Myra back to life," Dr. Stine said.

"How can you?" asked Judy. "All the body parts? It just doesn't seem possible."

I stared at a black chalkboard hung on the wall. It contained two neatly printed sections. "He's a genius," I said.

I BIO-BOOSTERS

- Anabolic Steroids
- Human Growth Hormone
- Amphetamine
- Beta-2 Agonists
- Erythropoietin

II LATER

- Regeneration of Tissue
- Gene Doping
- Gene-Modulating Technologies
- Electricity or Magnetic Fields
- Artificial Limbs
- Exoskeletons
- Embedded Nano Devices
- Species Brain Control

Dr. Stine proudly set a pointer on the edge of the chalkboard. "You may not understand the science. Earlier, I went after specific cancers, used vaccines, reprogrammed T-cells, and analyzed the DNA and RNA of twenty-five different types of cancer. Papa observes this list about my tools, my different approaches. Then I went deeper into robotics and cellular studies."

Judy strolled around the room and gazed at the microscopes, jars, freezers, lifelike drawings of robots and skeletons, and so on. "What about Myra's body?"

Dr. Stine said, "Robots have control systems, like our central nervous system. Sensors, similar to human senses, and, of course, a power source. Behaviors such as communication, movement, and the use of tools to interact with the environment develop. Behavior fascinates me."

Judy said, "Will she be one?" She walked toward the door, and it appeared that she'd bolt at any moment.

"No. No. Never. She'll be Myra—healthy, with no cancer. The same age as when she died. The real thing, not a robot." Dr. Stine couldn't take his eyes off of Judy, full of self-satisfaction and admiration.

"Phew," I said. "That's a relief. You learned from robots. Is that it?"

"Exactly," Dr. Stine said. "Exactly right." He continued, "I can cure flu. I can fix broken bones. I can restore life. And I..."

"Yes," I said. "Dr. Stine can do it all. You'll be there for Myra and me—to make her alive again."

Judy relaxed. Her facial skin sagged a bit and her blue-green eyes slowly lost the deer-in-the-headlight quality. At some level she'd apparently been frightened of the process, scared of Dr. Stine, and probably mistrustful of me. She laughed at last. "As long as you two don't kill me. While you're at it, can you remove these dots from my skin? It's one of Faulkner's novels I never understood."

"Of course, with time, my dear. I did a study for two years in Hamburg in a skin clinic. I'll remove the tattoos from all of your people. We undid scars and birthmarks all the time, my dear." He rubbed his hands in anticipation of the work ahead. "Another sherry. We're, as you say, teammates. We want to win." He sipped his third glass slowly. "You're a very attractive woman. Yah, very much so. Just the right size for me."

"Where is she? Where's her body?" Judy asked. "This is creepy."

I reminded her that we had Myra's skin on a scroll, that I'd saved her bones, and an undertaker colleague had preserved her vital organs.

"I'm in a classic horror movie," she said.

"Yes," Dr. Stine said, "but this is life. From death to life. The end to the beginning. Someday I'll be very famous—we all will be. Myra, too." He held up a photo of her.

I knew we were meddling in God's work, trying to create life. Rejecting death. Restoring a human being to the exact age and stage at which she died. Myra's life trumped everything.

Dr. Stine said, "There must be a consequence, too."

I didn't want to pursue the notion of a consequence, so we simply excused ourselves and left.

I knew the Bats' missions would consume most of my time—assignments in our quest for justice and fair play. But we had to find an antidote!

Chapter Six

The next day I couldn't get family out of my mind. I hadn't seen Joey or Mary, or either of you kids since the dots returned and we lived and slept on the Vampire. You guys, and I do mean Ben and Roberta, kept busy. You had your own friends, school activities, and homework and a busy social life. Mid-teens is a busy time, full of energy and full of angst.

The other reason is that I was saddened and embarrassed by the return of the dots. The chief's antidote had failed, and Dr. Stine promised to attack the problem and solve it easily—but no results yet.

More bad economic news appeared then. The authorities warned the public about the worsening drought and its effect on the remaining stores of wood and lumber. Prices went higher with the declining supply. Charcoal briquettes, a convenient fuel for stoves, remained available only in selected areas of the city, at particular times and days, and for a price few could afford.

There was a widespread suspicion that the major gangs and cartels controlled charcoal, as well as meth, coke, and pain pills.

I called Joey to get his advice. He kept in close touch with city hall and the leadership, if you could call it that, of the city.

Joey said, "It's not getting better fast enough, Dad. They need wood for power to run the infrastructure. Lumber is being hoarded by the city."

I said, "I'll burn furniture, if I have to."

I then told Joey and Mary that I'd be unavailable for several more weeks. They assumed I'd gone somewhere on vacation, so I didn't disagree.

"Joey," I said, "could you get me some political information?"

Joey said, "Uh, uh, uh. Political information?"

"I've got the phone now," Mary said. "What information, Dad? Joey has a new job with the city accounting department. Can't risk..."

I said, "Yes, I know that. No risks for him." Maybe I'd gone too far.

"Here, Joey," Mary said, "take the phone."

I said, "It is common knowledge around City Hall that the mayor is a crook—very corrupt. Want to double-check my info."

Joey's voice softened with relief. "What the street talk is like on the inside? No hidden cameras or mics?"

I chuckled. "Right. Just the street talk."

Joey said, "Sorry, Dad. She's just trying to protect me. That's all."

I said, "I understand. It's okay." The phone stuck to my fingers. I didn't really need this confirmation. I knew plenty by now.

Joey paused. "Here's what I've heard. When you need a zoning change, or to buy some land from the city—or to get a services contract... Well, the mayor has a cigar box on his desk that holds cash only."

"Is that it? Just bribery?" I said.

Joey said, "Well, rumors are that the mayor is about to be indicted for conspiring to commit murder, fraud, and interfering with a Federal investigation."

Mary said, "It's me again. Are you planning something, Dad? You and the others? Why doesn't somebody stop the drugs?"

"You're right, my dear. Maybe somebody will put a stop to the gangs someday." I was tempted to tell her more about the Bats.

Joey coughed. He said, "There are ways to help the community. The mayor stops them cold. I saw a memo on a big program to promote inclusiveness and reduce discrimination. Housing, education, and jobs."

"You're so right, Joey. Proud of your beliefs. That mayor can't last forever. Gangs will go." Could Myra and I **have been** wrong to reduce our expectations when Joey got sick?

Joey said, "Evil takes other forms. Can't help the current guys. Races need to talk. Tolerance and empathy."

I was very proud of Joey. His values and beliefs gave me hope for a better world. Myra smiled on us.

Mary spoke again. Her voice more relaxed and without the suspicion. "The kids are out tonight. When will we see you?"

"I'll be around in a few weeks. Hugs and kisses. Love you all very much."

"Same here," she said. She hung up.

I made a mental note to ask Dr. Stine to hurry up on the dots antidote ointment. We still had weeks to go on the blitzkrieg and I couldn't see the family until we finished the job.

My next assignment turned out to be politically delicate. The Bats requested that I evaluate our spy. I had misgivings about talking with the cousin of one of the Bats. He was a full-fledged member of the Diamonds gang. He was our man there, an informer for us, now suddenly a defector to their side. He knew a lot about the Bats and there were those who wanted him dead and gone immediately.

Cristo asked me to meet privately with him and make a judgment about him. I did just that.

A short man of no more than five feet, our mole told me he'd lost nearly fifty pounds since he got hooked on meth.

"What do you want?" he asked. He poured a huge dose of cream and sugar into his coffee as we sat in a boarded up diner near the docks. "No one trusts me now."

"You've done some good things for us," I said. "Warned us that Big Elmer was chasing Ricky Rubio. Told us that the Diamonds blamed the Ivories for the murders in Chinatown."

Our spy's hand shook as he held his coffee cup. His young face showed wrinkled signs of wear and tear, now greasy and sweaty. "Will you Bats kill me?"

I said, "You've been honest in a way. You don't want anything more to do with us."

"I'm a broken taco."

I gazed into his small, dark brown eyes, searching for the truth. "Why change your mind? Why tell people?"

He huddled in the corner of the booth. He appeared close to tears. "I don't like any of it. The Bats. The gangs. The drugs."

"Yes."

"All I told them was that your dots would go away sooner or later. That the Bats would go away. They don't know what you do." He gripped the edge of the table until his knuckles turned white. They were already flat and crushed.

Maintaining composure when interrogating him was easy. I liked him.

"See," he said, "I'm Mexican. My family is from Cuernavaca. I have three sisters and two brothers. Very poor."

"So?"

"I'm part of the Diamonds. We're Mexicans. I send money to my family."

"So, the Diamonds are playing a waiting game. Hope we kill Big Elmer. That's who they blame."

"That's it," he said. "I won't say..."

We shook hands. I wiped his sweat from my hand.

When I returned to the Vampire, I told Cristo to stay away from him, that he was naïve and foolishly honest, but couldn't be trusted any longer. "He is a druggie and a turncoat who will taste our justice later."

"Anything else?"

"Yes," I said. "It's just a gut feeling, I don't think he'd do much to defend Ricky Rubio. Ricky's a hot shot."

A few days later, the Bats were flying high again. Big Elmer, still under surveillance, and twenty of his bikers drove to the Diamonds' safe house on a rainy, dark night. The word on the street was that they blamed the Diamonds for the sniper killings of several Ivories. Wrong again, but a search for verifiable facts and honest ideas never got in the

254

way of their approach to life. They were out to kill Ricky Rubio and shift into the big time hard drug trade run by the Diamonds. At least, that's what our intel told us.

The bikers roared and rumbled on slick streets and alleyways, circling the safe house numerous times. Shots fired into the air called attention to the large number of attackers and probably scared everyone inside the dwelling.

Big Elmer pulled his massive black Harley to the front sidewalk and pulled out a bullhorn. He screamed, "You brown fucks! You killed my people! I want Rubio, the head brown fuck! He's dead!"

Bikers continued to shoot wildly in the air and circle the house. Screams could be heard inside the house. Many Diamonds scooted out the side door and were allowed to leave. They were desperate but unhurt.

"Ricky Rubio, come out you dumb fuck. You're dead meat. I'm top dog. I give the orders."

"Come get me you fat white cocksucker." That was a long sentence for Rubio. Fear led to this torrent of words.

Big Elmer yanked two sawed-off shotguns from his bike pack. One in each hand, he slid low between bushes in the front yard. "Last chance Ricky sweetie. You're toast. Your guys are gone."

Our team hid nearby, close enough to see and hear most of it, but far enough away in case we decided to us an RPG to finish off both leaders, the house, and a fair chunk of Big Elmer's Ivories bike riding thugs.

I said to Cristo, "Maybe they'll just kill each other. Benign neglect on our part. In a perfect world, we'd be the enemy—we shot the Ivories."

Cristo said, "We're trying to make it perfect."

I said, "Let's gas it up." We attached gas canisters on the end of long assault rifles and shot several into the front windows of the house. Anyone inside got caught in a fog bank.

Flames shot out of the first floor windows, sprinkling broken glass and burning embers over the lawn. Ricky was caught between a rock and a hard place, lethal gas fumes and blazing fire or a shootout with Big Elmer. Sacrificing a loyal Diamond as a surrogate,

he chose the latter. He faked it. The coward was safe.

Wearing a bulletproof vest and a military helmet, it looked to the world as if Ricky Rubio crawled out the back door, searching for protective cover.

A motorcycle rider yelled to Big Elmer, "Coming out the back."

Big Elmer circled the house and crouched ten feet from the Diamond he thought was Ricky, who slithered toward the safety of the alley. "You little brown fuck. Back to Mexico."

He shot the stand-in in the face with both shotguns at close range. Mush collected inside the helmet. It fell to the ground full of skin, neck, brains and bones in the form of Hungarian goulash. "So long, fuck face." Ricky fooled Big Elmer. He lived.

"That's enough for one night," I said.

Cristo said, "Are you sure?"

I said, "Not tonight. No need to get greedy."

Cristo stood and adjusted his face scarf. "We've both changed. Trained killers."

The "shooters" met nights later to decide on the next course of action, our short-term tactics. We noted a shaky coalition of the Ivories and Diamonds, a temporary collaboration on several, small money-makers, but not coke or heroin.

In addition to racial and cultural differences, neither gang enjoyed even a tiny commitment to social responsibility. Unlike the ancient Tong gangs of China, which used part of their criminal enterprise to help their own people, a distorted kind of social safety net, the Diamonds felt a responsibility and loyalty only to themselves and to the large Mexican cartels. The Ivories didn't think much beyond Big Elmer.

Cristo said, "We haven't shown any partiality. We've killed Diamonds, shot Ivories, stolen drug money, firebombed cars, interfered with poultry supplies, and let Ricky Rubio nearly get assassinated."

I said, "Sooner or later, they'll get on to us. We've been very lucky so far."

As ten of us hunched over a table with coffee and tea, we read and passed around the latest FBI report on Ricky. The painted gray metal felt cold and clammy when I laid the following report on it.

<u>Classified FBI Information</u>

<u>Ricky Rubio – Diamonds</u>

Ricky cooperates informally with Big Elmer on some deals, but not hard drugs. Short and stocky, he also wears a huge gold chain that reaches his waist. Ricky rose to power by knifing two guards while he was in a federal prison for kidnapping and assault. Known for his expertise with a Bowie knife, he also admires a German luger and an American Bushmaster with extra-long magazine. His motto is 'Kill first, then argue.' The Diamonds use young, illiterate Latino boys as mules and street salesman. The young males feel protected and valued whether they are on the street or in prison. Like large Mexican cartels, the Diamonds' violence is very public and terroristic. They often hang enemies from bridges or the murdered opponents simply disappear after the community observes their deaths. The Mexican population in the area has expanded while the Asian growth has stabilized. Therefore, the Diamonds are expanding their criminal activities from heroin and meth to government-sponsored services for the poor—soup kitchens and food pantries. They steal both food and money from them.

I sensed a growing tension among my compatriots, not as much painful guilt or shame that could, perhaps should, be there, but a mounting sense of fear and loathing for our task and what we'd accomplished. The vigilante war tipped the balance toward a better, cleaner, more socially responsive citizenry and government. No one— no gang or police or army—tried very hard to find us or pinpoint us as culprits in these attacks. The street talk said that the gangs were doing each other in.

I walked to a nearby wall, pounded it with both fists, turned to my peers. "The mayor is next. The community knows what he's done. Lives in a lavish mansion. That dirty pol deserves..."

257

"Hear. Hear." Coffee cups were raised and gingerly touched each other with approval—they were Styrofoam.

Cristo arose and placed his arm around my shoulders. He pulled me close. A weak smile crossed his face, then he burst into tears. "Not another assassination. Please. No." He went on, "We must stop. Now! We've enjoyed success, if it can be called that. We've hurt the gangs. They still exist but they have been warned and injured. Sooner or later, they'll stop blaming each other and find us and kill us."

"We must," I said. "The mayor and then that last dinner party. That's my surprise for later."

Quick agreement from our assembled peers. They stomped their feet and pounded on the able. In unison, "Do it," and "We must."

For some reason, I didn't feel I'd won the argument or was victorious. It was a kind of survival versus morality, good versus evil, even vigilante versus God. Simplistic, painful, and terrible dichotomies. Horrible, but the evil had to go in order to give the city a chance to thrive in these cruel and impoverished social and economic conditions.

As we were about to get down to the nitty-gritty plans for the mayor, a gentle knock on the bulkhead door interrupted us, followed by the appearance of an unprepossessing Dr. Stine. "I have good news."

Startled, I stood to shake hands with the doctor. "I think you all know Dr. Stine, or at least who he is." He was acknowledged without much warmth or welcome.

He said, "I'll be brief. I have the antidote—an ointment that will eradicate forever all tattoos. It's not cheap." With that he clicked his heels, did an about-face and disappeared through the doorway.

Cristo rubbed his hands together briskly, then ran them over his arms. "Thank God," he said. "No more Ninja outfits. Back to a normal life, if you can call it that in today's world."

I said, "I think the Bats should pay Dr. Stine whatever he wants. We'll be liberated once again. This time forever."

We danced. We sang. We cheered. We laughed. As others joined us, we told them the good news. More Bats laughed and stomped and drank. We were flying high. The chefs served steak and fresh vegetables to celebrate. This was a break we'd all been praying for, dreaming of, hoping to achieve, once our vigilante blitzkrieg ended successfully.

Amidst the revelry, Cristo said, "I'm on board now. The last of it. I did all I could. I've prayed. We take on the mayor soon. I've got a surefire way. Then we're finished." His powerful arms and massive shoulders even scared me. "No other choice." Tears or smiles gone now, just a serious, angular face of steely determination highlighted by bluish veins bulging on his temples.

Those who paid attention to him cheered even louder and longer. Others just jumped on the table and danced, so the bedlam kept up for hours. Twin ideas of striking at the heart of local corruption and then being freed of the dots were glorious—drunk or sober.

Judy sauntered over to our table. She reached out with both hands. "Want to dance? I'm a little tipsy."

I said, "Never was much at dancing. Let's go see Dr. Stine. He works very late."

She held both my hands and pulled me up from the table, then wrapped her arms around me.

"If that's the only way to be with you."

I said, "Judy, you play a pivotal role in Dr. Stine's effort to reconstruct Myra. More than you realize."

Chapter Seven

We followed stair-ladders down to the doctor's office and lab. Each of us slipped at least once or twice getting there.

Bent over a microscope, he said, "Aha, good of you both to come. I've put the antidote ointment into sixty tubes. Use it once a day for three days and then, voilà. Dots—books—whatever are gone forever. No one asked but the ointment physically vibrates the ink molecules to break them down before they are carted off by macrophages."

"That's wonderful, Dr. Stine," Judy said. "We're grateful, so very grateful. How much does it cost?"

He raised his head and adjusted his glasses. "The pleasure is mine. The money is for my ongoing research. Let's say three thousand per tube, that's $180,000 US dollars."

"Done," I said. "You're the best. Your skill is priceless."

Judy hugged him and kissed his cheeks. "We'll never forget you. The famous Dr. Stine. The product could sell globally for..."

Dr. Stine perched on his stool again. "The most important thing left on my research agenda is restoring Myra to life. As long as you're here, Judy, I'll take some pictures on my cell. Just stand up and give me several angles of your face and body." She did so. "Yes—that's it. Myra says thanks to you."

The alcohol relaxed Judy so that her poses were slightly risqué. She was a ham at heart.

"Papa's pictures of Myra's facial bones and location of eyes and nose and ears are so similar—it's almost uncanny. My job is much easier. Please go behind that screen. Take off your blouse and bra."

Judy said, "Are you sure?"

"Yes, yes," he said. "Just for a photo."

She did it. The photos were completed. I simply watched and listened. Judy was great.

Reminiscent of an oil painter hiding an unfinished portrait, Dr. Stine used a white cloth to cover an exoskeleton of Myra. He removed it carefully. "That's the outline of her body."

I gasped with adulation. I couldn't hold back my tears or the choking sobs. This man was clearly a genius. It was Myra to a "T."

"My robotic training paid off here. You saved the skin and bones and organs for me. They're next."

"Judy, if you don't mind, I'll x-ray you now—just to study your bone structure and organ placement."

"Fine, should I disrobe?"

Dr. Stine pointed to the divider screen. "Yes, please. There's a hospital gown there."

Judy joked, "You won't need my skin, will you?"

"No. Not at all," Dr. Stine said. He glanced at me and we both smiled quizzically at his answer. "We have that covered."

After the X-rays, Dr. Stine said, "Please sit here at the table. I want to remind you both of something. Myra, once my work is completed, will return to life minus her cancer cells. She'll be the same age as when she died. Once my efforts succeed, we'll be able to do this for others. If many were restored to life, our planet would simply be overrun by people. We couldn't..."

"Yes," I said. "That's obvious. But it will be a very expensive process. Slow to spread around the globe."

Frankly, this discussion unnerved me. My face contorted, relaxed, and then did it again. My mouth and lips were do dry. Myra would understand. There was a sense of foreboding. What was Dr. Stine, the genius, going to say next or warn us about, or try to prevent from happening? I had the shakes and my armpits literally dripped.

"You must die," said Dr. Stine.

"Do you mean me?" I asked.

"Yes, life for death. One-for-one."

Judy removed the gown and slipped on her clothes behind the screen. "Who dies? What the hell is this craziness? Who brings back the dead and then kills someone else? Dr. Stine, you're a murderer. Take me home, Papa."

Dr. Stine arose from the table. He walked to a wall chart. He grabbed a pointer. "See this. The world could implode with a major, unexpected medical discovery like mine—well, ours."

I said, "Before I take Judy home, I want to be very, very clear. When Myra lives again, I die. Is that it?"

"Yes," Dr. Stine said. "It has to be one-for-one. Otherwise, I won't create life, I'll destroy it. A death for a life."

I suddenly felt hot and cold and sweaty over my impending death—mostly cold. I couldn't back out. I'd swallow the Doc's pills or let him inject me with poison. Myra would be alive but upset with me. I'd be gone. Cease to exist. Not alive. No memory of anything. No experience of life. No sharing. Not even my selfishness to ward off.

Could I have arranged it any other way? I planned on trying everything I could think of with Dr. Stine but I knew he wouldn't budge. Incorruptible, at least on the point he made of a life for a death. It made perfect sense for a population statistician.

The global census grew far too fast anyway and given all the problems in the world, how to feed and house and clothe the next generation loomed as nearly impossible to solve.

The Bats could and would help me fend off Dr. Stine. It didn't seem fair to involve them in our very personal agreement. Okay on the cream and ointment to remove the dots, but not this.

I was afraid. I suffered with guilt. I was plagued by doubt. Then I became angry over the whole arrangement. Why should I die? Couldn't we exchange a suicide somewhere else for Myra's life? Plenty of suicides and homicides and accidental deaths in the world to trade. Plenty of elderly seniors who had given up on life. Why did Dr. Stine focus only on our family? Just because it was Myra, my wife, that will be restored to life, why does her husband die? I had agreed but, now that I thought about it I don't know why I did. Any human death could be a counter-point to…

Judy spoke as she stormed out of the lab. "I love Papa. I want him. You're a mad scientist from some bizarre movie plot. I should report you to the police or a medical society."

I followed her. Judy was impressive. She was devoted to me, without much coming back to her. Judy wanted me to live—with her.

I wanted Myra to live. I wanted a long, loving reunion with her after the gangs and corruption were destroyed. And the dots just a distant memory.

I couldn't wait to see Myra, to feel her smooth flesh, talk to her, hold her and love her. Dr. Stine recaptured the life cycle at the exact point of death. Myra would not go backward to the fetal stage, nor would she go forward to old age. She'd be Myra again, but free of the cancer that ate her alive.

The agony of not living my life, not sharing our final pilgrimage together, not being close to Myra left me sad and lonely whenever I thought of it. Yet, Dr. Stine's dictum made very good sense. Immortality would choke humanity altogether. Restoring all human life, after death, would lead to a population catastrophe unless a mechanism like Dr. Stine's proposal was implemented. My death made room for Myra.

The Bats' blitzkrieg would last for several more weeks. The dots would go away, so what should I do? Would there be time for a meaningful reunion with Myra—time to renew our love and need for each other? When she knew the eventual outcome, her feet would hurt horribly. My mouth would shut tight as I winced in pain. The angst and sadness and disappointment and anger could overwhelm the love and respect and sharing.

The obvious hit me. I'd have the chief tattoo my story—the vigilante story—on my skin. Myra would have a full record of the Paper People's life on the Vampire, their evolution into the Bats, from victim to victor, from slave to freedom, from homelessness to creating a better home for everyone. Myra could have my story to read to our grandchildren, just as I read her account to Ben and Roberta.

It wouldn't be a realistic family tale unless we coped with serious problems. The Irish know best that sooner or later the world will break your heart. Sooner or later, you break your own heart!

Chapter Eight

First, we had more work to do as the Ninja look-alikes, more justice to mete out, more pain to inflict and more violence to perpetrate. We now faced a corrupt government official and cruel, suspicious gangs that enslaved communities by fear and extortion and manipulation.

Sometime later, the pay phone near the dock rang, an emergency number, with a call for me. I shivered at the thought that Joey would phone me, using a number I told him to use only....

"Hello," I said. My hand trembled and I had difficulty holding the phone.

"Dad, Ben's in the hospital. An overdose. He'll pull through."

"Thank God. I wish I could be there. I can't. You'll understand someday that..."

Bats didn't go out during the day and, at night, we wore the black outfits. I wanted to rush to the hospital but my family did not know that the dots had returned. I couldn't be seen this way, with the likelihood of their imminent, complete removal by Dr. Stine's discovery. It wasn't just embarrassment, but the very real possibility of being discovered and followed to the Vampire by rival gang members. I was sure that they had evidence or rumors about us—maybe even our location.

"Any other details?" I asked.

"Well," Joey said, "we thought we'd lose him. He and two buddies ingested something at the mayor's daughter's sixteenth birthday party. The mayor called 911 and the EMTs. Ben's out of ICU and in a ward now. Swears he's through with drugs and agreed to rehab."

"Very sorry. So very sorry. Put Ben on the phone," I said.

Ben said, "Papa, I'm ashamed. First and last time but it felt so good. Not worth dying for. Don't worry."

I said, "Last time sounds good to me. Take care of yourself. There's a big surprise ahead. You'll understand it all later. Remember, I'm with you and I'll always love you and Roberta. Please give the phone back to your Dad now."

"Joey, thanks for the update. You and Mary should not blame yourselves. The city is swimming in drugs."

I talked to myself for a moment. I realized how important my grandchildren were to me. An OD experience for Ben conflicted with my image of him. Suddenly, he's a teen into experimentation with drugs, not clear on what, how much, or how pure was his choice. Being one of the guys, fitting in with his friends, going along with the crowd—that's what a young man does. How to encourage the independence of mind, the ability to choose the unconventional path? Ben would learn from his mistakes, the unfortunate consequences of this drug deal.

And at the mayor's house to boot. Was it lax discipline by that family? Did they encourage the booze and drugs blow-out with these adolescents? I'd read that some parents directly promote acting-out, while others are more subtle in their passive-approval of lousy teen decision making. It was another black mark on the mayor's list of crimes—bribery, corrupt contracts, pay-offs from gangs, votes based on cash, and so on. Now here's Ben at the mayor's house—under the mayor's supervision—involved with drugs.

It only reinforced the observation that the urban landscape was rife with almost anything that could be swallowed, ingested, or inhaled, patched, taken intravenously or with just a simple needle.

I would do anything for Ben and Roberta. I'd kill for them but nobody would believe me. I'd give my life for them. The Bats would take care of the mayor. The hospital and detox and Mary and Joey would support Ben's recovery.

Once back on the Vampire, my rage boiled over. I smashed a chair on the floor. I threw bowls and glasses at the wall. The mayor must die! I was furious that drugs like coke and heroin and meth were so available, sold and distributed to kids by the gangs, with the blessing and payoffs to the top echelon of city government. Dirty, filthy pols—couldn't believe a word they said. My legs nearly buckled, my heart raced, and I prayed for strength to carry out the end-game for the mayor.

In my mind the planning for the mayor's finale advanced quickly. I immediately met with Cristo.

265

He said, "We'd better keep the specifics to the two of us. If too many people know the details..." His light stubble failed to cover the few dots on his cheeks and chin.

"Why so secretive?"

The powerful and muscular, athletic middle-aged Cristo said, "Our man inside the Diamonds gang has revealed more about us." He drummed his fingers on the table. With that, he jiggled his enormous pecs up and down.

"He's told them of some of our plans. I don't want them to know where we live. They don't know about the "mayor" or the "final dinner" and its aftermath. We must move swiftly."

I bared my teeth. "A real Judas..."

"Yes," Cristo said, "when we finish off all the gang members, he'll get what he deserves. He's a turncoat."

The niceties escaped me at that moment. I couldn't get Ben and drugs out of my mind, though it only fired up an appetite for the mayor's hide. That would send a message destine to reverberate throughout the city and county government. Corruption must not pay off in the long run. Getting into bed with gangs and drug cartels can be momentarily lucrative, but jail or death or kidnapping should happen sooner or later.

I pushed my chair back. "Let's get the mayor now. My idea is to shoot down his personal helicopter with one of our RPGs."

The fortyish, energetic, testosterone-fueled Cristo said, "Hold it. That's too quick and painless. Make him suffer." Dressed all in black Ninja attire, he stood ramrod straight, arms stiff at his sides, with no hint of his mood behind the black scarf. "In the movies they get a guy hooked on coke or black tar. Then they drag it out. Torture him. Ask for money. Get it. Then kill him anyway."

I said, "We don't have time."

"Right," Cristo said. "Let's shoot him down. An eye for an eye. He's evil—the devil personified." He crossed himself and mumbled something I couldn't decipher. "I can make it happen."

The two of us made our way down several levels in the ship to the place we stored our arms and ammo in a screened, locked cage.

Cristo removed a box marked 'RPG' and grenade ammo for it. He ran his hand lovingly over the label 'RPG.'

He said, "I've wanted to fire one of these ever since training with it. It's a rush. To see it whistle through the air and hit the target. Wham-o." He smacked his lips.

Cristo ripped open the box. The RPG launcher used three sections, each attached to the other. The scope-site was separate and had latched pull-up eye pieces.

Later that night, while we stalked the mayor's house, Cristo told me an interesting story that captured our world. He said that he had an old computer but hoped that it could be repaired and used again. "I took it to a small repair store in Chinatown," he said.

I said, "I have a feeling that the plot thickens, my friend."

He stroked his beard, fidgeted with his beautiful, almost mystical, hands with the fingertips of each pressed on its corresponding mate.

I said, "Stop praying and tell me what happened."

"It's not a pretty story."

I said, "I didn't think so. Our depleted supplies and horrible repairs don't last long."

"You understand suffering, Papa. You understand sacrifice. You understand..." He touched my arm.

"I can't stand the suspense."

"Well, the shopkeeper, a handsome young Asian entrepreneur, said 'I can't fix it, sir. So sorry. No parts. Try an abacus. I use one.'"

Cristo said, "So, there you are. An abacus!"

I said, "Electricity for only seven or eight hours a day, if we're lucky. Gasoline when available, with a two-gallon maximum." My lips scrunched up. In fact, my whole face turned red with rage. "I'm sick of it!"

Cristo nodded with drawn face and milky eyes. "I hope the worst is behind us."

I said, "The mayor's a creature of habit. Like all of us. He leaves his gated compound at 5:00 a.m. every day. Lands the copter on the helipad on top of the city building. It's still dark." I had tracked him in advance of this occasion.

Cristo's eyes narrowed. For a brief moment, he became the aged patriarch. His face drained of color. Lines and bags rimmed his eyes. "I'll do it when he leaves. He'll never know what hit him. I'll perch on the wall near his mansion."

I don't want to go into all of the gory details of the mayor's demise, so here's a snapshot of the event. The RPG hits its mark! The main rotor sheared off and twirled counter-clockwise to earth. The cabin and smaller rotor exploded and burst into flames and smoke, which threw the mayor's bloody legs into the air, while the captain's hat lazily flew down with them. Both bodies split and flew into tiny fragments, which we observed with the pleasure of a successful job well done by amateurs to war.

We weren't as careful as we should have been. Buoyed by the helicopter's fire and explosion, I slowly sauntered to the wall to congratulate Cristo. Two policemen, the mayor's guards, screamed and ran toward us, guns drawn. Two shots from Cristo's assault weapon ended the life of one of them. The second cop, red-faced and breathing heavily, given the unexpected crash and his dash to the wall, got off a lucky shot. He hit my shoulder before Cristo quickly finished him off with a bullet in the head. That Cristo was such a powerful warrior— fearless, skilled, an inspiration to his fellow "troops."

My wound bled profusely, and then stopped abruptly as Cristo used a handkerchief to put pressure on it. Soldiers would call it a flesh wound. Dr. Stine could patch me up in no time.

As we drove to the dock, I asked Cristo about the firearms. He drove fast but carefully. He said, "The arms group gets this stuff by a circuitous route. The rocket launcher and the grenades are from a Polish company. Sent through Canada. I.D. numbers and place of manufacture are removed. We pay a lot for this. Slows the police."

I said, "They probably use an abacus."

Cristo couldn't stop laughing. He said, "If they trace it to us, our dots are gone and we'll have left the Vampire. Mission completed." He scratched the scrawny beard under his mask while only a few dots remained on his chin and forehead.

I found Dr. Stine in his office when we returned to the ship. He leaped off his stool, nearly stumbling to the floor. "There's blood."

"Yes, I was shot during an incident."

He said, "Don't tell me. I'll disinfect the wound and..."

"Thanks, Doc. Knew I could count on you for help."

"But of course." He sutured the skin and forced on a tight bandage. "There's more for you to see, Papa, much more." He pointed to the chair at the edge of the table.

I said, "Oh, my God. It's the spitting image of her. Judy's size. Her eyes are closed but the body, the face, the clothes, the..."

"She's almost back," Dr. Stine said. "A few shocks and some work on her hair and she'll be yours again."

I lost control for a moment. Through my agonized, blinding, tears, I kissed the robotic-likeness of Myra. "Yes, Myra, I love you. You're almost mine again."

Back home to a sleepless night. I returned to the dock early the next morning. The mayor's death was plastered all over the front page of one of the few copies of the weekly newspaper and carried as breaking news on TV. Some mourned the loss. Most felt little for such a well-known crook. His pilot was unfortunate collateral damage. No way to avoid his demise.

I couldn't help questioning our timing. If we had finished off the mayor sooner, maybe, just maybe, Ben wouldn't have found drugs so accessible. Another part of me answered, "There will always be another mayor—maybe worse."

I called Joey. He said, "Dad, Ben is fine. He's in treatment. The mayor's death has spread through the city government—faster than a contagious virus. People are suddenly talking about honesty, and FBI investigations. Even prison time for..."

I said, "Time to clean up the city. Way overdue. Love to the family."

The police didn't try very hard to figure out where the RPG originated or who fired it, or why. The assumption was that the mayor was protected by the Diamonds, and by the cartels with which they were associated. They just didn't do their job. A targeted assassination of an elected official didn't happen very often. They called it "urban terror", possibly a foreign radical extremist.

The police chief quoted in the newspaper as saying, "We'll provide much more security in the future for the new mayor." Once the incumbent's long-time buddy, he was fired the next day by the City Council. And on and on it went. A real housecleaning with the head of the snake blown to bits and pieces, only slushy debris left in his helicopter crash and explosion.

Two nights later, we met with the other members of the "shooters" group. They were annoyed at being left out of the information loop, but pleased and proud of the outcome.

Judy said, "What's next? I heard that the gangs are onto us, but they don't quite believe what their eyes and ears are telling them. They're so suspicious of each other."

"If only their paranoid myopia lasts a bit longer," I said, "we'll be home free. Big things are ahead for the Bats."

Chapter Nine

The blitzkrieg entered its final phase. I was glad. I wanted it to be over. Take some time to evaluate what we'd done and what remained to be finished. My doubts and fears were held in check—somehow. I felt ashamed that I enjoyed the vigilante experience to such an extent. I suppose that knowing our goals were noble, made it easier. But I did enjoy the mayhem, the chaos, the murders and the killing. I was pleased that the Big Kahuna was one of our final acts. I prayed that our luck continued and that the dinner would come off successfully. We referred to it as the "final dinner" though several insisted it was a sacrilegious reference to the "last supper."

As usual, Cristo's private contacts provided the Bats with inside information. A major cartel from northern Mexico and a large coalition of white supremacists organized the dinner for the two gang leaders. Dedicated to peace, cooperation, and territorial integrity, it was a rare opportunity to break bread with a fierce competitor and to divide the criminal pie.

Foolishly and inexplicably, they chose the Vampire dining area for the meal. Perhaps they reasoned that a mothballed destroyer was safe. Lucky for us, we had it wired for sound and video. We were there. We were also very suspicious of the choice. Was it a back-handed means to observe the Bats, to find out more about us, even to harm us?

Ethnic food, well, really the kinds of food each gang, or leader, preferred comprised the two courses of the meal.

Members of the "shooters" team huddled around the loudspeaker and several video receivers located in a crowded technology room one level below the dining room.

Cristo said, "Get the obituaries ready."

Ricky and Big Elmer arrived, shook hands, and sat at the simple table laden with a fruit basket and a box of Mars bars.

Big Elmer said, "Oh, yeh, that's candy I love." He grabbed a handful of the bars and shoved them into his jeans jacket.

271

Ricky noted his crude behavior. "My family. No Sunday dinner in Nuevo Laredo."

Big Elmer blinked. He picked up the feeling. "Is that in California?"

Up went Ricky's hands with a gesture of calm. "We're here to make peace. I'm still head... You tried to kill me—I lived. No hard feelings."

The social behavior of these gang leaders revealed how different they were, how limited in thought, and how much conflict could develop during their meal. Severely limited in conversation, Ricky preferred immediate violence to rational discussion.

We weren't surprised, only hoped they'd just end it all in a blaze of gunfire. At least, that was my hope.

Big Elmer choked on a Mars bar. He spit it out on the floor. "What territory do I get?"

"We'll draw straws," Ricky said.

"Bullshit. My people are in the north. I'll take it. No one goes there," Big Elmer said. He wolfed down another bar of candy and threw the wrapper on the floor. "Bring me a Coors."

"Okay, you get the north. I'll take the south," Ricky said. "We control it now. No interference." Ricky clapped his hands and the servers appeared. "This course is mine. Beans and rice covered by mole sauce—plenty of chiles and spice. Then slices of queso cheese."

As the gang leaders were served the Mexican food, Judy said, "They are the scum of the earth. At least they didn't eat Chamorro, that wonderful slow-braised crispy pork shank from Mexico City. They deserve hell."

The video showed Ricky gorging himself. He said, "If we argue, how do we solve it? Shoot to kill?"

"Yeh, that's it," Big Elmer said. He burped twice after chug-a-lugging his fourth bottle of beer. "Give me another."

The waiter said, "Another candy bar or Coors, sir?"

Big Elmer said, "Both. Oh, fuck it. My food's next. It's grilled rabbit, possum, and squirrel. I shot them little fuckers."

Judy said, "They're so stupid and mean. They don't discuss or negotiate in good faith. Their color blinds them. No hope for racial tolerance here." She stood, clenched her fists, and stretched.

Cristo pushed his chair back. He said, "Decent people of different colors or religions or backgrounds must meet together—to talk and listen—and to realize…" He arose and then sat down again. "The deeper we go into ourselves, the more we're like our fellow human beings."

I padded around the cramped space several times. "Yes," I said, "we have an opportunity to influence our new arrivals. We must teach them ethnic and racial justice."

Cristo gazed at us with unblinking eyes, his face set in stone. Only his lips moved. "You see what we're up against. Evil. Corruption. Their food has been poisoned with cyanide. They will die very quickly. Maybe they'll eat pressed duck from Paris or a roasted backstrap from Oregon with the devil in hell."

We applauded. A jury of sorts had sent the condemned gang leaders to the gallows. Big Elmer could never become the third antichrist. The verdict was death. The community could prosper with less danger from these gangsters and their cartels. I wondered what Cristo had in mind for the gang members.

Cristo said, "During the shootout, the leaders are dying or already dead."

"Shootout?" Judy said.

"Well, the gangs will arrive now to share dessert and cognac with their leaders. Five Bats wearing gas masks with special filters carrying MP5 weapons will fire Agent 15 (B2) gas into the dining area from a spray tank. Finish off any of the one hundred or so people still alive. That's the shootout. It starts with drug intoxication—then erratic behavior and lack of physical coordination."

"Very clever," Judy said.

Within moments the shootout began. It ended quickly, as the screams and gunfire died down. Silence from the dining area.

273

The "shooters" and "gassers" left. The disposal squad, of which Cristo, Judy and I were members, took over when the dining area air became safe for breathing without masks. We had a horrifying yet simple task, to clean the area and rid the Vampire of this human trash.

A few gangsters still gurgled while white foam oozed out of their mouths and nostrils. Not a pretty sight but justice has a heavy price. Dead bodies lay everywhere, some near the doors apparently seeking escape, most just on the floor tangled up or piled one on the other. We didn't question their location or what had transpired in their final minutes of life.

The plan was simple. Four large lifeboats from the Vampire, really motor launches, were lowered into the water. The bodies were brought out on cots and stacked into the lifeboats. With bodies piled in three boats, each steered by one of us and a fourth boat pulled behind empty in the capable hands of none-other than Judy. Bats were diverse and inclusive in their version of vigilante justice. Then out to sea, maybe ten miles. No shrouds. No coffins or urns.

Cristo looked tired and old and weather-beaten, his face deeply lined as he held a requiem for the dead gangs. He said, "It's a kind of funeral, really a mass for them." He coughed and spit into the salty, cold night air. "It's more solemn and serious. Not just dumping them into the ocean as chum for hungry fish."

No formal music or chanting, except three-foot waves whipping against the sides of our launchers in a rhythmic beat. Lap. Lap. Lap. Water music for us.

Arms above his head, Cristo said, "Dear Lord, we return these men to you. Violent men who killed and tortured and hooked so many children on drugs. Perhaps the next life will provide redemption. Eternal peace will not come easily. I hope..." He slipped into the well of Judy's boat, sobbing and gasping, obviously the weak and frail and bent Cristo.

We lit each of the three boats afire with kerosene. Bright orange-red flames momentarily shot up. The odor of burnt flesh was distinctive and nauseating. The boats gradually disappeared into the ocean with their heavy loads of cooked corpses. The bluish, distorted and burned faces of the dead joined the swirling fish, clinging algae, and assorted shells as they slowly floated to the sandy bottom.

They wouldn't last long, most stripped of burned flesh and gristle before they found a resting place. Only the bones remain. Who or what ate bones in the ocean? I didn't know. Maybe some would wash up on the nearby shore as a symbol of the sea cleansing itself of crime!

Judy ferried Cristo and me back to the destroyer in the fourth launch.

I removed my thinking cap during this episode, especially the part where my conscience resides. We had gassed, shot, and dumped unceremoniously over one hundred burned bodies, fellow human beings, into the dark waves of the sea. Most only suffered briefly but that didn't help much with my feelings. I froze my emotions the best way I could, vowing to return later to the right or wrong of our version of the criminal justice system.

We knew what they had done and what lay ahead for society if they weren't stopped. My family, you grandchildren could look forward to better opportunities and a richer, more honest lifestyle due to the Bats. Other mass murderers may have felt some of the same things, but usually their rationale had to do with ethnic cleansing, religion or race or nationality. We killed gang members and criminals, when the corrupt police and courts failed us repeatedly.

Back at the Vampire, I said, "Hurrah! We'll burn our Ninja outfits."

"Yes—good-bye Vampire—hello to our lives. No dots. No gangs," Cristo said.

Cristo appeared older again, almost bony, as he smoothed out his black Ninja shirt and tugged on his slacks, which hung loosely since he'd lost weight. "We don't debate any longer. Just seek revenge. Kill, maim, burn, and all the rest."

I said, "Ezekiel in our *Bible* argued it's okay to arm ourselves when faced with evil-doers."

The Father Time version of Cristo said, "Don't forget that the scriptures preach love and peace and forgiveness."

"You're getting old and feeling weak and stressed out." I placed both hands on Cristo' shoulders and kissed his forehead.

275

"Yes," the elder, bent Cristo said, "I am. But I have a valid viewpoint. A healthy community is... No gangs is good. But the devil will..."

I said, "At least the city won't suffer as much. Less fear. Maybe the feeling of trust in the government will return." Standing at military attention, for some reason, I saluted, then saluted again.

Cristo could barely stand. He said, "We can't fool ourselves."

"Do you think God will forgive us for what we've done?" I coughed and nearly choked.

Cristo said, "I hope so. We defended the city. Brought fresh hope. Used only the force we needed."

I said, "I wasn't prepared for all of this. My humor was skin deep. I was an only child—got A's in school and usually succeeded—but never tasted defeat or pain or much suffering. Just wasn't..."

Cristo said, "Myra knew better."

I said, "I still need her with me."

The youthful, charismatic version of Cristo took over now. He rubbed his hands together, not to warm them but to give himself a moment to think. "We're damned if we do and damned if we don't. Bad choices."

I pulled him aside. "The different parts of you are complicated but...Your friendship and leadership are so important to me."

Cristo said, "And yours, to me."

The puncture wound scars on his palms stood again out at that moment. I couldn't recall if I'd noticed them earlier. "Your hands are so expressive. They say so much."

Cristo held them out to me and turned them over several times. Then he placed his right hand on top of mine. "We are brothers. I'll miss you."

I sensed that we would not see each other again, that this was probably good-bye. I hadn't said it and neither had he. His secret belonged to him. I didn't need an explanation.

Good-byes are felt and understood between people, often inferred from what's not said. This was one of those moments where words weren't necessary, might have been an obstacle to genuine feelings and deep emotion between men.

Now, I could turn my attention full-time to my quest for Myra's return to life. I'd done what I could for justice and sanity in our community, which could be short-lived. Myra! Myra! Myra!

Chapter Ten

I couldn't wait to return to the garage before dawn. The chief arrived a day later at 9:00 a.m. for our first tattoo appointment. He carried a small sports bag full of dyes, pigments, ointments and several types of stylus. He was very proud of an advanced, experimental, technologically-sophisticated loupe which he could use in the dark.

He was virtually unchanged by the years. I couldn't help but admire the exotic Samoan body art covering his huge shoulders and arms. He sported a two-inch wide black stripe down the center of his shaved head, suggesting both beauty and movement, reminiscent of decoration on an antique Corvette.

"You forgive me?' he asked. Sheepishly, he peered down at his sports bag.

"Yes, of course, I do. We found a new antidote."

He said, "Bad when dots come back. So sorry. Good job now."

"I got rid of the hair. My skin is a little looser these days." I pinched several areas on my arms and chest.

The chief said, "It'll be good story. I know what to do. You say... English better."

I sat on the only comfortable chair. "Let's work twelve hour days. I want it finished in a week or so."

He stood near me and unpacked his bag. "No problem. Why do this?"

"Memories."

I didn't invite her, yet Judy dropped by the garage apartment during chief's first day. She brought some oatmeal cookies and a bottle of cold Prosecco. We exchanged pecks on both cheeks. She had a kind of European ambience—hair sleek and off of her forehead, pale rouge, no lipstick, and large hoop earrings. The Prosecco fit her style, but not the cookies.

"Papa," she said, "that's some body."

The chief said, "Hello" and immediately returned to his work. He then removed the loupe. "Remember me?"

Judy said, "Yes, of course. Got rid of your books—finally. Here you go again."

I said, "It's for Myra. She'll know everything that happened to me and the Bats and you and Cristo. The chief tattoos the events as I tell him. Ouch! That spot hurts."

Judy's gaze locked on my arm where the chief worked industriously. She lightly scratched my bald pate. "You really think that crazy little doctor can do it?"

"I'm crazy, too."

"Hold still, Papa. Don't move," the chief said.

Judy poured us each a glass of wine. She said, "To the dots and to Myra." We clinked glasses. The chief sniffed his glass but did not drink. Judy and I shared his glass when we'd finished our own.

She put the glasses in the small sink after rinsing them. "Best of luck, gentlemen. I'll miss you, Papa. Very much. Things could have been so different for us. But I suppose…"

"Yes," I said. "In another lifetime. I hope you understand. I like you very much. Trust you. I think I…"

She paused at the door. "You couldn't go on without Myra. No new life. You found such a clever way to end it all." The creaky door shut and then blew open. She closed it again.

She hit the nail on the head. I couldn't live without Myra, but with Myra alive again, I would be gone. I puffed up my mouth, and then my cheeks. My forehead turned red. This deserved a world-class scrunch—the agony, the loss, the pain. And the joy!

I knew also that Myra's feet would be plenty stiff and hurt her for months. Maybe her toes would curl up like a ballerina.

As she closed the door, the chief said, "Hot for you. She like big Samoan man?" He flexed his pecs and biceps, lifted his shirt to show off his washboard abs.

"Suck it up, chief."

His hand trembled with raucous laughter, so he pulled the stylus away for a moment.

Judy suddenly opened the door and reappeared. She turned and ran to me. She pounded my chest until it turned red. I wrapped my arms around her. She sobbed and beat her head against me. The chief walked outside.

"I hate you," she said. "I'm here. Myra's dead and gone." She pulled away but stood close to me. Her skin clear and free of dots, now the luster of her long, dark hair and dark eyes shone brightly. I gazed at her as if for the first time.

She said, "You're a different man now. A vigilante. You've killed. Myra wouldn't want you. I do."

Judy pulled a handkerchief from her purse and wiped her teary eyes. "I didn't think this thing with Myra would work. I played along just to be with you. We'd be happy together. I'm alive and I want to..."

"You knew. I thought you understood that..."

"No. I thought Dr. Stine was a sicko, a whack-job. I thought you'd realize that and forget about the past. Myra is... She's gone."

Stunned by her outbursts, nonplussed by the ferocity of her feelings, I became immobilized. "Myra's my wife. She'll be back here. You've been a good friend."

She headed for the door. "I guess I'm the martyr in this story. Not only lost you but helped bring it on myself. Call me if and when Myra..."

"Judy," I said. "Please understand. You're wonderful. A tremendous person. Believe me. I wanted you but Myra was there day and night."

The chief returned.

"I need a break, chief. Some time to think."

That afternoon I leafed through a photo album while the chief poked my back and shoulders. I'd dictate him a page or two, then recall events from the past. The pictures were mainly of the family, none from recent experiences with the Bats.

The wedding of Joey and Mary brought the first wave of joyous tears—such beautiful poses. The chief said, "Why cry?"

"Memories. Happy memories."

Everyone appeared so young, so vibrant, and so healthy. Birthday cakes surrounded by a smiling Ben or Roberta as they grew up. The summer holiday when the whole family tried camping. The emphasis here is on "tried" since a huge black bear scared us to death as he tipped over our tents, and then had the audacity to eat food we'd hung on a clothes line.

Then that Christmas with the tall, ornament-laden tree and the piles of presents for Joey and Mary and the grandkids. Myra gave me a refurbished short-wave radio and I saved for months for a pearl bracelet for her. Those were the days. Those were the days.

I recalled how heated up Myra became over one of Mary's decisions.

"Myra," I said, "you've had reservations about Mary—never told me all of it. She's not smart enough for Joey, she wouldn't help Joey's medical condition the way we did, she has a different religion."

"She's his wife. Let's leave it at that."

Myra stormed out of the room and slammed the door behind her. My consolations didn't always work out. I read her mind perfectly but she didn't like it one bit. She tried to keep the peace with Joey's wife, but not seeing you grandkids during one summer holiday was the last straw. She had to draw the line and solve it. So I took care of it.

Oh, Myra, we were on a journey for sure, not a ship like the Vampire, but we lived as best we could understand the awful choices and the lifestyle that we endured; the hardships of the global crisis, the racial and ethnic conflict that involved gangs, and the community terror, especially concerning drugs.

Killing the enemy—the gangs—isn't a final answer. We're all better off. We did what we had to do. We need spiritual changes, so that nature, herself, won't die. Love preserves but the problem of evil in the world won't disappear. The battle goes on. We will be forgiven for our part in that battle. You'll continue that struggle even when I'm gone. You are strong!

I simply couldn't live without you. I tried to stay, too, but it wasn't possible. Believe me, I tried everything I could think of. I'm part of you, our love lives on, and you'll be there for "us"—at weddings, births, and graduations.

The photos stirred up such powerful, vivid memories. They were the past, the world that was reality at that point. The people, our family itself, have changed and that world we knew is gone, in some ways, beyond recognition. And yet, everything is the same! Joey and Mary are together and married, you kids are older and more mature. Myra will overcome cancer and the dots and return to life as she knew it.

I didn't tell the chief my entire plan. After he completed the story, he'd need a week or so to keep the tats wet and clean, then maintain the moisture with no sun. My old buddy, the ex-coroner would be ready to prepare my skin for the scroll. He agreed to send the rest of me to my undertaker friend for the crematorium. No substitute for long-time friends.

I wanted Myra to secure my ashes in a metal container, and keep it in the cave where she would read the story.

The arrangements were set to go like clockwork. Finish the tats. Prepare my skin. Crematorium. Myra then reads the story to our grandchildren, Ben and Roberta.

What about Myra and me? We'd see each other and treasure each other. Then I'll tell her part of the story, and let her know she is cancer-free. The wonderful feeling—knowing she could live overpowered me. I couldn't find words or thoughts or ideas to capture it.

I suppose it was the dream of a reunion, the make-up-for-lost-time fantasy version. There we were together again holding each other in a loose embrace, gazing into the other's eyes, crying and sobbing but unable to let go. The pain and suffering of the cancer evaporated, quickly morphed into a feeling of relief and peace. The serenity of a future life together folding into old age and the end. The end for both of us, together to help and support each other, probably lie a little bit about each other's health and appearance and bodily functions.

In my half-awake state, I imagined us. We sunned on a secluded beach, pouring dark oils on each other, then kissing away the residue dripping onto lips and nose. After tanning, we rode white horses up and down the rocky sand, blue-green waves crashing into the feet and slender legs of our mounts. We raced, then rested, then raced again. It was a tie, no winner, both winners.

Our tennis game lasted long enough for us both to remember why we stopped years ago. The coordination left us, the balls floating lazily much too high in the air. Creaking joints in arms and legs forced the issue. Our old wooden rackets missed the ball time and again. It didn't matter. We slammed the ball at each other, near each other, then away. The "each other" made it memorable and joyous.

I hoped that Dr. Stine would relent and let me live. I could persuade him. I'd bribe him with the Bats stolen money. He'd relent. The goal of a life for a death could be applied to his next case. Not me. Not us. Not now. Please God, make him change his mind. I'd agreed to his terms but it was an impossible choice. Myra must live again!

After the tennis, we dried off and ate oysters washed down with goblets of champagne. We toasted each other. Our good luck. The restored life together. The second chance to live out our natural lives, which we had taken for granted so many years earlier.

Our plan to go to Mexico on the cheap for a few weeks took hold. We wouldn't need much. Some rice and green vegetables and ripe fruit might be available. Simple shorts and shirts and swimsuits would do us just fine. I could explain and describe the last few years slowly— the Bats, Dr. Stine, even Judy's role in…

I must write a letter, just in my mind for now, to the family. Time to say goodbye. Myra, you will be alive soon! You'll be angry and upset with me for a time, then understand that it was my love for you that brought you back, unfortunately to widowhood. That was the trade-off. It may appear from your vantage point to be selfish on my part yet you may eventually see the love and respect and care which prompted my actions. I didn't want it that way, you here and me gone, but the good doctor offered me no choice.

Believe me, I'll try everything I know to get him to relent. But he's on the right track, as his discoveries could lead to a population explosion with ramifications far worse than the current global crisis. No one regrets the correctness of his approach more than I do. It's some comfort to know you'll have this book account of the Bats and our escapades living on the Vampire.

I want you to know that I did find Judy to be a very attractive and interesting woman. She cooperated fully with Dr. Stine as the model and stand-in for you, for I guess her similarity to you in body type and, to some degree, temperament drew me to her. With her husband dead, there could have been romance were it not for my single-minded pursuit of your return. She made herself available several times yet understood that I held back because of you. No, because of me.

As long as I knew you'd be back, I shut off any strong emotions for Judy. Maybe it wasn't fair, but she realized it and still offered to help me in any way she could. She thought the good doctor and I were crazy at first. She didn't think it could happen, only a possibility, yet she became an enthusiastic participant in the restoration of your body—and soul.

There were times when I could have, and should have been more attentive to Joey, Mary, and our grandchildren. During our time as the Bats, I couldn't go everywhere, especially during the daylight, that I preferred. The fear of recognition by our enemy gangs kept most of us on board the Vampire during the day. I could have offered more wisdom and perspective to Ben regarding the use of drugs, especially when he didn't know what they were or their purity, or the effects. Remember Ben, the community can hurt us, making speedballs easily available. It puts white, and brown and yellow people at each other's throats. They don't know each other or have positive contacts. Not just your fault what happened. Roberta, forgive me, but I could have given you my views on boyfriends during the mid-teens, and more. Please forgive Papa.

I don't want your pity or tears but want you to always remember how grateful I was to have known you and enjoyed you both as my grandchildren. There is a special bond between us which can never be broken, much more than just genes and generations. A very unique feeling, a kind of love that is a bit paternalistic, but is much more than that, the kind of trust and love that only a grandfather experiences—pride and joy without the enormous responsibility of parenting. Ice cream!

Speaking of parenting, one of my real pleasures, a very poignant pleasure, is observing your parents as they've raised you. Watching my son Joey be a father to Ben and Roberta gave me goose bumps. You'll understand some day if you become grandparents. We live on through our descendants, but our own children reflect their upbringing in the ways they love and support and even discipline their children. And so it goes. Naturally, I'll miss graduations and proms and marriages, but I'm there with you. Don't forget me. I love you all, more than I ever really knew. My gratitude for your lives knows no bounds. Goodbye, Papa.

I hate to sound a sour note, but watch out for the new guy on the block who goes by the name of Chen Xi. He's the nephew of the leader in China. Get this: a black crew cut, designer Italian suits, brown horn-rimmed glasses. Looks like a successful young businessman from Hong Kong. Wears a heavy, gold Rolex near a tattoo of a Ming dynasty warlord. Likes French cuisine and Cuban cigars. Sophisticated and educated, so lets others kill for him. Lives in a renovated hotel suite with two teenagers, recent immigrants to the U.S.A.—not sure if girls, or boys, or both.

Once Myra returns, the plan is for me to be gone. A life for a life is Dr. Stine's decision. I've helped bring her back but without me— as a widow. I don't know how unhappy she'll be with my choice. I hope she understands but it may take a long time.

She'll be there with you, Joey, and Ben and Roberta. A good mother and attentive grandmother. Please take care of her. She's a proud, strong woman but she'll be lonely and needy without me. I didn't have any choice. I did what I thought was the right thing to do. Some people might think it was a stupid, suicidal gesture on my part. They're wrong. I love life but I love Myra more. I haven't lost my life, better I've given her life back to her. Help her see this.

Try to have her forgive me for what the Bats did. We defended the community and ended the reign of the two worst gangs and the crook and thief who led the city. I'm not the same person Myra married and knew. I've taken lives of others. I pray she understands and in her own way, forgives me. It could have been a miracle to have lived long enough to share life with her once again.

Chapter Eleven

It's nearly time for my loving Myra to return to life. I'm going to turn on the digital recorder so the chief hears the final pages of my story. He's prepared to tattoo the reunion with you, my dear Myra. I wouldn't want that left out of my story to you and the family, but I won't be here to dictate it to him.

The fantasy bubble—the dream, the goodbye letter—burst when I returned to Dr. Stine's office. He told me I'd have one hour with Myra, that the pill he'd give me when she resumed life would end mine in sixty minutes. "No chance for either of us to weaken."

Dr. Stine said, "You know I'm not just a doctor with an M.D. degree. I have a Ph.D. I worked my way through med school as a licensed dentist." He gazed at me but I wasn't sure he actually saw me. The lenses on his glasses were thick and smudged, so I didn't know where his eyes focused.

"Very impressive, Dr. Stine. Quite a pedigree."

"Danke schön. I feel ashamed that I couldn't use embedded nano-devices for Myra. Mine are tricky. Put one in Judy's brain and it could move Myra's arm. I'm nearly ready."

"Myra doesn't need it," I said. "Just make her like she was before the cancer."

"Yes, yah. That's it," Dr. Stine said. "I have too much power. Too much. I'm not comfortable." He removed his glasses and cleaned them on his soiled lab coat sleeve. The thick glasses hid the fact that he was cross-eyed.

I said, "It's power you use for doing good."

"Half and half. A death for a life means I commit murder, doesn't it?"

I rubbed my chin. I stood and stretched. A spark ignited my mind. Dr. Stine would murder me, or arrange an assisted suicide. The latter sounded better, but I was a goner either way. No wonder he felt uncomfortable about it. So did I.

I had been so single-minded, so hell-bent to restore Myra's life that I hadn't carefully considered how she would react to the event or what emotions Dr. Stine would experience. She wouldn't be happy to be returned to the world as a widow and Dr. Stine wasn't pleased to take my life, although it was a mutual promise to each other—a contract. A very messy situation, but I had to keep my eye on the ball. Myra must live again!

I begged for more time. I exaggerated—told him that the Bats had voted unanimously to donate one-half of their money to establish the Stine Life Foundation.

He smiled with gratitude but said, "It's best. See her briefly. Then leave. Otherwise, you may…"

"It's not fair. To either of us," I said.

"Not fair. It's all because of miRNA and robotics and me," he roared. "You know that wonderful, strange, little man. Nothing is fair in life or death." He shook his head from side-to-side.

"What if I promise never to tell anyone what happened? You can remove my new dots. We'll leave. Go into seclusion. Emigrate."

"Not possible," he said. He peered into his microscope, as if for support and strength to resist my offers.

"Well, maybe, I'll just have to kill you after Myra is alive."

Dr. Stine took off his latex gloves. He washed his hands. "We had a bargain. You're an honorable person. No deals."

"An hour?" I screamed in pain and sadness and anger. Then fell to the floor to growl like a wounded, dying animal.

"After you die," he said, "I have your instructions about who gets what part. Myra will remain in seclusion with me. Your skin and the scroll will be prepared."

The phone rang and he picked it up. "Phone call for you," Dr. Stine said.

I stood. "Who would call me here or now?"

"I did it. It's Cristo. He wants to talk to you." Dr. Stine's words were straightforward, but he put on a broad smile—sort of disarmed me for a moment. He handed me his cell phone.

Anxious to see Myra again, uncertain of what to say to her or how to explain these unpredictable events, I doubted if I could have a meaningful conversation with anyone else, let alone Cristo. He disapproved of my mission with Dr. Stine and would vehemently oppose my agreement with the doctor. Murder was murder, no matter the motive. Neither self-defense nor wiping out evil-doers this time. Simply old-world justice of a sort, a life for a life.

"Hello, Cristo."

He cleared his throat, then his weak voice, barely audible, spoke haltingly to me. "I pray for your soul, my friend. You've created life and taken a life—your own."

I choked back tears, part joy, mostly sorrow and shame. "Yes, I have. I need your prayers. I'm sorry to have disappointed you." My hand shook as I almost dropped the phone. I hoped the line would cut out—need new batteries—whatever.

"I've always loved you and Myra. That's the same—then, now and forever." Cristo said, "Only the Lord may…"

Then the sound—like a splat or cracking or shredding of his phone case. It must have dropped from his hand then broken apart. No need to say good-bye a second time but I did anyway.

"We love you, too. Forever."

Dr. Stine reached for the cell phone and returned it to his desk. He stood near me. I wanted Myra more than ever.

"Where is she? I want to see her. Enough talk."

"The money will help my research. Thank you. Myra is cancer-free. A few scars remain. Her skin was a challenge. My new brain nano-implants would…"

I said, "No one is perfect."

Dr. Stine led me to a tiny anteroom next to the lab. "You'll see the final electrical-boost that will animate her. It will be several minutes before she speaks."

I stood next to Myra, absolutely stunned. Was this real? Could it be her? A body-stocking protected her. Judy had been the perfect stand-in.

He said, "So?" He puffed up a bit, cleaned off his glasses with saliva and his lab coat, and touched her gently. He acted as the proud father, the creator of life, the only human being who could have done this.

Down on my knees before him, I cried and kissed his feet— really dirty, thin-soled, worn-out black sandals.

"Stop it," Dr. Stine said. "I'm not Yahweh. I'm not revivifying 'dry bones.' Ezekiel tells us only God unites physical matter with life-giving breath. The dead come to life."

I said, "To me, to us, you are God." I grabbed his legs and held on for dear life.

Dr. Stine said, "We'll argue theology and philosophy another time. Are you ready for Myra? This final jolt will do it." He pushed a lever on a tiny, black box which held many wires of different colors strung out onto several high-tech machines and video screens.

I couldn't wait to see her move, to talk to her, to hold her.

Her eyelids fluttered. Her lips moved slightly. Then her fingers trembled and there was an awkward shudder from head to toe. Much like a seizure, her torso shook repeatedly. Then no movement or sound. Silence. Minutes passed.

Myra said, "Where am I? Is this heaven?"

Dr. Stine said, "No touching yet. Let her get her bearings first."

"Can she hear me?"

Myra said, "Of course, I'm not deaf."

"My darling! You're with me again. You're back. Papa and Grandma are…"

She said, "Is it really you?" Her gaze took in me, the equipment, and Dr. Stine. Credibility was at stake.

"Yes. Yes. Yes. Really me and really you. You're alive."

Dr. Stine said, "Don't move yet. Please, Myra. Stay still and remain lying down a bit longer."

She said, "If this is true, I'm shocked. I'm exuberant. I'm so glad to be here. How could this happen? My cancer..."

Dr. Stine poured me a glass of water. He gave it to me along with two white horse-size pills. Without a word, he observed me swallow both. Then he took Myra's blood-pressure, removed his stethoscope to listen to her heart and lungs, and timed her heart rate. "In modern day language," he said, "Myra, you're good to go."

Myra and I embraced, tenderly as one might hold a China doll, unwilling to lose it but fearful of crushing it.

Slowly, awkwardly, I circled Myra several times, gazing at the unbelievable results of Dr. Stine's efforts—a perfect Myra returned to life without the scars of cancer or any evidence of dots or suffering and death. I twirled her round and round. Then I slipped my arms across her back and approximated a mambo step, next a two-step, finally, the twist.

"Slow down," she said. "I'm trying to get oriented to being alive again."

I said, "The excitement is bubbling up and through me and..."

"I'd better stop and rest now." She held me with both arms wrapped tightly around my back. It could last forever.

"Do you remember?" I said. 'The beard, the tennis games, even the horseback riding?"

Myra said, "Got to catch my breath. How's Joey and the kids? This is too..."

"They're fine."

"I still can't stand her. She's a know-it-all." Her arms relaxed and dropped.

"You mean Mary?" I asked.

"Who else?" She said, "It'll take me years to believe all of this. No book on me. You do."

"Yes, you'll understand soon enough. It's my story for you."

"Oh, my God, you're not sick, are you?" She held me at arms' length and carefully studied my body.

"No, no. My health is great, very healthy. Ecstatic that you're here with me. Dr. Stine did it. He's the world's greatest scientist."

She kissed me then. My face, my hand, my lips. Such warm, lingering, loving kisses. "My dear man, we're together again. You were so wonderful to me when I was sick and cranky at the end. I'll make it up to you. I promise."

I couldn't hold back the tears of joy and happiness, and of course, sadness. "The dots represent my story of life here since you left. We changed—did things differently. I hope the ends justified the means, because the means were violent and hateful. Major gangs are gone. Evil lives on."

"Why don't you simply tell me all about it, lying in bed with a glass of wine?"

Dr. Stine edged out the door without slamming it shut, carefully avoiding the loud bang for which the old iron ship's doors are famous.

"We have less than an hour together. My arrangement was that your life is traded for mine."

"What are you talking about? Are you crazy?"

"Believe me, I'd do anything to live out our years together. It's not possible. Dr. Stine will explain. You'll understand the whole story when you read my scroll to Ben and Roberta in the cave."

"It's all planned? I have no say in it? You jerk! You're just going to die within the hour? I'm a miserable widow. Alone. Who wants that?" Her face contorted in pain, the lines and puffiness became prominent and very red.

"I'm sorry. You'll feel differently when I'm gone for some months. I don't blame you for being upset. There was nothing more important than to see you alive again."

Myra turned and walked away from me. "You selfish old man. Just thinking of yourself and what you wanted."

I grabbed her from behind and pulled her closer. "You'll understand. Remember, I love you more than life."

291

My legs gave out. I'm falling. My fingernails scratch the painted surface. I…

POSTSCRIPT

A heavy silence hung inside the cave, suddenly interrupted by Grandma Myra's cough. She motioned Ben and Roberta to sit on either side of her, then lit a new candle and pinched off the weak flame of the first one.

She said, "There's your story. Now I see it all. Quite a guy. So dedicated and loving and loyal to me."

Ben said, "And you to him."

Roberta said, "And you to us."

Their three-way hug continued in the still of the cave, without movement from anyone.

Myra finally pulled away. She rolled the scroll tightly and laid the loupe neatly next to it. "Next year I'll read it again."

WRONGHEADED

by

NORMAN GIDDAN

Illustrations by Jamel Jones

CULT CLASSICS PUBLISHER

Chapter One

Few rain showers, much parched ground, still the warmth and blue skies of June held out hope. I needed hope...

My one-bedroom apartment, well, I could only use the living room and kitchen. So much stuff piled high the bedroom resembled the receiving platform at Goodwill. In several places it topped out at several feet. I'm ashamed to say it but...

"Hey, Boss, wassup?" Marty said. An unbelievable stunning mid-thirties Latina would not play sex games with me. She said it was disloyal to her wife, a Professor of English. Hell, she'd never know. Then, too, I fathered their son.

Oh, yes, I'm Kip. Both of us became PI's and formed a loose partnership. My wife died a little over three years ago. I drank and quit being a city cop. Marty hung it up over racist and sexist comments and behavior of her brothers in blue.

The TV blared the words "Breaking News." I said, "Hear this shit?"

"What shit?"

"An attempted murder of three big-time religious leaders. A pipe bomb, didn't explode. They lived."

"Uh. Who are they?" she asked.

"Believe it or not, quite diverse. Even inclusive. Chief Rabbi, from Jerusalem, Archbishop of Boston...head honcho of all Southern Evangelists."

"Why were they together? Suspicious. Overthrow the government! Take over the world?" Her eyes teared up. She closed them. Sad or angry or both.

"It's a crazy fucking world. That's all I know. Yessiree."

Marty stood and opened a huge, shiny black garbage bag. She shoved pizza boxes, empty beer bottles and cans, sandwich wrappers, and moldy cheese into it. The stink in the room noticeably improved. A half-liter of vodka remained on the table.

She said, "Out to the street, my lord..."

"Cleanliness is next to Godliness," I said.

Marty laughed. "No bullshit. Help. Only God knows what is hiding under this mess."

I started the coffee. We couldn't use milk or sugar—didn't have any. No eggs, bacon, hash browns, or toast either. Some reason. "That was a...some party last night."

"Uh, oh—somebody puked on the stairs. Dry and greenish."

"Maintenance guy will fix it. Comes with the rent." My grey running shorts and white t-shirt, surprisingly clean, fit me loosely. I needed a haircut and as I ran my hand over the dark stubble that covered my cheeks, chin and neck, I wondered what a real barber shop shave cost these days. I padded back to the couch, now cleared of the remains of the party... "Here goes six feet of nothingness."

Marty, long black hair straight and shiny, ruby red lips, and a hot body to kill for hugged me after I collapsed on the couch. "Don't care what's happened. Love you like a brother."

"That's better than a father. A lover?"

"Uhm. No way, José. We need gas money and more lunch money."

My cell phone played Mick Jagger. Stopped. I turned the speakerphone on, and then said, "Yes, Kip here."

Goldbaum, our lawyer turned referral agent, turned sometime friend, said, "You two go to the airport. Cabbie named Farouk is here most of the year. Owes me money. Gentle reminder."

I stood quickly and saluted smartly. "Yes, sir, immediately. We can fit it in."

"Good. That Porsche is yours for the weekend. Full of gas. See Jimmy at the agency. All arranged."

"No problem." He disconnected.

I jumped up and down. Danced. Happy. Excited. Elated. Tom Cruise style. "Saved by the bell. To the airport. Get Goldbaum's money."

Marty said, "Another week or so and this place would be liveable." She clapped her hands with gratitude. Several times. Then she hugged me again. And again. I loved it.

Some people thought we were brother and sister. Both of us a light cocoa color with brown eyes. Her hair longer and most lustrous, my nose bigger, and I sported a long scar from my right ear down my neck. My father was black but not my mother. Her father was Mexican. Marty's American mother lived for years in Mexico. Bi-racial is definitely in. Even our President...

Marty said, "O.K. Boss. Put on slacks and a sport shirt. We'll get the Porsche."

"You look perfect. White bell-bottoms and a white turtleneck. You must have known..."

Shook her head, "No, just lucky. Ten bucks in my purse. Lunch later. Let's go."

We closed the door to my apartment. "No need to lock it. Nothing worth anything..." We walked seven or eight blocks to the Porsche agency. The sun burned my retinas. Where the hell were the clouds to cover it? Clear, baby blue sky didn't help me. Marty wore cheap sunglasses from Walgreen's. She couldn't hide her Eva Mendes dusky beauty.

Goldbaum needed his employees, even down-and-out ex-cops, to look prosperous. His man Jimmy drove a new black Porsche with a huge wing over to the side of the building. "Thinking of buying…just the weekend."

I wanted to give him a $20 or $50 for his trouble. Shook his hand instead. "Thanks. I owe you."

We slid in. And I mean slid in. Smooth black leather with hand-sewn trim. Airliner cockpit. Pressed a button. The roar of power and torque and balance and timing ratio took over.

"You know, I feel successful," Marty said.

We pulled away. Hit the freeway headed toward the airport. I got it to 110 miles per hour, then quickly back down to 70 miles per hour. Used all six gears. God, what a feeling.

Marty's eyes, hidden by her hands, emerged into hyperspace. "Boss, a few good cases and we'll each have …"

I said, "Let's muscle Farouk. Then lunch…favorite diner."

"Okay. Doesn't he work for Goldbaum?"

"Yes," I said. "Don't know what he does. Works in New York, too."

A white Cadillac Escalade zoomed by us—going at least 90 miles per hour. A huge brown bear of a man at the wheel. He smiled. More of a smirk. With no cars in the middle lane, the Porsche heated up. The Escalade kept pace. Then by us again. Same smile. It turned into the airport and I followed. Hare's lose all the time to snails.

Marty peered at me. She growled. "Hormones again?"

"Arab lady in the car. The woman…more white."

"So what? Look at us."

I drove the circuit around the airport several times before Farouk's cab appeared. He stood smoking with one hand on the fender. Shirt too tight. Casual guy—thin, mustache, short dark beard. What did Goldbaum use him for?

Double-parked the Porsche next to his cab. He waved me off. "Move on," he said.

"You owe Goldbaum money. Pay."

"Who are you? Get out of…"

Suddenly the ground trembled with the sound of a crash. Then a huge black fireball bloomed tall behind the passenger entry into the building. Screams and cries and people running every which way. Next huge blue and red flames mixed with the dark smoke. An airliner crashed on take-off.

Detroit Airport crash

Marty and I ran inside the terminal. Still cops at heart, we needed to help if we could. I'll never forget observing the attractive tanned white woman leaning against a railing on the second floor—not moving, just stationary and staring out a window at the smoke and flames. Yes, the same woman who'd been inside the Escalade.

Marty pulled me toward the center of the terminal. The panic subsided a bit and people stood or sat stunned and cried. No physical injuries, just psychological shock and grief. They knew that everyone on board possibly died and they came close themselves every time they stepped on board a 747 or whatever type of aircraft.

Surrounded by hundreds of frightened and grieving souls, we threaded our way back to the Porsche. Farouk's cab probably found a way out of the traffic. He was long gone. Our car suffered no damage. I drove off, hoping to get back on the freeway before the authorities shut it down as a crime scene.

Marty said, "Terrorists? Radical Islamic extremists?"

"Maybe faulty wiring. Happened in New York. Blew a gas tank."

I called Goldbaum. "Message delivered to Farouk. All hell broke loose. Airliner crash. Explosion and huge fire. Fire engines and ambulances and police cars all over the place. Cops...Leaving."

The Porsche appeared untouched—keys in place. I used a side road on the northwest corner of the airport complex and reached the interstate moments before police closed it down.

Marty hunched in her seat, body throbbing, shaking, finally drenched in tears. She said, "Those people. Uhm. Dead."

"Horrible. Rare but it happens. So many Muslims live here. Detroit...could be terrorism."

I parked on the street in front of my apartment building. Once inside, I immediately turned on the TV. The story already international news. No group or cult or country took responsibility—at least not yet.

TV newscaster said all aboard, more than two-hundred, were killed. No survivors. Close to fifty Orthodox Rabbis from Israel...

"Some kind of tour. Organized trip," I said.

Marty's face darkened, eyes bloodshot, she nodded. She went on. "I've never been so close to so much death and destruction. The worst...How can fanatics..."

I gave her a beer, and ordered a pizza with salami and onions to be delivered. Then I opened a beer for me. I sat on the couch. Shock and the futility of the human race took over. I was one of the lucky ones. Lousy income, ex-cop, but I lived. Always the chance, the hope, the next day to look forward to. I was alive.

We choked down the salami and onion pizza. I'd given the driver too big a tip. What the hell. Several more beers. Then a second six-pack and the future looked brighter.

Marty slept and I watched the constant TV coverage of the crash. Interviews with local family members. Other families from all over the world would come later. I pulled the blinds to blot out a sunny, cloudless, blue sky…perfect flying weather!

I must have dozed. Around dusk both of us were awake, hungover but conscious. The pols and community leaders tried to reassure us on TV—they "were doing everything they could, a full investigation, go on with your normal lives."

Snippets from a panel discussion on TV caught my attention. Imam El-Khatoab said, "My sadness for all who perished whatever their faith. No Muslims were involved. We love America."

Then the Mayor of Detroit, a six-foot six-inch, 350 pound former NFL lineman. "I am Dwayne Washington. There is no evidence of pilot error or mechanical issues. All Jewish businesses and schools will be monitored and protected. The Israeli Air Force is sending trained experts here."

Last, the Israeli Consul General for Detroit said, "May God's mercy be with all of us. Three-hundred-twenty passengers and sixteen crew members are dead, including fifty Orthodox Rabbis and Chief Rabbi Mordecai Rothberg. We cannot rule out terrorism."

Marty sat up. She said, "What's all this Jewish stuff?"

My cellphone rang. It was Goldbaum. I put him on speaker phone so Marty could hear. He said, "Rabbis were on a U.S. tour set up in New York. Check it out." He hung up first.

I grabbed the last piece of pizza and guzzled half a warm beer to wash it down.

The cellphone rang again. "Before New York, talk to Betty Ibben. Got off the plane at last moment—sick—her husband died. Probably nothing." No questions—he cut off.

"Marty, please get her address. We'll see Betty… Use your contacts."

"On it, boss."

The next morning, Betty agreed to see us at her home—really a palace outside of Detroit. I told her an insurance consortium hired us. A few questions…

Betty, teary with sunken eyes, greeted us at the door. Sad but not suicidal. Depressed yet spoke clearly. No other adults in her home. No clergy. Very strong woman. Too strong?

"I'm Kip and this is Marty. Uh. Uhm. We work for attorneys and liability companies. We're private investigators."

Betty motioned for us to sit down. She poured tea. Couches and cushions arranged in an ornate Arabian style. Three teen daughters surrounded Betty on deep cushions.

She wore a purple pants suit, teal eyes and heavily tanned skin...about forty I'd guess but looked younger. Sexy in a way I couldn't describe.

Marty said, "We appreciate you seeing us. So sorry for your loss."

"Yes, he was a great man, great father..." She motioned to the children who moved closer to her. "I've told the police everything. Sick on the plane. A virus. I told him I would follow..."

"Why Israel?"

"For an Interfaith Tour. Been several times. Both John and I speak Arabic and Hebrew and French."

I said, "Why didn't John get off the plane with you?" Sipped my tea.

"Well, he offered...I said I'd see him soon. Stomach flu." She patted her belly.

Marty said, "So many dead. Many Rabbis. Anyone of Middle-Eastern descent? Well, you know."

"We love it here. Our children will go to college and work here. John...a successful business consultant." She poured more tea for us.

The three girls said nothing, looked wary, with half-closed lids, as if they had no sleep. She hugged the closest kid and kissed her tenderly.

Marty asked, "Anything unusual or suspicious on the plane?" She held her pen and notebook. Prepared to write.

"No—El Al checked us out very carefully. They're the best."

"What do you think happened?"

Betty shook her head. "The plane exploded and they all died. That's all I know. I saw it." She dried her eyes with a napkin.

We sipped tea, chatted about the fragility and uncertainty of life. She invited us to John's funeral—a ghaibana. Betty hugged each teen girl, and then escorted us to the door. Marty hugged her. I shook her hand.

We entered the Porsche. I asked, "Believe her?"

Marty said, "Not sure. Tanned white lady gets off plane. Then it explodes and Arab husband is dead."

"Hard to swallow, isn't it? Not sick now."

Called Goldbaum and gave him my assessment. He coughed twice, and then hung up. What the hell was he expecting? A confession of some explosive device that murdered Rabbis? Could have said thanks. Or, at least you did your best.

He called back. "Two grand will be delivered to your apartment. Nice clothes and both go to New York City, ASAP. Check out the Rabbis' tour. I'll text details and pave the way. You represent accountants and liability lawyers."

I laughed and peered at Marty and said, "We're rich, my dear."

Chapter Two

A whirlwind afternoon. Sport coat and dark slacks for me.
Black pants suit for Marty. Round-trip tickets on American Airlines.
True to his word, Goldbaum texted the name 'PS.com" with an address
near Lincoln Center. Head guy named Abe. A beehive of activity.
Sparked by cryptic directions from our lawyer-mentor-savior.

I peered out the window of the plane. Above the clouds.
Sparkling stars. Familiar constellations. What did it all mean? Would I
land on a different planet? Would my dead wife Nellie see me—greet
me—love me again?

Marty slept on the red-eye special.

I chilled out and recalled the old days, the family times…death.
My wife Nellie…both of my folks and all the grandparents gone.
Enough to feel like an orphan. It's not just cemetery time. It's more
than that. Much more. Always felt alone and different even as a kid.
My family still lived and loved at that point.

Because my father, an African-American Army M.P. dragged us
around the world—Japan, Germany, South Korea. Hardly in one place
long enough to make friends—know teachers or each school's customs
and rules. Maybe it could be traced to rushing from all-white
grandparents, Mom's folks, to visit my Dad's black-skinned parents.
Diversity without much understanding or patience for a kid. From
Detroit to Tuscaloosa, it confused me. Half-and-half. Who was I? The
experts call it identity. What was mine? I wish I'd had sisters. They'd
have figured it out for me.

The next morning after a bagel and lox deli breakfast, we
decided to meet Abe. Full-length mirrors in the deli's men's room made
me look so good I didn't recognize myself. No need of a mirror with
Marty—my eyes don't lie.

A huge portrait of Abe hung in the PS.com outer office. He'd
stand out in a crowd. Slicked-back black hair highlighted a long nose, a
grey double-breasted suit with spread-collar and a dark tie. About forty,
he cut quite a figure in the sleek PS.com offices.

His secretary Tara wasn't exactly a slouch. She smiled at me for
a long time with upturned, full red lips and perfect teeth when I
introduced myself.

"Oh yes. Expecting you. Mr. Goldbaum explained…This is…"

Marty said, "My name is Marty. I assist Kip."

Tara was definitely not her type. I nudged her, which meant 'be nice, this Tara can help us.'

Marty then shook hands with Tara and threw her a brief, sheepish grin. "Modern offices. Uhm. Quite striking. Black leather and chrome."

"Yes, thanks. We arrange tours from the Middle East. Also a Muslim match-making service. Very high end. Some escorts…"

I said, "We'll need a quiet office to review the books and the tour information. We'll meet Abe first."

Tara stood and walked around her desk. In hushed tones she said, "His real name is Abe Cedarstein. He calls himself El Hajj. Fits in better here as…All those Rabbis…"

"Oh, yes, a great tragedy," Marty said.

I couldn't take my eyes off Tara. So beautiful. Huge turquoise eyes, in a seductive Marilyn Monroe style. Over the top white sweater with brown plaid short skirt and high cork wedgies.

Marty nudged me which meant 'stop staring and stalking.' Tara smelled so good—the hint of flowered cologne.

I sank into the deep leather cushion of the chair, absorbed with my own fantasies. Who would go on a tour with Tara so close at hand? What escorts? Match-making for Muslims? Sounded like a Broadway musical. They marry their own but don't most religious groups—not always of course. Was this a Jewish guy Cedarstein pretending to be an Arab?

Abe emerged from his office. Unfortunately, he looked just like the picture in the waiting area—too damn slick—too sharp, too sleek—too something. The designer gold cufflinks and initials on his French cut shirt became visible as he reached for us. We shook hands.

"I'm Abdullah—or Abe—nice of you to come here." He led us through his office door.

Marty said, "Beautiful offices. Very. Uhm. Uh. My taste, too." She peered at the modern oil paintings and the book-lined shelves. The poem written in Arabic encased in a 2"x5" gold frame.

Abe said, "It means life is tough, so go ahead." He stood and touched the poem.

"All we need is a small office to look over the books—receipts, tour plans, match-making, tax and phone records."

"No problem," Abe said. "We have nothing to hide. Nothing." He sat again. Huge, ornate chair.

Marty said, "Don't Muslim families protect women? Hide them from outsiders. Keep them at home. Find spouses…and…"

"Not always. We help, too. Of course, it's very expensive. Very, very expensive." Sardonic smile on his lightly glossed lips.

I said, "What's the short version?"

"Well," he said, "we're using a new method to sequence an individual's personal genome. Genetic compatibility. Boring you?"

"Oh, no," Marty said.

"Everyone—or most people—are open to some version of love, or intimacy, or marriage. We discover what it is. We even seek a personal footprint…a failed love or a divorce. Rich oil sheiks pay through the nose." He opened his hands as if holding a pot of gold.

I asked, "How much?"

Abe said, "One-hundred-thousand dollars per person. That's confidential, my friends." He stood again. "Tara will show you my brother's office."

Tara entered as if on cue. "This way," she said. She beckoned with her arm. "Ike's office—was his—he died last week. Wheelchair—very sick."

Walls lined with file cabinets. Computer and cell phone accounts and records stacked neatly on a library table.

"Everything is marked and dated. Call me if you need anything."

I walked her to the door.

She said, "Something's funny here. That wife Betty from Detroit saw Abe recently. The Rabbi's wife Eve called for an appointment. Might be the tour stuff. Lawsuits. Not sure."

Tara toyed with the top button on her blouse. It was driving me crazy with lust. "See you later."

"I hope so," she said.

By 6:00 p.m. I was exhausted. So was Marty. We'd read and studied reports, tax forms, calls, meetings, income. It all matched. Nothing unusual. Very profitable business. Maybe Abe could use…

Marty said, "Here's a receipt for $500,000 marked 'Final Solution.' Didn't the Nazis …?"

I pounded the table in frustration. "Shit. Not much for a day's work."

A knock at the door. Tara came in and said, "Anybody got the munchies?"

Marty shook her head. Mine moved up and down. Her 'no.' My 'yes.'

Once outside, Marty walked in the direction of our hotel. I followed Tara to a cab stand. Seated in a yellow cab, I called Goldbaum and gave him a quick summary.

He said, "Not much." Hung up.

The remainder of the evening is still a blur—a wonderful, exciting fog—a mist I'd like to recapture.

Now inside her apartment, Tara ripped off her blouse and sweater and threw her arms around me. "You're such a beautiful man, Kip. So talented. So smart."

"I'm just a horny…"

The one-bedroom appeared nondescript to me. Neat and clean but junk modern furniture. The bed grew into something else.

As lust goes, the sex became sensational, but brief.

Both of us climaxed in moments. We held each other and gracefully outlined legs and arms and torso with our fingertips.

"What happened" I asked.

"Something came over me. Been a while. My daughter is not here. She's at my mother's house. We're alone."

The second time—slower and more loving, not so hurried. We undressed completely. Then kissed and hugged and murmured sweet nothings. With Tara panting on top of me, I said, "What's your last name? Mine is…"

This time reminded me of two volcanoes shooting lava and flames and smoke at the same time. Neither of us spoke. We shook and held on for dear life. Then sleep.

"McNeil," she said. "That's me. Tara McNeil."

"I'm Kip…" I was inside her again.

"It's not important."

My head kept spinning…so sudden…so fast. Could it be? Love at first sight? Or lust at first sight? A bit of both.

Tara rolled over. She said, "Your skin is so smooth. Your eyes. Dark eyes. Beautiful face.'

"And you. Wow! So loving and so beautiful and so soft. It's been a long time…everything about you…" I stroked her thighs tenderly.

"This is just the beginning," she said. "The future is ours." She kissed one hand. Full, soft lips.

"I know you," I said. "At least I feel like I do. Not just great sex. More like…"

"Old souls. Forever. Eternity."

"Could be longer."

Tara hunched up and leaned on her elbow. "How much longer?"

I laughed. "Let you know when we're better acquainted. Trust me."

"Do you and Marty…"

"No. Once to make her son Roberto. That's it." I held her tightly.

Tara and Kip

Breakfast at 6:00 a.m. Tara scrambled eggs with spicy bologna. We stared at each other, part recognition and part regret that we didn't know each other except sexually and part something else that I couldn't explain to myself.

The seat on my cheap dinette chair shook loose. We laughed.

Tara said, "Abe's brother. Next, the plane crash. Then Betty came, next Eve. It's all weird. They make so much money."

"We met. That's not weird. Be together again…promise. Anything else?"

"Yes. Abe takes women into his office, he says, 'No calls for one hour. Uhm. Okay, Tara?'"

I laughed out loud, and then chuckled, finally a sly smile. "So?"

"Well, some of them, uh, uh, like Eve Rothberg, then work for him. Never laid a hand on me."

"Not unusual. Bosses need sex. Reduces stress levels." I stood and massaged her shoulders. Wonderful feeling as she began to breathe deeply and rhythmically.

"Stop it," she said. "You're not Abe and I'm not…"

I moved away from the table. Sat on a leatherette chair directly across from her. "What else? He's slick but not a rapist…no crime."

Now she arose and peered at my eyes and face for what seemed like minutes. "He killed his brother." She wrung her hands as her eyes clouded with tears.

I moved around the table. Now I held her close to me. "Too much Kool-Aid. Why would you say that?" I kissed her hair and her forehead and neck.

Tara pulled away. "His brother was sick. Used a wheelchair. One day he had a meeting with Abe. Collapsed, found dead. I think...personal opinion...Abe poisoned him."

I took her seriously. No jokes or witty remarks. She meant it. Intuition or rationale? Hated Abe?

"Do you have any evidence or facts? Anything to back up your claim?" I sat down. Sweaty and depleted.

"Well," Tara said. She walked around the kitchen. "Abe's part of the business made much more money. Now going to help his brother's wife and kids."

"Guilty?"

"As close as Abe can come to self-understanding or guilt or shame? Didn't even take a day off when his wife died. A real asshole. There's more."

"Why don't you quit? Call the police."

"I love my job. It's exciting. I need the money. My daughter. I'm alone."

I kissed her lightly on the lips and opened the door quickly. Hate long goodbyes.

She rushed to the door. "I think...could love you." Slammed the door shut.

The whole thing scared the hell out of me. Love does that. Lust not so much. Somehow I knew in my heart that this might be...could be...would be love.

My wife Nellie died three years ago, so no guilt or shame. She'd love Tara too. She'd approve beyond a reasonable doubt—beyond any doubt. She told me to get on with my life. I waited too long to follow her wishes. Now...why the fear or anxiety or nervousness? Love just does that to me. Could the excitement foster it? Is there a 'Cops.com' matchmaking that feeds it?

I'm on my own with Tara. The amazing thing is that it's so good for her and her daughter. We fill a gap—not just desire. We need each other.

I strolled happily to the nearby cab stand, and then returned to our hotel. Felt triumphant. Rang Marty's room. Read her the text message from Goldbaum. "Come back ASAP. See remains of plane crash."

We checked out of the hotel, and went straight to the airport. Back to Detroit. Slept part of the way—my own red-eye.

Flying in the middle of the night—so smooth and silky—coffee or wine didn't tremble or spill. Perfect sleeping weather.

Marty said I appeared relaxed but smug. No fool, that Marty. She talked and I listened…in a way more than I wanted to know.

"So, boss, I married this guy—José Manchaca. I was pregnant…his son. Didn't love him. My dad insisted on the marriage. Then a stillbirth—no son—just José. The fucker slapped me, pushed me, fucked me everywhere and anywhere—drank tequila and… Well, the only peace I knew was when he drove a truck and was gone.

"I knew I liked women. Who wouldn't after José? We lived in L.A. and I worked as a maid and housekeeper. The lady of the house had a lot of lesbian friends. It was romper-room. Got tired of all that sex. No love…no commitment or family life. Moved to Detroit and found the love of my life. My English professor. And my son Roberto.

"Became a cop after I scored tops on the police exam. My police brothers continually harassed me. You can imagine. Tried…let's say to sexually manipulate me. I quit. Fuck them. Fuck cops."

We landed. I hugged Marty. Kissed her cheek.

A message on my cell phone directed us to an abandoned airplane hangar near the Detroit airport. Goldbaum said to "blend-in" and see what they have.

Detroit weather was good. About 80 degrees, sunny and low hanging balloons of white-gray cotton in the sky. Sometimes the sun hid in the fluffy cotton—for just a moment. Did this mean good things were ahead for us? So far, the beautiful June weather didn't help us one bit. Nada!

We arrived at the hangar. I shook hands with the boss…identified himself as Frederick K. Thurnly, C.I.A. No smile, just a muted red, striped tie with a dark navy blue suit and plain white shirt. I'd have known him anywhere. At least, who he worked for—C.I.A., F.B.I., and D.I.A.

His dark brown eyes and clean shaven cheeks with short sideburns seemed perfect, unless you looked for friendship and mild warmth. He said. "Two yahoos. Finally here. Ahem."

"I'm Kip. Uhm. This is my partner, Marty. Goldbaum sent us."

"Way ahead of you, buster. Miles ahead. Follow me…"

We followed. Marty put a finger to her lips. It meant 'be nice, we're being paid for this.' Silence.

Thurnly said, "A few body parts. Charred and broken. Not much of the plane. Piece of the fuselage, section of a wing and the end of the tail."

I observed three tables of "stuff" and the partially assembled plane itself. "Matched the D.N.A. to passengers, yet?"

Thurnly stood near me. "Not possible."

"Oh," I said. "Don't bullshit a yahoo."

"New explosive. No trace of D.N.A. No fingerprints. No fingers. Not many…" He smiled a victory version, like he'd won the N.B.A. title game.

Marty fell for it. "Uhm. No D.N.A. Not possible."

Thurnly sat on a fold-up metal chair. "Here's the short explanation. A Harvard biochemist says—hell—you can both read his note." He gave it to me.

It read: "The airplane explosion is due to genetically engineered microbes. Instructions to proteins are written in three letter sequences called condons, which specify one of twenty amino acids. Some chemical agent has changed billions of years of natural selection so we can't recognize D.N.A."

A short, fat, bald guy in his mid-forties appeared out of nowhere. "I'm Sol." Shook hands. "Mossad. Thurnly's telling the truth. No I.D. No D.N.A. Want to see a video clip?"

"Sure, if it will help us learn…"

"Give you a quick snapshot of what Mossad does. Don't use same rules as Europe...even the U.S. Every neighbor…well, most…want us gone. You know, dead. Off the face of the earth."

"Bad situation," I said.

"You've no idea of the strain we live with. Survival is the name of the game."

Marty offered. "We respect you. Mucho."

Sol said, "I've set up a TV monitor. See an example of our interview methods."

"The brutality…the horror of them…scares the shit out of me," I said.

"Watch this. Maybe you'll understand us better. Just maybe. I'll turn on the monitor," Sol said. "That's El Debbag. Real player, skilled killer. Water in his mouth and nose—like drowning."

Sheik screams. "Stop. Stop it."
"Tell us the truth, you miserable fuck."
Sheik says, "Yes. I…I did it. Used Pimex…Alone."
"Bullshit. Kill him. Food for the fish in the Mediterranean."

Sol turned off the monitor. He said, "Dead Rabbis aren't chopped liver, my friends."

Marty ran out the door towards the car. She said, "I can't..."

I walked toward the door. "Torture didn't work."

Sol said, "Not this time."

Thurnly and Sol both laughed. Too loud and too long.

Thurnly said, "Tell your boss not to pay the insurance claims quickly." He motioned me to stop.

I put my back to the door. "We were Detroit police officers. You motherfuckers need all the help you can get—even yahoos..."

Outside again, my old junk-heap of a car didn't start. The engine, what was left of it, needed a lot of work. Called a cab.

I held Marty who retched and then shook with apparent fear and disgust. "Wish I had that Porsche."

I called Goldbaum. "Dead-end. Nothing there. No D.N.A. Body parts cooked well-done and scattered sections of plane."

He hung up.

We struck out again with the hangar episode. No evidence for Goldbaum. Anger and mounting frustration at the bitter sarcasm of Thurnly. Then the outright hostility of Sol and Mossad—anything goes with him and them. Guess they have good reasons.

At home again, I felt lonely and lost so I looked up her number and phoned Tara at her apartment. "Hi there. Miss you beautiful. Wish we were together..."

"Me, too," she said. "It's been a horrible, terrible—the title of that children's book says—day."

"Tell me," I said. Sipping a beer and seated in the ratty, brown-beige patterned easy chair, I smiled and felt good. Just happy to hear her voice.

"You may not believe this...more receipts and payments. Abe hid them. His accountant covered it up."

Her voice hushed a bit on the last few words. Was someone with her?

"Alone?" I gulped the beer.

"Oh, yes. Don't be suspicious. A glass of wine. My daughter is asleep."

"So?" Opened another beer quickly.

"Well, Betty works for Abe. He fucked Eve Rothberg and now she works for him, too."

"What do they do? What kind of work? Set up tours? Match making?" I pulled myself up from the over-used sunken seat. Walked around the dining room into the bedroom.

"I'm a snitch," Tara said. "So is Farouk. He works for Abe and your lawyer. Both sides of the street."

"You're not a snitch...you're a good snitch. More like a whistleblower." I chug-a-lugged most of the beer.

311

Boston Harbor fire

"Oops—"blower"—sounds good—got to run. Daughter's having a bad dream. Crying. Love you. Love you."

"Me, too."

I finished the whole six-pack. Memories of time with Tara. Wonderful, loving, caring thoughts. Then sleep on the part of the bed that was empty—free of boxes and clothes. Barely enough room for me.

My interrupted dream became a premonition of more trouble ahead, not clear what or where. Goldbaum's call woke me and got me going again. It was midnight!

He said, "Sit down. Seventy-five priests dead in Boston. A day or so later two-hundred-thirty-five evangelical ministers in Memphis hotel. Get ready to travel. Maybe better luck. Ho! Ho!"

Marty's snoring stopped. She rushed to the bathroom. "No tears. Just pee."

"Crazy call from Goldbaum. Priests and Evangelical leaders— mass murders in Boston and Memphis. What the fuck is going on?" Scratched my head and rubbed sleep from my eyes.

"Got to be radical extremist terrorists. Killing religious leaders. Jihad, boss."

I said, "Probably but could be C.I.A. or Commie. End religion here or start World War III...Create chaos and blame Muslims." Slipped on pants and shirt and running shoes. "He'll want us to investigate. See what's happened. Who done it? Why? Says we're 'nonthreatening'. No fool." Marty said, "Uh. Huh. Just woke up. Things are bad enough here...Besides, Goldbaum wants the upper-hand, cops, government, and insurance companies. Makes money."

"We go to Boston first. Harbor closed...seventy-five priests dead...party boat exploded—precaution at all Catholic institutions." I did jumping jacks and then fifty sit-ups. Belched several times and felt better.

Marty peed again. She turned on the T.V. "Jesus H. Christ, he's the oldest fucking one, Cardinal Minelli."

Minelli said, "I flew immediately. Just arrived from the Vatican. The Pope prays for the souls of the priests. Sends his deepest condolences." Overcome with emotion, the Cardinal coughed and cradled his head in folded arms on the table. Head and shoulders shook with grief.

We packed overnight bags and took a cab to the Detroit airport.

Chapter Three

Then the red-eye to Boston. Erratic sleep. Hope for a better outcome. Solid evidence that Goldbaum could use as a liability attorney. Who? Why? Where?

The "where" was easy. A party boat loaded with expensive wine, catered food, gambling equipment and priests simply exploded in Boston harbor.

"Let's start with the Chancery," I said. Moved to the street and hailed a cab.

Our cabbie took the long, scenic route—Old North Church, Kennedy Library, Faneuil Hall Marketplace.

Marty said, "You need to know the rest of my story. Hated men...a long time. When I was thirteen, some priest held me down and the nun did me. Been a happy lesbian, but scared shitless of priests."

The Chancery, a huge red-brick historic building stood majestically.

I said, "Marty, I really need you on this one. Buck up."

We were welcomed and served tea and scones with Archbishop O'Reilly's lawyer. He blamed radical Islamists or maybe Russia or China, not anti-Catholics. No help from him. No tears either behind those rimless glasses. A cold, hard fifteen minute interview.

He implied that it was not an accident, added that Goldbaum had paved the way for our visit. He failed to say he'd be available for further assistance.

As we walked out the front door to the waiting cab, he said, "Sorry you can't stay for lunch."

Marty said, "Fuck him. Didn't even show us around... Diocese owes millions to the abused...Uhm...nobody with a beef would have done it. They want money."

"Exactly." For some reason I held the cab door open for her. "Didn't even offer us a glass of red wine."

I felt a gnawing bubble in my throat and stomach. My facial scar felt hot—probably looked red, too. This could be a dead end again. How many chances would Goldbaum give us? We didn't get anybody riled up, but then we hadn't come through for him either. Can't control the chain of evidence or the legal facts.

I told the cabbie to go to Hangar H about two miles from the main terminals at Logan Airport. For better or worse, Thurnly would be finished with what's left of the boat and the priests. He traveled fast and worked quickly…impatient S.O.B.

At the double-doors of the hangar stood Thurnly. He said, "The Jew lawyer sent both of you again."

"Yes, what do you have for us?" Marty asked with hatred in her voice.

I wondered what he thought of the whole LGBT community.

"Not a thing for you." He swung the doors open and we entered. "F.B.I. and C.I.A. and local cops been over everything. Nothing for you."

I said, "You mean no D.N.A. and no priests."

He said, "You're not so dumb."

Marty peered at the table of small boat fragments and tiny pieces of torn bloody cassocks. "Anything of the Archbishop? Give us something." She appeared ready to slug him.

"Well, an old drunk reported two real beauties in wetsuits ran on the beach," Thurnly said.

"That's it?" I asked. I felt like slugging him myself. Marty coughed, warning me to stay calm.

We walked to the door and returned to our cab. Maybe ten minutes had… I said, "What an asshole. Oh, my…"

Marty nodded. "You're right, boss. If he had something, he'd probably hide it…hates Islamic terrorists."

"And blacks and gays. Probably Asians, too."

Marty said, "Maybe the two beauties just came from the Mary Kay convention. By the way, fifty thousand people predicted to be at the candlelight vigil march tonight."

I called Goldbaum. Gave him an update. He said, "Probably same chemical as Detroit. Two hotties?" Then he cut me off.

Marty said, "We're not fired. South to Memphis, boss." She leaned forward and told the cabbie to take us to an airline that flew non-stop to Memphis that afternoon.

This time we flew in daylight. Wish it was night and dark. Loud thunder rumbled somewhere nearby. Lightning told me that it came close to our plane. Shaking the fuselage, electrical charges, that's all I knew. Hoped the captain understood more… I just wanted to land in Memphis. Didn't like flying though I faked it. No one knew.

Rain pelted the plane. Sideways mist of speeding water made it impossible to see outside. Bad storm. Continued lightning flashes—then the thunder echoes—Captain apologizing. Couldn't get around it. Explosive storm engulfed us. Said my prayers. Marty snored lightly and rocked imperceptibly.

The flight bumped and shook nearly all the way south. Pilot said due to high level storms which he tried to avoid but failed. Couldn't sleep so...Nellie... My wonderful dead wife.

She had a lump...in her thirties. Couldn't be cancer. It was. The worst kind. Fast-growing and lethal. Hospice arrived before I realized that it was over—Nellie's life, our marriage, the dream of kids and a family.

A strange time. She was brave and supportive. I collapsed, threw in the towel, blatantly gave up. Couldn't face the fact that she...her life could end like this.

Finally, she lay on a hospital bed in our living room, bald and thin and weak. We cried together. Then I cried alone. And then more tears until the drinking started. I'd brush my teeth sometimes, not always, before the first drink. Only left our apartment to buy booze and vitamin pills and pizza.

Everybody worried sick about me. I had little desire to go on. Quit the police force. Drank more. Went to AA—helped me cut back. Joined up with Marty. That whole thing took three years.

The plane's cable news channel replayed the Boston harbor massacre. Then pictured two-hundred-thirty-five evangelical ministers—the entire American Conference of Evangelists—killed in Memphis. Bodies now zipped into bags, nearly ready for relatives to pick up at the morgue.

Venue different, a Memphis hotel, probably same chemical in gas form, that leaves no discernible D.N.A. At least the cops and C.I.A. and F.B.I. knew who the victims were. Prints and dental records aplenty.

My stomach turned over several times. This was scary stuff. My hands trembled and my scar heated up. Even an ex-cop gets piss-ass frightened.

Marty hid her eyes again, then gradually peered at our TV screen. "What in the fuck? Omnious." She grimaced. Half-smile appeared. "I'd swear that Mexican guy I married did this. Died young in a truck accident." Held my hand very tight and hard.

The TV anchor read part of the obituary of Reverend Donnie Joe Pennington, leader of the evangelical group. "An orphan, Pastor Penny, grew up in the family of two American missionaries living in South Africa. His foundation donated twenty-five-million dollars to U.C.L.A. to found the Corinth Pennington Center for Addiction Treatment to honor his deceased first wife. More details of his life can been seen online at the Memphis LeaderGazette.com."

Marty fought off the tears but her bloodshot eyes couldn't hide the pain and confusion. "Three religious groups—mass killings. There must be a connection. Hope we don't...uhm...invade another country or...uhm...bomb the Middle East again."

316

We finally landed in Memphis, land of barbeque and the wonderful music of Beale Street. Good to be on the ground again. I kissed Marty's hand.

A muscular African-American man, crisp blue uniform with braids and badges, met us at the gate. "I'm Chief Jefferson. I'll get you started."

"Thanks," I said. "I'm Kip and this is Marty." Handshakes and nervous glances all around.

Chief said, "Police, F.B.I., C.I.A. flooding the place. Bar-B-Cue Deluxe...better than Nealy's."

We entered the huge police cruiser, a Suburban truck with more aerials than a cell tower. Hand-lettered "Chief" on the driver's door. Not the usual black and white, but canary yellow with snow white trim. He said, "President and our Govenor spoke out. God has a purpose. Praise the Lord. Praise the Lord."

"We'll see the reports. Interview a few folks. Be out of your hair quickly." I stretched my legs.

"That's fine. No kikes or fish-eaters here. Uh. Uh. Church leaders. Town shut down."

Marty inched toward us from the back seat—actually the middle seat of three sections. "At least there are bodies to bury."

Chief nodded. "No Ricin or Anthrax or Ebola—they think it's some new odorless gas. God-fearing leaders. Oh, my Lord."

I peered at him and asked, "Any terrorist group claim responsibility?"

"We don't need that," Chief said. "We know who did it. Fucking Arabs. Fucking Muslims."

"This is the third mass murder of religious leaders," I said. "No one is sure who's responsible. No one."

The Chief didn't like that. "You two fucking Yankees think you can just sashay into Memphis...show how good you think you are..." He honked the car's horn several times.

Streets downtown had police barriers and short metal fences on them. Most were blocked off. Killers were probably long-gone, in deep hiding somewhere far away. Downtown appeared to be a disaster zone, full of police, jeeps, National Guard troops, and SWAT teams with walkie-talkies. A dollar short and a day late, as the saying goes.

Once Chief gave a half-salute, barriers were moved quickly to let him drive through. We approached the hotel—scene of the crime—and the huge increase in extra-long TV vans, portable antennae, reporters talking into mics while being videotaped... A big crowd of people and equipment, though not much to show for it.

One of the largest scenes of domestic or foreign extremism in our country's history. According to the Chief, not a clue as to who did it, why it was done, and what the outcome would be. A lethal gas placed in the hotel ballroom's A/C killed everyone instantly, including the servers and bartenders.

"I'll drop you in front of the hotel, on your own. These badges," he handed them to us, "Uh, wear them…anywhere…everywhere."

As we started to enter the hotel, an oversized, two-story white electronic van caught my eye. More friendly then I remembered, Thurnly called to us. Handshakes all around. Gave me his new business card—the Deputy Director of National Defense Consortium. We patiently walked through what appeared to be a collection and systematic arrangement of every conceivable electronic toy. He called it his electronic heaven on earth.

So many buzzers, beepers, alarms and whooshes that Marty covered her ears and bolted for the door. I followed. The noise level, the multitude of electronic gear in one van—too much for us.

"Either the Middle East, Moscow, or San Francisco. Some group of crazies who want us to feel their pain, their fear, and their isolation," Thurnly said.

"Thanks for the tour," I said.

"Don't forget Russians still hate Christians and Jews—to this very day."

I called Goldbaum. Told him we'd met the Chief, seen Thurnly. Done a few interviews. All local and federal authorities continued to be stumped. Hung up before he could. I needed to win.

To my surprise, Goldbaum called back. He said, "Millions and millions and millions are at stake. Follow your instincts." He cut out first.

Marty leaned against the hotel inside pillar. "Once an asshole always an…"

"I agree one-hundred percent."

She said, "Wife of leader…then hotel staff. Then home. This is a dead end. No nothing."

"Wife first, okay?"

The lobby noise became impossible. An old hotel, no ceiling panels, so sound reverberated everywhere. Reporters, TV hacks and a few first-responders filled the adjacent "wedding room" to overflowing. The Chief now in the process of a press conference, looked to be even more of a cocky, insular, bigot. Worst of the Confederate south.

We escaped to the dull red used-brick sidewalk in front of the hotel. A uniformed cop, shiny black ankle boots and freshly starched shirt approached us. "Chief said to drive you all anywhere you want to go. No cabs yet."

I said, "Thanks. Like to visit with Mrs. Pennington."

Marty sat close to me in the rear of the cruiser. She smoothed her hand over the leather seats. "It's not the Holocaust or Rwanda or Hiroshima...I can't stand it."

The Memphis heat, sticky and humid. Tornado weather. Took off my sportcoat and rolled up my shirt sleeves. Still sweated through the shirt, back and armpits. How did the Chief stay crisp and cool in his uniform? Must be a Memphis secret? Eat more barbeque? Ribs or pulled pork?

The driver entered a circular driveway in front of a huge flamboyant white and grey stone mansion. We walked to the door. I knocked. A butler answered. I told him who we were and that we'd take just a few minutes.

"Yes, sir. Come in. She knew you were on your way, sir. Chief called." The butler pointed to the living room so we headed there.

Billie Jean Pennington, wearing a pink satin robe lay curled up on a gold-sequined curved sofa. Her maid served cookies and lemonade after we sat and introduced ourselves.

Billie Jean appeared to be about fifty trying to look thirty. Plastic surgery created plump cheeks and bloated, overly-full lips. Blue eyes slanted with a slight oriental touch hidden by continuous tears and occasional sobs.

"Such a good man..." she said. "I'm pissing green and ready for a fight. Who..." She uncurled and stood, padded to framed photos covering an entire wall.

Then kissed her husband's picture as she knocked it to the floor. "Donnie Joe was a true Christian leader. Replaced Reverend Lincoln— no drugs or stealing. I've got five kids and a big house and no husband and no father for them. Please God..."

Her eyelids fluttered and she appeared to faint. She fell on the photo and the glass frame shattered. The maid and butler revived her and helped her back to the couch.

"Thank you, Mrs. Pennington. So sorry for your loss," Marty said.

We walked out, then a few steps to the police cruiser. Neither of us spoke. I slammed the car door. Very hard and very loud.

We decided to meet the skeleton crews at the hotels closest to the crime scene. Due to the area lockdown few of the maids, bartenders, or desk clerks became available to us. The managers cooperated due to the intervention and instructions from Goldbaum via the Chief. Marty took odd floors and I took even.

Within two or three hours we'd canvassed four hotels. We said we were looking for two attractive women around forty years of age, probably sharing the same or with adjoining rooms around the time of the evangelical group's demise. Or anything that seemed unusual or abnormal. Whatever might be a clue to the hotel murders.

Marty said, "Nothing on the register or in anyone's memory that could help us." Seated in the manager's office at the site of the murders, she continued. "Uhm...Maria, a room service attendent on the third floor might have something. She saw two women in Room 312...wasn't certain if they were visiting the room or were registered in it. The desk clerk said it was occupied for one night by a Joan Evans of Wichita. Sounds like bullshit."

I found Maria. She showed me a torn piece of business card with what she thought was PMS.com on it. She said, "I have that...woman's problem."

I said, "No, it's just PS.com."

"Don't read English good."

"Thanks, Maria, you've been very helpful," Marty said. "Here's a hundred-dollars. For your kids."

Marie said, "Muchas gracias." She kissed both of us on the cheek. Then she curtsied.

I called Goldbaum and gave him a succinct summary. We hung up together.

Then called Tara. My sweet, loving, and whistle-blowing Tara. "Your intuition about PS.com is probably correct."

"Oh?"

"Yes," I said. "We've got two beauties, a PS.com business card and a receipt for 'Final Solution' the big boys overlooked."

Tara said, "Get them arrested? Prison?"

I shifted the cell to my other hand. "Not enough evidence. Why would Reverend Pennington get himself killed? Suicide? Maybe an accident. Why all the others?"

She said, "You're both on the right track. I just know it...My heart and soul."

"The only connection...PS.com and two beauties...points to Abe. But these women wouldn't kill their husbands. No way. We'll come to New York City. Sort it out."

"Oh, goody! Can't wait to see you," Tara said. "Maybe they are whores for sheiks or run tours or help with matchmaking services?"

Chapter Four

Another red-eye special to New York's LaGuardia Airport. Chopped liver and corned beef on rye with coleslaw—the perfect breakfast for us.

Beautiful sunny morning so we walked in the park near the PS.com office until it opened at 8:30 a.m. No suitcase or bags to carry—they must be in the Memphis hotel. Get them later. My scar heated up, usually a sign of action ahead.

The jogging and walking trails, leafy trees providing a broad canopy, held space for bikes, runners and baby carriages. Surprisingly empty on this morning, a hot sun leaked between the oak and cypress trees, creating a dappled effect that invited my special historical and philosophical view of our planet. Trees older than...green grass turned brownish soon...crushed stone trails easy on the feet. The quiet of the park echoed in my soul.

In Detroit the familiar aroma near fast-food joints—meat and fat and grease. In New York City the scents and odors pleased me. Heavy bagel dough baking, thick cuts of pastrami...aromatic with an almost herbal...and the dark mustard, sour pickles—the seeded rye bread—pungent pickled tomatoes. Blend these together... and you feel and smell the powerful sidewalk joy of strolling near eateries in the West Side of Manhatten. I pictured Zabar's...took a bite of air and tasted its deliciousness. Didn't need Zabar's yet.

"There they are. It's Karma. How lucky," Marty said.

Ahead of us, Betty and Eve ran slowly, then walked, then jogged again. They didn't see us or recognize us. We'd met Betty but only seen photos of Eve, the Chief Rabbi's wife from Israel. We followed at a distance of a block or so.

They jogged faster and ran to a statue of a Union Army General on horseback. We chased them, leaving us breathless. We crowded them.

Eve pulled up her sweat pants. She said, "We have no money...Uhm. Uh. Leave us alone."

Betty said, "You two again. What do..."

I pulled out my trusted Glock. I played a long-shot. "We know what you've done. We can cut you a deal." All in, as they say in poker.

Eve, a dark-haired fortyish version of the ash-blonde Betty—quite a pair—real beauties as the F.B.I. report told us. They appeared scared and sweaty and angry at being tailed by us, then confronted for their heinous criminal activities. Holding each other's hands, apparently deciding what to tell us.

Out of nowhere Farouk, Goldbaum's deadbeat cabbie from Detroit appeared. He interceded. I said, "What the...?"

He brazenly knocked the gun out of my hand. We struggled and rolled over and tried to choke each other. Marty picked up the gun.

Farouk said, "Boss...don't say nothing." Then he jumped up and ran away, a bit player in a crazy drama of crime and punishment. Must be playing both sides of the street—Goldbaum and Abe.

Marty handed me the Glock.

"I won't shoot. You need us. We need you. We're with the F.B.I.—C.I.A. Task Force." I slipped the gun back in its holster.

Eve hugged herself, chilled by the morning's events. She pulled her sweatshirt tighter around her bosom. "Abe's the fall guy. He did it. All the dead...Oh, God..."

Betty nodded. "Absolutely conned us. Slick son-of-a-bitch. You don't have any evidence that we...Go to hell!"

"Right," Eve said. "Perps and victims are dead..." She conveniently omitted herself from that list.

I said, "We can help you. F.B.I., C.I.A., Mossad and Interpol will take care of you. They want the top dog..."

Marty said, "We'll hide you both in a hotel room. Talk some more. Then..." She held out her empty hands.

"Uh. Huh. Off the record?" Betty asked.

"Yes, of course. You'll become material witnesses later. Testify in court."

They both nodded.

We stashed Eve and Betty in a nearby hotel under assumed names. Ordered Chinese food and bottled water to be delivered.

"Wait here. I'll be back. Marty will be with you."

I put my gun in Marty's purse. She nodded. She also had a .38 special.

Next came Tara. I rushed to her office. We embraced and kissed. She said, "Abe's out. Couple of hours. His couch..."

The woman took complete control of me. I wanted her cooperation and to tell her of my plan. She wanted me before all else. How could I refuse?

The next hour—or was it a day—could news be repeated. It was much too wonderful and enjoyable and heartfelt and ecstatic.

My pants fell to my shoes while her dress unzipped and then the magic. Softer and more gentle than I remembered, with occasional fierceness, then Tara's half-smile, and her cushioned lips remained on mine for an eternity. The other parts worked perfectly!

"Of course...I'll do it."

322

Eve and Betty – Killers Bonding

"Do what?"

"Whatever you want," she said. She rolled off the couch, zipped up her dress and slipped on her heels. "Whatever you ask."

As I dressed, I explained we had Betty and Eve, not enough evidence to convict Abe. Not yet. They'd rat him out to help save their own skins. We also wanted whoever paid for these ghastly deaths.

I returned to the hotel. Planned to interview Betty and Eve. I had to wait. They talked incessantly to each other...didn't try to stop them. Good listening. So I ate the leftover rice.

Eve said, "My dead husband, the hallowed Rabbi Mordecai Rothberg, despised women. Most, anyway." She pulled the hoodie over her head and covered her face. "I'd do it again."

"You paid Abe."

"Better believe it. Used all his insurance money," Eve said.

Betty ran her hands through her lustrous, blonde hair. Her hands trembled and tensed. Knuckles went white when she forced her hands together. She coughed and appeared to have trouble breathing.

"Feel okay?"

"I guess," Betty said. "Thought of John. My dear husband. I'm glad he died. Controlled everything I thought or did. Wanted me to become a Muslim so I converted."

"I paid for it. His death, too. Don't hate me."

Betty hugged Eve. Backed away. Then threw her arms wildly around Eve and kissed her cheeks. "Thank you. Thank you so much. Kids and I are better off."

She went on. "John always prayed at our local Mosque. He loved the Imam. Made him think. I went sometimes. In the back. Way back."

"I know. I understand. Horrible."

"Made me feel like shit. I didn't believe it. Just covered myself..." Betty now sat cross-legged on the floor and made a guttural, croaking noise. "The fucker."

Eve sat next to her. "The humiliation. The manipulation. Feeling of being second-class. Mordecai rubbed it in every moment."

Betty said, "Enough of those guys. We had a great time in Florida when I recruited you. Drinking and eating and swimming."

"It was wonderful. We hit it off immediately. No one suspected..."

"Yes," Betty said. "On the same page from the beginning."

Eve couldn't contain a raucous laugh. "Blending in with that Mary Kay convention in Boston. Our disguises worked."

Betty said, "I guess we don't have to be too careful what we say here." She peered at me. "We'll get Abe. Just like we got…"

At last, they squealed loud and long. Before any needle stuck them. Both confessed to being hired hands in Abe's scheme.

Betty admitted that her husband John used an explosive in a tiny tube of toothpaste to bring down the El Al plane in which everyone perished.

Both Betty and Eve claimed responsibility for the deaths of the priests in Boston. Planted a bomb on the paddlewheel boat.

Finally they told the story of hiding the deadly gas in the air conditioning that killed all the evangelical ministers, including the current honcho.

"Okay," Marty said. "You guys did it. The bottom rung. Who paid and who ordered it? By the way, neither of you shows any remorse or guilt or shame."

Betty and Eve smirked, locked eyes and then smiled at each other, but said nothing in response.

"Proud killers," I said. "We knew most of what you've told us." I padded around the hotel room, peering at the dirty window blinds, ugly green bedspread, and pea green worn velvet chairs. Layers of paint on the walls…a spotted, filthy ceiling. The room smelled of old age. Like death in a nursing home.

The décor matched my churning stomach. Did Betty actually kill her husband? Both women lost their mates. What about the fatherless kids?

Morality had to take the back burner. "Abe ordered and directed you both—employees of his or independent?"

Betty said, "A little of both. He told us what to do and how to do it. Supplied the chemicals."

"So far, so good," I said. "You two were the guns. Abe's the boss."

"That's it," Eve said. "We simply followed orders." She raised herself out of the chair, lay spread out on the bed. Sexy and suggestive.

Marty did not stare. I did. Would they trade sex for freedom? My hunch was that they would trade anything for something. Hit women are smart, protective, and take advantage of changing circumstances.

Marty gave me the 'be careful' signal. My scar heated up. I opened the window and let in some warm air. Cooled me off.

"Only Abe knows who paid PS.com. He paid us—thousands— Uhm. It must have been a lot," Betty said. She winced, inhaled and closed her eyes.

I said, "Why kill hundreds? Makes no sense. Was it just…"

Eve said, "It could have been the Russians or Communists. Hate all religion. Hate. Hate. Hate." More lies from her.

"Take off the head of the snake and..." Marty said. She wiggled her fingers.

I called Goldbaum to provide an update. He said, "Not enough." Hung up before I said, "Sting." Couldn't give him a preview.

Betty said, "Right-wing Catholics could have killed the evangelicals. You and Marty might be on the wrong track. Our own government..."

Marty said, "Terrorist tactics often give women strength."

"You bet, sister. Islam tells people how to live...strong emotional appeal...Sharia...God's law."

Eve retreated to a corner of the room and pounded the wall several times. "We'll do a 'sting'," she said. "No honor killings or slavery...gender equality...someday."

I said, "You ladies can philosophize later. Now it's 'sting' time."

I sat on the edge of the bed. "Here's the long and short of my concept. An Arab prince has his father killed at a large family gathering during a religious pilgrimage. You ladies do it for Abe. Reported in Cairo newspaper."

Not only did Goldbaum like the strategy of the 'sting', the Joint Task Force ate it up, too. Green lights all around, from local police, F.B.I., C.I.A., U.S. attorney, and Homeland Security among others.

And so it began. A trained New York actor plays the Prince. He gives Abe a million bucks in marked bills. He wears a wire. Eve and Betty meet with Abe and agree to leave ASAP for Cairo. They'll get their share of the money when an Egyptian newspaper reports the Sheik's death and that of the family members at the dinner.

I met with my old nemesis, Thurnly, over coffee. He agreed to coach the actor and arrange his garb. Thurnly said, "My guy, dark skin tone, neatly trimmed beard, sandals, and a white headdress. Gold watch and gold chain on the wrist. A Latin guy, no Jews."

I loaded my coffee with sugar and half-and-half, then stirred it. "The Prince can say he wants to use the matchmaking service. After Abe agrees, the Prince complains his father has treated him like shit...that he's fucked one of the Sheik's lovers...now she wants only the Prince." Tried to block out the thought of pushing Thurnly from the top floor of an apartment building. I could hear the police sirens and screaming crowd as his body lay crushed.

Thurnly said, "Good plan. Need a real drink. My own father died last year." He rubbed his eyes.

"Sorry for your loss. This is all pretend—fake—an act. You know the rest of it."

That evening Thurnly dictated a top-secret cable to his Cairo office. A phony obituary for the front page of The Cairo Gazette. The

Sheik died along with thirty-three of his extended family in a fire during the evening meal. Sheik Nasar ben-Sabati to be replaced by his eldest son Prince Ibrahaim ben-Sabati, now visiting New York City.

The cable ended with encrypted secure instructions to bribe editors, writers, typsesetters for the fake newspaper edition.

After Betty and Eve met with Abe, they returned to the hotel room. "We are to put this lipstick in water for five minutes. Then get the hell away from the tent. Fly back here immediately."

Two fist pumps—me, Marty, Eve and Betty—all around. After the second one, an open fist followed by saying 'explosion.'

Two days later, at the PS.com office, Tara said, "Abe, here are your newspapers—London, Paris, New York, Cairo and Tehran."

Abe reached for the Gazette. "Ah. Hah. Big fire. None escaped. Some Sheik died." With plenty of morbid sarcasm he said, "God is great. Praise…"

Tara handed Abe a black bag. "I peeked. Lots of cash."

Three religious leaders

At that moment, Kip and Marty burst into Abe's office.
Abe said, "What the…"

"Hello, you heartless son-of-a-bitch. We've heard tapes. Got you by the short hairs," I said. "The Sheik. A perfect sting."

"You can't prove a thing." Abe glared at her icily.

Marty said, "Who paid the money? Why kill so many?"

327

Six members of the Joint Task Force then stormed into Abe's office, guns drawn but held at their sides.

Thurnly laid the golden egg. He appeared smug and self-satisfied. "We can help you, Abe. Who paid for all this? No death penalty."

"Calm down," Abe said. "Put the guns away. I'll cooperate." He reached for the bag of cash.

"Speak up. Not much time..." I said.

"Three victims. That Chief Rabbi treated his wife like shit. The Archbishop abused a boy who became a rich doctor. The head evangelical stole a lot of money—grew suicidal." He went on, face covered with beads of sweat. "So, there it is—spousal abuse, sexual abuse, and financial abuse. They paid me directly."

"Why kill...?"

"That was my master plan—a new chemical. Mass murder to hide the killing of three individuals. Brilliant, no? No one..."

Each of us in the room—Marty, me, the Task Force members—appeared dumbfounded at that image. A concept of mass murder of so many innocent people, hundreds of religious leaders, to kill three abusive individuals.

Yes, we've become inured to mass murder. The deliberate and intentional use of it still seemed beastly and inhuman to me. To think otherwise left me in a position not much better than good old Abe. No cause, no group, no jihad, no religion, no theocracy—nothing but three people who had made their victims suffer pain, humiliation, and loss. They ruined lives, devastated families, harmed religious life, took leadership that would need at least a generation to rebuild.

Abe deserved the death penalty. If he cooperated with the prosecution, then he might live on death row for years. He could have fueled another mistaken attack and bombing in the Middle East, further harmed the world's perception of Islam. He could have led us into World War III, since it appeared to most, that Islamic terrorists had to be involved. Plain wrong.

Marty said, "Oh, my God."

Abe was led through his office by two Task Force members. No cuffs on him. He broke free, then grabbed and squeezed Marty around the neck. Stood behind her and pointed a small .22 pistol at her temple.

I stood too close.

Abe said, "Shmucks, drop your guns."

He smashed my face with his forearm. Broke my nose. Plenty of blood flowed. Backed off a few feet.

We all dropped our weapons. Made a loud, obvious show of it. He'd confessed. Couldn't get far. Maybe he wanted to be shot and die. A suicide by police.

Marty appeared stunned by the turn of events. She blinked her beautiful eyes, now wide with real terror, but no tears. Face immobile otherwise. Droplets of perspiration on her upper lip. I knew she didn't want to die especially from a .22 pistol—she loved .38's and .45's—bigger, more powerful, usually lethal. I loved Marty. She had some kind of plan, a strategy, that would fuck up Abe and save her own skin.

I stood back a few feet from Abe as the blood drenched my chin and shirt collar. Couldn't help her. Couldn't decide what to do. Jump him? Get shot at close range? Wait it out? The next move belonged to her.

If I moved too quickly Abe would shoot her and me too. She had guns in her purse. Could she find one without Abe realizing what she was doing?

Marty slowly reached into her purse, pulled out a snub-nosed .38, bent and twisted her body around and shot Abe twice in the abdomen. He bent over and I quickly grabbed Abe's .22 and shot him in the face. He fell dead. Sucking chest wounds gushing blood…red skin and pieces of bone stuck out of him.

Thurnly said, "That son-of-a-bitch got what he deserved."

The others, in stunned silence, simply holstered their Glocks. The hunt ended. So much bloodshed. So unnecessary. When rich powerful people—doctors, religious leaders, manipulative charlatans—murder, it's big time. But Abe's concept horrified all of us. Yes, he got what he deserved. Since Eve supplied money to Abe, she'd do more prison time than Betty. They'd die there if justice won out.

Marty slipped to her knees, then shook and cried and sobbed, her hands covered her face. I knelt beside her and held her close for a long time.

The end of a horrifying trail for me. A few clues but not enough. The sting did it. Abe knew. Finished…caput.

Holding Marty I tried to understand my feelings and emotions. Happy and so pleased that evil Abe bit the dust. Goldbaum would like it. Sad and gloomy that a fellow human being died. Wish he had a trial and conviction, but the state saved a lot of money this way.

Mostly, I couldn't understand, or refused to recognize the inhumane, chilling desire to commit mass murders. We can't predict violence, so I know that the murders of groups of innocent people is beyond our ken. There wasn't even a war…no tribal…no boundary dispute or rationale here…just one person in each spot.

I let go of Marty for a moment to wipe my brow and hide the tears. Close to barren emptiness, a hollowed-out core, a sense of the end. I then wept openly.

One of the authorities asked us to move as the room and hallway were now a crime scene. Paramedics taped my nose.

I updated Goldbaum.

He said, "Good. Criminal not civil. Bonus for you both."

Goldbaum called back. "A new Corvette for you. Matching platinum and diamond rings for Marty and her wife." He hung up without waiting for an answer.

We briefed the Task Force before heading to the airport to return to Detroit. They expressed appreciation and gratitude. Pink champagne in small plastic cups. Tasted cold and bubbly. Not sadness or loss. Just bye-bye Abe.

Even Thurnly shook my hand. Through gritted teeth, he said, "Good job. You two yahoos… I was wrong."

Marty and I returned to Detroit in grand style. Flew first-class, with many vodka tonics and rare roast beef.

Goldbaum came through—a man of his word. The bonus car parked for me at the airport. I tooted the horn repeatedly.

After a few hours of sleep, I drove non-stop from Detroit to New York City in my brand new silver 'Vette.

I called Tara. She rushed out of the lobby of her building as I drove up.

Exhausted from the long drive. Heart palpitations. Pulse too fast. Stomach cramps. Headache over my eyes. Perspiration dripped on the black leather seats.

Then magic when I peered at Tara. All the signs and symptoms and fatigue…gone…whoosh…just love and memories and hope.

"I love you."

She said, "Me too. I'll get my suitcase. My daughter is with my mother for a week. Then we can go. Anywhere. Everywhere."

Turned on the nine-speaker FM radio. Caught the end of a news broadcast. "The President has appointed a twelve member Interfaith Commission to identify, study, evaluate, and propose changes leading to the prevention of mass murder…" Good luck on that one.

The 'Vette's engine spit out more horses than…I thought of the big three. Rabbi Rothberg, Father O'Reilly, and Reverend Pennington. The Lord has a big tent. Sinners all.

Tara returned. She kissed my cheek.

"We're on our way. Hurrah!" The 'Vette purred. "This car is dangerous. So fast."

Kip and Tara -Vette

I glanced at her. "My wife Nellie died of cancer three years ago. I quit life. No more cops and robbers. Drank until the well ran dry. AA helped. Still miss her. Never stop." Held the leather steering wheel too tight.

Tara's fingers inched along my right thigh. They gently rubbed it. "It's okay. Very natural. You'll have my love. My daughter Teresa is ten. She'll love. All the love will push out the sadness."

"What's she like?" I asked.

"Well, uhm, active, smart, and asks a lot of questions. She'll want to know all about you. Even about Nellie."

"Interests and hobbies?"

"Oh, my. Yes. Plays soccer…likes gymnastics. Very creative—paints and draws beautifully. At least, I think so."

I kissed Tara's hand. "You're my good luck charm. You're my magic. Perfect for a new beginning."

She clamped her fingers tightly into my shoulder.

"Ouch."

"I'll never let you go. Never. Ever. First time, a mistake, not you."

A light wind bathed us. Blew away the dust of unpleasant events. Our hair fluttered in the breeze. Such a clean feeling on the skin, so fresh.

"Nellie and I…no kids. I fathered a son, Roberto, for Marty and her wife. Marty got pregnant. Wonderful kid. Uncle Kip…that's me… That's my secret."

"Want more? With me?"

"Can't wait. I want a home and family and you. More than anything in the world." It felt so good to say that.

Tara said, "I've got a secret, too. Teresa's dad got me pregnant. We were sixteen-years old and in high school. My folks made us get married." She spoke in a matter-of-fact manner. Made her peace with the long ago marriage.

"Past is past," I said. "New start for both of us. Forget. Baggage. Just learn from it and let it go." A gusty breeze, then a few rain droplets.

Tara's hand gently moved toward…Undid the zipper…Reached inside.

I pulled the 'Vette to a secluded side road, off of the interstate. Turned off the engine. Put up the top. Kept us dry.

Magic time. "Let's just…"

"Yes."

END

332

www.ingramcontent.com/pod-product-compliance
Lightning Source LLC
Chambersburg PA
CBHW062020170626
46813CB00001B/233